THAT SUMMER

A NOVEL BY

ALLEN DRURY

Also by Allen Drury

ADVISE AND CONSENT

A SHADE OF DIFFERENCE

THAT SUMMER

COWARD-McCANN, Inc.
NEW YORK

WEENDIGO (meaning 'cannibal'), myth-ical tribe of Indians . . . Indian stories tell of a terrible Weendigo with two faces and monstrous ears, who could see and hear everything . . . He lived far within the forest . . . The Great Weendigo had the power of self-transformation, and fre-quently he changed his form to gain his ends . . .

Encyclopedia Americana

GREENMONT, elev. 6,200; *club on the San Joaquin River; nearest town, Big Smith (see 'Towns Under 15,000'); 75 memberships; private*

'A Guide to California'

I STILL have their picture, taken at the Falls, and one of the bright red Italian-style beach sandals, encrusted with rhinestones, that Elizavetta was affecting that summer – the right one, that she always allowed to slide down and dangle off her big toe when she crossed her legs, lit a cigarette and leaned forward to plunge into some heated bit of politics or gossip. I know why I have saved the photograph, for it was taken on the night of the fire, but why I have the beach sandal, or even how it happened to come into my possession in that hectic month, is beyond me now. It was apparently just one of those things that went with being Elizavetta, that something about her should persuade a twelve-year-old that one of her sandals was a memento worth keeping of a summer long ago.

Of those who mean the most to one there are seldom physical mementoes, they aren't necessary, memory supersedes them. And so of the major I have only a recollection of kindness, a genuine friendship generously given, an attitude of adult respect I needed at that age and at that time; and a deep and abiding regret for a betrayal which, like so many other things that summer, was not really intended, not really meant, yet devastating and disastrous beyond recall for all of that.

Already, however, I see that I am giving you the impression that Elizavetta was some sort of *femme fatale* and that the major, largely by virtue of being a major, must have been a dashing and romantic figure. I have since known many women a hundred times more fatal that Elizavetta ever dreamed of being, and when I grew up and entered the army I discovered that not all majors are dashing. Our major wasn't a dullard by any means, but in some ways he was representative of the breed; and it was only because I learned a great deal of tolerance for others from him that I was later able to suffer his fellow majors, if not gladly, then at least with a sufficient forbearance to save myself from court martial.

Not that any of them, of course, ever got themselves into such an unhappy state as he did; or at least, not that I knew it. But when you go summer after summer to a place as ingrown as Greenmont, where everybody lives in everybody else's hip-pocket and the gossip rattles on incessantly by the pool, sooner or later everything gets itself known. So it was with those two. Elizavetta of course had grown up there just like the rest of us,

7

and that means that all her secrets were long since discovered. The major came late and for a while eluded Greenmont; but it got him, in the end.

Partly this was a deliberate process and partly it just came about, like so many things up there. It is one place that never seems to change, in its casual cruelties, its compensating kindnesses, its relaxed and sometimes rather inadvertent approach to life. I was just back recently, after a long time away, and it was all the same, almost exactly as it had been the day I left. This even extended to the lower tennis-court, where Louise and Jerry Drummond were galloping around on one side of the net making their usual wry, elliptical cracks, while on the other side Einar Magruder and Sally-Jane were giving as good as they got in their shrewdly biting and good-natured way.

'You know,' I told Louise, 'nothing ever changes, at Greenmont. When I left here ten years ago, you and Jerry and Einar and Sally-Jane were playing tennis, and now here I am back again and you and Jerry and Einar and Sally-Jane are playing tennis.'

'And still just as nasty as ever,' she said with a hoot, and I grinned.

'You said that, I didn't.'

'I knew what you were thinking,' she tossed over her shoulder as she turned away to deliver that contorted, slicing, effective serve of hers. 'We haven't all been through the wars together for nothing!'

And that, when you came right down to it, was probably where things went wrong for the major. He hadn't been through the wars with us, so to speak. He was something new – and things had reached something of an impasse for Elizavetta – and, well – everything happened as it did, and really, whose fault was it when you came right down to it? Or at any rate that is what we have all told ourselves many times since when we have talked about it.

'That's Greenmont for you,' Jim Buxton is fond of putting it when he philosophizes about that summer and all the others we have known together; and that, I suppose, sums it up. A comfortable – even, ironically – an impersonal, scapegoat, if anything as personal as Greenmont can be so described. We didn't know what an impasse things had reached for the major, there was no way we could. When I found out, I wasn't old enough

8

for it to do any good, and the others, with the possible exception of the Drummonds and Einar and Sally-Jane, weren't sympathetic and understanding enough until it was too late; and anyway, he wasn't the sort to talk about his troubles, particularly to summer strangers. Maybe things would have gone differently if we had known him better – although, knowing Greenmont, one is rather inclined to doubt it.

In any event, there was certainly nothing about the way that summer began that indicated to any of us that there would be any sort of crisis. This may have been because, that year, summer didn't get under way very fast. Greenmont is about 6,000 feet up in the California Sierras above the lush green furnace of the Valley, and wives usually pack up their kids and head for it right after school closes in June. Husbands rendezvous on week-ends for life amid the murmuring pines and the manzanitas, the cocktail parties and the cook-outs and the gossip by the pool. I wouldn't want you to think I'm kidding it, though, because Greenmont is really a very beautiful place, its cabins scattered along the great ravine carved by the San Joaquin River, the days of our youth and age remembered in the sunlight slanting through the forests, the high peaks looming above, the sun bright and clear and gently crisp, a lazy, drowsy felicity surrounding our snug, remote, closed-off, self-satisfied little world thirty miles from the nearest town, tucked away in back of the mountains.

But that summer, as I say, everything was slow. The Grangers were late coming up, the MacAleers, with troubles of their own, were tardy, the Smiths and the Grossmans and the Websters and the Buxtons didn't show until early July, and the upper end of camp, where the Drummonds and the Townsends lived, was equally leisurely. Even the Magruders, who usually opened the season in their sprawling cabin were late that year. So it wasn't really until mid-July when everyone gathered at the Meadows for the annual barbecue and board meeting that things really began to move. That was also the day Mrs Buxton appeared with the major and *that* began to move, too, although of course we didn't realize it then.

The Meadows (actually one big one, divided by the river) is where everybody congregates from roughly eleven in the morning to two in the afternoon, and then again, after lunch and

9

a nap, from about four until sundown. It contains the pool, the Grove, the badminton court, the golf-course (actually a rather tricky eighteen-hole putting-green wandering up the slope from the pool), and the upper and lower tennis-courts, so-called because one is actually on a level about five feet above the other. There are some who try to give the Meadows a significance they don't possess – 'The Meadows are rather like Market Street,' Mother Magruder, 250 pounds of amiably quaking malice, once observed in her lovable way: 'All the best people seem to live above them.' If you know San Francisco, you can imagine how that went over with those whose cabins are below: she must have made the comment forty years ago and nobody's forgotten it yet. But the Meadows do have their own real significance for us. Aside from being the centre of our activities, they're the place where everybody finds out about everybody else, so you can see how necessary they are to the life in Greenmont. Sometimes the Meadows can be quite vicious, but for most of us they hold some of the happiest memories we have. There was no reason to suppose on this particular July day that the major's arrival would affect this one way or the other.

Certainly there was no indication from Haila Buxton as her tall, angular figure went cooing about the benches in the Grove introducing him to everybody – 'You remember Major Steele, dear, from Fresno? But of course *you* would.' Of course nobody did, for this was the first time he had ever been up, but it said something about both Mrs Buxton and Greenmont that she should introduce him in this fashion and that everybody except Einar and Sally-Jane should say cordially, 'But of *course*. How nice to have you back again!' Einar, six-feet-three and twenty-two years of sceptical contentment, gave him a long, appraising look followed by a slow smile and a firm handshake, without comment. Sally-Jane dimpled and said sweetly, 'Now, Mrs Buxton, honey, you know perfectly well we've never met the major, but, Major, it *is* nice to have you here.' She sounded as though she meant it, too, which didn't always happen with Sally-Jane and other people, and from the major's pleased expression it was apparent that he understood this and appreciated it. There wasn't much the major missed, as we came to understand, which made subsequent events so puzzling; because people said, well, if you're so logical about everything else, why aren't you logical about love? Of course love doesn't work that way, and a good many of them had known it once, but you know how it is when people get settled down. They tend to forget those things, on the whole, except occasionally in the form of a casual jest such as Jim Buxton tried, somewhat unfortunately, to make about it once. And of course, a lot of them were partisan to Elizavetta and inclined to see it her way, and that complicated things too. Not that Greenmont took sides, as you might put it. It was a process more subtle and casual than that. But the major was an outsider, after all, and that made it difficult.

We in the younger generation at the time understood this with a candour our elders were at more pains to conceal. Looking down the length of the pool from the high-dive where eight or ten of us were soaking up the sun, we observed the major's arrival with a casually appraising interest.

'Who's that with Mrs Buxton?' someone asked.

'Major Steele,' he was informed.

'He's Not A Member,' Meg Magruder said definitively, and we all turned back to the pool to watch the youngest Granger trying to drown the next-to-youngest Smith. They were evenly matched and much more interesting than the major. Most of us forgot about him at once.

This business of being Not A Member is of course very important in Greenmont, because the original founders fifty years ago decreed that it should be a corporation limited to seventy-five memberships and seventy-five cabins. Sometimes rival clubs near by make sneering remarks about 'Snob Hill', and 'Millionaires' Gulch', and the like. But we just shrug and maintain a superior silence, because of course we only have three members who are millionaires, the rest range from modest to medium, and there isn't anything snobbish about any of us, actually. We just know we're better, that's all.

Being Not A Member, though, really does have an effect when you come to judging visitors to Greenmont, no matter how objective you may try to be. From wizened old Mr Stafford, the only Original Member we have left, who shakes his putter and mumbles to himself when a car he doesn't recognize drives through the Meadows, right on down to Pinky Grossman, the youngest child of the newest family, there's a sort of instinctive reaction that is really quite difficult to overcome. Even now,

11

years later, when I've been away for a long time and only get back very infrequently, there's still an automatic little pause when someone new appears at the pool.

'Who's that?' someone will ask, and on occasion I've found myself answering thoughtfully, 'I ... don't ... know. They're Not Members, are they?'

This attitude used to give Sally-Jane fits, which probably accounts in part for her attitude toward the major, then and later, and for the way she helped out the night he drove over the grade, and also for the way she took Elizavetta under her wing the night of the fire. Sally-Jane Harrell had quite a time with Greenmont herself, even if she had captured Einar Magruder – 'When the old folks weren't looking!' Louise Drummond cracked with her racy grin – and although they had dated steadily for two years, and although Sally-Jane had been up at their cabin almost the entire second summer (feuding all the time with Mother Magruder, which really intrigued every-body), Greenmont still hadn't really taken her in even in that third summer of their mutual acquaintanceship when the major arrived. You'd think they would have, too, if only to spite the Magruders, who were big, dark and bouncy with an air of deceptive good-fellowship that didn't altogether conceal a ten-dency to bite in the clinches, and who also were seemingly engaged upon an endless and instinctive campaign to outbreed the rest of the human race. This caused some comment too.

'Either the Board will have to authorize twenty-five new memberships or the rest of us will have to start moving out,' Jim Buxton said one time, and Father Magruder promptly cancelled their golfing date and wouldn't go around the putting green with him for three week-ends running.

Sometimes it did seem true, though. There were days when the Magruders took up one entire side of the pool, curly, young black-haired heads bobbing in and out of the water, curly, black-haired middle-aged heads gossiping at the water's edge, curly, black-haired old heads nodding on the benches, tiny black-haired heads stumbling about in the care of a couple of Negro maids. With the exception of Einar and Sally-Jane, the Mag-ruders were amused by Elizavetta and the major, and occasion-ally some half-heard snatch of conversation on the subject, punctuated by wild peals of laughter, would echo above the excited shoutings of the children in the pool. Of course that didn't help matters either.

Einar and Sally-Jane, however, were exceptions to this, as I say. In fact, they were exceptions to a lot of things, which I expect was why the younger generation liked them so much. They had only been married a month when the major arrived and spent most of their time lazing about the Meadows entwined in a way that made our parents impatient and us uneasy.

'Honestly,' Viola Townsend declared, and if she declared it once she declared it several times, right out loud in a voice that echoed across the pool, 'honestly, I do wish Einar and Sally-Jane would either go home to bed or act civilized!'

Sally-Jane heard this the third time around and made a face back, but Einar just laughed in his casual, independent way, and even though we sensed dimly that he must be engaged in something rather awful we couldn't help but admire him. He didn't pay attention to Mrs Townsend or Mrs Buxton or old Mr Stafford or anybody. He just paid attention to Sally-Jane and *they* could go to hell. We liked that.

And of course Sally-Jane got her innings, you could have expected that, because about an hour later she completely demoralized the Meadows for several minutes by suddenly shooting a wicked little smile in Mrs Townsend's direction and crying in a loud voice, 'EINAR HONEY DON'T DO THAT IN PUBLIC!'

Viola Townsend jumped as though she had been shot, and sought refuge in the Grove.

'I won't stay around that common little Sally-Jane one minute longer!' she cried bitterly to Myra Grossman, but of course Sally-Jane wasn't common at all, she was just having a little fun with Mrs Townsend. Sally-Jane was a child of nature just like Einar, which accounted for their purring satisfaction in one another, which of course in turn accounted for their elders' aggravation with them both.

As for Mrs Townsend, she really had a good heart in a lot of ways, but Einar and Sally-Jane, understandably, had it in for her to some degree and usually gave her a fairly rough time in an easy-going, joshing sort of way. Einar is good at this, because while he has a lot of pleasant characteristics that make him more popular than his family, he has a sharp tongue for those he doesn't approve of. There were some real pitched

13

battles, some real lulus, between him and Mother Magruder before he and Sally-Jane got married – so raucous on a couple of occasions that old Mr Stafford, who lived two hundred feet away on the path to the Mineral Springs, threatened to complain to the Board. Einar had emerged with his vocabulary in good shape and his willingness to let fly with it virtually out of control.

'Einar's going to calm down some day,' Bob Townsend predicted early that summer, 'if we don't all kill him first.'

Under it all he had a good heart and there was something about his kidding of Mrs Townsend that indicated he knew she did too. But he and Sally-Jane got a kick out of teasing, for Viola was always running up and down camp carrying the latest gossip about everybody. That made her fair game for those two, who had had occasion to find out what the results could be. Still, she wasn't like Haila Buxton, who never did anything spontaneously and whose gossip was always carefully calculated to serve some well-planned and usually damaging purpose. We often wondered why Einar and Sally-Jane didn't take Mrs Buxton on.

'After all, if anybody deserves it, she does,' Louise Drummond pointed out, but aside from mild asperities they held off, at least until the night the major tried to drive himself to perdition over the mountainside.

Not that I would want you to think that Mrs Buxton and Mrs Townsend and the Magruders and the other gossipers had things all their own way in Greenmont, for there were a lot of people like the Grossmans and the Whitmans and the Mac-Aleers and the senior and junior Bill Pursemans, orange growers, cattle ranchers, grape growers, peach growers, substantial people in the Valley, who didn't approve very much and didn't get involved too deeply in the web of gossip that went on all the time. But in their way, too, they contributed. Inadvertently, not really meaning to, just by being around – just by being part of Greenmont, with all that this entailed in attitude and reaction and the bright, appraising, cordial withholding of sympathy and understanding that was accorded those who were Not Members.

Even so, the major might have made out all right, for he was personable and likeable and as far as we knew hadn't had much trouble being friends with most of the world up to now – if it hadn't been for the situation as regards Elizavetta. And even

14

then, aside from a few deliberate attempts, first to encourage the romance and then to blast it and then, hastily and awkwardly, to try to put it back together again, Greenmont didn't really mean to be too meddlesome. It just couldn't help it: it was just the way things happened. 'Well, that's life,' Jerry Drummond said when it was all over, after the fire, and although Louise bawled him out for being so platitudinous at a time when everybody else was so upset, he was entirely right. It was just one of those things; although, of course, some of us helped.

Elizavetta (her mother had liked the Italianate form but had preferred the 'v' sound to the 'b' sound, so 'v' it was), did have some advantage, because she *was* a member, and had grown up at Greenmont every summer since her parents had bought the old Everett Montgomery cabin when she was five years old. She was now thirty-six, a fact which made her seem pretty ancient to us kids and also meant that for thirty-one summers, come war, come peace, Elizavetta Berrenger had been a fixture at camp. When her parents had died in an auto accident six years ago everybody had assumed that she would give up the membership and sell the cabin. But the pull of Greenmont was too strong.

'After all,' she explained to Mother Magruder, who promptly passed it on to everyone else, 'this is where I grew up and where most of my oldest and dearest friends are. I just couldn't imagine not coming up to Greenmont every summer. It just wouldn't seem right.'

This devotion, taken in conjunction with the many problems attendant upon her parents' death, immediately won her a special place.

'You *are* such a dear!' Haila Buxton exclaimed. 'You've no idea how much your decision means to all of us and what a wonderful example it is to the children!'

Shortly after that she got a job as librarian in Big Smith, thirty miles down in the foothills where the Drummonds and the Buxtons and the MacAleers have their ranches, and sure enough, regular as clockwork, she was up every week-end, sometimes with friends but more often alone; coming down to the pool as usual, playing a little bridge, giving an occasional cocktail party or wienie-roast, participating as always in the lazy flow of life in camp.

In a couple of years' time, possibly because of her daily association with books, she began to take up causes and people – 'Capital C, Capital P,' as Einar put it dryly after the first summer when she and Sartre had a mad, long-distance affair – and in this she was encouraged by Mrs Buxton. Then ran through Sartre that summer, Toynbee the next, hit T. S. Eliot and E. E. Cummings some glancing blows the next, and were beginning to get into painting and politics by the time the major came along.

Accompanying this rather frantic discovery of culture went changes in Elizavetta's appearance. Much too early, she began not only to talk like a character but to look like one. A certain garish, almost deliberate awkwardness came into her dress, a tendency to wear things that were too large, too bright, and too much. She experimented with lipstick too: the Garbo mouth was succeeded by the Crawford mouth and that in turn was succeeded by several other mouths ranging from the pale, colourless slit to the large, neon slash. Subtly, and sometimes not so subtly, Elizavetta Berrenger began to change from summer to summer like a large, earnest chameleon.

'Looks to me like a continuous dramatic production,' Jim Buxton remarked, but Louise Drummond hit closer home.

'Looks to me like a deliberate farewell to youth,' she said.

Whatever it was, by the time that summer rolled around Elizavetta had gone through three or four of these galloping transformations. When the major appeared she had arrived at what you might call her Mid-Mediterranean Period – the big, sloppy straw hat, the halter made from a red cotton kerchief, the bright yellow shorts decorated with modernistic squiggles that somehow didn't quite make it, the exaggerated mouth, the long, jewel-encrusted cigarette holder, the red sandals, the long black hair flying loose around the determinedly eager face. In conjunction went what might be termed the Grim Period in thought – the positive declarations for world government, the call to Deeper Thinking, the ominous implications of The Plight.

The Plight, which Louise soon began referring to behind her back as The Blight, was The Plight Of All Peoples. All Peoples were in a terrific Plight, which was certainly true enough, and Elizavetta and Mrs Buxton worried about it a good deal when they were together. This was practically always, because Elizavetta, although managing to look and act quite independent, at heart possessed another quality that appealed deeply to Haila.

16

She was a born disciple, and that was something Haila liked and was always looking for. Haila had a way of impressing new-comers and the young, and having grown up in her shadow for years Elizavetta filled the bill perfectly. It was really Mrs Buxton's urging, it had turned out later, that had tipped the balance in favour of Eliza's keeping the membership after her parents died, and it was generally Mrs Buxton who was there with the helpful suggestions on dress and the flattering encouragements to new ventures in the realms of politics, philosophy and the Active Mind.

'Why in the hell doesn't Haila leave that girl alone?' Jerry Drummond had exploded angrily one night when the two of them departed with the dutiful Jim Buxton after a particularly heated discussion on the Drummonds' deck, the pines aromatic and whispering all around, the mountains rising darkly against the stars, the river roaring quietly along in the distance.

'Haila needs worshippers,' Bob Townsend said. Jerry looked annoyed.

'Well, why doesn't she pick on somebody else?' he demanded, moodily poking the dying embers of the fire. 'She's turning that poor girl into a character before her time.'

'Not like the rest of us,' Louise shot out, 'who have reached our time and so it's all right, eh, sweetie?'

'Now, God damn it,' Jerry said, 'I'm serious. Eliza isn't going to have a chance to catch a man or anything.'

'I'm afraid you're right,' Einar agreed sadly. 'Or Anything. Who would want to Anything with Eliza?'

'Einar, honey,' Sally-Jane said firmly, 'I think you had better drop that subject right now.'

'Yes, ma'am,' Einar said with a grin. But the question did linger on, uneasily, in the collective mind of Greenmont: what was going to happen to Elizavetta, and what could anyone do about it? Because of course everyone really was very fond of her, it was impossible not to be.

'I don't think I've ever heard her say an unkind word about anyone,' Viola Townsend once remarked in a wondering tone that made Louise hoot right out loud.

'Yes,' she agreed, more soberly, after a minute. 'She's very thoughtful and very kind.'

Still and all, Greenmont couldn't help making its little jokes

17

at her expense, for she did seem deliberately to lend herself to them, in the way she dressed and the way she talked, and in what appeared to be her rather naïve and uncertain and mixed-up approach to life. Elizavetta was always good for a wisecrack or two, however kind and decent and thoughtful she was, when everyone was sitting around. Greenmont wouldn't have been Greenmont if that hadn't been the case.

Not, of course, that they were so perfect or had all their problems solved, either. Jim Buxton pretty well took the lid off that, in one of those abrupt unexpected moments of candour that sometimes slip past the mutually agreed-upon hypocrisies of old friends, one day later when they were all lying beside the pool discussing Eliza and the major as they putted sedately, if self-consciously, around the golf-course.

'I just can't understand it,' Bob Townsend said. 'I just can't see what those two see in each other, really.'

Jim tamped his pipe and snorted.

'Love does the damnedest things to people sometimes,' he said, and quite involuntarily his eyes met Haila's for a moment that began as something quite funny and became in a split second something quite embarrassing. Louise as usual came to the rescue with her sardonic grin.

'Let's just not dwell on that idea, darling, shall we? Let's not *any* of us dwell on *that* idea!'

But I guess maybe that is taking me a little far afield from Elizavetta and the major – although it isn't, really, because all these people got pretty well involved with them before it was all over.

Actually, everybody in Greenmont got involved with them. Everybody in Greenmont always gets involved with everybody, right down to this day. That summer, however, was one to remember. It got really serious before it ended, though when it began it seemed as light-hearted and uneventful as many another we had all spent together. The usual gossip, the usual back-biting, the usual sleepy, drifting days of tennis and swimming and lazing in the sun – or so we thought.

And so it was, only this time it really mattered to someone, and that made it quite terrible before it was over.

But, of course, that morning by the pool, none of us could know that.

18

ONE

If you were a Valley boy, the trip from Fresno to Greenmont was full of landmarks familiar as your hand, and a Valley boy the major was, born and reared in Turlock, noting automatically as he drove along Highway 99 the dry brown fields of wheat interspersed with the bright green fields of clover, the little dusty towns and somnolent little cities, the tidy vineyards and the cattle ranches, the peach orchards, and the rows of cantaloupes under their little paper caps, the geometric progression of irrigation ditches stretching away on every side across the Valley floor, the great range of Sierra Nevadas flung up white-topped on the east, a distant low-lying band of haze marking and obscuring the Coast Range far away to the west. It was one of those delicate, shining mornings in the Valley that begin with dew on the ground, a little, quick-dying wind, and a feeling of deceptive coolness that quickly burns off and gives way to a suffocating 100 degrees by noon. It would be good to get out of it for a while, he thought; physically good, and mentally good, too. Everything, in fact, was combining to make this trip to the mountains an ideal escape from the ghosts that harried him.

Not, he told himself with a growing certainty and satisfaction, that they were such fearful ghosts. He felt he finally had them under control, now, felt in fact a sort of near-humorous fellow-ship with them; was more certain now than he had been a month or even a week ago that he could handle them and whatever they might try to inflict upon him.

There had been a while when he had not been sure of this, and looking back upon that unhappy time so recently over, he marvelled a little that he should have emerged from it so well. But he had, he told himself, and for that he was very thankful; thankful, too, that the final seal was now to be placed upon his recovery by this journey to Greenmont, the chance to lie around and relax for a month, the opportunity to do nothing in the pleasantest possible fashion in a place he had often heard of but had not until now had the opportunity to visit.

That this should have come about by inadvertence rather than deliberate plan served to make it that much more enjoyable as he travelled on through the bright morning world. It lent a spirit of light-heartedness he knew he needed and he welcomed it. His eye caught the gleam of a little brook as he neared the edge of the foothills, a deep, secretive gully of green twisting through the bare brown ravines, with cottonwoods and willows hanging jealously over. Near at hand he saw a meadowlark on an old weathered stump. The bird gave its lovely, gurgling, liquid call and he tried the impossible task of whistling an answer to its silver convolutions. He felt like doing that sort of thing: it was that sort of morning. For the first time in weeks he was almost happy, and on the surge of it he thought with a kindly warmth of the old friends who had quite unexpectedly, and not through anyone's laboured plan, made it possible.

Probably he would never know exactly what, aside from the obvious, had prompted the MacAleers to select him to write to from their cabin at Greenmont two days ago, but the moment he had received the letter he had felt there was something inevitable about it. They were coming down from the mountains, Mary wrote, and were going to San Francisco and then on to Hawaii for several weeks 'to see if we can't work it out'. He had been startled by this, for it had been a long time since he had seen them, their contacts had been limited to casual notes at Christmas, and the old war-time intimacy had long since subsided. He had not even known that there was anything to 'work out'. They had heard about his situation, Buck scribbled in an accompanying note, 'through the grapevine' – whoever that meant, for most of the others in that particular group had scattered far in the service and lost track of one another, too – and they wondered if he would like to come up and use the cabin while they were away. They had always meant to invite him, but somehow, he knew how these things were, they just never had, and now this was the opportunity and maybe if everything became all right with them again they could make it a regular thing thereafter and resume their old friendship.

There was just one price for this, candidly stated and no problem for him – they didn't know what to do with Gray, the grandparents were in Europe for the summer and couldn't take

22

him, and under the circumstances they themselves couldn't very well have him along. So perhaps if the major wouldn't mind batching with the boy and keeping an eye on him—?

The major had called them at once, hearing their voices distant and squeaky along the frail line over the peaks and ridges, and shouting down the well of the years he had told them that, yes, he would be delighted, and it would be perfectly fine, and he would love to if Gray wouldn't mind. Gray wouldn't, Buck said, and a small, polite voice had observed cautiously, 'I hope you will like it here.' 'I'm sure I will,' the major had called back across the intervening miles of valley and mountains; and last night when the MacAleers had stopped by briefly they had told him that the boy was staying overnight 'up at the upper end of camp with some people you'll meet, Louise and Jerry Drummond', and would be at the cabin expecting him when he arrived next day.

'Watch out for Greenmont,' Buck had volunteered with an abrupt grimness that had startled the major, and he and Mary had exchanged a look he couldn't fathom.

'Best of luck,' he had said, rather more emotionally than he had intended. Mary had started to cry and for a little while everything had seemed bad again. But as soon as they left the depression had lifted and now, under the encouragement of the morning, he felt that things would go well from now on.

'Which is O.K. with me,' he said aloud as he began the slow, snaking climb through the meadows above Big Smith, 'because it's about time.'

And so it was, he reflected, although there might be some who would say that his own heart had made much longer the time it took to get over what he had to get over. But there had been the shock of it, to begin with, and then the gradual realization that it was not to be changed; and finally, most hurtful of all, the humiliation of coming to realize that it had never been as he supposed, that he had deluded himself right along, that this was a judgment rendered on him as a human being who had, in so important an area, failed.

And yet, he wondered still – although he tried not to wonder, for that only brought it back more strongly than ever – whether it had all been his fault. Somehow he could not believe it. Intelligence and experience and common sense told him it had not been ... although there, too, he must cease, for if it had not been, if the flaw had been there always, if from the first it had really been a mockery, then was that not a humiliation even deeper than the other? Did it not show that even in the beginning he had been gullible and unwise, and unable to judge something so empty for what it actually was?

Well. He told himself again that he was through brooding about that. The day was bright and beautiful, the morning coolness of the Valley was beginning to be replaced by the clear winds of the lower mountain ranges, and he must stop thinking about it. It was a perfect day, he was going to have a perfect time, the past was going to be exorcised once and for all by the drowsy magic of Greenmont. There he would make a fresh start and set for himself a fresh course in a life that after all had only run forty-three of its years and still had much more of good left in it.

'I *will* be bright and chipper,' he told himself, again aloud, and with an ironic amusement at this constantly running, self-conducted argument. 'By God, I've *got* to be.'

The pines were sleek and glistening in the sun, a soft haze lay on the higher mountains, far below he saw the first glint of the river's deep chasm as the car steadily gained altitude up the narrow winding road.

'Yoo-hoo!' Viola Townsend cried from the path. 'Hi, Drummonds, are you u-up?'

'We're u-up, Viola,' Louise called back from the kitchen. 'Come on in and have some co-offee.'

'Honestly, Louise,' Viola said, 'you make fun of everybody.' Her eyes took in with an instantaneous practised skill the big comfortable living-room bright with sunlight streaming through its windows, the magazines on the floor, fishing-tackle and tennis-rackets hanging on the knotty-pine walls, Jerry's swim trunks flung carelessly on one of the wicker chairs. 'I tripped on a rock,' she explained with dignity, 'which is why I said u-up.'

'Well, that's good,' Louise said, bringing out the coffee. 'I thought maybe you were beginning to get verbally cute, like

24

Haila. Let's go out on the deck. Jerry's almost through in the bathroom and he's quite apt to come out naked looking for his trunks. You don't want to be here when *that* happens, I hope.'

'No!' Mrs Townsend said firmly.

'Not that it's such a sight to see, of course,' Louise said cheerfully. 'However, though a poor thing, it is mine own.'

'Really, Louise,' Viola Townsend said, flushing, 'I just don't know what to do about you people. You and Jerry and Einar and Sally-Jane and *the things you say.* I don't know which of you is worst.'

'We just do it to keep you on your toes, Viola,' Louise said, leading the way to the big daybed under the oak at the corner of the deck and plopping down upon it comfortably. 'Now,' she said, settling herself among the pillows while her guest eased her ample form primly into a beach-chair, 'tell me what's new.'

'It was 105 degrees in Big Smith yesterday.'

'Oh? How do you know?'

'The Grossmans came up last night and Myra was over to say hello for a little while. They're up for the summer now.'

'That's good, Jerry was wondering if Roy was going to be here for the Board meeting.'

'The Robertsons and the junior Bill Pursemans got in last night, too,' Viola reported. 'The Johnsons and the Cartwrights are coming in this morning and the Talbotts will be in tonight.'

'My, you are a walking compendium,' Louise said. 'As always,' she added with a little bow.

'I just think people are interesting,' Viola said in a defensive tone, and Louise nodded heartily.

'Oh, indeed they are. Nowhere more so than in Greenmont.'

'Even if they aren't all clever, like you,' Mrs Townsend couldn't help adding. Her hostess gave her a cheerful grin.

'Come, now, Viola. Don't be catty. Where's Bob?'

'He and Jim Buxton had a golfing date at nine with Father Magruder.'

'We have a tennis date at ten with Einar and Sally-Jane,' Louise remarked. 'They beat us three times last week-end, so we've got to recoup.'

'What's going to happen to the MacAleers?' Viola asked abruptly. Louise frowned.

'I don't know,' she said, lowering her voice. 'Gray's in the bedroom sleeping.'

'Oh, is he staying with you? I thought they had some friend—'

'They do. He's coming up some time this morning, so we kept Gray overnight.'

'Haila was telling me he's a major in the Air Force,' Mrs Townsend said. Her hostess chuckled.

'You "thought" they had "some friend",' she quoted in Viola's innocent tone. 'You and Haila probably know ten times as much about him as I do. I'm sure you have him all catalogued.'

'We don't know very much about him,' Mrs Townsend said with dignity. 'Except he used to know them when Buck was in the service. Buck wasn't very specific when he talked to Haila.'

'Good for Buck.' There was a stir in the living-room and Louise glanced in quickly. 'Don't look, Viola, it's just like I said. There he is without a stitch. Sweetie! ' she called. 'Will you please wake Gray and help him get some breakfast? He's supposed to be down at his cabin to meet the major pretty soon, I think.'

'Right,' Jerry Drummond said, leaning his upper half coyly around the door to wave at Mrs Townsend. 'Hi, Viola. What's the dirt?'

'Jerry Drummond,' Mrs Townsend said firmly, 'you're too old to interest a woman as old as I am, so you might just as well go on and get dressed and stop behaving like some Romeo or something.'

'But I *am* some Romeo,' Jerry said. '*Some* Romeo! At least, Louise thinks so. At least, I *think* Louise thinks so.'

'Run along, sweets,' his wife said. 'You'll just have to guess on that one. And do get Gray up, hm?'

'O.K.,' Jerry said, and disappeared.

'For a man of forty-two,' Louise said placidly, 'he does have his little ways.'

'For a woman of sixty-one,' Viola said tartly, 'he can have them. Here come Einar and Sally-Jane, and I suppose that means more trouble for me.'

Louise laughed.

'Oh, come now, Viola, life isn't that bad. Hi, there, competition. Where've you been?'

'Getting the Cartwrights settled,' Sally-Jane said as she came up the steps to the deck. She was looking particularly cute this morning, dressed in tennis togs with her blonde hair in a bright halo around her pert little face.

'Oh, are they in already?' Mrs Townsend asked, and Einar smiled.

'Better run along and see them, Mrs Townsend. You might miss something.'

'Einar, honey,' Sally-Jane suggested before Viola could make a sharp retort, 'now, you just behave. It's much too beautiful a morning to start arguments.'

'It is beautiful,' Louise agreed, and for a moment they were all silent in the glory of the day, the great sweep of the canyon before them, the pines rustling and murmuring, a couple of blue jays flirting and screaming through the oaks and cedars and manzanitas, the river roaring along below.

'We saw some deer at the Meadows last night,' Einar remarked. 'There were three down by the pool about nine o'clock. We stood and looked at each other for about five minutes before they took off. It was,' he said softly, 'very nice.'

'Tommy Rupert claims he saw a bear near the Mineral Springs Wednesday night,' Louise said, 'but I don't believe him.'

'Tommy Rupert's a great one for tales,' Viola Townsend said. 'He's just at that age.'

'Some people never outgrow it,' Einar observed. 'How about some coffee, Louise?' he added quickly.

'Sure thing. I've got to check on Gray, anyway.'

'I'm up,' a small voice said from the living-room window and she smiled and waved.

'So you are, love. Did Mr Drummond get you breakfast?'

'Yes,' the boy said, appearing hesitantly in the doorway. 'I think I'll go down to our cabin now.'

'All right. Did you sleep well?'

'Pretty good.'

'Good. Bring the major up to the Meadows after a while, why don't you?'

'I will,' the boy said. 'I'm going to show him everything.'

27

'We want you to come and shag tennis balls for us too,' Einar said. 'We'll be on the lower court.'

'Maybe we will,' Louise said sardonically, 'if the rest of your endless family doesn't beat us to it.'

'Well, we'll be at the courts anyway,' Einar said, 'so you come along, kid, O.K.? We want you and the major to stick close to us these next few days, if you'd like to.'

'I don't know what he'll want,' Gray said thoughtfully. 'I don't know what he's like.'

'I'm sure you're going to like him,' Louise said. 'Would you like Mr Drummond to go down with you to meet him?'

'Oh, no,' Gray said politely. 'I'm not afraid of him.'

'Of course you're not, honey,' Sally-Jane agreed, giving him a hug. 'You run along and we'll see you later, all right?'

'All right. Good-bye, now.'

'Good-bye, child,' Mrs Townsend said. 'If you see Mrs Buxton, tell her I'll be down soon, will you?'

'All right,' Gray said. 'Good-bye.'

'Poor little thing,' Mrs Townsend remarked as he vanished along the path to the road and started the half-mile hike down through camp to his cabin, 'it's very tough on him.'

'It's tough all around,' Jerry Drummond said, coming out with additional coffee-cups. 'I only hope Buck and Mary can work it out.'

'What about this guy who's coming up?' Einar asked. 'You must know, Mrs Townsend. How will he fit in?'

'I think he plays tennis, if that's what you mean,' Viola Townsend told him, a trifle spitefully. Einar grinned.

'Well, that helps, I'll admit. I mean, maybe he can become One Of Us. Bridge at your place, barbecues at ours, cocktails at Haila's, wienie-roasts at Elizavetta's – *say*! ' he exclaimed suddenly. 'You don't suppose this will turn out to be Eliza's Dream Prince, do you?'

'Why, whatever makes you think that?' Louise asked sceptically, but there was no denying the idea was suddenly most interesting to them all.

'Oh, I don't know,' Einar said. 'Young, dashing, handsome – at least, I suppose he is, isn't he, Mrs Townsend?'

'I really don't know,' she said disapprovingly. 'He's more than forty, I know that.'

'Good for him!' Jerry Drummond said. 'You kids don't understand why I say that so feelingly,' he informed Einar and Sally-Jane, 'but it means something to us older types to know we're gaining reinforcements.'

'Sure, sure,' his wife said. 'Now, for heaven's sake, Einar, let's don't get camp started on promoting a romance. I couldn't imagine anything more horrible for both of them than to have us all sitting around shoving them at each other and placing bets on the outcome.'

'I'm willing to put up a little money right now,' Einar said. 'I can see the gleam in Mrs Townsend's eye already. Just wait 'til she suggests it to Haila.'

'Einar, honey,' Sally-Jane said reproachfully, 'that's cruel, now. That's real cruel to everybody.'

'Camp is, on occasion,' her husband said, giving her knee a friendly squeeze. 'Haven't you noticed?'

'Well,' Louise said firmly, 'I think we should all just leave well enough alone. If it happens, it happens. If it doesn't, it doesn't. I don't think we should any of us do anything about it one way or the other. Don't you agree, Viola?'

'Well,' Mrs Townsend said slowly. 'Of course. But – if he *is* nice, there's really no reason why – why it wouldn't *be* nice, is there?'

'Hell, let's give 'em a run for their money,' Jerry Drummond said. 'I'd like to see Eliza have a little fun, for a change.'

'Jerry,' his wife said in a tone he knew, 'I want you to stop that. And I want all the rest of us to stop it. I know this camp when it gets started on something like that. We don't know anything about this man, and it's none of our business. Anyway, we haven't seen him. He may be blind in one eye and have a wooden leg, for all we know. He may be a complete wreck outside.'

'Unlike Eliza, who's a wreck ins—' Einar began, but Sally-Jane reached up quickly and put her hand on his mouth.

'Now, that *is* cruel. You stop it, Einar.'

'Sure,' her husband said with a grin, rising and stretching to his full height, lifting his arms high above his head and bringing them down with an exuberant shout. 'Tennis, anyone?'

'Yes,' Louise said, jumping up. 'Want to come watch, Viola?'

'I'll walk down to the Meadows with you, I'm going on down

to Haila's for a minute. I *told* her I would,' she added defiantly at Louise's look, 'it has nothing to do with—'

'Well, it better not, I wouldn't want to have to fight you about it, Viola.'

'You won't,' Mrs Townsend said with dignity.

'I hope not,' Louise said. 'Einar,' she added with some vehemence as she went by him to get her racquet. 'I'm surprised at you.'

Einar grinned in his slow, unimpressed way.

'Maybe it will help relieve The Blight,' he suggested. Louise hooted and looked a little less perturbed.

'I hadn't regarded it just that way,' she admitted. 'But take it easy. People do get hurt, you know.'

'That's right, honey,' Sally-Jane said. She frowned at her husband. '*I'm* surprised at you, too.'

Einar grinned again and mussed her hair.

'Oh, hell,' he said, 'we don't mean any harm.'

'That's what scares me,' Louise remarked as they started along to the Meadows.

'Yes,' said Sally-Jane.

The major came to a fork in the road, a powerhouse far down to the right on the river's edge, its network of steel cables and great brown-glass condensers sparkling in the sun; a sign, 'Far Inn', on the left fork. He took the right. The car shuddered on a sudden steep grade, then moved forward in a steady climb. The last shadows of the night were slowly disappearing from their final refuge among the trees, the sharp coolness of the mountain morning was beginning to give way to the insistent persuasions of the sun. The river looked like spinach jade, dull-green, heavy and powerful, its deep pools feathered with white at the lower edges where the ice-cold water tumbled over jagged granite boulders on its implacable way to the valley floor.

The problem of regaining stability and peace of mind, he told himself, was not so much a matter of conscious effort, though God knew there had been plenty of that, as it was one of personal character. For a little while he had not known whether he had the necessary reserves or not. Then a calmer and less desolate mood had come to his assistance. If this was the way things were to be, this was the way they were to be, and he had best accept them and do the best he could to emerge from the situation with honour. Not that people were inclined to accord much honour to one in his position – somehow it always seemed to be something of a joke, something faintly funny that had happened while he was away in Korea fighting their damned messed-up war for them – but at least in his own conduct, he had come to realize, he could act with a dignity that might compel respect beneath the humorous reaction he found he was receiving. So this he had done, to the best of his ability, which was not always sufficient. Certainly it had not been on one or two private occasions, but for the necessary braveries of everyday living he hoped he had got by without putting his emotions too openly on display. It had not been easy, surrounded as he had been by the clever and uncaring wisecracks of a crowd whose loyalties didn't run very deeply or have much foundation in the heart.

It was strange, he thought, how well you could know people in the service and not know them at all. It was the nature of the life, he supposed, disjointed and wandering and not leaving much time for genuine attachments or understanding. You visited one another's houses, all filled with the grinding sameness of here-today-gone-tomorrow, you played bridge or went swimming or went out on the town together, and it was all very jolly and very close and very buddy-buddy. Then the party ended and everyone went home, leaving with each other names and faces and the memory of good times. But essentials were not exchanged, and nothing was left behind that really mattered. And if some military emergency arose and you were away from home for a while, then other things sometimes happened, the heart got damaged even more, sometimes it could not be put together when you got back.

The road became suddenly more winding. Thankfully, he was forced to drop this line of thinking that never left him for long and concentrate upon his driving.

He became conscious now that the air was becoming thinner, his ears were beginning to feel tight from the altitude. He swallowed several times and popped them open. He realized that he was climbing steadily higher into a really gorgeous day; and suddenly, too, he felt that he was really getting away from his burdens, that there was a genuine palpable division, aided

31

by nature, between what he was leaving behind and what he was about to enter. He felt elevated high above an old unhappy world, on the threshold of a new and friendlier one.

'What sentimental nonsense,' he remarked to a squirrel that ran suddenly across the road in front of the car, but the little beast did not stop to argue, it chattered sternly, gave its tail an angry snap, ran under an oak and disappeared down the side of the grade. It was the same world, wherever you were.

Still and all, he could not help a recurrence of happiness, almost in spite of himself, as the car climbed steadily on. Now the great canyon was narrowing, the mountains were crowding closer in, far ahead through the gap he could see much higher peaks where the snows never melted and where the grey rocks, bare of trees, suggested both the beginning and the end of Creation. High above on his right one of the nearer peaks loomed in over the canyon, near its summit a chunky outcropping of boulders mottled with lichen. Did it look like a frog? He remembered what the MacAleers had said last night: 'When you see Toad Rock you'll know you're getting close to camp.'

He gave the car a little more gas in anticipation and as he navigated an outside curve became conscious that he was being followed, not too far behind, by an old green convertible with the top down. Its bandannaed driver was feminine, its pace was about even with his own, perhaps half a mile back. Moved by some impulse of good fellowship he raised a hand and waved. After a moment of obvious hesitation the driver waved back. Why hesitate? he wondered. After all, a wave across half a mile of canyon didn't obligate anybody to anything. He smiled and shrugged. The road went suddenly around a shoulder of cliff, the other car slipped from sight, he was forced to tend to his driving again as the corkscrew trail plunged upward through the ridges.

He saw now that he was entering a burned-over area, noticed with a heightened interest that it must have been quite a fire; eight or ten years ago, he would estimate, and in its day a fairly awesome conflagration which had cut a swath perhaps a mile wide, from the riverside on his right over the road and on up until it disappeared out of sight high on the mountain to his left. He wondered in what season it had occurred, whether it had been during the summer months when Greenmont was fully occupied, whether they had all escaped, whether anyone had been hurt. A hell of a way to die, he thought with a shiver, if anybody had. He had spent his college summers with the Forest Service, and fire was no joke. He frowned and drove on out of the burned area into untouched forest again.

The road made a few last turnings, he saw a stable and some horses in an open clearing on his right, realized that the canyon was widening out into a valley perhaps half a mile long and half a mile across. He came to a well-kept general store, a few weathered cabins basking in the sun. He stopped at the store, bought some cigarettes, drove on a quarter of a mile to a locked wooden gate barring the road.

GREENMONT, it said on the arch. MEMBERS ONLY.

The green convertible, which had evidently passed while he was in the store, was drawing up before it. He honked and jumped out.

'Wait a minute,' he called. 'I'll get it.' The driver, a black cocker spaniel leaping and barking excitedly in the seat beside her, turned and smiled and held out a key.

'That's very kind of you. Don't let it throw you off if the lock doesn't work right away. You have to keep at it.'

'That's something I wouldn't know,' he said gravely; and added with a sudden little grin, gesturing at the sign, 'Not being a Member.'

She laughed.

'Don't let that throw you, either. There are nice people here.'

'I'm sure of it,' he said, and for a moment looked straight at her, the abundant black hair straying out from under the scarlet bandanna, the mouth over-painted and a little garish, the eyebrows thin and dramatically pencilled, some sort of Indian print thrown around her shoulders, an insistent air of over-dramatization that repelled him for a moment. Then she smiled and he found himself, somewhat to his surprise, smiling warmly back – her smile did things. He had an impression of something questioning, hopeful, kindly, capable of being hurt, in the wide, earnest dark eyes. A strange protectiveness came out of nowhere to touch his heart and he told himself sharply not to be a fool. He had felt protective once before and look what hell had come of it. But the feeling persisted for a second, agonizing and sharp with old memories – and, disturbingly and much to his

33

annoyance, new hopes. He turned away with an air of impatience she did not understand and wrestled with the lock.

'There!' he said finally. He bowed low with an elaborate mockery.

'Princess,' he said, 'enter your kingdom. I'll roll up the moat.'

'Thanks so much,' she said with another smile, taking the key. 'I hope you'll like it here.'

'I hope so.'

'Perhaps I'll see you at the Meadows.'

He nodded.

'I gather it's impossible not to see people up here,' he said, and again she laughed, a quite unselfconscious, happy sound that did not go at all with the garish get-up.

'We'll all try to protect you,' she assured him. 'Take care.'

He bowed again, she drove on through, and with a last wave was gone from sight where the road wound away through the trees, skirting the river, now close at hand as the canyon narrowed sharply once again.

He drove his own car through, stopped and got out to lock the gate; much more thoughtfully than he had opened it, and with an air almost of reluctance that he could not entirely define, although he told himself with a peculiar mixture of sadness and anticipation that he would probably understand it well enough the more he thought about it. How vulnerable he still was, really, he thought with a sudden bitter self-disgust; really, how vulnerable, for all his pretensions to himself that it was all over and he had it conquered.

Half a mile further on signs of habitation began to appear, the canyon widened out again a little, he saw dwellings set off amid the trees, rustic but substantial. The word 'cabin', he could see, did not, at Greenmont, mean a share-cropper's shack in the boondocks. At two or three of them people were sitting around on porches. Several waved. An abrupt turn in the road, a little hollow, two cabins neighbouring across a narrow ravine, a sign: SIERRA MIA. He had arrived.

⚜ TWO ⚜

He stepped forth into the mountain silence, the great warm quiet that has so many noises in it: squirrels chattering, jays and crows insulting one another, a flicker hammering busily on a hollow branch, the tiny flutings of quail, wind rustling in the trees, the river, muted yet not too far away, roaring along softly in the near distance. The ground was thick with pine needles, soft and aromatic underfoot, the air was fresh and invigorating. By the road a pair of monarch butterflies fresh from the cocoon, glistening yellow and black, danced lazily like little kites above the bear-clover. A bland harmony ordered the world.

He saw a two-storey cabin finished with hewn-log siding; big windows; a deck on the second level gained by a steep flight of steps; a garage and service area underneath; at the top of the steps, peering over, the solemn face of a twelve-year-old boy. The major, looking up, had an impression of big eyes, clean shirt and shorts, gangly brown arms and legs, unruly hair, an aloof and watchful expression. The boy, looking down, had an impression of a compact, solid presence, a plain but pleasant face, a friendly expression, an air of calm efficiency, masculine and self-contained. The major, moving around to unlock the car trunk, spoke first.

'Hi, skipper!' he said cheerfully, but apparently this was the wrong thing to say, for the boy's eyes widened and the aloofness did not decrease.

'My name's Gray,' he said politely. The major laughed.

'All right, Gray. Mine's Bill. O.K.?'

'Yes, sir,' the boy said, still politely.

'I saw your folks last night,' the major said, matter-of-factly yanking a tennis racquet out of the trunk and tossing it up so quickly the boy had to jump to catch it. 'They said I was to make you mind and see you didn't misbehave.'

'That's what they told me, too,' Gray said cautiously, leaning the racquet carefully against the deck railing.

'Shall we forget about that and work it out in our own way?' the major suggested. 'I'd rather, if that would be all right with you.'

'I'd rather, too,' Gray said, sounding more interested and not so reserved.

'Fine,' the major said, tugging away at a large suitcase that didn't want to come. 'Suppose we – God *damn* it, get out of there! – put you in charge and I'll do whatever you say. After all, it's your cabin. You'd think your folks would remember

35

that, wouldn't you?' He shrugged and grinned. 'Well, parents are funny.'

'Were they talking to each other?' Gray asked abruptly, and the major stopped grinning.

'A little.'

'Do you think it will be – all right?' the boy asked, and at the worry in his voice the major for a second looked quite troubled.

'I don't know, Gray,' he said quietly. 'I suppose I could tell you everything would be fine, but that might be pretending. And we don't want to start our friendship pretending with one another, do we?'

'I don't want to,' Gray said. The major smiled.

'Well, neither do I. So I can't tell you what will happen. You know how those things are – or anyway,' he said with a rather grim smile, '*I* know how they are – so I tell you what we'll do. We'll keep the house and hope for the best and maybe it will work out O.K. and they'll be back in a couple of weeks. Fair enough?'

'I guess so,' Gray said uncertainly.

'Good,' the major said, pausing to survey the two suitcases and bulging duffle bag stacked neatly at the foot of the steps. 'Now, why,' he demanded, 'do I always bring all this junk. You'd think with all the travelling I've done I'd know enough not to over-pack, wouldn't you?'

'What are they all?' Gray asked, and the major grinned.

'That one,' he said, kicking it, 'is filled with books. I thought maybe this would be a good place to catch up on my reading.'

'It's good for that,' Gray agreed. 'Greenmont is awfully good for just relaxing.'

'Wonderful. That's what I want, is just relaxing. Now. I'll get this stuff up there and you can tell me where you want me to sleep.'

'Do you want me to help?' Gray offered. The major nodded matter-of-factly, though a pleased little twinkle came into his eyes.

'I think that would be a real buddy.' The boy hopped promptly off the rail and came down the stairs.

'I'll take the book one. I like books.'

'It's heavy,' the major warned, and Gray gave him a smile that was suddenly quite trusting and no longer aloof.

'I don't mind.' He gave it a tug, grunted, and started, lop-sided but gallant, up the stairs.

It was just this moment that Haila Buxton came into the major's life, and, as he came to understand when he knew her better, the entry was typical.

'It looks as though *you've* made a friend,' a voice called archly, and with an impatient gesture, because that was exactly what he had done and this might well make the boy self-con-scious and set it back a week, he looked around in some annoy-ance at the porch of the cabin across the ravine. A tall, angular, stylish matron in mid-sixties, every grey hair and every fold of dress in exact place in the midst of this casual setting, looked warmly back.

'Hello, Gray, dear!' she called with a friendly wave, and Gray, having arrived at the top of the steps, dropped the suit-case with a thud and looked around. The major was pleased to note that the boy glanced first at him, however, and he had time to wink and catch a little answering gleam before Gray looked across the way.

'Hello, Mrs Buxton,' he said with some reserve. 'This is Major Steele. He's going to be staying with me for a while.'

'I know, dear, your mother told me before she went down,' Haila Buxton said, preparing to leave her own porch and come along the little path across the ravine. 'Did they get off all right last night?'

'Yes,' Gray said. The major noted with some amusement that his new pal didn't give an inch when he didn't want to.

'Well, that's good,' Mrs Buxton said. In a moment she was on the MacAleer's porch, hand outstretched.

'I'm Haila Buxton, Major Steele,' she said cordially. 'Welcome to Greenmont.'

'Thank you, ma'am,' he said. 'Everybody's making me feel at home.'

'Greenmont is like that. Everybody always feels at home here.'

'You can sleep in the back bedroom on the right,' Gray said abruptly. 'I have to go up to the pool, now.'

'All right, dear,' Mrs Buxton said. 'Why don't you run along and the major can come up with me a little later?'

'But I thought maybe Gray would show me around—' the

major began. But the boy was already down the steps.

'I'll see you later,' he said, and was gone.

The major shrugged and laughed.

'Such a strange child,' Haila Buxton said thoughtfully. '*Such* a strange child.'

'Oh, I don't know,' the major said, rather shortly. 'He seems O.K. to me.'

'Oh, he is,' Mrs Buxton said hastily. 'I don't mean to imply there's anything wrong with him. But so—' she too shrugged and a quizzical, understanding, half-humorous, what-can-you-say-about-situations-like-that? expression came into her eyes. 'So – elusive, somehow.'

'Well, he's my problem,' the major said, still rather shortly, 'and I guess we'll manage. This isn't my house,' he added with a smile that softened it somewhat, 'but I seem to have fallen heir to it in the abdication of its lord and master. Won't you sit down?'

'I was just going to suggest that you come over and join us,' Mrs Buxton said. 'Jim and Viola Townsend and I are having a little breakfast before going up to the Meadows. Quite Continental, coffee and doughnuts.'

'You mean you've just got up?' the major asked. Mrs Buxton smiled.

'It's only eleven,' she said comfortably. 'You'll learn that's part of Greenmont. Life doesn't begin until around noon. That's one of the reasons we all love it so.'

'Greenmont,' the major observed, 'seems to be quite a place.'

'You'll find out,' Haila Buxton promised gaily. 'Do come over when you get through unpacking.'

'It's very kind of you. It'll be a little while.'

'That will be fine. We do so want to know all about you.'

The major grinned.

'I can't promise that, but I'm looking forward to the coffee and doughnuts.'

It was only after she had departed and he had begun unpacking that he paused suddenly to reflect that in the short space of ten minutes a wedge had been driven between him and the boy, their friendship had been expertly attacked, and he was now under Mrs Buxton's wing and about to be presented to Greenmont as her acquisition instead of as his own man. He

38

decided with a rueful little smile that he was perhaps going to have to be a little more on guard than he had planned to be, here in this sunny, restful, pleasant place.

None of this, however, showed a few moments later when he took the little path across the ravine to be greeted by the voice whose arch inflections he was already beginning to anticipate.

'All settled in?' it asked. He smiled.

'I think so. It seems a very comfortable cabin.'

'Oh, it is. Major Steele – Mrs Townsend. And this is my husband, Jim.'

He saw another sixtyish matron, unkempt, dowdy, an essentially kindly but openly curious face. A tall raw-boned man with a little pinched, quizzical face, who seemed to be all knees and elbows, stared at him with a patient, good-natured expression.

'My pleasure,' he said, shaking hands with them both. 'There were also some people named Drummond the MacAleers told me about—?'

'They live next to me at the upper end of camp,' Mrs Townsend said. 'You'll meet them at the Meadows. How are Buck and Mary?'

'Fine,' he said non-committally, and then smiled and shook his head. They all smiled, a lengthening moment.

'That has been such a worry for us all,' Mrs Buxton said finally, sorrow in her voice. '*Such* a worry, really, for two years, now, when you stop to think about it.'

'Oh?' he said. 'They gave me the idea it was all rather sudden.'

'It may have been sudden in some ways,' Viola Townsend said, 'but we could see it coming last summer. At least Haila could.'

'Old Haila,' Jim Buxton said suddenly with a dry little chuckle. 'She sees things.'

'James Buxton,' his wife said with an air of coyness that struck the major as both automatic and absent-minded, 'stop calling me old. You know I'm all of a year younger than you are. But I'll admit that's a lot older than *you* are,' she added, placing a kittenish hand suddenly on the major's arm. He made

39

a very slight movement he knew had registered, for the hand was calmly and instantly removed and he knew it would not be proffered again.

'Oh, I don't know,' he said, 'I'm forty-three.'

'Well, you bear it beautifully,' she said with a comfortable laugh as they all sat down. 'Cream and sugar?'

'Please.' An acorn fell suddenly from the oak somewhere above and bounced sharply on the deck. A squirrel chattered in petulant annoyance.

'He lost it,' Jim Buxton said with a laugh. 'That's the third he's dropped in the last ten minutes.'

'They're such pests,' Mrs Townsend said. 'How long will Buck and Mary be gone, Major?'

'Didn't they tell you?' he asked innocently. Haila Buxton gave a merry laugh.

'We don't know everything that happens in Greenmont, Major.'

'I could have sworn you did,' he said with a chuckle that also sounded innocent. Jim Buxton snorted. 'I think they'll be gone about a month, Mrs Townsend. That's about how long I'm planning to be here, at any rate.'

'Well, we hope you will stay just as long as you can,' Haila Buxton said. Her husband grunted, folding one long leg over the other.

'Give these gals something to talk about,' he said. 'They need some excitement.'

'As for you, James Waldorf Buxton,' his wife said pleasantly, 'I think it's about time you went up to the Meadows and played some golf.'

'That's right, Jim,' Viola Townsend said. 'I wondered why you were sitting around. Bob left at ten.'

'Good,' Jim Buxton said lazily. 'He ought to have old man Magruder pretty well worn down by the time I get there.'

'Well?' his wife inquired with an amused patience. He looked at the major with a humorous shrug.

'They're set on driving me out. They want to get at you alone, boy.'

'Well?' Haila said again, the note of amusement in her voice increased to exactly the right degree. Her husband grinned and stood up.

'Take care of yourself, Major. We'll see you at the Meadows later on.'

'Maybe I should come along with you now,' the major suggested. Mrs Buxton laughed aloud.

'Certainly not! He's entirely right, we want to know *all* about you, so you just sit here and relax for a little. After all, it was a long drive from Fresno in the heat.'

'I was out of the Valley before it really closed in. It felt like another scorcher, though. It's been a fierce summer, so far.'

'Oh, have you been in Fresno these last few weeks?' Mrs Buxton asked quickly. 'I thought perhaps you had just come back from—' she gave a quizzical little smile as much as to say, you people go *everywhere*— 'from wherever you were.'

'You see what I mean,' Jim Buxton said with a farewell wave as he started down the steps. 'Keep your guard up, boy.'

'Run along, sweetheart,' his wife called lightly. 'Don't laugh at your own jokes so hard you fall in the pool. Really,' she said, turning back with a humorously confiding smile, 'Jim is *such* a good sport. You have to know him to appreciate him, but he is *such* a good sport.'

'I can see he must be,' the major said politely, and for just a second he was rewarded by a sharp little glint in his hostess' eyes. But she let it pass.

'Now,' she said briskly, 'do tell us all about yourself. Buck said you were in the Air Force, I believe?'

'Yes, ma'am,' he said. 'This is awfully good coffee.'

'Were you in Korea?' Viola Townsend asked. 'I have a nephew who was there in the Marines.'

'I hope he got out all right,' the major said. She nodded.

'Safe and sound. About six months ago. He was married last week.'

'Good for him,' the major said.

'You're a bachelor, I take it, Major,' Mrs Buxton said, and though his hesitation was split-second he could see she took note of it.

'Yes.'

'Recent?' she inquired gaily, and with a sudden annoyance he made no attempt to conceal, he said, 'Yes.'

'Oh,' Viola Townsend said in a tone of discovery, 'now I understand why Buck and Mary—'

41

'That's right,' he said grimly. 'Birds of a feather.'

'Well,' Haila Buxton said smoothly, 'I'm sure you'll find Greenmont a good place to – to—'

'To what?' he asked coldly, and saw that she was, for a moment, a little nonplussed by his tone.

'Why, rest and relax.' A certain challenge came into her own voice. 'What else do you feel like doing, at this stage of the game? Anything?'

'Nothing, Mrs Buxton. Just nothing else at all.'

'Well, that's good,' she said calmly. 'Do you like wienie-roasts?'

'I like almost anything,' he said shortly, 'as long as I like the people I'm doing it with.'

'I think Elizavetta is planning one tonight,' Viola Townsend said, and at the name, so awkwardly foreign in this completely native setting, he felt a little warning flag go up in his mind. Oh, no, he thought: don't tell me. But he knew already.

'Who's Elizavetta?' he asked. 'I don't suppose she drives a green convertible, does she?'

'Major,' Haila Buxton said with a smile, 'you've been hiding things from us. You already know Eliza.'

'We've met.'

'Oh?'

He nodded.

'Like I said,' he added with a smile, 'this is very good coffee.' She gave a hearty laugh.

'Oh, you military men! Always so secretive.'

'Did you meet in Fresno?' Viola Townsend asked, and Mrs Buxton gave her a chiding look.

'Viola, how can you be so crude? You can see the major wants to be mysterious.'

He perceived he had better drop this tack at once or create an issue that would have the whole camp buzzing before sundown.

'We met at the gate. It was hardly what you would call a formal introduction. I unlocked it for her. She thanked me. I said you're welcome. She drove on. I drove on. Period. Who is she, anyway?'

'One of our oldest and dearest friends,' Viola Townsend said. 'One of Greenmont's really genuine people.'

'Really Genuine People,' Haila Buxton repeated solemnly, with capitals. 'Such a dear. Such a dear! Such – a – *dear!*'

'That's good,' he said. 'I'm glad to know there are nice people in Greenmont. In addition,' he added with a smile, 'to the Buxtons and the Townsends and of course the Drummonds I'm to meet. And Gray MacAleer. And all the rest. How soon do you go up to the Meadows, usually?'

'Oh, she won't be there until noon,' Mrs Buxton said with the arch airiness he was already beginning to find tiresome.

'I don't care when she's there,' he said calmly. 'It's getting on, and I'd like to see the place. Since you drove off Gray, I guess you'll have to be the one to show me.' But his hostess did not rise to the bait. Instead she murmured pensively, 'That *strange* little boy. *Such* an unhappy time for him. Well, Viola, are you ready?'

'Would you like to play some golf, Major?' Mrs Townsend asked as she arose. 'I expect Haila has an extra putter if you do.'

'No, thanks. I'll run over to my cabin – *my* cabin, you see I'm at home already – and get my tennis-racquet, though. Maybe I'll find somebody who plays.'

'Almost everyone from ten to seventy does,' Mrs Townsend said proudly. 'We've had Valley champions from among our young people for the past twenty years.'

'Have you? Then I shouldn't have any trouble finding competition. And if I should, well, I'll just sit around and observe.'

'You'll find us a collection of characters,' Haila Buxton said with a comfortable laugh. 'A real collection of characters.'

'But pleasant,' the major suggested, so blandly that it again brought a little spark to his hostess' eyes. 'Of that I am quite sure.'

Back at the MacAleer cabin for a few moments, changing into sports shirt and shorts with swim trunks underneath, he stopped for a moment to listen again to the sounds of the warm sunlit day, the ceaseless talking of the wind-teased forest, the constant murmur of the river, the sounds of bird and animal life all around.

So he had divulged his great secret already, he thought, and already they were match-making, he could see that.

43

What a secret and what a match! The sorry secret of his divorce, how earth-shaking and profound! And the match, that strange, over-dramatic elderly girl with the garish make-up and the eyes that admitted more candidly than they knew that their owner could be hurt!

But as abruptly as it had come, his sarcastic mood vanished and he brought himself up short. The secret was earth-shaking enough, for him; and as for the girl, he promised her suddenly on an inner jest that was at once wry, defensive and kind. Don't worry, sister. You won't be hurt by me – because, he added quite grimly, I'm not about to let myself be hurt by you.

And yet when he returned to the Buxtons' cabin a moment later, he was asking himself, I wonder? – and both his companions noticed a little preoccupation in his manner, though their conversation on the slow uphill walk to the Meadows passed pleasantly and matter-of-factly as they pointed out which cabin belonged to whom, and filled his head with names and dates and little bits of intimate background gossip that soon clogged his thoughts like torn scraps of paper he knew he would presently have to sit down and sort out if he wished to find his way through this labyrinth of old friendships, old enmities, and family interrelationships stretching far back down the years.

⋗ THREE ⋖

'Eliza, pal,' Einar asked out of the side of his mouth as he stood at the lower tennis-court net waiting for one of Jerry Drummond's slice-shots down the sidelines, 'have you read any good books lately?'

'Pickings were pretty poor this week,' she said from the bench where she was holding a tight leash on an excited Smudge and keeping Gray MacAleer company between his quick dashes to retrieve balls. 'How about you?'

'I'm not reading much these days,' he confessed with a grin. 'That little Sally-Jane, she just keeps me so busy—'

'Honey,' his wife screamed, 'watch out for Jerry!'

'I – am – watching – out!' he cried, lunging for the ball and angling it deftly across-court where it landed at Louise's feet and caused an explosion.

'Oh, you stinker!' she whooped. 'Oh, you *awful* stinker! You know I can't get that kind of shot, you black-hearted blackguard!'

'Blast one right in his face!' Jerry urged, and his wife snorted. 'He never gives me a chance!' she wailed.

'Set-point,' Sally-Jane announced triumphantly and promptly muffed her first serve, which struck her husband in the small of the back.

'Sal, darling,' he said patiently. '*Over* the net, baby, *over* the net, please, not into my sacroiliac, O.K.?'

'I like your sacroiliac,' Sally-Jane said blandly. 'Now turn around and pay attention, because this one is going to be good.'

'No, it isn't!' Louise cried triumphantly, and it wasn't. 'Now, come on, sweetie, *let's bear down*!'

'Right,' Jerry said briskly, lobbing the next serve toward the back-court, where Sally-Jane struck at it futilely and let out a wail of anguish.

'That's good!' Louise cried. 'We've got 'em on the run!'

'We will have if you stop talking and sew up this point,' her husband told her, and with a sudden crow of triumph she did just that, lobbing the ball to Sally-Jane, who lobbed it back, and then driving it with all her force straight past Einar, who flailed at it wildly and missed.

'Five-all!' Louise crowed. 'Better get your excuses ready, chums. You'll be needing them in another two games. All right, sweetie, let's change sides and then *give it to 'em*!'

'Do you like tennis, Gray?' Elizavetta asked during the pause. He smiled.

'I like it the way Mr and Mrs Drummond play it. It's funny.'

'Out of the mouths of babes,' Einar said with a chuckle, mussing the boy's hair as he moved around the net. 'You tell 'em, kid.'

'That's all right, lover,' Louise told Gray. 'You have to excuse us old folks our little fun.'

'Oh, I enjoy it,' Gray said reassuringly, and just then Jerry delivered a terrific serve off the tip of his racket that described a surprising parabola and sailed over the fence. 'Excuse me,' he added to Elizavetta. 'I've got to get that one.'

'He's being an awfully good sport,' Elizavetta said when he

45

trotted off. Louise nodded hastily as her husband for his second serve delivered a cautious pat that fell dismally on their side of the net.

'He's a dear,' she agreed. 'Eat your Wheaties, Jerry!' she added sternly to her husband. 'Oh, oh!' she cried suddenly as her eye fell upon fifteen or twenty strapping Magruders moving slowly along past the courts to the pool. Her voice rose to a mocking shout. 'Here comes the medieval progress! Here comes the royal parade! Everybody out of the pool! Everybody out! Make way, here! Make way, peasants!'

'Hello, Louise,' Mother Magruder carolled happily, looking like a mammoth moving pyramid in the midst of her brunette brood. 'We hope you get beaten!'

'Thanks so much,' Louise carolled back cheerfully. 'Your children,' she said, repeating it with satisfaction when she saw Mother Magruder wince at this inclusion of Sally-Jane, '*your children* are giving us a rough time.'

'Play ball, Louise,' Einar ordered with dignity. 'Just ignore them, please.'

'Do you think they'll go away if I do?' Louise inquired with a grin. 'I might, if you could guarantee it.'

'I can't guarantee anything about my family,' Einar said, still with dignity. 'Thanks, kid,' he said to Gray, who was returning with the ball. 'Has your visitor arrived yet?'

'He's here,' the boy said tersely and plopped down again beside Elizavetta.

'Do you like him?'

'He's all right.'

'I think Elizavetta's going to like him, too,' Einar suggested and at that moment Jerry got over a serve that really did connect. They were all quite busy for a couple of minutes until Einar smashed a return to the Drummonds' backline and took the rally.

'Einar, honey,' his wife remarked sweetly, 'I do think you're puffing a little.'

'I have too many demands on my energies these days,' he told her cheerfully. 'Anyway, Eliza, you ought to see this guy Gray's got staying with him He's a real dream prince.'

'Einar,' Louise said, 'didn't we agree—'

'We agreed he was just what Eliza needs for a terrific

46

summer,' Einar said with enthusiasm. Elizavetta gave them a rather puzzled smile.

'I don't get it. Is there a secret I'm not in on?'

'No secret at all,' Jerry Drummond said, preparing to serve again. 'Just the handsomest man you ever saw.'

'You, too, Jerry,' his wife said, and Sally-Jane spoke up reassuringly.

'Elizavetta, honey, don't you listen to these old teases. They're always match-making, you know how they are.'

'Well,' Elizavetta said with a laugh that was quite genuinely amused, 'they haven't succeeded with me, all these years. Tell me,' she said, turning to Gray, 'is he driving a little black car?'

The boy nodded.

'It's a Karmann Ghia,' he said importantly.

'And he's medium height, and starting to get bald, and has a nice manner?'

'He's old,' Gray observed throughtfully. 'But,' he added, 'I like him.'

'So did I,' said Elizavetta promptly. Louise hooted.

'There, you connivers, take that! They've already met, the romance is on, and you can mind your own business.'

'No romance,' Elizavetta said placidly. 'He just opened the gate for me. Even Einar would do *that* for a lady.'

'Hm,' Einar said. 'All right for you, pal. If you find sand in your potato salad tonight, don't be surprised.'

'Your serve, muscle-man,' Louise said. 'Six-five and you're trailing. Come on, Jerry! '

'Anyway, Eliza,' Einar said as he prepared to serve, 'I think you ought to follow up on it. You never know.'

'Neither do you, honey,' said Sally-Jane at the net, 'so stop teasing and let's beat these old Drummonds.'

'Good as done,' her husband assured her, and after ten minutes of serious concentration by all of them, it was; except that it was the Drummonds who won.

'Well, I feel better,' Louise said, as they gathered, rather winded, in a group by Elizavetta and Gray at the bench. 'I was beginning to think we were *never* going to get back at the younger generation, over-fed, over-confident and over-sexed as they are. Oh, oh! ' she added with a sudden interest. 'Here comes another royal progress – and this time I think Haila's got your dream prince in tow, Eliza.'

And across the pool, now filling up with shouting children; the putting-green, now dotted with casually moving players; and the benches of the Grove, now filled with comfortably gossiping elders, they turned to look, where the road from the lower end of camp entered the Meadows, with a bright and interested stare.

~~§ FOUR §~~

Staring back down the green sweep of hill as it dipped across the Meadows to the pool and the tennis-courts beyond, he saw them standing so: his host the boy, a dark youth and a blonde girl, a wiry, pleasant-looking couple approaching middle-age – and the girl at the gate. There must have been a hundred people at the Meadows, the excited voices of children shouted from the sparkling water of the pool, the cries of their elders echoed from the putting-green, but for a moment these were all he saw, etched, in a curious silence that shut out other sound, against the clump of trees beyond the courts and the high peaks that soared above. He knew instinctively that they were watching him as intently as he was watching them, but before he could wave – which he rather wanted to do, because, after all, he knew the boy – Viola Townsend spoke at his side and broke the mood.

'There's Elizavetta now! ' she said in a cordial, excited voice. He turned and smiled.

'Elizavetta and a lot of other people. I hope you ladies are going to protect me.'

'We'll make sure you're safe,' Haila Buxton assured him gaily. 'Come along to the Grove and we'll introduce you to everybody. Hold it! ' she cried in mock alarm as they started down across the golf-course. 'Hold it, now, Bob! ' A threesome down the slope paused and waved.

'That's my husband,' Viola Townsend explained. 'And you've met Jim Buxton, and that's Father Magruder with them. And that dark boy at the lower tennis court is his son Einar, and that's Einar's wife Sally-Jane, and that's Louise and Jerry Drummond with them, and over there on the first bench in the Grove is—'

'Whew! ' he interrupted with a laugh. 'Slow down,. Mrs

48

Townsend. I can't keep up with all this. Give them to me one at a time.'

'Of course we will,' Mrs Buxton said, piloting him firmly toward the Grove. 'Hello, dear!' she called to Myra Grossman. 'You remember Major Steele, don't you, from Fresno? But of course *you* would!'

Ten minutes and twenty-three introductions later they arrived in rather breathless progress at the tennis-court and with some relief he said, 'Hi, Gray,' to his host. The boy gave him a sly little smile.

'You can call me Skipper,' he said, and grinned all over.

'I can, can I?' the major said with a chuckle. 'Suppose I prefer Gray?'

'Suit yourself,' the boy said, still grinning.

'Yes, dear,' Haila Buxton said. 'Let me introduce the major, now, may I, please?'

'O.K.,' Gray said. 'I think I'll go swim.'

'Good,' the major said. 'I'll join you in a minute.'

'Not on the high-dive,' his host told him firmly. 'That's for kids.'

'I wouldn't think of invading it,' the major said solemnly and turned away to the others. 'You're the Drummonds,' he said with a pleasant smile which they returned.

'We are,' Louise said. 'Two of the more obvious characters around here.'

'But nice,' Jerry assured him with a firm handshake. 'Or so we consider ourselves, anyway. This is Einar Magruder and Sally-Jane.'

'*You* remember Major Steele from Fresno,' Haila Buxton said automatically. Sally-Jane dimpled.

'Now, Mrs Buxton, honey, you know perfectly well we've never met the major, but, Major, it *is* nice to have you here.' Einar took his hand and gave him a long look before firming up the handshake and agreeing, finally, 'It is,' The major chuckled.

'Are you always so formidable?' he asked. Sally-Jane gave a merrily spontaneous laugh.

'Honey,' she said kindly, 'I think he has your number already.' Her husband smiled sleepily.

'I don't mind. Do you have a first name, Major?'

49

'I believe it's Bill.'

'Fine,' Einar said. 'This is Elizavetta Berrenger, who is sometimes known as Eliza to her ·friends and intimates. Of whom, Bill, we expect you to be one.'

'I hope so,' the major said, smiling at last directly at her. 'We've met – which seems to be a big thing, in Greenmont.'

'Almost anything is a big thing in Greenmont,' she said. Louise Drummond hooted.

'We're as inbred as the Jukes,' she said. 'We've all got each other's fleas.'

'That's not very elegant,' her husband told her, and over by the pool Mother Magruder looked up with a lively interest at their burst of laughter.

'What are you conspirators cooking up?' she demanded loudly. 'It's always something,' she informed the world at large, 'when that bunch gets together!'

'Me and my elderly friends are just getting ready to raise hell, Ma,' Einar called back. 'You needn't worry.'

'Oh, you match-makers!' she shouted merrily, and was pleased to note that a little uncomfortable silence fell abruptly upon them.

'Oh, hell,' Einar said vehemently. 'Come on, Sal, race you in the pool.'

'It was your idea, sweetie,' Louise called after him mockingly as he hit the water in front of old Mr Stafford, who was dangling his bony match-stick legs over the edge and reacted with an indignant splutter when the resultant tidal wave engulfed them.

'I'm going to talk to that boy,' Sally-Jane promised as she flipped on a bathing-cap and tucked the last blonde curl away in one practised, efficient motion. 'See if I don't!' she added as she dashed toward the pool.

'Well,' Haila Buxton said brightly. 'Who won your match, Drummonds?'

'We did, thank God,' Jerry replied. 'They were beginning to lord it over us in great style. How about a swim, Eliza? We have a few minutes before Annual Meeting. Bill?'

'Do we dare?' the major asked dryly. 'I mean, if we've already become a public issue—' But he was aware that Elizavetta was smiling and suddenly he did too. 'I'd offer to race you in,

Louise,' he said, 'except I think we're both too old to stand the gaff.'

'Race Eliza,' Louise suggested. 'She's younger.'

'I'm not that young,' Elizavetta said. 'And anyway, it apparently is a public issue – and I expect I should be up there in the Grove helping to get things ready for the meeting. I'm on the road committee this year with Rudy Whitman, and you know how important it is to Rudy that everything be in order.'

'Well,' the major said. An awkward little silence fell. Then he added, and could have kicked himself for adding fuel to this particular fire, 'I hope you aren't going to run away altogether.'

'Oh, she won't,' Viola Townsend promised brightly. 'We won't let her!'

'Indeed we won't!' Haila Buxton agreed. Louise Drummond gave her racy grin.

'You see there's no fear of it. Your interests are going to be protected, Bill.'

'Yes,' he said; and, with a sudden defensive crispness that sounded cold, 'assuming I have any interests.'

'Let's go, boy,' Jerry Drummond said heartily, taking him by the arm. 'That water comes right down off the snows and it's so cold it's going to knock you sideways, but it sure does make a man feel good.'

'At your service,' he said, still in the same crisp tone, and turned away, but not before he had caught a fleeting expression of puzzlement and pain in Elizavetta's eyes. He turned back and held out his hand.

'Princess, I like your kingdom. But keep the natives off my back, will you?'

'I'll try,' she said, giving his hand a squeeze and looking, he was relieved to note, more relaxed. 'Maybe we can swim after the meeting, if you like.'

'We'll see,' he said. 'Perhaps we can play some golf or tennis this afternoon, in any event.' Haila Buxton broke in briskly.

'Well, now, you two, there'll be plenty of time for that, because the major is going to be here for a whole month.'

'Oh, sugar plums,' Louise Drummond said dryly. 'All right, Bill, on that happy and auspicious note I *will* race you in.'

Two minutes later as he pulled himself up, shivering but exhilarated, on to the concrete apron along the edge of the pool, she arrived with a brisk splash at his side and looked up at him thoughtfully from the sparkling water agitated by constant diving and swimming all around.

'Was that trip necessary? I mean, people can get hurt, you know.'

'How can you stand to stay in that water?' he inquired pleasantly. 'Aren't you frozen to death?'

'You get used to it,' she said, scooping a waterlogged blue dragonfly on to the concrete with a practised flip of the hand. 'A little. I repeat, that sounded a trifle harsh.'

'My God,' he said. 'You people. I've been in this place two hours and you've got me signed, sealed and delivered. Haven't you got anything better to do?'

'That's the trouble,' she said with a laugh. 'We haven't. But don't bite Eliza. It isn't her fault.'

'Just don't push me.' He shook his head with a sudden impatience. 'The whole thing is absurd, anyway. Utterly absurd. In any normal context things don't happen this fast, in the first place, and in the second place—'

She gave a sudden grin.

'In the second place, who said you were in a normal context? We who love it call it Greenmont.'

'Yes,' he said, unamused. 'Well: just lay off, or none of us are going to be friends.'

'I'm on your side, brother,' she informed him as she prepared to shove off with a vigorous back-stroke across the pool.

'Can I count on that?' he called after, but, not having looked before she leaped, she had crashed into an outsized inner-tube bearing two small Whitmans and a teen-age Webster, and her answer, if any, was lost in the confusions of getting everybody shaken out and right-side-up again.

And that was what the wayfaring stranger got, he told himself ironically, for going along too amicably with the bland envelopment of this lotus-eating atmosphere which drew you in before you knew it and suddenly made everyone's intimate concerns everyone else's. There was something about the place, apparently, that made privacy almost impossible; and, with it, a certain acceleration of mood and emotion that did not bode altogether well for someone whose feelings happened to be in as uncertain a state as his were at the moment. But of course he could not tell them that: that would be an abandonment of privacy even beyond the expectations of this insistent and in-grown community. And so he had snapped out and offended someone who might conceivably be a real friend. That was a fine foot to get off on. He sighed suddenly. The day, though physically reaching the zenith of its warmth and serenity as the sun stood high and hazy blue mist filtered down through the forests, did not seem so relaxed and comfortable as it had.

Up in the Grove he could see people beginning to gather in rows of wooden chairs for the meeting. He realized that the pool was emptying of adults. Einar and Sally-Jane waved and disappeared among the trees, Haila Buxton and Viola Towns-end called, 'See you later – we'll call you after the meeting, for the barbecue!' – and Louise came by and said, 'Relax!' which he accepted with a smile but resented a little because he told himself he felt perfectly relaxed.

Abruptly he and the children were left in command of the pool. He felt he should probably stay for the barbecue, but he also felt the need to get away for a while from this cloying, all-pervasive camaraderie. He swam two quick, shivering laps across the pool, got out, dried himself, put on his shoes, picked up his tennis gear and walked, thoughtfully and alone, across the deserted Meadows and down the winding sun-speckled road to the MacAleer cabin.

'Where's our boy-friend going?' Einar whispered to Louise in the Grove. 'I hope we haven't offended him.' She snorted. 'Why don't you worry about things like that before they hap-pen?' she whispered back, and they both looked at Eliza, who was just starting upon an earnest report on estimates for black-topping the turn in the upper road near old Mr Stafford's cabin. There must have been something peculiarly intent in their gaze, for she looked up suddenly in mid-sentence, saw in the distance the disappearing figure of the major, stopped abruptly and then had to search quite hard for the next word before she found it and, suddenly quite flushed, went on.

'Now, what do you suppose made him run off?' Jerry Drummond demanded when the meeting was over and they had finished going through the barbecue line and were settled around the end of one of the long wooden tables in the Grove. 'I thought we were doing our best to make him feel at home, and off he goes. I don't get it.'

'Maybe he finds us a little overwhelming,' Jim Buxton suggested. 'It happens.'

'Well, I don't know why, I must say,' Viola Townsend remarked with some asperity. 'Haila and I did everything we could to get him started right.'

'Maybe that's why,' Jim said with a practised chuckle that over the years had been perfected to skirt the edge between agreement and provocation. His wife gave her equally perfected response.

'Oh, you!' she said, giving his arm a coyfully playful pat. 'Always joking!'

'Somebody has to, darling,' Louise remarked. 'Can you get the catsup down this way? Ask Janie Purseman.'

'Well, what *do* you make of it?' Bob Townsend asked. 'Seems to me like a funny time to go skulking off.'

'I don't think he went skulking off at all,' Sally-Jane said indignantly. 'I must say, I think you-all are terrible. Here the poor old major comes up here for a rest and right away you start picking on him. It isn't fair. And furthermore,' she added, stabbing vigorously at a piece of barbecued beef, 'it isn't funny.'

'I think he's touched Sal's tender heart,' her husband remarked with a grin. 'She's a born mother hen.'

'I am *not*! I must say I don't understand *you*, either, after all the opportunities you've had to find out what this place can do.'

'Well, now, everybody,' Louise said, 'I think we had best leave this fascinating topic because here come Eliza and Gray and it might be better to just drop it.'

'Oh, I don't know,' Einar said lazily. 'Hi, Eliza, sit down here with us. I thought that was a good report you made. Too bad Bill didn't stay to hear it.'

'Now, you stop,' Sally-Jane said firmly. 'Einar Magruder, I

54

want you to stop!'

'I think you'd better, Einar Magruder,' Jerry Drummond said. 'She sounds as though this time she means it.'

'You know, I think she does,' Einar said admiringly. 'That little gal can put her foot down firmer than anybody I know. But I am sorry he missed it, Eliza. It was good.'

'All right,' Sally-Jane said, picking up her plate. 'I'm just going to move somewhere else with people I like better.' But her husband threw both arms around her waist and pulled her back.

'Don't fight, children,' Louise said. 'Viola, these watermelon pickles of yours are delicious. I thought it was a good report too, Eliza. Do you suppose old Mr Stafford will be satisfied now we've voted the money?'

'Old Mr Stafford has been a member of this club for fifty years,' Elizavetta said with a smile, 'and he's been dissatisfied every single minute of it, I'm sure. Is there room beside you, Haila?'

'Of course, dear. Viola will move over.'

'I don't know to where,' Mrs Townsend said, rather huffily, 'but I'll try.'

'Just push Jerry off the end of the bench,' Louise suggested. 'He likes to sit on the ground.'

'Seriously, about the major, now,' her husband said. 'Do you think we've been hard on him, Elizavetta? I thought we were all being pretty decent. *I* was trying, anyway.'

'Maybe you were all trying,' Elizavetta suggested with some irony, 'too hard. But,' she added quickly with a characteristic generosity, 'I thought you were all nice to him. I was proud of you.'

'That ought to make you feel ashamed of yourselves,' Louise told them quite severely. Einar grinned.

'I still think he's the perfect beau for you, Eliza. Seems a little moody, but I think he's nice.'

'I don't think he's moody at all!' Elizavetta said with a sudden real indignation. 'I think he's a fine person and I wish you'd leave him alone!' And, flushing, she looked intently at her plate and started eating furiously.

'Well, well!' Bob Townsend said with a hearty laugh. 'Can this be love?'

'Sounds like it to me,' Jim Buxton agreed. 'Yep, sounds like it to me.'

'We could ask,' Louise said pleasantly, 'what you know about it, Jimsy boy, but that probably wouldn't be kind.'

'Now who, at this point,' Sally-Jane asked of nobody in particular, 'is worried about being kind? Or at any point, for that matter?'

'I think,' Gray announced clearly from around Haila Buxton, 'that he is one of the nicest people I have ever met.'

'Yes, dear,' Mrs Buxton said. 'I'm sure he will be pleased to know that.'

'Yes, he will,' the boy agreed matter-of-factly. 'He likes me, too. Can I have some more beans, please?'

'More beans for the inner man,' Bob Townsend said heartily, heaping them upon the proffered plate. 'How are you making out, youngster?'

'All right. And some more meat, too, please.'

'Everything going all right, is it?' Bob Townsend repeated and Louise Drummond said, 'Honestly, Bob,' in an annoyed tone of voice. 'Pass the meat and help yourself, too. It's delicious.'

'Why, yes, it is,' Bob Townsend said in a rather surprised voice and, after looking owlishly about for a moment, returned to his meal. The clatter and chatter from other tables surged over them, Myra Grossman calling over some comment about the pickles, Viola Townsend shouting back, several assorted McCalls, a Talbott and a Magruder or two chiming in. Everybody was beginning to get a well-fed feeling and a sated look. Einar made a quick grab for a piece of French bread on Sally-Jane's plate and there was a brief, intimate scuffle that made Viola Townsend quiver. Louise turned hurriedly to Elizavetta.

'What's new in politics? Anything new on the plight of the world?'

'Well,' Elizavetta said, lighting a cigarette, leaning forward, and coming to life abruptly. 'It seems to me things have grown considerably more serious in the past week. Don't you think so, Haila?'

'They have,' Mrs Buxton said soberly. 'They *have*. Goodness, what will become of us!'

'Now, looking about this bucolic scene, Haila,' Louise said

dryly, 'do you really think anybody cares?'

'*I* care,' said Elizavetta fiercely. 'And Haila cares. And Viola. Why don't you ever care about anything, Louise?'

'But I do,' Louise protested mildly. 'I just don't make a profession of it, that's all.'

'I suppose I do!'

'No, sweetie, you don't. I just don't think it's necessary to be quite so serious about it sometimes, that's all.'

'How can you make fun of it,' Elizavetta demanded, 'when Greenmont and all of us are – are sitting on top of a volcano?'

'Goodness,' Louise said with real annoyance in her voice, 'are we going to have to sit on top of that damned volcano all through another summer? That's why Greenmont means so much, to me, at least. You can forget the damned volcano for a while and enjoy this fantastic little island in the sky. Frankly, I love it and I'm shamelessly glad we have a cabin and can come here.'

'That's all it is,' Elizavetta said firmly. 'An island. But the plight of all peoples is getting worse all the time we're lolling about up here.'

'Of course it is, dear,' Haila Buxton said severely. 'And despite what frivolous people think about it, one cannot help but be concerned if one has an ounce of social conscience. *Just one ounce!*'

'I'll pick up my ounce when I get back down to the Valley,' Louise said. 'Ounces mean something else to me up here.'

'Well,' Elizavetta said, tapping out her cigarette and speaking in a more kindly tone, 'I know you don't mean to be uncaring, Louise. After all, none of us wants to face unpleasant things in pleasant surroundings.'

For a second Louise looked quite genuinely annoyed. Then she laughed.

'You're wonderful, darling. What would we all do without you?'

'I don't know what the major would do without you, I must say,' Einar remarked. 'If he knows what's good for him, that is. I only wish he had been here to see you under a full head of steam, Eliza. You were mag*ni*ficent.'

'Somebody has to keep in mind what's important,' she said defensively, and her eyes under their heavy mascara suddenly looked quite hurt. 'I know you all make fun of me all the time,' she added wistfully, 'but *somebody* has to.'

'Nobody makes fun of you, dear,' Haila Buxton said indignantly. 'At least not *thinking* people.'

'Oh, come on, Haila,' Louise said. 'Let's get the table cleaned up and call it quits for one meal, shall we? Don't worry about us, Eliza. You know how we are. It doesn't mean anything. And you're entirely right, of course.'

'I really think you ought to be polite to her,' Gray remarked seriously, and they all laughed as Elizavetta gave him a hug.

'I have one champion, anyhow,' she said. He smiled up at her thoughtfully.

'I think *he* likes you, too.'

'There, you see, Eliza?' Jerry Drummond demanded triumphantly. 'You haven't got a thing to worry about. *He* likes you, too.'

'Come on, sweetie,' Louise said firmly. 'Let's police the area and get on home for a nap, shall we? More tennis this afternoon, competition?'

'We'll come prepared,' Einar said. 'How about you, Eliza?'

'No, thanks. I thought maybe Gray might ask the major if he would like to play some golf with me this afternoon. Tell him I'd like to if he would.'

'O.K.,' Gray said. 'He will.'

'Well, I guess that sews it up,' Bob Townsend said jovially to Jim Buxton. 'Now the girls can stop worrying.'

Jim Buxton snorted.

'You don't know the girls.'

⋙ SIX ⋘

A singing silence lay upon the great cleft in the Sierras: summer noon, mountain noon, spellbound the world. He was aware of the cabin, the trees, the sun, the speckled shade, the birds and squirrels, the river tumbling in the distance – it was as though he were perceiving them through his skin with a heightened awareness even as their physical impact diminished under the somnolent persuasions of the hour. The busy fret of morning had given way to a drowsier pace. The birds were quieter, the squirrels were off somewhere in the woods, the river seemed hushed and sleepy and far away. He heard a car grind up the road, pass and dwindle. No other human sound disturbed the stillness, no doors slammed, no voices called. He might have been a thousand miles from nowhere, alone in the aromatic universe, last man on earth and emperor of it.

Going quietly about the kitchen in swim trunks and bare feet, making sandwiches and pouring a glass of milk which he took out on the deck, he was aware that the peace of the place was beginning to flow back into him. The conversations at the pool became less annoying and began to subside into perspective. He should not let himself be too irritated by the things these people said, he should not respond too quickly to the obvious goads with which they sought to draw him out. He should remain as calm as he appeared to be – if, he told himself wryly, he did appear to be. Louise Drummond hadn't thought so: 'Relax!' Relax, indeed. He told himself again that he must certainly do so, and that with it he must also carry within him, quietly but tenaciously, a little more caution and a little more care if he did not wish to run the risk of some further laceration of his feelings, some new situation that might turn out to be, despite whatever hopes and idealism and goodwill might be put into it, just one more disappointment for a heart that had known its share and desired no more.

Still and all, he couldn't help liking Greenmont and the people in it. Some of them were characters, obviously, as in any ingrown place whose residents had been returning year after year over many years; but on balance he decided they meant well. In fact, as he went back over the events of the morning, he could not escape a growing amusement at their tribal ways and their mass approach to the outlander. He had permitted himself to grow a little testy about their determination to promote a romance with Elizavetta, but after all she was part of them, they were her friends, they wished her well and wanted to be helpful. If this was not particularly helpful to him, he couldn't blame them: they could not know that. And, too, he was forced to admit ruefully, he wasn't really holding back as hard as he knew he probably should be.

The reasons for this he could not, at this particular moment, analyse exactly: or, perhaps, he did not prefer to analyse them exactly. Certainly in this rather absurd, rather frumpy, overly-made-up and overly-dramatized – and with how little basis for drama! – girl, who seemed pleasant, but not otherwise notable, he could hardly see very valid reason for becoming emotionally entangled. Not, of course, that anyone ever had to have any very valid reason for becoming emotionally entangled. But you liked to think that you operated with a certain intelligence in that area, even though you knew, of course, that no one, really, ever did.

He had to confess, however, as he bit thoughtfully into a jam and peanut butter sandwich and watched the shadows of a thousand leaves chase themselves back and forth across the deck in obedience to a little warm wind in the trees above, that for all her rather improbable aspect there was something basically attractive and appealing about Elizavetta – a certain kindness, a warmth of being, an impact of personality that seemed to exist in spite of, rather than because of, the carefully stage-managed appearance that presumably was intended to set it off. Eliza, he suspected with a smile that was itself quite kind, was much more innocent and much less experienced in the ways of the world than she tried to make out. Basic decencies could not be concealed that easily, nor would they appear to the sensitive if they did not exist.

Or would they? He frowned suddenly as he contemplated this casual generality that had come so glibly out of his musings. He had thought that before, and the end result had hardly borne it out. Perhaps he was falling again into the fatal habit of moving too fast, assuming too much, accepting too willingly the surface of things without waiting to discover their inner reality. He knew this had proved unwise and might prove unwise again – just as he knew also that it was his own responsibility that this was so. If his own heart was too innocent and idealistic and kind, under the layers of its living, he should not blame anyone else for the scrapes it got him into. It was, basically, his own damned fault.

Even so, you could hardly lead a life of always being suspicious of everyone. You had to accept some people and some things at face value, otherwise you would never find any kind of peace in the world. You had to trust someone some time. You had to believe in something, even something as tenuous and naked to destruction as the meeting of two hearts.

Or did you?

He frowned again. Somewhere off in the woods a squirrel chattered, quickly stilled; a blue-jay screamed, but muted; the drowsy humming sank to a deeper, yet more placid note as nature went half-heartedly about her thousand tasks in the midday laze.

Or did you?

If he came up to this remote and closed-off little enclave suffering from ironies and hurts its close-knit denizens would never know, and found himself thrown with someone they had obviously decided he should be thrown with, was he wise to indulge the jest without some adequate self-protections? These, he knew, could easily be made as defensive and brutally selfish as he wished to make them. He had met the Elizavetta type before, and there was one very practical way to approach it – a cold-blooded summer romp, into the hay for what you could get, wham, bam, thank you, ma'am, and *do* have a good time next summer. But that would hardly be fair, though he was convinced it would be quite possible. He suspected, in fact, that several of his new-found friends fully expected exactly that to eventuate. He and Einar, he was sure, could speak the same language in that sector, and possibly the Drummonds as well. Yet he was aware already that there was a genuine concern for Elizavetta's welfare beneath the casual cattiness with which they went about it, and when all was said and done, he had to admit that he found it justified. Quite aside from questions of his own self-respect, he realized he was beginning to share it. He had observed in this world that those who go around deliberately hurting others eventually, in life's patient and impartial justice, get hurt themselves; and he did not relish the prospect of that. Easy though he was sure it would be to begin and consummate a casual affair and dismiss it as casually after, he did not believe it would be best. The fact of the matter was, he liked Eliza.

'I like old Eliza,' he said half-aloud and laughed at his own sardonic mood. But it was true, he did; and while he reflected pragmatically that his body could use it, his heart and his mind could not condone so wanton a misuse of another's personality. If there was to be anything, it had to be something more than that. Otherwise he would suffer too, in some way deeper and more lasting than he wished to undergo.

But having said all that, and having painted what he told

61

himself wryly was certainly a noble picture of a noble soul, he still hungered for closeness and some sharing in a genuine sense with someone who could give him comfort and help him regain the forward momentum he seemed to have lost in recent months. If it wasn't here, if it didn't exist in this opportunity so ubiquitously being offered him by Greenmont, what then? Wouldn't he really be better advised, after all, to accept what was available and make the most of it, returning to the Valley in a month's time heart whole, fancy free and body eased to seek a more permanent solution, if he was lucky, somewhere else?

He got up with a sudden impatience and stood for a moment staring off at the jagged peaks above, hazy with heat and distance. Around and around, he thought with a savage bitterness: around and around. Why couldn't he let this be the place to bring it to a stop?

Possibly, he told himself abruptly, he was trying to arrive at too many conclusions too fast. Perhaps he was dismissing out of hand the chance that the foundation for a real understanding did exist in this earnest, awkward, rather ridiculous girl. It could be he was down-grading her too hastily, writing off too soon a heart that might be as genuinely anxious for solace as his own. It could be he was saying good-bye to something he had not even taken the time to say hello to. It was possible that once again, if in a different way, he was being foolish and that, having once cared too much, he was willing too quickly to care too little.

He sighed and ordered himself to stop agonizing and snap out of it. The one who made him agonize was far away and no longer gave a damn – if she ever had – and he shouldn't give a damn either, particularly not to the extent where it could interfere with a relationship that might provide him with everything he wanted. The little he knew of Elizavetta seemed to indicate that she was nice enough and decent enough, and perhaps kind enough. Why not give things a chance? It didn't all have to be decided at 1 p.m. on the MacAleers' front porch.

He went into the kitchen, washed his dish and glass, put them away and went into his bedroom. Everything seemed far away, the insistent peace of midday sapped and overwhelmed his energies. He stripped naked, flung himself down and slept.

SEVEN

Two hours later, prompted by some half-overheard, half-understood words from next door in Viola Townsend's positive tones – 'and I do think Elizavetta is getting quite excited about him' – he dreamed of her hazily for a moment or two and finally came awake with an erection that made him laugh aloud. What would Eliza make of *that*?

He jumped up, took a cold shower with a hoot and a holler, hustled into his sports gear again, grabbed a putter and golf-ball and started down the hall. Opposite the door to the other bedroom he stopped abruptly. A sound of sobbing came surprisingly from within. He entered to find Gray face-down with a pillow over his head.

'Hey,' he said, sitting on the bed and putting a hand on the boy's shoulder. The sobbing increased in volume.

'Hey, hey, *hey*,' he said gently, pulling the pillow off and tousling the boy's hair. 'What's the matter, buddy? What's wrong?'

'I won't tell you,' Gray said in a muffled voice. The major made a mildly disapproving sound.

'Now, is that any way to treat a pal? How can I help you if you won't tell me what it is?'

'I don't want you to help me!' the boy said, still muffled. The sobbing swelled again.

'Well, now, that's a foolish thing to say. We're in this thing together, aren't we? You're supposed to look out for me and I'm supposed to look out for you. Isn't that what we agreed this morning?'

'Ye-es,' Gray said doubtfully, rolling half over and looking up at him with tear-filled eyes.

'All right, then. If you won't let me help you when you need it, how can I expect you to help me if I need it? And I may, you know.'

'Why?' Gray demanded, giving a couple of gradually subsiding sobs and sounding more interested and a little sceptical.

'Just because. I may. They may be after me, you know.'

'Who?' Gray asked with a touch of scorn. 'The cops?'

'Greenmont.'

'Oh Greenmont,' the boy said, and his eyes filled with sudden tears as he rolled back face-down. 'I hate Greenmont!'

'What's the matter, Skipper?' the major asked softly. 'Have they done something to you?'

The boy gave a muffled wail in which the words 'made my parents mad at each other' came clearly through. The major sighed.

'Oh, I don't think they did that.'

'Yes, they did, too!' Gray said, rolling over and staring up at him again. 'They're mean.'

'Well,' he said rather helplessly. 'Who's mean? Mr and Mrs Drummond?'

'No.'

'Mr and Mrs Townsend?'

'No.'

'All right, who, then? Sally-Jane and Einar? Mr and Mrs Buxton? Your other friends?'

'No.'

'Well, who, then? After all, buddy, you can't go around saying things about people without something to back it up. Who's mean?'

'They aren't mean *alone*,' Gray explained scornfully between sobs that seemed receding. 'They're mean *together*.'

'Oh, I see. You mean they—'

'I mean they made my parents mad at each other!' the boy said with another wail and rolled back under his pillow.

'Oh,' the major said, realizing it wasn't very adequate but momentarily at a loss for other comment.

'*That's* what I mean,' Gray added from beneath the pillow. The major stood up. 'Sit down!' his host commanded tearfully. He grinned and sat down again, gave a gentle tug on the pillow, which was resisted, and suddenly yanked it off entirely. There was another wail.

'*No!*'

'No, look, pal. I know it's tough on you being here alone with an old crock like me—'

'You're not an old crock!'

'Well, all right,' he said amicably. 'I don't think so, either, but you must admit I *am* pretty ancient. However. The important thing is that your folks left us here together because they thought we could get along—'

'We *do* get along!'

'—could get along,' he went on calmly, 'without a lot of storms and upsets. Now, I'm not going into all the details for you, but I just want you to know that *I'm* not very happy, either. So what do you want me to do about it?' he demanded, suddenly burying his face in the pillow. 'Boo-hoo?'

There was a small conflict of laugh and sob at his elbow. The laugh won out. He removed the pillow.

'That's better.'

'You made me laugh,' the boy said accusingly.

'I should hope so. I can't have you bellowing around the place all day long.'

'I didn't bellow all day long,' Gray said indignantly. 'I just bellowed—'

'You just bellowed so it woke me up.'

'You were already awake. I heard you in the shower.'

'Well. You were pretty loud, anyway. Now, I don't know what Greenmont did to your folks, but I do know it would like to do something to me, so why don't you pull yourself together and come up to the Meadows with me? I need protection.'

'What does it want to do to you?' Gray asked, looking interested.

'I think it has designs on me and the fair Elizavetta,' he said. The boy's eyes widened.

'Oh.'

'And don't ask me to tell you the facts of life about that, because that isn't my responsibility.'

'I *know* the facts of life,' Gray said solemnly. The major grinned.

'Pretty damned silly, aren't they?' he asked cheerfully. His host gave a rather uncertain smile.

'I guess – that depends.'

The major laughed.

'You can say that again, buster,' he said, pulling the boy to his feet, turning him around, giving him a friendly swat and a shove toward the hallway. 'No, come on, scoot. Into the bathroom with you, wash your face and get your tail out here in a hurry. I want to go up to the Meadows and find out if my ladylove is waiting for me.'

'She is. She said she wanted to play golf, if you wanted to.'

'I want to. You can join us, if you like.'

65

The boy gave him a sudden pleased smile.

'We can have a pact.'

'We certainly can,' the major agreed. 'You and me against Greenmont. We'll show 'em.'

'Can't Eliza be in it too?'

'Do you want her in?'

Gray nodded thoughtfully.

'I think she needs protection, too.'

The major smiled.

'Well, we'll see.'

'Will you ask her?'

'Have I got to?'

'I think you should,' the boy said seriously. The major grinned suddenly.

'You're a character, buddy. Hurry it up. I'll wait for you on the deck.'

'Ask her, I said!' Gray called as he turned away.

'I'll give you two minutes.'

'Oh, all *right*,' the boy said in a disappointed tone, and vanished within.

⌘ EIGHT ⌘

He could not, in this circumstance, entirely escape a certain renewed uneasiness. Age twelve does not cry for strangers unless deeply disturbed, and even though he had been able to talk the boy out of it with relative ease, it was obvious Gray thought he had genuine cause for being resentful of Greenmont. What was under the bland and comfortable surface of this snug little, smug little world? More than he knew, apparently. He stood motionless on the porch, lost for a second in musings more sombre than he liked. It was thus Haila Buxton saw him, for a moment completely absorbed, unself-conscious and unaware, as she stepped out on her own deck across the ravine and gave him a hearty greeting.

'A penny for your thoughts!' she cried gaily. He frowned.

'I was just wondering what you did to the MacAleers,' he said thoughtfully, and was pleased to note that she looked quite flustered for a second. But she recovered with a quick laugh.

'Not a thing but be a good friend to them. Are you about

66

ready to go up to the Meadows?'

'I think I'll go with Gray this time.'

She said, 'Oh,' in an exaggeratedly aggrieved voice. 'Well, I know Elizavetta will be waiting for you.'

'Oh, I hope not,' he said drily, aware that his host had come out on the deck and stopped hesitantly behind him. 'Come on, boy,' he said firmly. 'We'll see you up there, Mrs Buxton.'

'If you want some competition on the golf-course,' she called as they started up the road, 'maybe Viola and I can join you for a foursome.'

'Fivesome,' he said cheerfully. 'Can't leave out my partner, here.'

'Fivesome,' she agreed with equal cheer. 'We'll see you soon.'

'Gosh, do we have to play with *them*?' Gray demanded as soon as they got out of earshot. The major chuckled.

'We don't have to play with anyone but Eliza, and if she isn't there, we don't have to play with anyone but ourselves. Does that satisfy you?'

'Yes,' the boy said with a smile. 'Except I hope she will be there.'

'Don't be match-making like the rest of them,' the major said. 'I've got enough troubles. Tell me about your pals up here. Who do you like to play with, mostly?'

'Well,' Gray said thoughtfully, 'there are *lots* of Magruders—'

'Yes, I've already noticed that. Do you like any of them?'

'Not as much as Einar. Nobody likes any of them as much as Einar. Of course I don't play with him, because he's older. But I like him, though. I play with the Purseman kids, and Tommy Rupert, and sometimes with the Whitmans and Grangers – we have a bunch,' he finished abruptly.

'Do you enjoy them?'

'We have fun,' the boy said indifferently. 'Mostly we just relax and don't do much. That's what the grown-ups do, too.'

'I gather that's the main activity. How early do I have to make you go to bed?'

'When I get ready,' the boy said with a grin. 'We usually get in by ten, though. You don't need to worry.'

'I'm not worried. You know your way around here a lot better than I do. Let's say you turn in at ten while I'm here, then, O.K.?'

'How about ten-thirty?'

The major chuckled.

'Are you bargaining with me?'

The boy grinned.

'Ten-fifteen?'

'All right. You're a tough trader, but it's a deal.'

'Good,' Gray said, looking pleased. 'When can I expect you?'

The major laughed.

'You mean I have to check in with you?'

'You don't know your way around here as well as I do,' the boy pointed out solemnly, and jumped out of reach with a giggle.

'That I don't, but I think you'd better not worry about when to expect me. You expect me when you see me. I'll most likely be in bed by eight every night.'

'Not if you like Elizavetta,' Gray said as they came up around the bend and the Meadows opened out before them crowded with afternoon golfers, a few late swimmers shouting and shivering in the pool, people chatting comfortably on the benches in the Grove. The first sharp edge of evening was just perceptible in the air, on the mountains the light was beginning to turn, flatter, brighter, more golden, as the trees cast their first long shadows down the slopes.

'What if I don't like her?' he asked. Gray grinned.

'I bet you do. Anyway, there she is.'

And so she was, sitting sedately on a bench near the first hole of the golf-course, wearing some sort of green contraption and the usual excess of make-up; a little uncertain, but quite determined. He smiled and waved.

'You're very prompt.'

She laughed.

'I knew if I sent you a message by Gray you'd be sure to get it, so I got here early.'

'You were sure I'd respond to it, then,' he said, and for a moment their eyes met quite candidly.

'I hoped so.'

'Well,' he said with a smile, 'and so I have. It doesn't look too crowded, does it?'

'It isn't bad.'

'Good. Where's the rest of the pack?'

'What a way to talk about my friends,' she said with a laugh and gestured toward the lower court where he could see the Drummonds and their favourite competition once more furiously engaged. 'There *they* are, and as for the Buxtons and the Townsends, you'd know more about that than I would. They went down to Haila's after the barbecue.'

'Yes. Mrs Buxton tried to trap us, but we took evasive action, didn't we, Gray?'

'We got away from her,' the boy said with satisfaction.

'I'm afraid there's a certain rapport lacking there,' Elizavetta said, smiling over his head at the major.

'Do you think there's cause?' he asked bluntly. 'The way I hear tell, things might have been different at that cabin if certain people hadn't interfered.'

'I don't know,' she said, and he could see that was going to be the end of it as far as she was concerned. 'Shall we start? Maybe Gray can look after Smudge for me.'

'Can't I play?' the boy asked in some alarm. The major nodded.

'Of course you can. We've got a pact, Elizavetta, and we want you to be in it. It's a defensive pact against all-comers. Designed to protect strangers in our midst, temporarily abandoned children – and you, if you'd like to belong.'

'Do I need protection?' she asked humorously. The major smiled.

'Maybe you do. From Mrs Buxton, possibly. Or from Greenmont, maybe. Or maybe even,' he said with a sudden quizzical air, 'from me.'

'Oh, I hope not,' she said, still humorously but with a questioning note that made him suddenly feel quite grim, though he spoke flippantly in reply.

'So do I. So in-deedy do I. Anyway, Gray and I have voted you into membership if you'd like to join.'

'Nothing,' she said with a mock gravity, 'could be a greater pleasure. And honour, I might add.'

'You're in. Smudge will have to find somebody else to watch over him, this game.'

'I'll tie him in the Grove for you,' the boy said. She handed him the chain and he ran off.

'It's been a long time since anybody offered to protect me,' she observed in a voice that began humorously but wound up sounding quite forlorn. He decided it was time to break that mood.

'Lady,' he said lightly, 'your worries are over. Do you want to lead off?'

'All right,' she said, giving him a smile that regretted his refusal to carry the conversation further, and stepping down on the green she sent a straight shot smartly off to within a couple of inches of the cup.

'Wow!' Gray said, materializing at her elbow. 'Are *you* good!'

'You're next, buddy,' the major said. The boy squared away with exaggerated deliberation and sent his ball three feet wide of the hole and eight beyond it.

'*Gosh*,' he said in a dismayed voice.

'Leaves it up to me to make a record, doesn't it?' the major asked, and quite by accident he dropped his ball neatly in the cup for a hole-in-one. There was an immediate outcry from all around.

'Leave it to a stranger!' Louise shouted from the tennis court. 'Sure shows us up!' Bob Townsend shouted from the road where he and Jim Buxton were just coming along. 'Watch out everybody!' Mother Magruder cackled from the pool, 'this man's *good*!' He was suddenly uncomfortably aware that the entire Meadows had been watching their little game. For a moment he did not know whether to laugh or be angry. Elizavetta came to his rescue before he had time to make up his mind.

'Your lead,' she said placidly, ignoring them all. He smiled up at her as he stooped to retrieve his ball.

'Want to concede yourself two and Gray three?' he asked.

'I think it would probably be four,' the boy said honestly. 'Why don't they mind their own business, anyway?'

'Right now,' the major said, 'we're their business. Bet I can't do it again.'

And sure enough, more flustered than he liked to admit to himself, he found he couldn't. It took him five strokes to make the second hole. Once again the matter was worthy of comment.

'Have to do better than that if you want to stay in this league,' Einar advised him from the court. 'Don't let 'em bother you, boy!' Jim Buxton encouraged from up the hill. 'Oh, *my*,' Mother

70

Magruder exclaimed on a wild wheeze of laughter at the pool, 'did you see *that*!'

'Gosh,' Gray said indignantly, 'they aren't going to let you do *anything*.'

'You must admit,' Elizavetta said calmly just as he was on the point of explosion, 'it *is* chummy.'

At this he had to laugh, and after a moment, shaking his club in the general direction of the tennis court, he shouted back in good humour, 'If you're so good, come on over here and we'll take you on!'

'You're sweet, Major, honey,' Sally-Jane responded. 'We've almost beaten these old Drummonds again and we'll be over in a minute.'

'Does that include us, too, Major?' Haila Buxton asked coyly, coming alongside with Viola Townsend in tow. He looked at Elizavetta with a shrug he tried to keep humorous. She winked.

'Ladies,' he said with an elaborate gallantry, 'the more the merrier. Come right ahead.'

'*Gosh*,' said Gray.

Half an hour later, having organized into a laughing, joking, noisome caravan of eight – minus the boy, who announced that he was going to play with the Granger kids, and disappeared – they were effectively tying up the golf-course and filling the rapidly cooling late afternoon air with hilarious shouts of glee and good-fellowship. Clubs were tossed for partners and he found himself paired with Sally-Jane against Elizavetta and Jerry Drummond, Einar and Haila Buxton, and Viola and Louise. A tentative suggestion from Elizavetta that they break up into two foursomes was shouted down merrily, and Haila Buxton led off with a flair. Several young Magruders, blue and chattering from having stayed too long in the water, came over from the pool; the Whitmans and the Grangers gathered around; the Talbots abandoned their own game to watch, although invited to play through; and the Meadows perforce ground to a halt while their happy band occupied centre stage with whoops and jovial ribbings.

Thus put on display, he found that his game went rapidly to pot despite encouraging remarks from Sally-Jane designed to assist his ego and morale. Finally Louise decided to take him in hand and he began to get better. 'Just say the hell with it,' she advised cheerfully, and after a moment he did and astounded them all with another hole-in-one on the ninth.

From then on it went better. He and Sally-Jane wound up second behind Louise and Viola Townsend, both of whom showed a surprising skill, Louise's a practised determination and Viola's a sort of reckless whacking at the ball. Einar and Haila Buxton came in third after wrangling with savage good nature on every hole. Jerry Drummond and Elizavetta ended in the cellar. The major didn't know what it all proved, exactly, except that it had very definitely prevented any further private conversation with Elizavetta. He mentioned this casually to Louise after the game ended and they were all sitting, relaxed and gossiping, on the benches by the first tee.

'I don't quite get it,' he remarked quietly when the rest were busy bickering away in their usual fashion. Louise looked surprised.

'What?'

'I don't know. I thought this was supposed to be a romance you were all promoting for me, yet the minute I get my lady-love alone you descend on us like a flock of black crows, or maybe I should say vultures. How come?'

'I love your comparisons,' she said with a chuckle. 'So flattering to us all. Why, did you want to be alone?'

'Not necessarily, but I sure as hell can't make time in the middle of the Fourth of July parade.'

She hooted.

'That's Greenmont for you. We can't stand to keep hands off something once we've started it. Not that I, I might add, was particularly in favour of starting it.'

'Oh?' he demanded, rather more sharply than he had intended. 'Why not?'

She shot him a sudden shrewd grin.

'You sound as though you resent that. I do believe you're beginning to like the idea.'

He shrugged.

'Oh, well,' he said with an elaborate indifference, 'there are worse ways to pass the time.'

'I hope you regard it more seriously than that,' she said, quite

72

severely. 'We expect you to treat our Nell right, stranger. Anyway,' she added, more lightly, 'you'll really have to make time if you're going to make any, because she works, you know.'

'Oh, does she?' he asked, and was surprised to find that the news aroused a genuine concern for a second in his heart.

'Sure. She has to go back down to the Valley Monday morning and open the library in Big Smith, just like all the other working stiffs. And she won't be back until next Saturday, so if this is a romance it's going to be a week-end one. Unless, of course, you want to go after Haila or Viola.'

He laughed so abruptly at the thought that from the bench in back the dominant of these two ladies leaned forward.

'*Now* what are you two gossiping about so cosily, Louise? We'll begin to think you and the major are having secrets!'

'You'd be surprised, Haila,' Louise said cheerfully. 'If we told you, which we aren't going to. So just lean back, dear, and try not to eavesdrop. We'll tell you all we want you to know.'

'Well, all right,' Mrs Buxton said comfortably. 'Just so you don't take him away from Eliza.'

'She won't,' Einar remarked. 'Eliza's got this deal sewed up, haven't you, pal?'

'Einar,' Elizavetta said calmly, 'when are you going to grow up?'

Sally-Jane laughed merrily, a happy little sound.

'Yes, Einar, honey. When?'

'I didn't know you objected,' her husband said. 'Why, only this afternoon—'

'That will do, young man,' Sally-Jane said firmly. 'Aren't those some deer up there on the mountain across the river?'

'That's right,' Jerry Drummond said approvingly. 'Create a diversion for him Sal. It's the only way to keep him under control.'

'Unfortunately he doesn't divert very easily,' Sally-Jane said, and then blushed prettily at their laughter.

'As a matter of fact,' Viola Townsend said in a tone that indicated she refused to be amused, 'there *are* some deer up there, aren't there?'

'Let's go see,' Louise suggested, linking her arm through the major's and leading him forward to an open expanse of the deserted golf-course, now half in shadow, half in the rays of the rapidly failing sun.

'Is this another local custom?' he asked with a touch of sarcasm. She smiled.

'One of the minor and more pleasant ones,' she said, pointing. 'See?'

A mile away across the great ravine, half-way up the side of the mountain opposite, the deer could be seen, little brown objects moving slowly as they grazed among the oaks. The shadows were deeper now in the forests, the light on the higher ranges had turned from gold to purple. A little wind was rising, sharp and invigorating, carrying with it the promise of a crisp night. For a time they stood silently watching, a little group of humans hushed and quiet in the spell of twilight and the innocence of the natural world.

'There are people who like to kill those graceful things,' Elizavetta broke the silence finally, 'but up here, we just like to watch them.'

'I'm afraid you're a sentimental bunch,' the major told her. 'But,' he added, and found, a little to his surprise, that he suddenly meant it, 'I like you.'

'I should hope so,' Haila Buxton said, restoring a note of briskness to the proceedings. 'Eliza, dear, you have a lot to do to get ready for the wienie-roast. Why don't you take the major along to help you while the rest of us go home and fresh up a bit? We'll see you around seven. All right?'

'Well—' Elizavetta said uncertainly. The major spoke up with an equal briskness.

'That sounds like an excellent idea. Why don't we do it just like that?'

'All right,' she said, seeming to capitulate suddenly though he could not for the life of him see why she had hesitated in the first place. 'If that's all right with you.'

'Perfectly fine. If you see my young charge running around loose anywhere,' he added to the others, 'bring him along, will you?'

'I talked to him about it this morning,' Elizavetta said. 'He'll be there.'

'Good,' he said, 'then we're all set.'

'You see?' Louise said with a puckish grin. 'You didn't have anything to worry about, after all.'

The sun was suddenly gone, a real coolness, sharp yet pleasant, entered the air. The sky darkened, shadows became impenetrable around the trees, a sense of the wilderness fell abruptly on the world: the forest came nearer. A little emanation of mystery and fear crept out of the underbrush as they walked slowly along together towards the upper end of the camp. It was not present in daylight, it would be gone as soon as night came fully down, but in the in-between of dusk – who could say for sure what might not be lurking in the woods? He shivered suddenly and laughed to cover it.

'What?' she asked. He smiled.

'I hear the Weendigo walking.'

'It doesn't roam these woods,' she said with a little laugh. 'Greenmont wouldn't let it.'

'Smudge wouldn't let it,' he said, tossing a stick. The dog went rushing away into the gathering darkness, his excited yelps restoring the everyday. The major laughed.

'Funny what your mind does, this time of night. You can see all sorts of things in the trees.'

'You must have seen some things some time that made quite an impression on you.'

He smiled.

'They used to be Japs. And later they were Communist Chinese and North Koreans. We shot a lot of Weendigoes in those days.'

'I don't think you had a very happy time of it,' she said. He shrugged with a sudden impatience.

'Oh, well. That was long ago and not very pleasant. And not very important now. How long have you been coming to Greenmont?'

'Almost all my life.' They passed lighted cabins, snug enclaves of light and warmth amid the trees. 'The Grangers and the Websters,' she explained to his questioning nod. 'They're in cotton around Weedpatch and Taft. They're nice people. In fact, most people up here are.'

'So I'm constantly being told. I wonder why everybody is so defensive about it?'

'Are we?' she inquired placidly. 'Well, I'm sure we don't mean to be. But I suppose we do seem a little smug, the first time a stranger meets us.'

'You do, a little. Although I suppose maybe that's a mechanism for putting a stranger in his place. It's probably instinctive, after all these years.'

'Heavens!' she said with a laugh. 'How severely you must be judging us!'

'Oh, I don't think so,' he said with a sudden bitterness he could not have explained. 'No, I don't think so. It's just talk. Don't mind me.'

She turned her head and studied him for a moment, though they could see little enough of one another in the deepening night. After a moment she looked away with a puzzled sigh.

'I'm sorry you're so unhappy,' she said gravely, 'but possibly being here for a while will help.'

'What makes you think I'm unhappy?' he demanded with a genuine exasperation in his voice. She did not recoil from it as he half expected she might.

'You've seemed unhappy to me ever since I saw you at the gate this morning. I don't know why.'

'Oh, well,' he said with a laugh, and it was not too bad a one, 'if this is just woman's intuition, then I'd suggest you not worry about it too much. I'm all right.'

'Haila said Mary MacAleer said—' she began. He interrupted with a defensive irony.

'Haila said that Mary said that So-and-So said that Somebody said that such-and-such happened,' he chanted. 'Only,' he concluded with a heavy sarcasm, 'it didn't, really. What a life you all lead up here! Truth or Consequences, *à la* Greenmont – or rather I should say *Un*truth *and* Consequences.'

'Well,' she said in a tone of hurt withdrawal, 'here's my cabin, anyway. If you'll wait a minute I'll switch on the outside light and you can begin building the fire.'

'With pleasure,' he said crisply and stood silent for a moment while she went in, snapped on the inside lights and an outdoor spot hanging from a tall pine against the house. He saw a rambling cabin, a big deck extending out over the river which rushed along, narrow and precipitous, just beneath; some tables, some benches, some plastic-webbed chairs, a stone-and-mortar fireplace on the river side. Civilization was suddenly re-established, the mountain night pushed back.

76

'There's some kindling and firewood and old newspapers by the back door,' she called. 'If you want to clean up afterwards, the bathroom is straight back through the cabin. I'll be in the kitchen getting things ready.'

'I think I can manage.' For a few minutes he was busy fixing the fire, giving to it an almost savage industry that submerged thought to some degree, though not as much as he would have liked. Was he that obvious to every female who happened by. Apparently so, for in one way or another he had received the same song-and-dance from all of them today.

'You realize, of course, don't you,' he called on a sudden wryly sarcastic impulse, 'that you've been selected to make the world look brighter to me?'

'What's that?' she asked in a startled voice, coming to the kitchen window. 'I don't understand you.'

'Come out here,' he said, and after a moment she did so, appearing at the door with a tomato in one hand and a paring-knife in the other, a bright red apron thrown over her green dress and a gaudy gipsy ribbon holding back her hair.

'I said,' he repeated carefully, 'that you realize, of course, don't you, that you've been selected to make the world look brighter for me.'

'I don't know what you mean.'

He laughed.

'I'm sure you don't,' he said with a mock solemnity.

'No, really,' she said in a tone of genuine concern that sounded, absurdly, close to tears.

'I mean,' he said, more kindly, 'that I get the idea a label has been put on me reading "Yours".'

She laughed in a hurried, flustered, protesting way.

'Oh, you mustn't mind Haila. She can't help it.'

'Well,' he said quizzically, 'watch out, Eliza! I'm not a horse that stands hitched without a struggle.'

'It isn't my doing!' she said defensively. 'It's just Greenmont.'

'You know something?' he said humorously, yet with a real seriousness underneath, 'I think you let Greenmont run your life too much. I think it would do you good to break away from Greenmont. That's what what I think.'

'Oh!' she said, and to his surprise and concern there suddenly were genuine tears in her eyes. 'You just don't understand. You just don't!'

'No,' he said, more gently, 'I guess not. Well, I'm sorry. I didn't mean to upset you. You go back in the kitchen and finish getting things ready.'

'Oh, yes,' she said, turning blindly. 'Yes, I think I'd better.'

And what, he wondered with a biting self-disgust as he resumed fiddling with the fire, gave him the right to come up here to this tight little world and act like Everybody's Bastard to a nice young-old maid who was doing her best to hang on to peace of mind by pretending that everything was all right and not thinking too much about her situation? He was a hell of a one to act superior, to blunder in and force her to look at reality. Where did he get the right to be so high and mighty?

Of course, he reflected with a returning ironic ruefulness, that was what he got for expecting a woman to react logically. He should not have let himself be misled by the fact that an hour ago at the Meadows she had apparently been all for it, for so she had – on her terms. To have it presented to her baldly as a circumstance precipitated by her friends, to be put in the pathetic position of having to accept assistance in so intimate a situation – that was what hurt, he could see, now that it was too late and the damage had been done. But, damn it, she should have defences – and, he was now certain, she had none.

Which put the burden of being kind, of course, right back where he had sensed right along it would have to be, upon him. And what a strong reed that was for them to lean upon. Oh, sister, he thought, we're really a couple of beauts, we are. This is really the blind leading the blind, this is. Be my guest in Cripples' Paradise, and maybe we'll get out alive and maybe we won't.

With a sudden bitter impatience he kicked a pine-cone into the night and automatically Smudge went yelping off after it. The Weendigo behind a tree? The Weendigo was in him, and that was why he had shivered in the dusk.

Well: here she came out of the cabin with a bowlful of tomatoes and a platterful of wienies, and down on the road he could hear voices approaching. Here was reality, and better come back to it fast if one would drown out the demons that laugh on the edge of human yearning.

'There's the two love-birds!' Bob Townsend bellowed heartily from the path. 'Look mighty cosy there, boy!' Jim Buxton cried jovially. Elizavetta shot him a stricken glance and he had just time to frame the words, 'Don't worry,' and gave her what he hoped was an encouraging smile when the Townsends and the Buxtons entered the area of light and reality began taking over.

'Well, dear,' Haila said comfortably, 'this *is* nice.'

'I brought some more pickles,' Viola Townsend said. 'I wouldn't have, except that everybody seemed to like them at the barbecue.'

'Thanks so much,' Elizavetta said, carefully setting down her burdens as far along the table from him as possible. 'They're wonderful, Viola.'

'Jim,' Haila said briskly, 'you take orders for drinks, dear, and I'll help in the kitchen. I expect the others will be along in a minute. Gray is with the Drummonds.' The major nodded.

'I expect he can take care of himself,' he said. *Better than I can*, he thought.

'Well, Major,' Viola Townsend said, easing her way into a wicker chair with an air of prim indulgence, 'are you beginning to unwind a little?'

'Am I wound up?' he asked, with a deliberate blankness, and for a moment she looked slightly taken aback. Then she smiled.

'You'll see,' she said encouragingly. 'A day or two in this place and all your worries will be over.'

'I'm sure. How long have you had your cabin, Mrs Townsend?'

'Bob and I have been coming here for twenty-seven years,' she said with satisfaction. 'We bought the place right after we moved to Oakland.'

'You must have seen a lot of members come and go in that time.'

'Not so many,' she said thoughtfully. 'It's like a big family. Members don't change much over the years. The Grossmans joined three years ago and the Drummonds were the last before them.'

'Oh, are they new?' he asked in some surprise. She gave a jolly laugh.

'Ten years. That's *almost* new, by our standards!'

'What do you want, Major?' Jim Buxton called from the

kitchen. 'I know everybody else's drinks by heart but I don't know yours.'

'I'll bet you do. Bourbon and water would be fine.'

'Good enough. Say, that was quite a golf game you folks had today!'

'It was a hum-dinging lulu,' the major agreed. 'I can see I'm going to have to practise up.'

'Not on my account!' Haila Buxton called merrily. 'I like you *just* as you are!'

'Did I hear Haila say she liked something?' Louise called from the path below.

'She says she likes me,' he called back. 'Just as I am!' he added emphatically. She gave a hoot as she came into the light, an arm around Gray, Jerry following just behind.

'Treasure that remark!' she ordered. 'Haila doesn't pass around compliments as though they were acorns, do you, darling?'

'Actually,' he said, 'it wasn't exactly me she said she liked. It was my golf-game.'

'Major,' Haila said with a gracious chuckle, appearing in the doorway with a tray of rolls and condiments, 'I like *you*. Believe me, I like *you*.'

'Now you *are* getting the accolade,' Jerry assured him. 'This doesn't happen once in a blue moon.'

'What's the matter?' Einar inquired, arriving with Sally-Jane, clad in a pink wool pullover and jodhpurs, carried feet first, bottom up, and struggling prettily, under one arm. 'Did somebody say something nice about somebody?'

'Einar!' his wife said, drumming futilely on his back with her fists. 'You put me down. Einar, you put me down!'

'Oh, I don't know,' her husband said casually. 'This makes me feel like a caveman. Don't you feel like a cavewoman? Anyway, it isn't often your friends get to see this side of you.'

'Einar!' Sally-Jane said. 'Put me down!'

'Please,' he said grandly. 'You'll upset old Mr Stafford.'

'To hell with old Mr Stafford, *put me down!*'

'Well, I hate to do it,' he said, complying reluctantly, 'but I suppose if you're going to make a federal case of it—'

'Goodness!' she said, looking flushed and excited and as pretty as a rosebud in the rain. 'What a man!'

'Yea, boy!' her husband echoed with satisfaction. '*What* a man! Bill, I hope you've recovered from your hectic afternoon, and that you and Eliza have been making great progress since we saw you last.'

'You're so tactful, Einar,' Louise said. 'Why don't we all gossip about the junior Bill Pursemans instead?'

'What about the junior Bill Pursemans?' Haila Buxton asked alertly, and they all paused to listen.

'Well, I don't know exactly,' Louise said, 'but Janie Rupert dropped in to borrow some coffee just before we left, and she said Helen had suddenly taken one of the cars and gone down to the Valley.'

'That's odd,' Viola Townsend said. 'Now, why would anyone want to go down on Saturday night?'

'That's what intrigued us,' Jerry Drummond said. 'Janie said she had sort of been worrying about them, lately.'

'So have I,' said Mrs Buxton thoughtfully. 'So – have – I. You remember what I told you, Eliza, dear?'

'I don't want to listen,' Elizavetta replied with a strange desperation in her voice that astounded them all. 'I just don't want to listen to all this hateful gossip!'

'Ho, ho!' Louise exclaimed cheerfully. 'There's your answer, Einar. They haven't been hitting it off at all, and Eliza's mad at the major and the major's mad at Eliza and—'

'No, see here—' he began, but their hostess forestalled him with an obvious determination to be calm.

'I just don't see why it's necessary to gossip about everybody all the time. That's all.'

'Well, dear,' Haila Buxton said archly, 'I don't recall your ever being so concerned about it before.'

'Maybe she's always been concerned,' Jim Buxton said, 'but she's just been too afraid of you gals to say anything. Here, have a drink, everybody!' he added with a laugh that was just hearty enough to reaffirm his charter as comic. For a time they were diverted by this, while the river rushed along beneath the deck and the pines murmured overhead in the crisp, invigorating night.

'Anyway,' Viola Townsend said thoughtfully, 'it *is* peculiar.'

'I brought your jacket and a flashlight,' Gray said into the silence. 'It's pretty cold.'

81

'Thank you, buddy,' the major said. 'I'll put it on right now.'

'That's a little man,' Haila Buxton said kindly.

'We stick together, in our cabin,' the major said.

'I'll bet you do,' Einar said, relaxing lazily in a hammock with Sally-Jane cradled in his arms, 'but, now, seriously now, let's don't change the subject. Greenmont has a right to know. How's it going, Bill?'

The major shook his head and smiled.

'Hunky-dory, caveman. Just simply hunky-dory. I lack your technique, but I'm getting there.'

'I think you're all rather obnoxious!' Elizavetta said suddenly, and she went in and closed the door firmly behind her.

'Well,' Haila Buxton said, rising with a little smile all around 'I see this calls for tact. Better start the fire, Major,' she called over her shoulder as she went in. 'We'll be ready to eat shortly.'

And a few minutes later, their hostess back with Haila at her elbow and apparently restored to a reasonable good humour, everyone crowding around the fire roasting wienies on long sticks, old friends joshing one another with a somewhat softer note now that drinks had worked their persuasion and food was under way, a certain drowsy glow began to settle over the party. He found that he too was beginning to relax. He was assisted in this by Sally-Jane, who hopped off her husband's lap and made the major her special project for the evening with a kindness that came rather surprisingly from her pert little person. He sensed that it was genuine, however, and before long they were chatting away amicably at a great rate by the fire.

'There!' she said finally. 'You can get along with us just as well as anybody.'

He laughed.

'That sounds rather formidable. How well does anybody?'

'Oh,' she said, 'we aren't so bad.'

'Tell me,' he said, 'how does a group like this get together up here, anyway? You're such a hodge-podge of ages and interests.'

'Well,' she began, and he interrupted:

'I know – "That's Greenmont for you." '

'Well, it is. We started playing tennis with the Drummonds quite by accident last year and that started that, and the Buxtons and the Townsends have always been close – Viola,' she explained, her voice dropping, 'is such a born stooge for Haila, and the men like to play golf together – and the Townsends' cabin is right next door to the Drummonds', and we started going there and Viola began dropping over, too, and everybody's always been fond of Elizavetta, and so – well, there you are. It's like that all over camp, though. Age doesn't matter up here, it's such a never-never land.'

'It is,' he said with a twinkle, 'but I didn't know you were old enough to realize it.'

'Oh, yes. And listen: don't mind my oaf of a husband. He's a dear, sweet lad with a tongue like a bull-dozer and I love him dearly, but I know he can set people back on their heels sometimes. He does it deliberately, of course. Slap him down if it gets too bothersome. He really likes you very much.'

'I'm getting rather fond of him, except we may have to have an understanding pretty soon if he doesn't lay off Eliza. She can't take it like I can.'

'I don't think either of you can take it,' Sally-Jane said, staring at him thoughtfully. 'Which is why we probably all ought to be shot for even thinking about the two of you at all.'

'Oh, I don't mind, really. I suppose I need to be taken out of myself.'

'Yes, you do,' she agreed soberly. 'You need it badly. What happened, anyway?'

'Oh, come now,' he said lightly. 'Do you really want to know?'

'Certainly. I wouldn't have asked.'

'Well,' he said, rising abruptly to his feet, 'that will have to wait for some other solemn occasion when I'm talking to the self-confident young, because I really do think I must go and assist our hostess with the dessert.'

'Oh,' she protested. 'There you go, getting away again. Just as we get you pinned down, you think of some excuse for getting away. How can we help you, when you do that?'

He chuckled.

'Who said you should?'

'No, really!' she began, but he was gone to the door to open it for Elizavetta. Sally-Jane turned back with a puzzled expression just in time to intercept a toasted marshmallow proffered by Jim Buxton and dimple at him prettily for it. They fell to talking about golf scores and the major was relieved to notice that she seemed to have given him up, at least temporarily. He expected that persistent little S.-J. would probably be back.

In the meantime, there was his hostess, and as he smiled pleasantly into her eyes for the first time in more than an hour he was gratified to see that she seemed calm and unperturbed once more.

'It's a nice party,' he said. 'I'm glad I came.'

'So am I.'

'Even if I never was formally invited.'

'Oh, well,' she said with a smile, 'it was just sort of understood. Have you had enough to eat?'

'Ample. I'm sorry if I—'

'That's all right,' she said hurriedly. 'It doesn't matter.'

'I hope not.'

'No, really. It doesn't. Would you want to pass the dessert tray for me?'

'How much is everybody allowed?' he asked, turning toward the others and aware that they were, as usual, observing with a casual diligence. 'I wouldn't want Louise to over-eat. Or you, either, Mrs Buxton.'

'I think we know each other well enough by now so that you can call me Haila,' she said with a gracious air.

'I'm overwhelmed,' he said simply. Louise snorted.

'That's the proper response. As for me, I'm thin as a rail and can eat like a horse. What is it this time, Eliza? Fudge-cake and vanilla ice-cream?'

'Isn't that what I always have?' Elizavetta asked with a trace of irony. 'You'd be shocked if I tried anything else.'

'Good old Eliza,' Bob Townsend said jovially. 'We can always count on *you*!'

'That's right,' Einar agreed solemnly. 'As steady as these eternal hills.'

'Well, sound the organ and start the hymn,' Louise said. 'And call me Grabby,' she added, helping herself to an extra-large piece of cake as the major went slowly from hammock, to chair, to chaise-longue, to sofa, to bench, around the deck. 'Is Gray getting enough?'

'I don't know,' the major said. 'How about it, Skip? You've been so quiet all evening I've sort of lost track.'

'I can take care of myself,' the boy said quietly from a place alongside the fire. 'I'll bet I've eaten twice as much as anybody.'

'He has, too,' Sally-Jane said. 'I've had my eye on him.'

'Well,' Gray said with a shyly pleased smile, 'I've eaten quite a lot, anyway.'

'Snap off the light, Eliza,' Jim Buxton suggested. 'Let's enjoy the fire for a while.'

And as she did so and they quietly finished dessert the peace of the night established its hold upon them. It was quite cool now, the major was thankful for his windbreaker, and above through the pines the dim outlines of the mountains and the twinkling beacons of a million stars loomed enormous overhead. The steady, insistent rush of the river beneath their feet, the sighing of a little wind through the trees, the occasional snap of a coal and the hypnotic fascination of the fire began to induce a relaxed and congenial mood.

'Oh, I wandered today to the hill, Maggeee—' Louise began, half-mockingly, but they took her up on it and in a moment they were all singing along softly and pleasantly together. He had the feeling they were eons from anywhere, stranded on some outward shoal yet at the same time curiously secure and wonderfully uncaring and happy. A feeling of kindness, of closeness, of friendship close to love for them all swept over him. He was one of them, they were his friends, and he began to think perhaps he need no longer be afraid.

'Well!' Viola Townsend said promptly at eleven o'clock, 'do you know what time it is, Bob? We've got to run along if you and Jim are going to beat Father Magruder tomorrow.'

'Yes,' Haila Buxton agreed. 'Come along, James. We'll walk Gray down for you, Major.'

'S.-J. and I think we'll take a dip in the pool before bed,' Einar announced. 'Anybody game?'

'At 11 p.m. and fifty degrees?' Louise demanded. 'You must be insane, sweetie. However—'

'We can't afford not to can we?' her husband suggested. 'It's a clear test of youth and stamina.'

'It's a great sensation,' Einar explained to the major. 'The air's freezing, the water isn't much better, and you're torn between getting out and turning to ice or staying in until you freeze to death and sink to the bottom. It's one of camp's wilder experiences. Coming?'

'It sounds wild, all right,' he agreed. 'Also insane. What would you recommend, Elizavetta?'

'I can't go,' she said. 'I've got to stay here and clean up. But perhaps you should. As he says, it's quite an experience.'

'I'll try it some other time. I'd better stay here and help you get things in shape.'

'Oh, that isn't necessary—' she began, but he began picking up dishes in a business-like manner.

'I'd like to.'

'Of course he would,' Bob Townsend said with a knowing chuckle. 'Come along, you people, can't you see they want to be alone?'

'That's right,' he said cheerfully. 'That's exactly right. So you just run along.'

'Is it the pact?' Gray asked in a sleepy voice. The major laughed despite Elizavetta's look of concern.

'It's the pact,' he said. 'The pact versus the pack. Right, Eliza?'

'I don't like the sound of that, somehow,' Louise said with her irreverent grin, 'but maybe we deserve it. Lead on, water nymphs!'

'You could have gone with them,' Elizavetta said as the group went down the path, flashlights flickering and disappearing when they reached the road and moved off among the trees.

'Oh, well. You'd rather I stayed, wouldn't you?'

'I don't know,' she said in a puzzled tone.

'Why not?' he asked sharply, because it suddenly seemed to matter. 'Are you afraid of me?'

'I don't know,' she said again, still in the same puzzled fashion.

'Well,' he said shortly, 'maybe I had better go and catch up with them.'

'No!' she said quickly. 'No, don't do that.'

'Do you know what you want, Elizavetta?' he asked, and more challengingly than he would have expected from her, she shot back:

'Do you?'

For a moment they stared at one another rather blankly across the dying fire. Then she made a self-conscious gesture and gave an awkward laugh that attempted to dismiss the subject.

'Whatever are we talking about?' she asked. 'I think I'd better get busy and put these things away.'

'I warn you, Eliza,' he repeated quietly, 'I'm not a horse that stands hitched without a struggle.'

'I realize that,' she said quickly, turning away. 'I'm not offering to hitch you, am I?'

'That's good, because I wouldn't want you to.' A sudden expression of pain came into her eyes.

'Anyway, it's all Greenmont. You said so yourself.'

'Well,' he said quietly. 'Maybe we'd better finish cleaning up and say good night.'

'Not as enemies, I hope,' she said with a nervous little smile. He smiled back.

'No, not as enemies. Where do you want all this trash put?'

'Burn what you can and put the rest in the garbage can by the back door. They collect it on Monday morning.'

'O.K.,' he said, and for a time they were briskly busy about the cabin, burning paper plates and cups, disposing of the heavier trash, washing and drying the flatware.

'Now,' he said finally, 'that looks more civilized. Nobody'd ever know there'd been a party.'

'Maybe there wasn't,' she said with a touch of whimsicality.

'Maybe not. Although I think perhaps something happened.' He grinned and added more lightly, 'I don't know just what, yet.'

'You love to talk in equivocations, don't you? Is it really a good device to hide behind?'

'You should try it some time,' he said cheerfully. 'You've no idea. How about a swim now?'

'Oh, they'll have been in and out by this time,' she said with a laugh. 'You don't linger at poolside in the middle of the Sierra Nevadas in the middle of the night.'

'I didn't mean them. I meant us.'

'Oh . . . Well – I really don't think – that is, I mean—'

'That's right,' he said grimly. 'They certainly would talk, wouldn't they? O.K., Eliza, I'll see you tomorrow morning. Maybe we can have some more golf, if we're real brave.'

'No,' she said in an anxious voice. 'No, please. I don't mean to be a spoil-sport. It's just that—'

'I know what it's just that,' he said drily. 'It's just that you're afraid of me and afraid of them, and between the two of us you're never going to do anything you want to do. I said I'd meet you for golf.'

'You don't have to be brutal about it,' she said as though she might cry, and abruptly he turned back with a stricken look.

'Elizavetta,' he said quietly, I'm sorry. I have no right to talk to you like that. I am sorry. I'm not fit to live with right now and I shouldn't impose myself on anybody, let alone someone as nice as you.'

'I'd like to help you,' she said, looking forlorn.

'I'd like you to,' he said, and for a long moment again they stared at one another with a rather helpless air as the river plunged and roared beneath their feet and the trees rustled overhead.

'Well,' he said abruptly, 'what time do the clans gather in the morning?'

'Around eleven or so,' she said slowly; and then, on a sudden impulse that surprised him greatly, 'Why don't you come up about ten for breakfast?'

'How can I get away from Haila?' he asked, humorously but not daring to be too much so for fear she would become frightened and change her mind. But a modest and minimum sort of daring seemed suddenly to have taken residence in her heart, and she gave a nervous, excited little laugh.

'Get up early and sneak out. They won't know until you've gone.'

'Maybe I'll do just that,' he said with a smile. 'Maybe I just will.'

And before she could have time to answer, or perhaps change her mind, he turned suddenly and went leaping down the path, beginning to whistle as he went, until the whistling and the bouncing reflection of his flashlight against the pines were swallowed up and lost in the cool velvet night.

'It's late,' a sleepy voice said accusingly from the other bedroom. He paused in his undressing to grin.

'Go to sleep!'

'Did you stay with Elizavetta?' the voice asked, slightly more awake.

'I did,' he said, and snapped off the light. 'I'm getting into bed, now. Good night.'

'Did you kiss her?' the voice persisted. He sat up with a laugh.

'Will you go to sleep before I come in there and tan your little hide?'

'Well, did you?'

'No, I didn't, and the reasons for that are something you won't understand until you're a lot older than you are now, so go – to – sleep!'

'Oh,' the voice said in a disappointed tone. 'I'll bet she wanted you to.'

'I don't really think she did, this time,' he said. 'But,' he promised rather grimly under his breath, 'she will.'

'Oh,' the voice said. There was a deep yawn. 'Well, good night.'

'Good night to you, too,' he said cheerfully, and burrowed under the blankets. Two minutes later he sat up again and on an impulse he could not quite understand and at once regretted, asked into the darkness, 'Do you want to go up there to breakfast with me tomorrow morning?'

But there was no answer from the other room, and after a moment he shrugged.

'Well, then,' he said, still aloud, 'I guess I'll have to go alone and we won't have a chaperone and Greenmont will go wild.' He grinned happily in the darkness. 'Then to hell with Greenmont!'

And dropping back, he was conscious for a second of the utter completeness of the night, swallowing the cabin, swallowing Greenmont and the great cleft in the Sierras where it lay, engulfing, encircling and encompassing the world, before he fell into a motionless and drowning sleep.

TEN

The morning lay bright and sparkling before him; a virginal sweetness – very fitting, he thought wryly – dominated the air as he dressed and prepared to sneak quietly out of the cabin after leaving a note that said, 'Gone to E.'s. Don't tell anybody. Secret Pact.' Off in the distance the river sounded louder in the early hush, near at hand the jays had begun to scream, a couple of squirrels were quarrelling bitterly on a lichen-covered rock. Somewhere far off up-canyon something cracked loudly, possibly a tree falling. Very high overhead, the first he had seen cross the mountains since his arrival, a lone aeroplane travelled in the sun against a fantastically deep blue sky, a tiny silver sliver tossing down in its wake a faint, fading drone as it gleamed for a moment or two and then disappeared over the peaks to the south. The first slanting rays of light shot down through the trees, the wind stirred and rustled in the leaves; the air, though cool and sharp, bore an elusive but insistent promise of the midday warmth to come. The world seemed younger than he had known it for a long time, poised on the threshold of a day that might well hold anything, everything – or, as he reminded himself with a caution by now so customary as to be almost instinctive – nothing.

That, however, was a thought that he did not hold long against the enchantment of the morning, as he managed to get with a fair degree of silence out of the cabin, down the steps and started on his way up the road. The day was too beautiful and invigorating for such a mood: it was suddenly just too good to be alive, for such thoughts to long prevail. The Buxton cabin seemed silent and still asleep as he hiked quickly by, a small, foolish, rather adolescent but none the less enjoyable excitement beginning to fill his heart at this innocent little adventure. Whoever would have thought that breakfast could have such drama, he asked himself with a grin: and added sardonically, Golly gee.

And all, he thought with a continuing wryness as he trudged along, because he was allowing himself to slide perilously close to giving it an importance he knew it did not deserve and should not have. It was ridiculous on the face of it to suppose that there was in this shy and inhibited heart he was about to see again the slightest comfort for a being as bruised by events and emotion as he. What could Elizavetta possibly know of the sort of complete commitment he had gone through, or the rending savagery of having to get out of it under the conditions he had? Obviously, nothing. Yet this was the girl he was actually coming to regard as a possible salvation, beginning to build up in his mind an image, born of need, of an understanding that in the greatest likelihood simply did not exist. It was not wise, it was not fair, it was, in fact, extremely dangerous to the peace of mind and ultimate happiness of them both. And yet – and yet. When did the mind ever stop to be rational when the heart was involved? And what made him think that a heart such as his, which probably had less chance of subjecting itself to reality in that area than most, would be satisfied with anything less than a complete surrender of logic if he once began to give in to it?

But already, he knew as he came up the rise and turned the corner into the Meadows, lying dewy and deserted in the sun, he had begun to give in to it. He was already half-prepared to believe that Elizavetta was what he wanted. He was already on his way to a rationale which would tell him that he had really found, here in this remote little world so quivering with self-awareness, a companion for the journey to take the place of the one who had so hurtfully withdrawn. How absurd and how stupid – and how ill-equipped he was, in the present state of his emotions, to remain true to the knowledge of just how absurd and stupid it was.

That was the trouble with defences, however; they were good only as long as you wanted them to be, and once you began to let them down they took advantage of you by disappearing much more rapidly than you were prepared for. If you weren't ready to see the process through, you shouldn't begin it; and he had begun it, ready or not. That in turn, he was now aware, could impel some approach to the situation more insistent, more impatient, perhaps even harsher than the tentative approaches he had made so far.

He walked down the slope of the golf-course, crossed over the river and went past the pool, ice-blue and placid, mirroring the mountains and the sky in its unruffled surface. Water-beetles, water-skaters and a hundred glistening dragonflies flirting over the silent water held sway where small Magruders and little Talbotts would presently disport. A mocking-bird on the high-dive called to him loudly, the air was beginning to turn steadily warmer as the sun crept down the ravines. From somewhere there came on the wind the smell of bacon, he heard a screen-door slam and the sound of voices. Greenmont was beginning to come awake.

He hurried on, crossing the tennis courts and starting up the upper road past a turn-off marked 'Mineral Springs'. An old man appeared suddenly on the porch of a weathered cabin, looked startled, then gave him an abrupt wave with an air of grumpy and suspicious good-fellowship. This must be old Mr Stafford who, he suspected, probably didn't like any of his neighbours well enough to spread the word about the major's early-morning walk. He called, 'Good morning, sir!' and waved cheerfully back. The old man, looking a trifle more interested, said gloomily, 'I suppose you'll be cutting across my corner going to Soda Springs just like all the rest of them!' and popped back in as abruptly as he had come out. The major shook his head with a smile and walked on.

Now the smell of cooking and the noise of human activity became more insistent as the canyon's narrowing crowded the cabins closer together in the upper end of camp, but as far as he knew he still had been unobserved by anyone save old Mr Stafford when he reached Elizavetta's path and turned off the road to climb the abrupt little hill to her cabin. Here, too, things were in a state of preparation, pans rattled, a drawer banged shut, there was the sound of silverware. He picked up an acorn and threw it at the kitchen window. Smudge barked excitedly inside.

'I've set things up on the deck,' she called at once in a voice that sounded, disappointingly, quite casual. 'Make yourself at home and I'll be right out.'

He stepped out on the big wooden platform above the river, which seemed to rush along even more vehemently in the morning shade and sun than it had in darkness last night.

'Can I do anything?'

'No, everything's coming along fine. Did you sleep well?'

'Like the dead. And you?'

'I always sleep well at Greenmont.'

'Even with a wandering stranger disturbing your rest?' he

asked, leaning on the rail and staring at the crystal water as it raced down from the distant snows. The door opened behind him and she came out with a laugh as the dog rushed forward to dance around his feet.

'Even so,' she said, depositing her burdens on the table which now, in contrast to last night's bare informality, carried a white cloth, a bowl of silver-painted pine cones, a general air of something special. His hostess, too, he observed, looked flushed and excited for all her casual tone. Absurdly, all this struck him as quite encouraging.

'Well,' he said. 'Maybe I can do something to change that.'

'How?' she asked, and flushed even deeper.

'I could tell you, but I don't think you're ready for it yet. Anyhow,' he added hastily, as she looked quite startled and half-turned to go in, 'I think I got up here without being noticed. Haila didn't let out a peep.'

She smiled.

'She wouldn't, if she saw you. Until later, when it might throw you off balance.'

'Bring out the rest of it and let's sit down,' he said, suddenly impatient. 'I want to ask you about Haila and Greenmont and a lot of things.'

'Heavens,' she said with a flustered smile, 'am I going to be cross-examined?'

'It'll be for your own good,' he said cheerfully, last night's scruples seeming to have vanished somewhere in the morning's bright mood.

'If you'll allow me the same privilege,' she said, with more spirit than he expected. Then she laughed. 'Truth or Consequences.'

He grinned.

'Some truth. Maybe some consequences. Hurry it up, now! Smudge and I are hungry.'

When they got to coffee, the sun turning steadily warmer, its rays flickering down through the trees and falling pleasantly on the deck, a sudden feeling of recklessness came to him. Whatever he wanted to do suddenly seemed dangerously simple and easy in this relaxed and dream-like atmosphere.

'Now,' he said, leaning forward confidently with his elbows on the table, propping his chin on his hands, 'I think you need to be taken in hand, Miss Berrenger.'

'*I* need to be taken in hand?' she said with a little startled, eager laugh. 'Why me?'

'Oh, I just think you do.' He paused and then, prompted by the mood and the morning and the candour of Greenmont, which he knew now could have its uses, went crashing ahead. 'For instance,' he said thoughtfully. 'Your dress.'

'What?' she asked blankly, and he thought for just a second that he should retreat from this at once before it was too late. But something told him immediately that he was right, the only way to break through these reserves was to plunge straight on.

'Here you are, just quietly entertaining a gentleman friend for breakfast, and yet you put on something that's so – so elaborate.'

'Elaborate?' she said, staring down in a puzzled way at the enormous flowered print, the gaudy green sash, the orange fingernails, the gleaming red sandals buried in rhinestones. 'Is it elaborate?'

'It looks to me,' he said crisply, 'like Madam LaZonga. Why dress like a gipsy when you're not a gipsy? Why not dress like a nice girl, which you are?'

'Oh!' she said, as though not knowing whether to laugh or cry. 'How dare you say something like that?'

'It's just Greenmont,' he said, and believed it for the moment. 'We all say exactly what we think, in Greenmont. Furthermore, there's your make-up. It's about five times too much.'

'Oh!' she said again, and this time he thought she would cry, except that he hoped she would get angry instead. But she did neither, only staring helplessly at the woods across the river's narrow chasm.

'And your dog,' he added in the grip of a recklessness that seemed determined to force some conclusion. 'Mr Smudge! Mr Smudge the First! And then Mr Smudge the Second! And then Mr Smudge the Th—'

But his purpose was achieved.

'Oh, stop it!' she cried angrily. 'Just stop it! Wouldn't you want to have a dog if you – if you—'

'If I were afraid I wasn't ever going to live?' he asked with a deliberate cruelty. 'Well, maybe. But I wouldn't name him Smudge. Smudge, for God's sake! I'd name him something a dog wouldn't be ashamed of, wouldn't I, Smudgy?' And he reached down and rolled the cocker over, where it lay in ecstatic abandon while he scratched its belly.

Now, he could see, she was both angry and crying, and there struck him abruptly the feeling that he had gone too far and that this might really be the end of it. And with a curious self-perception he knew perfectly well that this was what he really hoped, even as he hoped with a parallel fervour that it would not be, but would help instead to bring her, if not at once then before long, into his arms.

'I don't see what right you have to come here and treat me like this,' she said. 'We all try to make you feel at home, we all try to help you, I extend my hospitality to you, and – and this is what I get for it. You talk to me like this!' She dabbed angrily at her mascara, which was beginning to run in black rivulets down her cheeks. 'I don't know why!'

'I think you need someone to talk to you like that,' he said, more gently. 'Someone who really cares what happens to you.'

'I suppose that's you!' she said with angry scorn. He bowed.

'I suppose it might be. If you and the fates were willing.'

'What an extraordinary person,' she said finally. 'I suppose you're so perfect yourself that you just can't refrain from advising others even if they're – even if they're – they're perfectly—' and on an angry sob she finished: 'happy!'

'No,' he said calmly. 'I'm not perfect at all. And I'm not happy, either. But I am more honest than you are. I'm not afraid to admit it to myself.'

'Do you think,' she asked in a half-whisper, 'that I'm afraid to admit it to *myself*?' She made a sound that could have passed for laughter, though it was empty of amusement. 'I don't notice you admitting it to anyone else, even if you do admit it to yourself!'

'I've just admitted it to you, haven't I?' he said quietly. 'Doesn't that indicate anything to you?'

He had the feeling that for the first time since their meeting at the gate she was actually looking at him, for which he gave some small thanks. The scrutiny lasted for several seconds.

'How terribly you must have been hurt,' she said then, still in the same half-whispering, half-wondering voice. 'How much someone must have hurt you.'

'Yes,' he said with a sudden anger of his own. 'Yes, someone did. Does that make it any easier for us to understand each other? Or will you just blab it all over camp like everybody else?'

'How much,' she repeated slowly. 'How much! Do you think anyone can help you after that?'

A harsh black pain seemed to fill his heart and mind.

'I hope so,' he said in a bleak voice. 'I still keep hoping so.'

'Forgive me,' she said. 'I had no idea—'

'Nor I,' he said, standing up abruptly. 'No idea, and no right. You go on and live your life, Elizavetta, and forget that I ever blundered into it. This is your place and these are your friends. I'll only be here a month and I'll try to stay out of your way. If,' he added bitterly, 'your friends will let me, which I doubt.'

'Don't go,' she said, tense and unhappy in the speckled sunlight on the deck in the bright clear morning. 'Please don't go now.'

'I think it's best we both have a chance to think it over. I'm sorry I hurt you. It was a poor return for your hospitality. I suppose I'll see you at the pool.'

'Wait!' she said, but he was already gone, off the porch and down the path and out of sight as she remained seated stiffly at the table, staying there motionless until she began presently to hear again the river as it rushed along, the sharp crack of an acorn striking the roof, the call of quail, and all around from cabins near by the comfortable, familiar, everyday noises of another morning in Greenmont.

⋙ ELEVEN ⋘

How he made his way to the Mineral Springs he was not entirely aware, but presently he found himself there, sitting on a boulder overlooking a broad stretch of the river into which the effervescent waters of the springs bubbled down from small, orange-encrusted openings deep in the naked rock. He cupped his hands and scooped up a mouthful, turbulent, acrid, bitter yet invigorating. The taste was enough of a jolt to bring him out of wherever he had been and restore some semblance of balance to the day.

Whatever had become of the controlled resolve with which he had set out from the MacAleer cabin an hour ago? Whatever, really, had precipitated so odd and hurtful an exchange! Extraordinary, she had called him, and extraordinary he must be, to have engaged in so fantastic a performance, punishing her, in a sense, for the crimes of someone else, trying to work off his own pain by transferring it to one who was so innocent, so ill-equipped and so ill-prepared to bear it.

Or was she?

'How terribly you must have been hurt,' she had said; and a moment later, 'Forgive me'; and a moment after that, 'Please don't go now.' So she must have understood it; understood it and been prepared to take upon herself the responsibility for its having come with such unexpected hurtfulness out of the part of his heart where he held it, not too successfully, enchained. Dismayed but not repelled, she had asked him not to go, though in his blind striking-out at her perception of his pain he had not done so. She had been ready to help him, he could see that now, but he had been too involved in his own self-centred turmoil to let her do so.

He put his hands to his eyes and rubbed them in a weary, defensive gesture.

'I am no good,' he said aloud to the sparkling morning, but nothing seemed to listen. A water-ouze lit suddenly on a nearby rock, bobbed up and down a couple of times in its nervous characteristic way, then ducked out of sight on to the bottom of the stream, foraging busily for grubs for several minutes before it popped up again on the opposite side. Above his head a chipmunk scurried out and swayed precariously on a branch extending far over the water, observing him with beady curiosity before it gave a squeak and dashed back to safety. The river roared and chuckled and clucked and gurgled as it swept on through the broad stretch before him and then narrowed again to tumble headlong over quartz boulders flecked with fool's gold. That's for me, he thought with a cold bitterness: fool's gold for a fool.

And suddenly, out of his unhappiness and self-contempt, there came an overwhelming mood in which the last vestiges of common-sense and caution, the last reluctance to commit himself, the last defences, seemed to go down and be swept away. It suddenly seemed terribly important that he apologize to Elizavetta, regain her respect, beseech her understanding, impress upon her that he was someone to be thought well of, to be granted his good-will, to be accepted at his own evaluation, to be admitted to her heart. Even as he told himself he was in no condition, to judge anything accurately, even as he tried with one last failing attempt to look at it objectively, he realized that she had become instantaneously of overwhelming importance to his life. It was ridiculous, it was absurd, it made no sense – and it had him.

He realized that he was bracing his feet against the rock as tensely as though the river itself were threatening to draw him into its roiling depths and carry him to his death. He laughed shakily and told himself he must light a cigarette and calm down. Ahead lay what was now the serious conquest of Elizavetta. Ahead lay Greenmont, with all that it meant for their two poor hearts and uneasy, beleaguered hopes.

✑ TWELVE ✑

'Well,' Viola Townsend said as she dropped an air-mattress on the concrete apron by the pool, took off her beach-robe and prepared to settle down, 'has anybody seen love's young dream this morning?'

'Love's young dream, Haila hopes,' Sally-Jane said. Viola bridled.

'I don't think you have any right to speak like that. I think it would be very nice all around.'

'Well, I don't think it will happen,' Sally-Jane said flatly, 'if we don't all leave it alone. I think he's still all tied up in knots about his divorce.'

'He certainly conceals it well,' Mrs Townsend observed with a sniff. 'Nobody seems more self-contained. I think you're over-sentimentalizing the whole thing.'

'O.K.,' Sally-Jane said indifferently. 'Suit yourself. But don't be surprised if Haila produces a real explosion with all her meddling.'

'I don't think she's meddled at all,' Mrs Townsend said,

puffing slightly from the exertion of lowering herself to a sitting position on the air-mattress. 'She's only been doing her best to make them feel comfortable with each other. I don't see,' she added with a rising inflection, 'how you can say something like that, Sally-Jane. It's just plain disrespectful and impolite!'

'Girls, girls,' Einar protested mildly, shifting his head in a vain attempt to find a more comfortable position on the concrete. 'Let's don't have a public brawl about it this early in the morning. Wait until later, when everybody's here.'

'And as for you, Einar Magruder,' Mrs Townsend said, 'I don't need any of your bright remarks this morning. I declare, a sharp tongue to you is just as natural as – as—'

'I can think of a few things, honey,' Sally-Jane said sweetly, 'if you're running out of similes.'

'Very well,' Viola said, surging to her feet with a vigour that both startled and alarmed them. 'I don't have to stay here and listen to that kind of talk from you two! I guess I can go somewhere else!'

'Don't do that,' Einar said. 'Here come the Drummonds and you might miss something. Not only that, but here comes the major and you *really* might miss something.'

'I didn't know he knew old Mr Stafford,' said Mrs Townsend in a tone that resented it, settling back down with an uneasy reluctance. 'When has he had time to meet him?'

'We have kept him pretty busy,' Einar agreed, 'but maybe he just ran into him on the road on his way up to Eliza's for breakfast.'

'Oh?'

'I have a husband who gets up early and talks to people like old Mr Stafford for fear he'll miss something,' Sally-Jane said. 'He's the busiest little gossip of the lot, only you all don't realize it.'

'Well!' Viola said. 'Breakfast with Eliza! I do hope he's going to sit with us so we can find out all about it.'

'Wouldn't blame him if he didn't,' Einar said, 'but it can probably be arranged.' And rearing himself to a half-sitting position and raising a long, brown, muscular arm to wave, he yelled, just as Louise Drummond did the same, 'Hey, Bill! Over here!'

'Two minds,' Einar said, flopping back, 'usually empty, but

99

this time with but a single thought. You people just get up?'

'That swim last night made us so sleepy we couldn't have staggered out any earlier,' Jerry said, spreading a couple of beach towels on the grass alongside the concrete apron. 'Where do you suppose the major ran into old Mr Stafford?'

'Probably brooding on his troubles at the Mineral Springs,' Einar suggested. Louise reached over, scooped up a handful of water and dumped it on his chest. 'Don't DO THAT!' he roared, jumping violently. 'I can't stand these familiarities from married women this early in the morning.'

'All right, sweetie,' Louise said, 'but I think this had better be Lay Off The Major Day. Maybe he was brooding on his troubles. If so, it's none of our business.'

'He doesn't look to me,' Viola Townsend said with a sceptical glance, 'as though he'd been brooding on anything.'

And, aided by some recuperative ability, and old Mr Stafford's irascible good nature as he shuffled along beside him bemoaning the good old days in Greenmont, the major did appear for all outward purposes relatively carefree. When old Mr Stafford bade him farewell with the news that he was going to walk to the gate and back to get the juices circulating, he came over and dropped to his haunches beside Einar.

'Well,' he said, 'what's new on Helen Purseman?'

'What?' Viola Townsend said, looking blank.

'I said, what's new on Helen? She went down to the Valley on a mysterious mission last night. Remember?'

'Oh, now, see here—' Louise began with a grin, but Mrs Townsend replied with complete seriousness.

'I stopped by there this morning, just pretending to borrow some bacon, you know, if they had any, only they didn't, and Helen was back.'

'Helen was *back*?' he exclaimed. 'Great heavens!'

'Oh, listen,' Louise protested, but Viola was not to be deflected.

'She only went down to get a friend of theirs who was coming in on the train from San Francisco,' she explained earnestly. 'She picked her up in Big Smith and came right back and got in about midnight.'

'Damn!' he said. 'If I'd only known. To think I stayed awake for hours last night, just worrying about Helen. I wish you'd let me know, Mrs Townsend.'

'You know, Bill,' Einar said, reaching out suddenly to yank the major's ankle so that he perforce had to sit down abruptly on the concrete, 'I think you're beginning to be One Of Us.'

'I'm getting the pitch,' the major said, stretching out. 'I ought to be pretty good in another week or two. What have you all been saying about me?'

'Why,' Mrs Townsend began, 'we haven't been saying—'

'Oh, yes, you have. I'll bet you've all been wondering how late I went home last night—'

'You went by our cabin at 11.46,' Viola said promptly. Louise hooted.

'We also know you went back for breakfast,' Einar said.

'When did you have time to find out? I didn't know you ever got out of bed except to swim and play tennis.'

'My, aren't we sharp this morning,' Einar said complacently. 'My, aren't we all sharp. Was it a good breakfast?'

'Delightful.'

'Where is she, then?' Einar inquired, opening one eye and giving the major an appraising glance.

'Still fussing around the cabin,' he said, trying to make it sound sufficiently off-hand. 'I expect she'll be down after a bit.'

'Good,' Einar said, closing the eye. 'Wouldn't want to miss that.'

'Is anybody going in before the pool gets too crowded?' he asked abruptly, standing up and stripping to his trunks. 'How about you, Sally-Jane?'

'Sure,' she said, giving him a pretty smile. 'I'll race you across and back.' And with a leap she was into the water and half-way over before he could move.

Puffing and blowing on the other side, she looked at him shrewdly.

'Was it a good breakfast?'

'First-rate,' he said crisply. She nodded.

'I thought so.'

'What do you mean by that?'

'Nothing,' she said with a charming smile, 'I just thought so. Say! Isn't that Elizavetta going by over there on the road?'

'Don't you know whether it is or not?' he asked shortly, but after a second he forced himself to look while Sally-Jane examined him brightly. The enormous flowered print, the gaudy green sash and the rhinestone-encrusted sandals went by in a hurry under an enormous flowered hat, as though they didn't want to be seen. He wished he were in Fresno or somewhere, and apparently she did too, for she did not look to right or left.

'Hey, Eliza!' Einar shouted. 'Aren't you coming in?'

'After a while,' she called back hastily. 'I have to take something down to Haila.'

'Well, hurry back,' Jerry Drummond called after her rapidly departing figure. 'We've been waiting for you.'

'I know what she's taking to Haila,' Sally-Jane observed with an angry little snort. 'Her troubles. *Honestly.*'

'I'm sure,' he said carefully, 'that will be very helpful.'

'She always seems to think so,' Sally-Jane said, 'although I must say I can't see why. How much longer do you want to delay it?'

'What?'

'Rejoining the others. It's inevitable, you know. Come on, I'll race you back.'

He smiled.

'You're a caution, you are. Doesn't Einar ever find you a little disconcerting?'

'Ha! Not that boy. We deserve each other.'

'I'll bet you do at that,' he said with the first impulse of genuine amusement he had felt in a couple of hours.

There was a shout of glee from the golf-course, crowded with players, and they could hear Jim Buxton crowing, 'Oh, *baby*, what a putt!' The benches in the Grove were filling up, more and more children were racing noisily into the sparkling water, on the tennis courts the Websters and their guests and the Ruperts and theirs were engaged in vigorous doubles. The sun was turning slowly from warm to hot, the blue mountains stood clear and sharp against the blue sky. Two thunder-heads, perfect white galleons of cloud, drifted slowly over, too high and too distant to be threatening. He climbed out beside Einar and stretched out again on the concrete with a sigh that was almost relaxed.

'Is every day as perfect as this?'

'Where every prospect pleases,' Einar said, 'and man is the

only lousy thing about it, or whatever the hell the quotation is as if I didn't know. That,' he added out of the side of his mouth in a confidential murmur, 'was quite a brush-off we got. You got.'

'She told me she was going down to Haila's,' he lied with a disinterest he knew he must show. 'She said she'd be back.'

'Hmph,' Einar said. 'Well. All I can say is, I'm damned if *I'd* want my romance courtesy of Haila.'

The major reached out and gripped the wrist beside him, which tensed under the sharpness of his touch but was not pulled away.

'Listen,' he whispered savagely. 'You watch your tongue, sonny-boy, or you and I are going to have trouble.'

Einar gave him a slow look and a smile.

'I'm with you, pal,' he murmured. 'Relax.'

'Everybody's with me,' he said, releasing the wrist. 'That's the whole God-damned trouble.'

'Hey, Louise,' Einar said in a normal tone, jumping up and giving her a slap on the rump. 'A couple of quick laps before too many kids get in the way, O.K.?'

'O.K.,' she said, shooting them both a speculative look, though she had not been quite close enough to hear their muted exchange. 'Come on, Jerry. We'll be back in a flash, Viola. Take it easy, Major.'

'I am taking it—' he began sharply and then forced himself to laugh. 'I'm taking it so easy I'm almost dead.' And he rolled over, buried his head in his arms and exposed his back to the sun with an elaborate pretence of getting a tan.

In the humming silence thus created around his head, with the shouts and splashings from the pool and the jovial out-bursts from the golf-course muted by his flesh, he asked himself if there was any way at all out of this agglutinous web of in-timacy and answered himself instantly that there probably wasn't. How would one go about it? Say: 'I'm mad and I won't play with you other kids?' Obviously not. The slightest with-drawal, however managed, would instantly be interpreted for what it was, a running-away. And if he became more aggressive and more resentful of their continual supervision, that would simply be taken as a declaration of war. Then their interest, instead of being mildly jocular and basically friendly, would turn to a sharper and more spiteful mood that might do real harm to himself and Elizavetta – not only to their relationship, whatever it might be, but to themselves as people with feelings that could be hurt and perhaps permanently damaged. There was really, he supposed, no way out of it except to keep right on as he was doing, trying to hold his emotions under control and trying as best he could, to play along. Greenmont had him in check, and about all he could do was co-operate as gracefully as possible.

Not, of course, that this made things any easier with Elizavetta. He sighed, quite without pretence at concealment, and glanced over quickly at Mrs Townsend. But, mountainous and uncorseted in a glistening black bathing-suit, her face covered with a handkerchief which rose and fell rhythmically in the middle she too was taking the sun. A small voice at his other shoulder disclosed, however, that he was not unobserved.

'What's the matter?' Gray asked. 'Don't you feel good?'

'Shh,' he whispered. 'You'll bother Mrs Townsend. Lie down here beside me and talk quietly, if you want to.'

'Elizavetta's down at Buxtons',' the boy said, complying. 'I think they're talking about your fight.'

'What makes you think they're talking ab—' He caught himself abruptly. 'What fight?' The boy said, 'Shh!' with a mischievous little grin, succeeded immediately by a serious expression.

'I heard you,' he said solemnly.

'*Heard* us? the major demanded angrily. 'Didn't your parents ever teach you—'

'I didn't mean to,' Gray protested hastily. 'You left that note, so I thought I would come up and have breakfast too. You didn't tell me not to!'

The major gave a tired nod.

'So what happened?'

'Well, I got up there when you began to talk about her dress. You sounded kind of excited and nervous, so I hid. I think you're right,' he added stoutly. 'All her clothes look funny.'

'Don't change the subject,' the major said, feeling a sense of humiliated chagrin that was still, somehow, close to helpless

104

laughter. Here in Greenmont, it was all so expected. 'Why didn't you let us know you were there?'

'I wanted to, but I just didn't know how. And then you left and it was all over.'

'Does she know you were there?'

'Oh, no,' Gray said solemnly. 'I waited until she went in and then I ran. Smudge barked, but she probably thought it was just a squirrel.'

'Some squirrel,' he said, realizing that it was pointless to be angry, there was nothing to be gained by it now. 'More like a nut, I'd say.'

'Then you aren't mad?' the boy asked with obvious relief.

He sighed again.

'Oh, hell, no,' he muttered drily. 'I'm not mad. No,' he said seriously, 'I'm not mad. But I want you to promise me one thing, mister: I don't ever again want you eavesdropping on anybody, understand? If you stumble into a situation like that where two people are talking and don't know you're there, you let them know, understand me?'

'Yes, sir,' the boy said fervently. 'Oh, yes, sir! '

'And don't tell her you know, because it would bother her terribly. And don't tell anybody else, either.'

'Oh, I *wouldn't*.'

'All right. Now I want you to do something for me. I want you to go down to Buxtons' and tell Elizavetta I'm waiting to see her at the pool. Will you do that?'

The boy looked worried.

'What will Mrs Buxton say?'

'I don't give a damn what Mrs Buxton says. You go do as I say. It's part of the pact, O.K.?'

'O.K.,' Gray said with a sudden relieved smile and took off so fast he almost ran head-on into Louise as she emerged from the pool.

'My goodness,' she said. 'Where's he going, to deliver a message to Garcia?'

The major laughed.

'You're uncanny, lady. You've no idea how uncanny you are.'

'I've been called many things,' Louise said, banging her right ear vigorously to knock out a water-bubble, 'but not often that.

105

Where are those cards, Jerry? We'll have to put the major in his place with a good stiff game of canasta.'

An hour later, deep in a six-handed game while the kids screamed and frolicked in the pool and the Meadows buzzed with life on putting green, benches and tennis courts, he lost himself for a while in the general conviviality, though he could not avoid a heightened awareness of the point where the road entered the clearing from the lower end of camp. But neither Haila nor Elizavetta appeared, and presently he gave up his occasional casual glances: about time, he decided with a mixture of annoyance and amusement, since no matter how casual, they always evoked some appropriate comment from his companions.

'I expect she'll be along in due time,' Viola Townsend remarked comfortably at one point. 'Major, honey, pay attention to your game,' Sally-Jane advised kindly at another. And Einar finally, though with some care about the tone in which he said it, murmured thoughtfully, 'Must be quite a sewing-bee down at Haila's,' when he caught the major looking up.

Still later, the sun now high overhead, the full warmth of the day beating down into the fragrant river-canyon, Viola's beach-robe thrown over his shoulders at their insistence that he avoid too much exposure the first day out, he found himself coming to the conclusion that he should simply out-sit them. This was not very subtle, but he was damned if he would go back to the MacAleer cabin and risk running into Haila and Elizavetta together. Sooner or later Elizavetta would have to come by, either to join them, which she apparently did not intend to do – Gray reappeared, looking a little disturbed, but didn't come near, which was indication enough – or to return to her cabin. If he waited long enough she would inevitably pass by and then, if it were as late as it appeared likely to be and if the Meadows were as deserted as he expected in late midday, perhaps they could talk again.

Since there was no point in trying to fool people who weren't to be fooled, he said frankly, 'I think I'll stay here and wait for Elizavetta,' when the group broke up around 1.30 and the Drummonds invited him home for lunch.

'Well, good luck, sweetie,' said Louise.

'Give a shout if you need reinforcements,' said her husband.

'I don't think I will,' he told them with a grin that looked self-confident, 'but if I do, isn't Einar's cabin closer? I'm sure he'd be glad to come and help.'

'You'll be lucky if he doesn't come back in ten minutes looking for something he's forgotten,' Sally-Jane said. 'Come along, beach god.'

'I just want to listen,' Einar protested. 'You wouldn't mind that, would you, Bill?'

'Shove off, beach god,' the major said. 'You've got enough to take care of at home.'

'Oh, well, if you put it that way,' said Einar with a lascivious grin that prompted Viola Townsend to become very busy.

'I think I'd better be running along,' she said hastily. 'I'm sorry I have to take my beach-robe, but—'

'I'll sit in the Grove,' he said. 'It's cooler there, anyway. I'll see all you nice, interested, observant, chummy, close-knit, perceptive people this afternoon.

Louise chuckled.

'I can see you're beginning to understand our fine points,' she said.

⋖§ THIRTEEN §⋗

After their departure the Meadows gradually emptied around him. The Websters and the Ruperts finished their respective tennis games, the noisy foursomes on the golf-course one by one broke up and went home for lunch. The last protesting child, a Talbott, emerged shivering from the pool at the indignant insistence of a parent shouting from a nearby cabin. The placid peace he had seen in early morning, emphasized now by the heat of midday, returned to the big open area that formed the hub of camp. With it came a drowsy feeling that there was nothing else in the universe, no Valley, no Fresno, no world, no time, no past, no future; only the present, perfect and complete in its absolute moment of being; only Greenmont, hidden away in the Sierras, self-contained, untroubled, inviolate and secure.

Into this suspended world Elizavetta came presently walking, and abruptly his tensions returned, magnified by the delay, the

107

protracted visit to Haila, the ignoring of his message sent by Gray. Why had she chosen to be so stubborn when he had suddenly found that she was so important to him? Why had she subjected him to so capricious and petty a testing? But he reminded himself in time that nothing of this must be allowed to show in voice or manner or she would, he did not doubt, quite literally run away. When he called, it was quietly. She paused, gave him a startled glance, and started on.

'Wait!' he said, echoing her own admonition of the morning. 'Please don't go.' And as she paused irresolute near the bench he went on in a tone he made conversational. 'Did you have a nice visit with Haila?'

'Oh, yes. Yes. We had a good talk.'

'I hope you didn't condemn me too drastically,' he said with a little smile. She gave the smallest of half-smiles in return.

'We talked of a great many things.' She looked about. 'Where is everybody?'

'It's almost two,' he pointed out with another smile. 'Home eating lunch, as decent people should be.'

'Oh, that's right,' she said in a flustered way. 'I guess I'd better be running along myself.'

'So soon? I've been waiting quite a while for you.'

'Haila said you probably would be,' she said, and despite a quick flare of annoyance at this quoting of the oracle, he kept it under control. But he could not help asking bluntly, 'What else did Haila say about me?'

She looked vaguely off at the mountains. Presently she spoke. 'She said I shouldn't judge you too harshly.'

'Well, thanks,' he said drily, 'for small favours. Did you take her advice?'

'I don't know,' she said; and with a sudden unhappy vehemence: 'I don't know!'

'I wouldn't blame you for judging me harshly,' he said after a moment. 'I deserve it.'

'I don't, really,' she said, sitting down cautiously on the far end of the bench. 'I just don't know how to – how to deal with you, is all. I'd like to be your friend, but – I don't know what to expect. It makes it difficult.'

'I know,' he said softly, surveying in his turn the distant, looming peaks. 'I am difficult. But I don't really want to be.'

'That's what Haila said,' she informed him quickly, and this time a real irritation entered his voice, try though he did to keep it out.

'Is there anything Haila doesn't know?' he asked sharply. At once she looked upset and withdrawn.

'I'm sure she tries to be helpful to everyone. I don't think she wants to hurt anyone deliberately.'

'Well, I'll admit I don't know Haila as well as you do.'

'She did say,' she offered earnestly, 'that you were one of the most attractive men she had ever met.'

'Doesn't get around much, does she?' he said with a flippancy he at once regretted, for she looked surprised and hurt.

'I don't know.' She stood up. 'I do think I'd better be getting back to the cabin for lunch.'

'I suppose,' he said rather forlornly, 'that I should too. Be getting on back to mine, I mean.'

She hesitated a moment, but then said what he expected.

'Yes, I suppose you had.'

'Will I see you later on?'

She paused.

'Do you want to?'

'If you want me to.'

'Don't always put the burden on me!' she said with a sudden flare of indignation that startled him. '*Do you want to?*'

'Yes,' he said with equal anger. 'Yes, I do!'

'Ah, ah,' Einar called mockingly from poolside, making them both jump. 'Voices, voices. People will hear you.'

'Why don't you just go to hell?' the major demanded harshly. Einar gave him a bland look.

'I forgot my sun-glasses. Obviously I had to come back and get them. Going up to your cabin, Eliza?'

'Not yet, thank you,' she replied with a firmness that clearly surprised Einar. 'I don't like to walk with sneaks.'

'Oh, come on!' Einar protested, looking, comically, quite dismayed. 'I just arrived a second ago. Honest. And I did forget my sun-glasses. See? Here they are.'

'No, thank you,' she said. 'Not today.'

'Well—' he said uncertainly, and then turned away and left them with an unhappy air. The major laughed without amusement.

'Good for you. He needs to be put in his place.'

'He doesn't mean any harm.'

The major laughed again.

'Nobody means any harm. That's what makes them all so harmful. To you and me, at any rate.'

'I wonder,' she said in a remote voice, 'whether they could possibly do us any more harm than we could do ourselves.'

He did not respond for a moment. When he did it was in a gravely troubled voice.

'Is that the best you can think of me?'

'I don't know what I think,' she said with a tired sigh. 'You aren't so easy to think about.'

'No,' he agreed bleakly, 'I guess not. But it's very important to me, suddenly, that you think well of me. When you do think of me.'

'I guess I do,' she said, and shook her head with a puzzled expression. 'I guess so.'

'I'll be expecting you for golf at four,' he said, trying not to sound too hopeful. She gave the briefest of smiles.

'I don't know. I'll have to see.'

'Please.'

'I'll have to see.'

'Please,' he said gravely.

'Oh, why do you keep after me!' she cried unhappily. 'I said I'll have to see!'

'Very well. I'll be here.'

'Now I must go,' she said, turning away. 'I must!'

And as he offered a hand she did not take, she turned and hurried past the pool and the tennis courts to disappear along the upper road.

At the MacAleer cabin ten minutes later he found he was not to be excused a further exercise on the subject. Gray was asleep but their next-door neighbour was on the job. He had scarcely finished washing down a sandwich with a glass of milk when the door opened across the way and she came down the path through the little ravine and up on to the porch where he sat with an uneasy tenseness in the soft drowse of mid-afternoon. Her tall, gaunt figure was immaculate as always, her high-boned

face as always perfectly composed, her manner brisk but kindly.
He braced himself for another open onslaught upon his feelings,
but it soon became apparent that he had underestimated Haila.
Her approach could not have been more pleasant.

'Why didn't you come over?' she demanded with what
appeared to be a genuine cordiality. 'Any time you want a free
meal, just holler. Jim and I would be delighted. Not having
any children, you see, we're always alone, so it's nice to have
company. Particularly,' she added with a coy little smile, 'such
very *nice* company.'

'That's very nice of you,' he said cautiously, gesturing her
to a chair. 'I'll remember that.'

'As a matter of fact, we were thinking that it would be quite
delightful if you and Elizavetta could come for dinner tonight.
With the Townsends. And Gray, if you like. Or have the Drummonds grabbed you already?'

'No,' he said, unbending a little, 'the Drummonds haven't
grabbed me.'

'Well, then. It's all set.'

'Is it?' he asked, staring into the bottom of his milk glass as
thoughtfully as though it were a highball. 'Are you sure of that?'

'*She* agreed,' Haila said with an air of triumph. He tried not
to appear either surprised or pleased, easy enough since he
didn't know exactly what he felt at that particular moment.

'Did she?' he said, still staring into his glass. 'Then you think
I should too?'

'I think it would be very nice if you did.'

'Why?' he asked, suddenly abandoning the milk glass and
looking squarely at her. Stylish, attractive, all-knowing and composed, she looked back with a tender, poor-child-do-trust-me
expression.

'Because she needs you,' she said softly, and at the words, so
completely pat yet said with such fervent conviction that he
could almost believe she meant them, an impatient expression
shot across his face.

'Oh, come on,' he said harshly. 'What fairy-tale did that line
come out of?'

'You poor dear,' Mrs Buxton said gently. 'You poor, poor
dear. How much the world must have hurt you.'

'Damn it to hell,' he said, making no attempt to be gentle-

111

manly, 'will you women stop mooning about how much I've been hurt! That's my business. It's none of yours.'

'But you've *made* it our business,' she said in a tone of gentle reproof, 'by thinking so highly of Eliza.'

'I don't think so highly—' he began angrily, but ended more slowly '—of Eliza.'

'There,' she said in the same gentle voice. 'You see? You can't deny it.'

'Why should I?' he asked with a distant gesture towards humour. 'You would none of you believe it.'

'Of course we wouldn't,' she said comfortably. 'Then we can expect you for dinner?'

'Tell me,' he said, with a flippancy he did not bother to make friendly, 'do you always get what you go after?'

For a second the mask of cloying goodwill dropped and the little dangerous gleam he had seen before came into her eyes. But she only laughed merrily.

'That's what Jim says!' she confessed with a girlish candour.

'I'll bet he does. I'll *bet* he does. By the way,' he added quickly, 'I'm being a poor host. Can't I get you some milk?'

She laughed again.

'No, thank you. It's a little early in the day to start drinking milk.'

'You're so right. I don't know why I ever touch the stuff. Well,' he said abruptly, standing up, 'is that all?'

She gave a little tug of readjustment to her skirt and patted her perfect silver hair.

'Sit down, Major,' she ordered with a kindly chuckle. 'Stop acting like a fretful horse, and sit down. We have many things to talk about.'

'We do?' he said, still standing. 'I wasn't aware of it.'

'Elizavetta likes you very, very much,' she said, completely unperturbed by his deliberate rudeness. 'Very, *very* much.'

'And what if I were to like Elizavetta ve-rry, ve-rry much,' he inquired with a mocking inflection, 'what difference would that make to the affairs of nations and of men?'

'Not much to them,' she agreed with another chuckle, 'but much to Greenmont! We all, you know,' she added with sudden solemnity, 'love Eliza dearly. We are her *friends*. She is our *pet*.'

'How lucky for Eliza,' he said, and this time she took him up on it at once.

'Yes, it is,' she said crisply. 'It's good to have friends who really care for you. I take it you do not have that pleasure, Major.'

'Call me Bill,' he said, and sat down again because it suddenly seemed hardly worth the trouble to stand up.

'There,' she said serenely. 'I told you it would be easier for you to sit down. Of course we want to be *your* friends, too, you know. None of this would be happening if we didn't.'

'I'm drowning in it. So Eliza likes me very, very much, does she? I gather you think this is a good thing in spite of all my faults?'

'We want her to be happy. We want *you* to be happy. I think we have concluded, even on so brief an acquaintance, that this would be an ideal solution for everything.'

There was a pause, and in it a car churned up the road and dwindled away into silence. A woodpecker hammered on a tree, and through the leaves above the warm wind stirred.

'Major,' she said earnestly, 'let your heart trust love! '

'Oh, my,' he protested, not knowing whether to laugh or swear. 'Oh, my, oh, my. How corny can you get? These are people who are involved here, not sayings your mother used to have on the parlour wall.'

'We want to be your friends, Major,' she said with a wistful firmness. 'Don't underestimate our power to help.'

'Or hurt.'

'Any hurt that comes out of this,' she said softly, 'you will bring upon yourself. Only you, will bring it upon yourself. Remember that, Bill.'

'What do you want me to do, then?' he asked with a sudden capitulation, for all at once it seemed pointless to go on fighting this flood-tide of molasses. Who knew, maybe it was genuine, maybe he should accept it, maybe it would all work out. In any event, he felt, abruptly, too tired to fight back. 'If she likes me and I like her, what then? If she really does.'

'Oh, she really does,' Mrs Buxton said with a pleased expression. 'She really does. Well, *I* think it's quite simple. All you have to do is act friendly and loving, and so will she. And that will be that.'

'She told you about this morning, of course.'

Haila nodded with an air of gentle regret.

'I think it was – unfortunate. But not fatal. I think she was more startled than anything else.'

'I was a little startled myself,' he confessed with a return of wryness. 'But it seemed like a good idea at the time. Why *does* she get herself up the way she does, anyway? You must admit I have a point, aside from everything else.'

'Elizavetta is a *nice* girl, but a little – exaggerated – sometimes, in what she does. It's just a little trait. I think you may find – I think you may ... just ... find, that things will be different this afternoon.'

'Oh? That will be nice.'

'I told her I thought she might try to dress a little more to suit you,' she said placidly. 'I think she agreed.'

'Well, isn't that nice,' he said admiringly. 'I can't think of anything more delightful than to feel that she took my suggestion at your insistence.'

'Major,' she said, and the cordiality definitely ceased for a moment, 'you must remember not to be too bitter, here in camp. We are all friends and we enjoy getting along with one another ... But, there!' she said with a merry laugh. 'What a serious thing to make of something that isn't serious at all. I just told her I thought you might like it better if she took some account of your ideas. She didn't have to agree. The important thing is that she *did* agree. Isn't that so?'

'If you think that's the only significance of it, then I suppose that makes it so. Only of course you don't, any more than I do.'

'Now, Bill, Bill,' she said in the same merry tone. 'I refuse to let you spoil this beautiful day by picking a fight with an old lady. I've got to get back to our cabin now and take a little nap before we go up to the Meadows, but we'll be expecting you for dinner. Remember, you promised!'

'Did I?' he inquired with an elaborate surprise as she stood up. 'I don't remember it, but if I did, I guess I'll be there.'

'*Good*. Will you be playing golf again this afternoon?'

'I think Elizavetta and I may be playing golf. Alone.'

'All right, Major!' she said with a cheerful peal. 'All right, you stubborn boy.'

'All right,' he echoed. 'Watch your footing going down the steps.'

'I'll bet you'd love for me to break my neck,' she said gaily. 'But I won't, Bill. I won't!'

'Gosh,' said Gray behind him as he watched her go, trim, beautifully groomed, unruffled and serene, 'why doesn't she?'

'What did I tell you—' he began, but the boy smiled up at him without concern from drowsy eyes.

'I just got up,' he said with a yawn. 'Just this very minute. Anyway, don't you wish so too?'

The major laughed.

'Just between you and me, buddy, it's not a thought two gentlemen should have, so we'll banish it, shall we?'

'Sure,' Gray said, rubbing his eyes. 'But it sure would help Greenmont.'

Haila Buxton, however, the major knew, was one of those women who are indomitable, insufferable, indestructible and inescapable, and no hope of intervention human or divine could remove her from direct participation in his affairs. Quite successfully she had assumed control of his little romance. Whether she had actually suggested that Elizavetta moderate her appearance he would never know, but she had certainly made it impossible for him to think anything else if it happened; and what she had done to influence Eliza's thinking directly, he could only imagine. The fact that Eliza was waiting for him at the Meadows when he arrived at four was enough to make him wonder if Haila hadn't told her she should do that, too. The thought brought an impatient and annoyed expression to his eyes for a second and he knew she saw it, for her tentative welcoming smile was momentarily shadowed. Thank *you*, Mrs Buxton, he thought grimly. But when he saw what she was wearing he smiled with a peculiar reverse elation.

'So you didn't after all,' he said; and, when she looked puzzled, 'change your dress.'

'Oh. What an odd thing to say. I thought you wanted me to.'

'I did,' he said, conscious that on nearby benches several

Cartwrights and Bakers were listening while pretending not to, 'but – when you get ready for it. Not because anyone else tells you to.'

'Who else would?' she asked in some surprise. 'My friends seem to like me as I am.'

'O.K.,' he said with a wry expression that conceded he wouldn't carry it further. 'I guess I'm the only scoundrel in the lot.'

'You're not a scoundrel,' she said with a sudden smile. 'I don't think you could be a scoundrel if you tried.'

'I hope you're right,' he said mockingly; and then, with an abrupt sobriety, like a shadow on the sun: 'I hope you're right.'

She gave a nervous little laugh.

'There you go being serious again. Let's play golf and forget about it for ten minutes.'

'Right. I'll try to do better today.'

And rather to his surprise he found that he did, though again there were various lively comments from around the course as they went along. He found today that he could parry them without irritation, and as they progressed Elizavetta too seemed to relax and become more comfortable. By the time they finished the game and came again to the benches they were laughing and outwardly carefree together.

'That's a happy sight,' Louise observed, wandering over from the tennis court and flopping down on the grass at their feet with a winded air. 'I'm glad somebody had a good game.'

'Did they beat you again?' Elizavetta inquired sympathetically. Louise chuckled.

'No, indeed. For a couple of spavined old hacks, Jerry and I do fairly well. But I must confess we are spavined. Two solid days of this and I don't see how he manages to run the ranch all week.'

'You just don't know the iron man you married,' her husband said, collapsing alongside. 'This keeps me youthful.'

'Me, too,' Einar said, sitting down beside the major and giving him a rather wary look. 'Bill, how are you?'

'I'm fine, thank you,' he replied with a non-committal politeness. 'And you?'

116

'O.K., I guess,' Einar said with a revival of his usual buoyant grin, 'providing I can get back in Eliza's good graces. How about it, pal?'

'How did you ever fall out of them?' Louise asked. 'I didn't know it could be done.'

'It happens. O.K., Eliza?'

'Well—' she began thoughtfully, and then gave him an amused smile. 'Just don't let it happen again.'

'Lordee, no! Heaven forbid.' He looked brightly at them both. 'Everything all right with you two again?'

'Einar, *honey*,' Sally-Jane said. 'Really, now. Don't spoil it.'

'It's a legitimate subject of curiosity,' her husband said cheerfully. 'You know we're all interested. You don't mind, do you, Bill?'

'Oh, no,' he said drily. '*We* don't mind, do we, Elizavetta?'

'I think,' Louise said decisively before she could answer, 'that we should all go to our cabin and have a drink before dinner. We'd like you and Eliza to stay for dinner, too, Bill.'

'We can't,' he said solemnly. 'We promised Haila.'

'Oh?' Einar said, and then changed his tone with elaborate haste at the look in the major's eye. 'I mean, oh?'

'I did, anyway. I don't know about Eliza.'

'I said I would,' she remarked calmly. 'But a drink beforehand would be nice, Louise. Let's go.'

'We'll send you off to Haila's looping,' Louise said cheerfully. 'That way, it won't be bad at all.'

But actually, he found when they walked later down the darkening road past the brightly-lighted cabins and came presently to the Buxtons' sitting neat and complacent amid the trees, it didn't start off badly; and he hoped that with a little luck it might be maintained on a level where it wouldn't end badly, either. Certainly the cocktail hour had been pleasant enough, spent in casual gossip about the Grangers and the Moores that didn't particularly hurt anybody but did reveal to him still another layer in Greenmont's constantly unravelling cocoon of interlocking memories and relationships. While he carefully sat away from Elizavetta and did not seek in any way to monopolize her conversation, it seemed to him that in some

117

quietly unexpressed way they were moving back into an understanding at once closer, easier and more exciting in its promise of things to come.

On the walk down to the Buxtons' their conversation, while meticulously non-commital, was reasonably calm and comfortable. As they arrived to a hearty, 'He-*llo*, children!' from Haila, he thought that perhaps by the time the evening was over they might be able to establish on some relatively permanent basis their evanescent, shifting, uncertain association, with all its starts and stops and hesitations and impulses. With a grim humour he hoped so: the pace could get wearing, in time.

For a while, as Haila moved about efficiently in the kitchen with Elizavetta helping, he found that talk with Jim remained on the golf-course, which was perfectly all right with him. Notes were compared, tricky holes were discussed, the problem of the fifteenth, lying near the bridge over the river that divided the Meadows, was gone into with some thoroughness. There came a point, finally, however, when his host looked at him shrewdly over his highball and inquired calmly:

'How are things going for you up here in our happy wilderness, boy? The natives treating you all right, are they?'

'I can't complain,' he said with a show of amiable indifference. Jim said, 'Sure?' in a quizzical tone. 'You know,' he added, crossing one long leg over the other and cocking his head on one side in a characteristic gesture, 'I could almost think maybe you meant that. Except I'm not sure you do.'

'Why not?' he said, aware that their voices had instinctively lowered even though the women were chatting busily in the kitchen and couldn't possibly overhear. Or could they? He wouldn't have been surprised, nor, obviously, would Jim.

'Just a hunch,' his host said with a comfortable smile. 'Living with old Haila you get so you develop hunches. She has so many herself.'

'What's that, Jim?' his wife inquired from within, and they both started guiltily, then grinned at one another. 'Are you taking my name in vain out there?'

'No more than usual,' her husband informed her with a wink at the major. 'Get on with your work, there. We're hungry.'

'It won't be long. Don't you two old gossips say anything we ought to hear!'

118

'Is there anything you ought to hear?' Jim asked with the chuckle that indicated he was being permissibly flippant. 'Or rather I should say, is there anything you don't hear?' But they had resumed talking and after a moment he turned back to the major.

'So you like it here, eh?' He nodded towards the kitchen. 'Do you like her?'

'I think so,' the major said; and with a sudden flippancy of his own, 'A man has to do something to pass the time.'

'Now, you don't mean that the way it sounds,' his host said calmly. 'Not about a nice girl like Elizavetta.'

'No,' he said, feeling surprisingly ashamed. 'No, I don't. I like her.'

'Good,' Jim said comfortably. 'That will please Haila. She wants you to like each other.'

'So she's told me,' he said drily. Jim took a long drink of the highball.

'Old Haila means well. At least' – he grinned a little – 'she always starts out meaning well.'

'Did she start out that way with you?' the major asked. His host lost the grin, started to be offended, thought better of it.

'She did,' he said softly. 'Once upon a time, she did. Sometimes,' he said with a rather rueful laugh, 'she still does.' He shrugged. 'We get along. What more can you expect of a marriage?'

'Not too much, I guess,' the major said grimly. 'At least so I've found.'

'Pretty rough time of it, eh?' his host suggested, watching him shrewdly. He nodded shortly.

'Pretty rough.'

'Tough luck. Must have taken something too seriously.'

'Everything. But shouldn't one? I mean, how can it ever be what you want it to be, if you don't?'

'There's an in-between,' Jim said thoughtfully. 'Important when it should be, not important when it isn't.'

'I suppose that's what you've got,' the major said with a sarcasm he did not bother to moderate. His host smiled without offence.

'We get along,' he repeated. 'The nightingales stopped singing about twenty years ago, but old Haila and I, we get along.' He

119

gave a pointed little chuckle. 'Better than you did, obviously.'

The major shook his head in a baffled way.

'You wonder and wonder where things went wrong, but you never really understand, do you?'

His host smiled blandly.

'I wouldn't know,' he said with a certain deliberate complacency the major knew he had invited, and deserved. 'I've never had the problem.'

The major laughed harshly.

'You people up here are so damned smug. It's no wonder I don't—' But his host lifted an admonitory hand and gave him a sceptical, appraising look.

'Don't what, boy?' he said comfortably. 'You're doing all right. We all like you. Relax. Have another drink!'

'By George,' Bob Townsend boomed heartily from the steps, 'that sounds like a wonderful idea. You can count me in on that!'

'He's already had two at the Websters',' Viola explained as she bustled towards the kitchen, 'so be sure to make this one very, very light, Jim, if you please.'

'Some people always like to spoil the fun!' her husband said. 'But I suppose us poor old husbands are in no position to argue.'

'That's what *I* always say,' Jim Buxton agreed with his authorized chuckle.

'It does simplify things, doesn't it?' the major agreed with a dangerous pleasantness. Bob Townsend gave him a surprised glance.

'What's the matter with sunshine, here?' he inquired cheerfully. 'Oh, Haila! Something's eating the major. Better come out here and smooth his ruffled feathers.'

'Dinner will be ready in just a second,' she called, 'and that ought to soothe even the most savage breast. Which I don't really think,' she added, popping her head out the door to give him a merry wink, 'the major is. Right, Bill?'

The only answer to that was a laugh. He produced it.

'You people,' he said, shaking his head. 'You people!'

'We people are about to eat a sumptious meal,' Jim Buxton said, returning with the replenished drinks. 'Old Haila's outdone herself this time, tablecloth, candles, best silverware and

120

all. By the way, where's Gray?'

'He's at the Websters',' Viola Townsend said. 'Micky invited him to stay to dinner and spend the night, so he said to tell you he'd see you in the morning, Major.'

'I suppose he's perfectly safe,' he said. They all nodded vigorously.

'Everybody's safe at Greenmont,' Bob Townsend said. 'After all, Bill,' he said, slapping him on the back as they started in to the table, 'we're all friends here!'

'Sure, sure,' the major said with a smile he made quite genuine. 'Lead me to that meal, Haila. I can hardly wait.'

Later they sat on the deck, the stars fantastic above, the massive ridges looming along the canyon's edge in the velvet night. For a time they made the rounds of camp in casual after-dinner gossip, the emotional situation here, the financial problem there, the small difficulties or triumphs somewhere else. Again he was given to understand how close they all were, how knowledgeable about one another, how self-protective. Eventually there came a lapse and into it his hostess said, quite abruptly and apparently in all seriousness:

'You know, I can't think of anything better than a true understanding between two hearts!'

There was a moment of surprised silence, broken by her husband with his customary air of carefully calculated amusement.

'Well, bless my soul! Now, what brought that on?'

'What you and Bill were talking about before dinner,' she said, smiling at the major's startled look. 'I couldn't help thinking about it while we were eating. It just seems so true!'

'I told you, boy,' Jim said with a chuckle. 'Can't keep anything from old Haila!'

'We didn't hear a thing, really,' Elizavetta said calmly in response to the major's questioning glance. 'I think she's just shooting in the dark to see what she hits.'

'Child,' Mrs Buxton said with an air of amused candour, 'you know me too well. But it's still entirely valid, Major, don't you think?'

'It seems obvious,' he said warily, and received support from an unexpected quarter.

121

'Of course it does,' Viola Townsend said blankly. 'Why ever did you bring it up, Haila?'

'Eliza's got it pegged,' Bob Townsend offered. 'She just wants to stir things up. As for me, you defeated your purpose with that food, Haila. It's made me too sleepy to be philosophical. You don't mind if I just sit this one out, do you?'

'Sit away,' she said cheerfully, 'but I still think it's something we should all be thinking about.'

'Why?' the major demanded, though he knew this was exactly what she wanted him to do and he shouldn't. But before she could reply Eliza intervened.

'Yes, I don't really see why, either. Isn't there something more important we can talk about?'

'My dear,' Haila said softly, 'there is *nothing* more important to talk about. *Nothing*, in this world.'

'So what shall we do?' he asked, with a reasonable humour but unable to keep a little edge from rising in his voice. 'Have a profound discussion about it while you try to embarrass Elizavetta and me?'

'Oh, *Bill*,' his hostess said in a gently chiding voice. 'Oh, now, *Bill*! What an assumption! No one wants to embarrass you and certainly no one wants to embarrass Elizavetta. It just seems to me—'

'It just seems to me we'd better drop it,' he suggested crisply. 'I'm suddenly awfully tired of playing games with other people's feelings.'

'But—' she said with elaborate dismay.

'If you don't mind,' he said with elaborate courtesy.

'Sounds as though he means it, Haila,' Bob Townsend said lazily. 'Maybe you'd better mind.'

'Maybe you had, old girl,' Jim Buxton said. 'The boy sounds mighty fierce, all of a sudden.'

'I'm not fierce,' he said, amicably but with an unyielding note in it. 'I'm just tired of it, that's all. So just – cut it – out.'

'Well, really—' Viola Townsend said.

'I think I agree,' Elizavetta said suddenly. 'I don't know what you had in mind, Haila, but I think perhaps you had better forget it.' She stood up. 'I think I really must run along. It's getting late and I have to get up at six tomorrow morning to go down to the Valley for work. I'd better be getting back.'

'Of course you'll see her to her cabin, Bill,' Haila said quickly, and the only way he could keep himself from making an angry reply was to talk directly to Elizavetta as though their hostess had never spoken.

'I'll walk you up to your cabin.' She nodded as though it had been settled long since.

'I'd be happy if you would.'

'Well, children,' Haila said with a comfortable laugh, 'you see how things work themselves out in spite of yourselves.'

'Thanks for the meal, Haila,' he said evenly. 'It was delicious.'

'Drop in when you get back,' she suggested as they all rose in farewell. 'We'll probably still be here playing bridge.'

'Oh, I may not come back. I may spend the night, if Elizavetta will let me. Who knows?'

His hostess gave a peal of laughter.

'Major, you are a rogue!'

'That's me all over. Come along, Eliza. It's a long walk.'

'Yes,' she said, giving him a glance at once relieved and uneasy. 'It is.'

⤢ FOURTEEN ⤡

For a time as they trudged up the road, their flashlights casting quick reflections ahead along the rutted blacktop winding through the towering trees, an earnest distance carefully maintained between them, they did not speak. Many cabins were already standing dark and silent as they passed, much of Greenmont seemed well on its way to bed, but the Grangers', the Bakers', the Swifts', the Elliotts' and the Ruperts' were still alight, and from the Magruders' as they passed came the sound of boisterous voices and an occasional wild whoop of laughter as Mother Magruder addressed her vigorous brood. The Meadows were still brightly lighted and in the Grove a group of adults and youngsters were using the badminton court for a raucously happy game of volleyball. He could see Gray and Micky Webster darting around with the rest. Otherwise, the place was deserted as they came to the first bench in the Grove and in tacit agreement sat down.

Overhead the stars were enormous and unreal, blazing across space with the unearthly clarity the thin atmosphere of the high

123

mountains gives them. A tiny sliver of new moon lay far away in their luminous depths. His emotions were at a singing tension now that he and Elizavetta were alone, but for the moment he did not see quite how to proceed with it. In a tone he made carefully casual he commented upon their hostess instead.

'She's a strange woman,' he said without preliminary. 'I wonder if she's really real.'

'Oh, I don't know,' Elizavetta began thoughtfully. 'I think she—' But he forestalled it.

'I know,' he said with a gentle mockery: 'she means well. Do you ever stop being charitable to people?'

She gave a little laugh.

'I shouldn't think that you, of all people, would want me to,' she said with the quiet irony that always surprised him, it was so out of character; at least, the character she tried to suggest to the world by her appearance. He laughed in quite a genuine amusement.

'Score one for you.'

'No score,' she said, sounding more reserved. 'Just a comment.'

'Mmmmmm. I have to watch you, sometimes. I forget that, now and then.'

'Why?' she asked simply. 'I don't deliberately try to score off people. I'm not like that.'

'What are you like?' he asked, aware that a car was working its way up the road and in a moment would top the rise and catch them in the flood of its headlights as it swung into the Meadows. 'Do you know?'

She sighed.

'Yes, I think I know. Why does it matter?'

'Who knows?' he responded with a little flippancy. 'Let's just say it does matter, to me.'

She was silent for a moment. He was increasingly conscious of the volleyball players shouting behind them in the Grove, the nearing car.

'I'm sorry,' she said finally. 'I'm not sure that it matters to me – that it matters to you.'

'But—' he began, turning towards her with a sudden sharp dismay, and just then the car arrived and caught them full in its headlights. Abruptly it stopped and Einar called out:

'Hi, there, love-birds! Want to come up to our cabin for a drink? We're still serving.'

'No, thanks,' Elizavetta called back. 'We've got to get on home to bed. Or I've got to, rather.'

'There's a Freudian slip,' Einar trumpeted cheerfully. 'How about you, Bill? Stop by on your way back, if it's not too late, that is.'

'Ignore him, Bill, honey,' Sally-Jane advised in a disembodied voice from behind the headlights. 'He isn't as cute as he thinks he is.'

'Oh, yes, he is,' the major said, rather grimly. 'Far more so, in fact.'

'O.K.,' Einar said happily. 'Stay all night, if you like. See if we care. See you next week-end, Eliza.'

' 'Night,' Sally-Jane echoed, and the car zoomed off leaving the Meadows once more quiet in the velvet-covered universe. Behind them the volleyball players resumed their noisy game.

'I wish they weren't always so specific,' Elizavetta said with a tired little laugh.

'Why shouldn't they be?' he asked quickly, for now the way seemed open. 'Why shouldn't we be? Is there any reason why not?'

'What?' she asked in a startled voice. 'What did you say?'

'I said,' he repeated with great care, 'why shouldn't we be, too? Is there any reason why we shouldn't?'

'What do you take me for?' she demanded in a disbelieving tone, and at the question, so stock-theatre in sound yet so inevitable under the circumstances, he almost completed, 'Jack Dalton!' But it was no time for levity, though nervous tension almost provoked it. Instead he said evenly:

'A grown woman of – what is it, thirty-four, thirty-five? – who can do what she pleases if she likes someone enough. Just as I am a man of forty-three, similarly independent. The conclusion seems obvious.'

'Does it?'

He leaned forward eagerly.

'Who else is there to consider?'

'Are you really that all-alone in the world?' she asked in the same disbelieving voice. 'Really so unresponsible to anyone or anything? I don't know much about you, but I can't believe that. It doesn't ring true.'

'Responsible to my own heart,' he said, aware that it sounded like more from the same melodrama, yet helplessly impelled to go on with it. 'Maybe responsible to yours, if you will let me.'

'That's what I'm talking about, in case you haven't understood.'

'I understand it,' she said; and, after a moment – 'I guess.' Abruptly she stood up, brushing her hand across her eyes in a puzzled gesture. 'I must get back. I have to get up at six.'

'I was told to see you to your cabin,' he said with a desperate kind of jauntily uncertain humour, 'and I intend to do it.'

'I don't think you should. I think we should say good night here.'

'I don't.'

'I do.'

They stood for a moment unmoving by the pool.

'I really don't know what you see in me,' she said finally, 'except a funny-looking old – old maid who doesn't dress the way you think she should. I think you must be making up all sorts of dreams about me in your own mind that really don't exist at all. I'm just me. And that,' she added with a sudden quiet bitterness that moved him powerfully, 'isn't much.'

'Look,' he said, taking her arm with sudden decision, 'I'm seeing you home. Come on.'

For a second it all teetered on the edge of another unhappy parting, and the knowledge that it did lent the moment a fearful tension in his heart. But after a brief hesitation she turned as he directed and they started across the tennis courts to the upper road.

'We'll have to sneak by the Talbotts',' she said with a sudden shaky amusement, 'or there'll be more comments.'

'Let's run,' he suggested, and they did for a little way until they were past the Talbotts' and several other still-lighted cabins, and she stumbled suddenly and they had to halt.

'In the movies,' he said with an unevenness promoted equally by nerves and lack of breath, 'this sort of sprint ends with the hero and heroine wind-blown but happy, laughing hysterically and falling into each other's arms. Laugh hysterically and fall into my arms, please.'

But this, of course, was the wrong thing to say, for she drew away immediately.

'I think you'd better go back now. I've got my own flashlight and I've been walking this road for thirty-one years. I won't get lost. I know my way home.'

'To an empty cabin,' he said bleakly. 'And I to an empty cabin.'

'But I to my own empty cabin,' she said, not unkindly, 'where I belong. I'm sorry you don't belong, but really – I don't know what I could do that would—'

'You can let me stay,' he said angrily. 'Is that so very difficult to understand?'

'No, I can't!' she said unhappily. 'No. I can't.'

'Yes,' he said savagely. 'You can. I shall see you to your cabin, and then you can. Come along!'

But he knew even as he took her arm and they started again up the dark road through the dark trees to her cabin, that it was probably not to be. The onrushing unity of emotion such moments require, while present in them both, was not present in sufficient degree in her. The knowledge, of course, made desire even stronger in his heart. At her door they stopped and he snapped off the flashlight while Smudge crashed against the screen and barked excitedly inside.

'Now,' she said. 'Good night. Please, good night.'

'You're afraid of this God damned camp. That's what the real trouble is.'

'Please.'

'Please, yourself,' he said harshly.

'Why do you keep after me?' she exclaimed bitterly. 'What am I to you?'

'Why don't we find out?'

'You're turning me into something I'm not at all. You're making me up. I'm just odd old Elizavetta Berrenger with Mr Smudge' – she began to cry – 'Mr Smudge the First—'

'Please, please,' he said, coming closer, but with a sudden movement she stepped inside and closed and locked the screen-door after.

'Don't you want to?' he asked in an agonized whisper.

'Good night,' she cried. 'Oh, good night!'

'O.K.,' he said dully after a moment. 'I'm going.'

'Will you still be here when I come up next week?' she called as he turned away. He gave a harsh, unhappy laugh.

'Does it matter?'

'It does to me.'

'You aren't talking sense.'

'I hope you will.'

'I'm captive,' he said bitterly. 'I'll be here.'

'I hope so,' she called as he turned quickly and went down the path, but he did not answer; nor, this time, did he leap or whistle. She saw his flashlight glimmering through the trees for a minute or two and then it was gone. A little wind talked in the trees, the river rushed along noisily under the deck, the stars blazed fantastically overhead. She gave a sudden sob she could not have explained exactly and stooped in tears to pat her bouncing dog.

For a long time after he walked back down the empty road, past the now-deserted Meadows, past the still-raucous Magruders' and the still-busy Buxtons', he stood on the porch of the MacAleer cabin staring up at the glittering universe. How narrow yet how enormous the gap between happiness and unhappiness, desire and fulfilment: how small and awkward the chances that govern the human heart! If it could only have happened as simply and naturally as he had thought he wanted it to, how wonderful it could have been. If, if, if. The wind sighed in the pines, in the distance the river, always present, always there, raced along with its muted roar. The dark mountains pressed hard against the blazing sky. The sky pressed back, afire with its million stars.

Surely there must be one for him up there, he thought with a weary wryness; *surely*, there must be.

And so there was.

Even as he looked, it fell to its death behind the mountains.

TWO

It is not surprising, perhaps, that his dominant emotion in the first lazily drifting days of the ensuing week should be one of self-contempt. To such graceless and grotesque extremes, he told himself bitterly, is one reduced by the ridiculous imperatives of need. How laughable the whole episode, really, from the first glimpse of Elizavetta at the gate, to his abrupt emotional commitment, to his begging like a schoolboy on the doorstep While The Virtuous Maiden Said Nay! How laughable desire, and how desperate and inescapable when time and circumstance collaborate to give it an importance it would not deserve in other, more temperate moments. Look at it reasonably, he urged himself with a sardonic harshness, knowing reason had nothing to do with it. Be reasonable, and say it isn't so.

But it was so, for all of that; and as he began to sink deeper into the casual Nirvana of Greenmont, rising later and later on each succeeding morning, playing a little golf and tennis in a world of women whose men were mostly down in the Valley making a living until the next week-end, dining out on a friendly catch-as-catch-can basis at various cabins, he was forced to recognize it for what it might portend. Desire compounded by denial established its own insistent rules. It was of course made further difficult by the atmosphere of highly knowledgeable intimacy in which he must, if he could, find a solution.

He was quite sure Eliza had seen no one prior to returning to the Valley Monday morning, and he made it a point to notice that no letters came in from her to anyone at the community mail-box at the Meadows. None the less, with an apparently unanimous instinct, in one of those mysterious mass extra-sensory perceptions that seemed to be so characteristic of Greenmont's approach to things, he found himself surrounded almost immediately by the general assumption that some sort of crisis had occurred on Sunday night.

This ranged from Gray's, 'Did you and Elizavetta have another fight?' to Louise's, 'I hope it wasn't too bad, sweetie,' to Einar's cautiously philosophical, 'Well, sometimes it takes

131

longer than it does other times.'

He supposed this must have been because he looked worried, though he tried to be, and hoped he was, sufficiently bland and non-committal as he shrugged off Gray with a surprised, 'Now what makes you think that?' told Louise lightly, 'It was absolutely *fierce*,' and scoffed at Einar, 'Beach god, if you knew all you think you know about every conceivable subject under the sun, including me, you'd be quite a boy.'

This wholly convinced Gray, partially diverted Louise and fooled Einar not at all. That bronzed young hulk, staying in camp on vacation from his job as a lawyer in San Rafael, rolled over lazily at poolside and opened one sceptical eye.

'Come on, now, buddy, who are you kidding? If I know Eliza, you got the indignant virgin treatment.'

'Well,' the major said tartly, 'you don't know Eliza.'

'There was something, then,' Einar said with relish. The major sat up abruptly and flung out his arm in an impatient gesture that embraced the world of chattering women and shouting children all about.

'Look,' he demanded sharply. 'Try to stand by me, will you? You're practically the only other male in this woman-ridden place this week. Don't give me a hard time, too.'

Einar grinned and held out a lean and muscular hand.

'When you put it like that, how can I resist?'

And he gave the major a quick and apparently genuine handshake, and dropped the subject. This gave the major the flattering and encouraging hope, which he could not quite trust, that he might just possibly have enlisted Einar for the duration.

Haila Buxton, of course, was another matter as he realized on Wednesday when she and Viola Townsend came and sat beside him on the bench where he was idly chatting with Louise after a fey twosome around the golf-course.

'I *do* wonder,' Haila confided with a gentle, purse-lipped worry, 'if anything is wrong with Eliza. She usually writes me a note on Tuesday, just to let me know how things are going in Big Smith. But nothing came in this morning.'

'I thought you were going down tomorrow,' Louise said. 'Maybe that's why she didn't write. I'm thinking of going with you, as a matter of fact. I want to check the house for Jerry and pick up a few little things in town.'

Haila nodded.

'Jim has some people coming in at the ranch on business and I've got to be there to give him advice.' She gave a comfortable little laugh within the sisterhood. 'Men are so helpless.'

'They can be made so,' Louise agreed blandly. 'What time are you going?'

'Eight. Why don't you come by for coffee about 7.30 and we'll leave right after?'

'I'll be there,' Louise said. She sighted carefully down her golf-club at her left foot and inquired in a casually thoughtful way, 'What do you think *is* the matter with Eliza?'

'I don't know,' Haila said, her eyes resting on the major's. 'I ... really ... don't ... know.'

'Well, don't look at me,' he said with a grin that was genuinely amused by her portentous aspect. 'I really don't know, either.'

'Now, Bill,' she said. 'I think you're keeping secrets.'

'He wouldn't tell *us*,' Viola Townsend said, looking so comically indignant about it that he laughed aloud.

'Mrs Townsend,' he said, 'you know I'd tell you everything. Everything.'

'Hmph. Anyway, we'll have lunch with Eliza tomorrow and find out.'

'Well, goody for you,' he said, though he felt a sudden dismayed concern for what they might do to upset things that already rested on so delicate a foundation. Louise laughed.

'Don't worry, Bill. I'll keep an eye on these girls. I won't let them ruin it.'

'I don't doubt your intention,' he said with an expression he made suitably whimsical, 'but I'm not so sure of your ability.'

'These two? We've been fighting for years, haven't we, Haila? You'll see. I'll make them behave.'

'You're always so droll, Louise,' Haila told her. '*So droll*. If you're worried about it, Bill, why don't you write Elizavetta a note? We'll take it down to her.'

He hesitated, long enough for Louise to give a hoot.

'Doesn't trust us, Haila,' she said cheerfully. 'That's obvious.'

'Why should he?' Haila said with a hearty chuckle. 'We're all such despicable cads, capable of reading people's mail and everything.'

'No, it isn't that,' he said slowly. 'Frankly, I just don't know quite what to say. Let me think about it.'

'Very well,' Haila said. 'Special delivery leaves at 8 a.m.'

'I'll drop over if I decide to.'

'Don't wait, though, Haila,' Louise suggested.

The major smiled.

'That's right. I regard it all as distinctly chancy.'

'I must say I don't see why,' Viola Townsend objected. 'We'd be perfectly glad to do anything we could to help.'

'I know that,' he agreed, without irony. 'But it's still chancy.'

And chancy it remained, as the day wore on, for though he contemplated several times how to begin such a letter, nothing seemed very satisfactory or even adequate.

To ask forgiveness would be to concede a crime he didn't really believe he had committed, when all was said and done. And to explain the ultimate origins of his emotion and the awkwardly abortive conclusion towards which it had pushed him on Sunday night would be to get into an area he did not want to re-enter, for Eliza or anyone else.

At first it did not seem necessary that he re-enter it. But later in the afternoon, at the hour when the sunlight was beginning to withdraw from the forests and on the mountain across the way the deer were beginning to graze, there came to him the realization that he was afraid to re-enter it.

This was not a noble conclusion to reach, and he did not think very much of himself for it, but he was forced to admit it was the fact. To go back down that dark passageway was not a journey he wished to undertake, at least in a letter to someone else: it promised to lacerate him too much. And how would you state it, anyway? There was this guy, see – and this gal, see – and they got married and didn't live happily ever after – though the guy hoped they might – but the gal knew they wouldn't – and there you are, and that's how it was. See?

That wasn't the ticket, he thought with a sudden wry little smile as he sat in the Grove watching the lovely purple light of California evening fall across the jagged peaks while the air sharpened and the earth turned faster towards night. No, that wasn't quite the ticket. It had been both that simple – and not that simple. And no hesitant, awkward, embarrassed letter to anyone was going to portray it as it was or make understandable the exact combination of regret, humiliation, anguish, sorrow and pride that had brought his emotions to so chaotic a pitch.

He could not remember the exact moment at which they had formally met, though he could remember without any difficulty at all the fact that there had been an instantaneous interest about it for them both. He had been stationed in Alabama, outside Montgomery. There had been a dance arranged by the towns-people. He and his friends from the base had gone. Some time during the evening he had seen her, tall and dark – as a matter of fact, rather like Elizavetta without the make-up, now that he thought about it – mingling in and out of his glances around the room, seeming to come by some inadvertence of drift or direction ever closer to him. He could not recall now when this casual encircling had ended, or which of them had spoken first, or even the first dance they had danced together, though she often told him with a chiding petulance that she could. It didn't matter, because by the time the evening ended they knew they would see one another again, and soon. And so they had, and within two weeks it was decided they would marry. Within two months they had.

He took her home to Turlock to show his family, and everyone was suitably pleased and impressed.

'You you-all types go over big in my home town,' he told her. She smiled with her quick slanting look and told him that he had obviously gone over rather well in her home town too. Everything seemed right and fine and hunky-dory and the guy settled down with the gal and proceeded to live happily ever after.

Except that somehow it didn't work out that way. For a time, of course, it did. But the time did not last as long, it seemed to him, as it should have. Expressions of love that were perfectly genuine for him and apparently wildly ecstatic for her were succeeded before long by a certain subtle inattention on her part.

'I don't really think your heart's in it,' he had told her on a night scarcely three months after their wedding. It had sounded more bitter than he intended and an ugly argument had flared at once, ending in a desperate coupling that left them physically and mentally bruised.

'I don't want to get into anything like that again,' he told her evenly next morning just before he left the house, and a strange expression (of what? amusement? He could not exactly define it) came into her eyes.

'Whatever you say,' she replied calmly. 'I wouldn't want you to get yourself really involved in anything.'

'That isn't fair,' he said with a sudden blinding anger. 'You're my wife, of course I want to be involved with you.'

'Really? Well, have a good day at the office.'

And the door, for the first, but not the last, time, had closed with a sardonic thunk! in his startled and upset face.

There followed a period of deepening tension during which he tried various alternatives without much success. Elaborate ignorings were succeeded by passionate reunions, only to be succeeded again by elaborate ignorings.

'Is it because I'm so much older?' he asked once, more conscious than he felt he should be of the ten-year gap in their ages but trying in bewilderment to centre upon some reason for their growing hostilities.

'Oh, no,' she replied lightly, again with an infuriating amusement. 'I like older men.'

'If I ever catch you—' he had flared at once. But she only smiled with something close to contempt.

'Don't worry. I'm the best little girl you ever saw . . . Daddy.'

As far as the world knew, they could not have been happier. In all the facile, quick-springing friendships of the service they played their part with an outward ease that brought envying compliments from many of their friends.

'You two love-birds certainly have it made,' Buck MacAleer remarked admiringly not long after the four of them first met at Luke Field near Phoenix. Neither Buck nor Mary had understood their burst of laughter, linking them for a moment in quite genuine harmony. Fortunately it had been taken to mean agreement, and the MacAleers' admiration had continued unabated all during the months before he and Buck were sent to Korea. Indeed, there was no reason he could ever determine why they should not have it made. All he knew, with a steadily deepening misery, was that for some reason that always seemed to escape him, they didn't.

Looking back upon the early weeks of their marriage, he wondered sometimes if he had placed too much reliance upon an aspect of kindliness, of sympathy and warmth and gentleness, that could have been more surface than substance. Yet he could not bring himself completely to believe it, even in his most bitter moments. Surely one who seemed at first so outgoing, so considerate of his welfare, so understanding and, apparently, so deeply in love, could not have been pretending. Why should she have pretended? It was true that she came of a modest family, that her parents were dead, that she was a stenographer trapped in a small town who obviously wanted to get out; but all these circumstances were so trite and so obvious if used as an explanation of her willingness to marry him that he rejected them out of hand. She was a beautiful girl – again he was struck by the resemblance to Elizavetta, or at least to Elizavetta as she might conceivably be if she put her mind to it – and with many friends younger than he. He could only conclude, when he came to the end of his incessant arguments with himself, that she had genuinely preferred him above all others. Either that, or there was some reason too deep for him to fathom. There was, it seemed to him, no way to come to grips with the situation on any rational basis. She never denied herself to him, there was no obvious inclination to use sex as a weapon. She just wasn't there, in the ways that really mattered.

Certainly there had never been any doubt about his own feelings. Having been footloose until forty, he succumbed completely when the day finally came, giving himself to her with a commitment that to him, at least, seemed final. She 'wouldn't want him to get himself really involved in anything', would she? How extraordinarly and viciously unfair! He was sure no one had ever been more irrevocably involved with anyone.

'What am I supposed to do?' he finally demanded in complete exasperation, adding in bitter mockery an obscene suggestion.

'Now, *that*,' she said, 'wouldn't look very dignified, would it? But,' she added thoughtfully after a moment, 'why don't you try it?'

So, because nothing else seemed to work, he had, and for a time they had entered upon a period of frantic animalism that had exhausted them both and settled nothing. It seemed to him in retrospect that for a couple of months they had never gotten out of bed, although somehow life had managed to go on and

137

he had received high commendation for his work as the edges of the Korean whirlpool reached out and began to claim him. For all their hectic partnership, however, he had come no closer to her heart, nor she to his. The only thing it accomplished, it seemed to him, was to give her more fuel for her amusement and so, in some inexcusable and infuriating way, more dominance over him.

Towards the end he began to have the terrifying thought that perhaps she was one of those beings who indulge in love for the purposes of humiliation. If that were true, he told himself, he indeed was lost.

None the less the dark strivings went on for a while longer, lent an extra edge by his own desperation, as though in the secret places of the human body could be found the secret places of the human heart. It was only when he got his orders for Korea that it ended, and then without conclusion.

'What have we proved?' he asked. She shrugged.

'Good health. We couldn't have stood it without it.'

And even so, for a few brief moments, their parting had been tender and filled with some of the mutual generosity that had seemed to surround their early days.

'Take good care of yourself,' he said with a show of lightness. 'You belong to me.'

'Do I?' She smiled. 'I've never known.'

'It will be better when I get back,' he said earnestly. 'I promise.'

Much to his surprise her eyes had filled with tears.

'So do I,' she said, clinging to him desperately with a sudden fierce grip. 'Oh, so do I.'

But that, of course, was make-believe. He could see now that it must have been, for the letters grew shorter and less regular, and presently, though he continued to write faithfully twice a week, they were coming only once a month, scraps that told nothing and conveyed nothing across the endless ocean and the barren, starving land. Twice he flew home on leave for brief, uncomfortable periods in San Francisco, where she had taken a tiny apartment on Russian Hill. It did no good; the baffling listlessness had returned to their relationship.

He returned to Korea to write yet more anxious, more desperate letters as his marriage slipped away. For some perverse reason lying deep in human nature it seemed the more worth keeping the more he understood its emptiness. Although he would not admit it to himself, his pride became involved: it became a matter of preserving self-respect that he should re-establish what clearly was moving beyond re-establishment. A note of pleading for which he despised himself entered his letters. It failed to arouse even the mockery of previous times, and he presently realized that he had sunk so far that he would have been happy to have even that. It did not come.

The war staggered to its empty close, he came home to San Francisco to find the apartment occupied by someone else. His wife had gone to Los Angeles.

'You might have told me,' he said when he found her there.

'I didn't know it mattered,' she said indifferently. 'It doesn't to me.'

'It does to me!' he said with a bitter protest, though he knew the time for protest was almost past.

Her expression did not change.

'I'm afraid that's your problem.'

So it apparently was. So it apparently always had been, though to this day he did not know why. But faced at last with the implacable certainty that it would never change, he had done finally what he probably should have done long ago, had pain and pride only permitted it: he had finally let go. Or so, at least, he had told himself, though he knew then, as he knew now, that he never really could. To really let go, you had to be the one to do it; and he had not been. He had not let go: he had been let go of. And thus, apparently with no deliberate intent to do so – which made it hurt the more – she bound him to her still.

Sometimes in the whirling days and nights of anguish that followed their divorce he had thought bitterly that if only she had given him the satisfaction of a rival, it might make sense. But she said, and his hasty investigations seemed to prove it, that there was no rival.

Thus it had been the most crushing of rejections, a personal judgment rendered upon him as a person, not because someone else had taken dominion of a heart he was unable to hold, but simply because he was unable to hold it, on any terms. He was convicted of a failure he could not admit himself responsible

139

for, confronted by a faceless nothing whose existence he must deny or go mad. His joking reference to Elizavetta about the Weendigo, that fearsome unseen legendary Thing that roams the woods of the distant North, had not been so fanciful, after all. It roamed his heart, leaving mockery and desolation behind, and no amount of agonized, self-justifying recapitulations of the past could remove the spoor of its bitter passage.

And yet, he told himself dully on many occasions, his was a decent being and his were good intentions. He wanted only good things for those with whom he came in contact; he wanted only to be friends with them and to be of service to his country. He was not selfish, he was not harsh in his dealings with others. He had a heart, if truth be known, quite full of kindness and love. Contrary to all he had supposed as he reached maturity, this apparently was not enough to secure these benisons in return. 'You want to be kind on your own terms!' she had flared out at him once. The charge, as unjust and hurtful as her complaint about his lack of involvement, had wounded him fearfully. Could that be he, who meant so well? Surely it was only the distortions of her own twisted glass that disclosed his lineaments in so harsh and dreadful a light!

Yet, disturbingly now, there returned the memory of other voices at other times. In the service his record was excellent, his bravery in Korea soon became a legend along a tiny sector of the bitter frontier where the tides of conflict robbed of purpose and victory robbed of meaning ebbed and flowed in the world's unending sickness. Yet in that place, too, there had been the curious misinterpretation, not so deliberately personal or hurtful, but still arising to dismay him.

'You're the perfect soldier,' one of his friends had told him with an odd mixture of awe and puzzlement. 'You don't care about *anything*.'

He had dismissed the comment with a laugh and a mocking, 'Sure, sure, buster that's why I'm doing all this dirty work, because I don't care about my country, or liberty, or anything.'

It was only later in the privacy of his hut that the remark came back with a painful insistence, coupled with other remarks less innocent of intention.

'I wouldn't want you to get yourself really involved in anything ... You want to be kind on your own terms ... You don't care about *anything*.'

How could others so completely misunderstand a human heart? His mind could not conceive it then, nor could it now as the afternoon hastened still faster to its ending, the little cool evening wind began to rise, the Meadows began to empty of all but the most persistent lingerers.

This was not the Bill Steele he knew, this cold, selfish, self-contained, unemotional, uncaring individual that others seemed to see – that some others seemed to see. Certainly his family had never seemed to see it, though he did remember, now that he was forced by Greenmont and its quickly manufactured romance to face himself candidly, some intimations along the way that some of his contemporaries in high school and college might have considered him a little distant, a little apart, some-one who seemed to them to have a curious and unsettling in-difference at the heart of him that made others a trifle wary, a shade uneasy.

'But I just want to be loved,' he protested to his unhappy mind, and recognized at once with a wry justice the banal stupidity of the complaint.

Who doesn't? his mind responded sardonically.

But to the ultimate question of why some succeed and some do not, it furnished, despite his further musings, no clue.

Maybe then, he decided finally as the Meadows emptied still further, leaving only himself on a bench in the Grove and Louise and Einar playing a last game of tennis on the darkling court, maybe the thing for him to do was *be* involved, if that was what everybody demanded of him. Maybe he *should* be committed, not in the intense and suffering way he was accus-tomed to inside, but in a more public way much beyond the restraints imposed by a characteristic hesitation and delicacy. Maybe he *should* be kind, not on his terms – if that comment, despite its bitter exaggeration, had some truth in it – but on someone else's. Maybe he should dramatize things and make a big show of his feelings to the world, or at least to someone in it. Maybe, having allowed Greenmont to push him so far so fast in the direction of Elizavetta, he should abandon even the last restraints of caution which he knew were still controlling his heart despite its apparent willingness to accept the situation, and plunge forward without thought of self-protection or the necessary provisions for possible retreat.

Maybe that was how he could find the bauble everyone sought and none save the luckiest kept for long.

But when the game ended on the lower court and Louise came over for a final moment as Einar gave an exuberant shout and sprinted off towards home and supper, he still could not quite bring himself to do it.

'Got that letter written yet?' she asked, contorting her way into Jerry's lumber-jacket against the now insistent edge in the twilight air.

He smiled with a hesitation she did not miss and gave a quizzical shrug.

'Nope . . . Just tell her I said hello.'

She looked surprised.

'Just hello? Seems a little bare.'

'Less bare than nothing.'

She smiled.

'I can't argue with that.'

Yet when he came to the MacAleer cabin to find it brilliantly lit and Gray in the kitchen struggling valiantly to open a can of beans with an antiquated opener, the first thing he said was:

'What time do you expect to come home tonight, old buddy? Or are you planning to stay in?'

'I'm going up to play with Tommy Rupert. Can you get this old can opened so we can have supper?'

'I'll try,' he said, shucking off his sweater and rolling up his sleeves. 'Why don't you set the table and let me worry about the food?'

'It's my cabin,' Gray said, a trifle stiffly. 'I've got to take care of things.'

'True enough,' he agreed cheerfully. 'I can help, though, can't I?'

'O.K. I'll be getting in about ten, I guess. Are you going out?'

'Not tonight,' he said, opening the beans and dumping them in a pot on one of the front burners. 'I'm going to stay home and think.'

'About Eliza?'

'Maybe. Is that all right?'

'I think you should,' the boy said seriously. 'Maybe you can get it straightened out O.K., if you do that.'

'Oh?' he said, fixing lettuce and slicing tomatoes while Gray leaned against the counter at his elbow. 'Are things as bad as that?'

The boy frowned.

'That's what everybody says at the Meadows.'

He stopped slicing for a moment and stood arms akimbo to stare at his earnest ward.

'Oh they do, do they? What do you say?'

Gray looked suddenly shy.

'I think you should make up with her. I think she's nice. I like you, too,' he added firmly. 'I want things to be all right for you.'

'Well, thank you, buddy,' he said, genuinely touched. 'It's mutual. I must say I don't quite know how to go about it, though.'

The boy looked surprised.

'Just tell her.'

'Mmmhmm. Some day you'll realize it isn't that simple.'

'I don't know why not!'

'Well. You will.'

'Well, you have to do *something*,' Gray said in some exasperation. 'You can't just *sit* there.'

'I'm not sitting,' he said mildly. 'I'm standing up and getting your supper. How's that table setting coming along?'

'I'll *do* it,' the boy said. 'Don't worry about that ... Anyway, I still think—'

'Better hurry,' the major said firmly. 'We're almost ready.'

'Oh, all *right*,' Gray said. 'I don't see why, though,' he added as he got a couple of plates and some silverware and put them on the polished slab of redwood that served for a table, 'why you can't just tell her.'

The major gave him a long look, so blank for a moment that it almost frightened the boy.

'Maybe I will,' he said slowly. 'Maybe I just will. I may want you to take a letter over to Mrs Buxton for me later, so check in when you get back, O.K.?'

143

'O.K.,' Gray said, looking pleased. He paused at the door.

'I'm glad,' he said. The major, staring thoughtfully at the sink, did not respond. The boy added hesitantly, 'Aren't you?'

The major rubbed a hand that trembled a little across his eyes.

'I don't know, buddy. I just don't know.'

Nor did he three hours later, after he had written his letter, after Gray had returned from the Meadows and been sent off with it to Haila, after the boy had come back again and gone to bed and the major was left alone in a deck-chair beneath the violent stars. None fell for him tonight. Too large to be real, too bright to be believed, they shone down upon him impassive and impersonal, bound on some secret business of their own along the endless highways of the universe. His mind did not know serenity, his heart did not know peace. What had he done, under the pressures of the emotional moment and his own unhappy seeking? What consequences would come of it, bearing what burden for the coming days? And what, above all, could he possibly hope for from the awkward, uncomfortable heart of this awkward, uncomfortable girl – a heart as lonely and unhappy and inadequate, possibly, as his own, its importance to him pushed out of all proportion by his own turmoil and the carefree callous encouragements of the in-grown, all-involving camp?

He remained on the deck under the stars until it grew too cold to stay. Before he went in to bed he stood for a moment at the railing listening to the river, much louder now in the night's feral stillness, his eyes, haunted and unhappy, searching among the enormous pines as they marched the ridges that mounted towards the peaks above him, self-contained and unapproachable against the improbable sky.

What did it all add up to, the desperate striving of the heart? And whoever understood, or knew, for sure?

He sighed and went in. It was very late. No human sound anywhere came from the sleeping camp.

TWO

'It isn't,' Einar observed as he flopped down alongside with a grunt at the pool next morning, 'that I mind your keeping secrets from me. Everybody has to have secrets. It's just that I thought we were becoming real buddies – real *friends*—'

'What in the hell,' the major demanded with a fair show of unconcern, though his heart suddenly began to pump furiously, 'are you talking about? Do you know?'

'I don't know, exactly,' Einar said, rolling on to his back and stretching out full length to luxuriate in the high noon sun as it burned down upon them from an absolutely cloudless sky. 'Something was going around among the kids this morning that sounded intriguing, though. Mighty intriguing, I must say. Ah, well,' he added drowsily, muffling a yawn and pretending not to notice the major's instinctive, almost flinching, movement. 'Ah, well. Life's little mysteries.'

'*God d*—' the major said, starting in a loud tone but abruptly dropping his voice to a violent whisper as two of his companion's many siblings became suddenly attentive nearby, '—amn it, what in the hell are you talking about?'

'Mysterious communications,' Einar said comfortably. 'The Message to Garcia. The Purloined Letter.'

'Who purloined it?' the major demanded in the same sharp undertone. 'Do you mean to tell me that little bastard Gray—' and quite comically his tone changed from one of anger to one of sudden, almost childish, hurt. 'I thought I could trust *him*.'

'You can trust several people,' his companion said, equally low and, abruptly, equally serious, 'if you just will. Gray didn't do anything. Tommy Rupert got it out of him quite by accident when they were playing last night. Sally-Jane just happened to send me up to borrow some coffee from Janie Rupert this morning and she told me all about it. Anyway, nobody *read* it. We just know you wrote it, that's all.'

'That's all,' the major said bitterly, staring off at the distant peaks, now bright and shining, clear and distinct against the bottomless blue. 'My God, that's all.'

'Look,' Einar said reasonably. 'Don't take life so hard, Bill. We all want this to work out for you, you know. And as for Eliza, bless her heart and all its earnest worries, we're all for her, too. So take it easy. I dare say your prestige will go up enormously when it gets around that you're seriously after the girl.'

'It better not get around,' the major said in an ominous tone. Einar gave a whoop, terminated abruptly as he glanced at the major's expression.

'I'm sorry,' he said, more soberly, 'but you know Greenmont. By now, you surely know Greenmont. How can you stop it? I'm sure even old Mr Stafford knows. At least he looked awfully perky about something when I passed him on the road going up to Janie's.'

'Oh, Lord,' the major said with a sigh, and when he spoke again it was in a lowered voice as though only to himself: 'How can I ever work my way out of this?'

'We'll help you,' Einar said. 'Take a swim. Play some golf. S.-J. will be down in a minute and we'll take you on at canasta. Relax!'

'Relax!' the major echoed bitterly. 'Everybody is always telling me to relax and then doing their best to make it impossible.'

'Don't fuss. Don't *fuss*. That's the main thing. Don't mention it to Gray, he didn't let it slip out – if I know Tommy he probably twisted his arm to get it, literally. And don't mention it to anybody else. Just grin and shrug it off. That's the way to handle Greenmont. The only time this place can get you is when you let it. Kid 'em along and tell 'em to go to hell. It's the only way to survive up here.' He gave a sudden cheerful grin. 'I know.'

Which, the major thought as Sally-Jane appeared prettily decked out and her husband uncoiled his steel-muscled length to seize her suddenly from behind and toss her screaming into the icy water, was probably very sound advice. There was no real conspiracy in this pleasant place, he was letting his imagination become morbid if he thought so. Just a string of interferences, the majority inadvertent, only a few deliberate, and most of them, he was willing to concede as he thought about it further while the Meadows filled with roistering children and their busily chattering mothers, done with the best of good will towards both Eliza and himself. There was nothing organized about it, he was letting himself edge towards a dangerous area of fantasy if he permitted himself to think so. How oddly the mind could work things around if you once let it begin to run away with you!

The best thing to do, just as Einar suggested, would be to grin and shrug it off. This would not be easy, for the knowledge that his sending of the letter – and possibly, for he did not entirely trust Einar, its contents as well – was now the common property of Greenmont, made him feel terribly self-conscious as he glanced carefully, through half-shut, hooded eyes, at the busy benches of the Grove and the bright little enclaves of gossip along the concrete apron of the pool. But in a moment he was able to rise naturally enough and stand poised for a dive at the deep end.

'Who wants to play tag?' he shouted, and from all corners of the pool came screams of excited agreement from a dozen kids, all of whom started converging on him at once. 'That's the spirit!' Einar shouted and started to surge towards him with a powerful crawl stroke. He flung himself over the heads of the nearest children and sprinted towards the far corner as Sally-Jane gave a squeal and joined in the rush to capture him. The next fifteen minutes were very busy as he tried to elude his pursuers, failed, was tagged, tagged Einar in turn, joined in pursuit of Sally-Jane when Einar tagged her, and then himself became the quarry again when she caught him near the diving-board. The game roared from one end of the pool to the other and ended in a froth of screams and splashes. Exhausted, he drew himself up out of the water and collapsed beside the two of them on the beach towels Sally-Jane had brought along from the Magruder cabin.

'You look as though you feel better about the whole thing,' Einar told him approvingly. He managed to muster a winded grin.

'It'll last until Haila comes back from the Valley,' he said with an attempt at jocularity that struck him as rather brave, considering the uneasy sense of anticipation that kept tightening his stomach every time he thought about it. Sally-Jane gave him a sober look.

'Major, honey,' she said with a firm little line in the corner of her mouth, 'if Haila says one word, you call on us. There's nothing I'd love better than a good excuse to tangle with Haila.'

'Don't try it,' her husband advised, turning his back to the sun. 'You'd be outweighed and outclassed.'

'Out*classed*?' she demanded, hitting him a swat across the shoulders with her bathing-cap. 'What do you mean, outclassed?'

'Strictly in bitchery,' he explained gallantly as she hit him again, his voice muffled by the beach towel he had clutched protectively around his head. 'I didn't mean in pleasanter graces.'

'I should hope not,' she said with a chuckle, snuggling against him like a fluffy little cat. 'Bill and I are a match for Haila any day, aren't we, Bill?'

'I hope so,' he said, though abruptly the relaxed mood brought on by violent exertion seemed to be going and he felt himself sliding once again towards a morass of uneasiness as he began to feel for the first time the full enormity of his letter and what might spring from it. 'I intend to do my best.'

'No man can do more,' Einar murmured, half asleep. 'Wake me when she comes and we'll have at it, smiting her hip and thigh.'

'And a lovelier hip and thigh,' Sally-Jane observed with an irrepressible gurgle, 'the realm of man doth not disclose.'

The full enormity of his letter ... That, he had not really begun to appreciate until just this moment. It hit him full force in the midst of the serene and lovely day. The enormity of his letter: perhaps that was more to be feared than anything anyone might wilfully or accidentally make of it.

His mind tipped abruptly towards despair as he remembered its harsh, demanding phrases, its intensely personal tone, its assumption that she too must be moved by the same hunger of need and the same desperate search for understanding, its battering insistence that she respond in kind with all thoughts revealed, all secrets told, all defences abandoned.

However could he have done such a thing? He must have been mad to bare his feelings so, to crash so insistently into the heart and mind of another with his own blindly selfish imperatives. How could he, *how could he*?

The full enormity of his letter ... With a shattering clarity he realized it now, a crime against a fellow being almost too

148

monstrous to contemplate, acknowledged too late . . . too late.

For several minutes he lay face down in the sun, his head sheltered protectively by his arms, his mind oblivious to the vigorous swirl of life along the pool. This was what he had reduced himself to, then, this wandering heart wailing for surcease to another heart that was, in all probability too shallow to grant it . . . And yet, was not this assumption, also, too much of a piece with the others that had prompted him, finally, to write? Was he not again discounting Eliza? And had it not, in fact, been a basic discounting of her, a basic disrespect, which had prompted him to write in such language at all?

'How inevitable it all is,' a friend of his in Korea had remarked one time. 'The words you know you shouldn't say, the things you know you shouldn't do, the letter you know you shouldn't write . . .'

Yet that had been at the ending of a love affair, and his own indiscretion had come at its beginning. Or was it a beginning? Was it anything at all but his own exaggerated imagination, inflamed by the exaggerated half-kindly, half-scoffing interferences of this tight little dream-world behind the mountains where he found himself a temporary sojourner?

Well . . . suppose it was? His mind made one of those sudden relieving transitions that sometimes compensate the thoughtful for thinking too much, an abrupt reversal, an assertion of independence and justification as unexpected as his previous descent into sadness.

What if it was all imagination, was he supposed to apologize for it? Was he supposed to humble himself because he had honestly expressed the honest sentiments of an honest heart?

What was so wrong with what he had written, anyway? Whatever others might think of it – and he was already bracing himself for that – it was a genuine statement of a genuine emotion, an act of affirmation in a world that did not permit too many. Affirmation was what everyone seemed to want of him: very well, he had obliged! Suppose it had been too violent in some places, too insistently demanding in others, too self-revealing and self-castigating in still others? What of it? He had trusted another: that was his crime, if any. And what had made him conclude, so quickly and with such a foolish lack of faith, that she was unworthy of his trust?

Eliza, after all, was the one he had written to, not Haila, nor Viola, nor Einar, nor Sally-Jane, nor Louise, nor Gray, nor – nor Greenmont. What if they did all come to know that he had written it, or even, at worst, come to know its contents? The decision ultimately would be rendered by just one heart, the heart he had held before him in imagination while he wrote. His fate – if anything so tenuous and summer-fragile could be given so pompous a designation – would be decided by Eliza, not by Greenmont.

For no reason he could have explained he suddenly felt a great faith in her ability to understand. Elizavetta must be what he thought she was, for it was necessary to him that she be.

Buoyed by this new-found certainty, created of nothing more stable than his need for it, he sat up, prodded Sally-Jane and Einar awake and challenged them to a game of canasta which went on until they finally stopped for lunch around 2 p.m. He strolled back down to the cabin in a strangely light-hearted mood, ate an apple and a sandwich and then dropped into a sleep whose profundity was more measure of the state of his being than he knew.

His mood held when he awoke, held when he reached the Meadows again at four, broke when he saw Louise walking towards him across the golf-course. Her expression indicated trouble and he knew, at once, that of course he had been expecting it all along.

'Sweetie,' she said, placing a hand firmly on his arm and propelling him to one of the more secluded benches in the Grove, 'I've got to talk to you. Seriously. Before you mess things up irrevocably for yourself and a really very nice girl. It's quite important.'

'I'm not going to run away,' he said, though he wanted to. 'And anyway, I've already messed them up, haven't I?'

'Well, I don't know,' she said, staring at him thoughtfully as though seeing him for the first time. 'You've certainly upset her, there's no doubt of that. She cried most of the way through lunch, though she wasn't very explicit, at least to Viola and me. Haila took her aside before we left and they had a little talk—'

'They would,' he said bitterly.

'They would. And that's why you weren't exactly wise, possibly, to write whatever it was you did, because I know Haila has it all now. I've never seen that tight-lipped routine of hers put on with quite such a flair as she gave it on the drive back up here. You would have thought matters of gravest import and solemn fate were involved. Not that they aren't,' she said hastily, giving his arm a squeeze, 'but you know Haila. She does overdo it sometimes.'

'So now I suppose the next step is for her to convoke the membership and tell them all about it,' he said with a tired mockery. 'That would be about her speed, wouldn't it?'

She smiled.

'Haila isn't quite that bad. She has her faults, but she's a little deeper than she seems on the surface.'

He smiled in wry agreement.

'Oh, she's deep, all right. I've never doubted that from the minute I met her. Deep and clever and shrewd and determined – especially about other peoples' lives. I suppose that's because she's made such a mess of her own.'

'She isn't that simple, either: it isn't so bad, from where she sits. Haila can be a good friend, you know, as well as a powerful enemy. I'm sure she considers herself the kindly older counsellor leading you both towards paths of happiness and light. Of course you may have run off the road a bit at the moment, in her mind, but if I know Haila she'll soon be putting you back on it again and getting everything fixed up.' She chuckled. 'Most people are content to live their own lives on their own terms, if they can. Not Haila. She wants to live *everybody's* life on her terms.'

He sighed.

'It's frightening, isn't it? At least it frightens me, though the rest of you seem to be used to it.'

Louise gave a strange little smile, filled with the years and the patient knowledge of old friends that the years bring.

'To us she's just Haila. We've known her so long. She's just one of the things that go with Greenmont being Greenmont, like so much else up here. But that doesn't solve your problem, does it? I think Eliza is really upset. I get the feeling she's never met anyone quite like you.' She smiled. 'Can't say as I have either, to tell you the truth. But I'm in a position to be a little more

151

objective about it than she is.'

'You mean she isn't?' he asked with a quickening of something that could have been hope were the whole thing not so absurd.

She looked quite solemn for a moment, most un-Louise-like, he thought.

'I don't think so any more. I think you've accomplished one thing. I think you've gotten through.'

'To what?' he asked with a quizzical sadness. 'What's there to get through to, that's what I can't figure out.' He shook his head in bitter puzzlement, staring at the shadows once again beginning their descent on the mountainside across the way. 'I can't really figure out why I want to, either. Though I thought for a little while last night that I knew.'

'I suspect you know more about that than I do. More than you're letting on to me, anyway. As to what's there. I'd say – a very decent heart. A hurt one – hurt because it's always been too afraid to let itself get hurt, if you follow me. An uncommitted one – that's always been too afraid to be committed ... If you follow me.' She gave him a sudden, sharp, shrewd glance. 'You do follow me, I trust?'

'I follow you,' he said. 'But where, I know not.'

She shrugged.

'Wherever you'll let yourself go, I'd say. If somewhere, then somewhere. If nowhere – then nowhere.' She turned and smiled at him with a genuine friendliness. 'It's up to you, sweetie. Maybe you have to decide what you're looking for before you can know what you've found. Or am I getting stupid in my old age?'

He smiled.

'Stupid is the last thing I would ever call you, my dear Louise. Viola, yes, but—'

'That's another thing. Viola's already rattling around this camp spreading the word, if I know Viola. She's almost finished working the upper end and is now about to come through the Meadows on her way south. If I know Viola, and I do know Viola. So I think you should be deciding just what you're going to do from here on in, because Greenmont is going to be expecting something, you know.' She gave a little grin. 'You can't just leave us all dangling. It wouldn't be fair.'

152

'What would you propose?' he asked in a tired tone.

'What do you want?' she asked with a challenge she hoped would be sharp enough to jolt him. It did. He looked at her with a sudden naked helplessness.

'I don't know...I just don't know. I guess I want what everybody wants...someone I can rely on. It's as simple as that, I guess.'

She nodded thoughtfully, then turned to study his face.

'Do you think *you're* somebody someone can rely on?' she asked and, if anything, he looked more helpless than before.

'I don't know that, either. Maybe that's the trouble...Maybe I'm just no good for anyone. Maybe it's in me, whatever it is.' He shook his head with a despairing motion. 'Maybe I just don't know how to love.'

She laid a hand on his arm and spoke in a softer tone.

'Does anybody? We just try. Maybe you need to try a little harder.'

'But – I – have – tried,' he said in a low, agonized tone. 'I – am – *trying*. And it just doesn't seem to do any good. It doesn't do me any good, it doesn't do anybody else any good. I just can't make it, somehow.'

'Oh, come,' she said, more lightly, giving his arm a squeeze. 'Life isn't all that bad.' But his expression did not change.

'It is for me. You don't know how it is for me.'

'No,' she conceded soberly. 'Nobody ever knows how it is for anybody, really, no matter how close you may be to them. I remember one time when Jerry— but,' she broke off with an abrupt chuckle, 'that's another story. *That* is definitely another story. If I were you, I would just ignore everyone on this for the rest of the week and then I think I'd go to Eliza when she gets up here this week-end and throw myself on her mercy. I don't know what you wrote, but she's a nice girl, even if she is a little shocked by it at the moment, and she'll forgive you.'

'Do you think so?' he asked without much hope.

'I'm sure of it,' she said firmly.

'And what about all these – these vultures around here?' He gestured vaguely towards the Meadows, its population of shouting children, slowly strolling golfers, and final twosomes on the tennis courts beginning to take on a going-home-to-supper aspect as the evening declined and the air began to sharpen.

'What am I supposed to do about them?'

'Ignore them. Laugh it off, if you can. You don't have to say anything.' He gave a bitter little smile.

'That's what Einar says. You both make it sound so simple, you old hands in Greenmont. Then you all turn on me and make it impossible.'

'Einar's an intelligent boy,' she said thoughtfully. 'And a friend of yours.'

'You, too. I think you really are. But, you wait. By tomorrow morning you'll both be at me again in spite of your good intentions.'

'Oh, no, we won't. Not any more.'

'You can't help it. It's too much of a habit with all of you up here.'

'Well, at least,' she said with a twinkle, 'we'll try damned hard, anyway.'

'If everybody will just leave us alone,' he said slowly, 'I think maybe we can work it out.' He smiled bleakly. 'It's a big If.'

'I'll begin right now,' she said, jumping up and waving to an ample figure bustling busily towards them down the road from the upper end of camp. 'Viola! Hi, Viola! Wait a minute, I want to talk to you about something important. *Very* important ... That ought to stop her,' she confided with a chuckle. 'If there's anything that can top a secret, in Viola's mind, it's another secret. Although I'm blessed if I know exactly what I'm going to tell her, now I've got her stopped!'

The major rose, waved to Viola and then turned back to take Louise's hand in his.

'Thanks for everything.'

'We're your friends,' she assured him. 'Greenmont's really a very friendly place.'

'Like a grizzly bear.'

She gave her racy grin as she turned away.

'You just have to understand us. It takes a little doing, but it can be done.'

The voice he expected to hear called out to him as he reached the MacAleer cabin. Its tone was friendly but commanding, its owner obviously did not expect him to refuse her invitation, though that was what he contemplated for a second. He turned at the foot of the path leading across the ravine and faced her where she stood above him.

'What is it, Haila?' he demanded sharply. 'What do you want of me?'

'I just want you to come over for a drink, dear,' she said calmly. 'And to talk about Eliza.'

'Well,' he said curtly, 'I don't want to talk about Eliza.'

'But we must,' she said gently. 'We must get this tended to before it goes completely wrong.'

'Nothing will go completely wrong,' he said with a harsh impatience, 'if you will just stay out of it.'

'Bill, Bill. How mistaken you are, about so many things. Now stop being a stuffy, silly boy and come up here.'

'I'm not a stuffy, silly boy—' he began, and suddenly broke off with a grim little laugh. 'What absurdities you reduce things to! As though everything in the world were three years old. Well, it isn't. It isn't.' Abruptly he wheeled and started up the stairs to her deck, so quickly that she fell back a little before him, losing for a second her air of perfectly lacquered calm. 'Now, what is it?' he demanded, dropping savagely into a chair. 'Just what is it you want of me, anyway?'

'The first thing I want,' she said crisply, 'is for you to remember that I am sixty-three years old, which is old enough to be your mother and I think entitles me to some courtesy. If not respect.'

'Very well. I'm sorry. I apologize.'

'That's better—' she began, but he went on in a level voice.

'Just remember that I too am entitled to some respect. As a human being who has a right to some privacy in his emotions and his feelings. Isn't that right?'

'It depends on what you do to the emotions and feelings of others, whether or not you deserve respect,' she said calmly, sitting down on a porch swing and draping her skirt carefully over the cushions. 'Isn't *that* right?'

He smiled without humour.

'So you get respect, regardless of what you do to people, just because of age, but I don't get it unless I earn it. Well, well. That's Queensberry rules, all right.'

'It is for a gentleman.' She leaned forward, tapping his knee

155

gently with an admonitory finger. 'Bill, we must discuss this matter calmly, now. It won't do us any good to bicker. We both have the same thing at heart – I think. We both want what is best for Eliza.'

He made an impatient movement.

'And me, too, I hope.'

'You too, but not you exclusively. If you're thinking in terms of you exclusively, then it's even more important that we talk. That *would* mean hurt for Eliza. I won't let you hurt her, Bill. I've been like a mother to Elizavetta ever since her parents died, and I won't let you hurt her now. She's been sheltered and protected—'

'Too sheltered,' he said bitterly. 'Too protected.'

'—sheltered and protected, and she isn't used to people who express themselves as – as strongly, perhaps, as you do. Or as you did in that letter.'

'So she told you about it.'

'Of course she did. She tells me everything.'

'Did you read it?' he forced himself to ask. She shook her head.

'I don't read people's mail, Bill, unless they ask me to. She didn't show it to me. But she told me enough about it so I think I understand it very well.'

'Then,' he said in an agonized half-whisper, 'for God's sake show a little charity.' He was suddenly very conscious of the rustling woods all about, the last of the light dwindling out on the distant ridges, the dark, secretive shadows drawing in around the porch, soft in the distance the river tumbling along. A squirrel ran out on a branch, a last blue-jay screamed, a car churned up the grade and whined away towards the upper end of camp.

She allowed the silence to lengthen until his whisper in retrospect seemed a shout. Then she spoke softly.

'Bill, what makes you think Eliza has the answer for you? Isn't it, perhaps, all in your imagination? Wouldn't you be better off if you just left Greenmont and forgot all about it? Wouldn't you really be happier? Don't you think?'

'So that's it,' he said, still speaking close to a whisper. 'I'm supposed to be noble and go away.' His voice abruptly grew stronger. 'Well. Not until she tells me to, Haila. And you can't

156

make her do that. Or can you? Maybe you can.'

'I haven't tried to. I think her own common sense will tell her that. Don't you? Really?'

He gave her a sudden glance, full of pain, but challenging.

'Why?'

She looked at him with a gentle, sad expression and shook her head in her oh-you-poor-child fashion.

'Bill, Bill! Surely you know the answer to that.'

His look did not change.

'You tell me.'

'Because, dear, you are so much more – more mature, than she is. You've been out in the world more. You've had an experience, with your marriage, that – that she just can't comprehend. Even though,' she added with a less gentle note in her voice, 'you apparently tried to make it very explicit to her in what you wrote. That's what I mean, dear, don't you see? Eliza just doesn't comprehend – things like that.'

'Eliza is thirty-five years old, or I miss my guess,' he said harshly. 'She's at least been reading books all these years, if she hasn't been doing anything else. I suspect she comprehends a lot of things. Including a lonely heart. She has one herself, doesn't she?'

'Eliza has her compensations,' she said. The major gave a scornful laugh.

'What? Mr Smudge?'

'The comfort of a kind and generous heart that knows it has rarely been selfish or deliberately hurtful to anyone,' she said quickly. 'Can you say as much?'

'My God, my God!' he said with a bitter anguish. 'I've tried to be unselfish to people! I have *never in my life* been knowingly hurtful to anyone. I've done my best to be kind and generous—' his voice trailed away and she responded in a softly considerate tone.

'But somehow it just hasn't worked, has it? Somehow it has all gone wrong, somewhere. Don't you see what that indicates, dear? That it's something in you, something you can't escape. Something you shouldn't ask Eliza to try to solve for you, if you can't solve it yourself.'

He gave her a tortured look and spoke, finally, in a low and tortured voice.

157

'How damnable you are,' he said, and she did not flinch from it. 'How horribly you twist things to your own purposes. How terribly you undercut and undermine a man's morale. How has Jim ever stood it all these years!'

And even then she did not flinch, though her face grew white for a second and a harsh line came about her tightly held lips. But when she finally spoke it was in the same gentle voice, out of an invulnerability made twice as terrifying to him by his own vulnerability.

'Bill, Bill! What does it profit you to get bitter and personal? Jim and I have had many happy things together – many happy things. And at least, dear – we *are* together. And we're going to stay together as long as we live.' She gave him a kindly, pity-ing look, made more galling by his knowledge that she had calculated it exactly, and added softly: 'And that's more than you can say about your marriage, isn't it, dear?'

'Haila,' he said, rising abruptly to his feet and speaking in a voice that trembled on a ragged edge between firmness and hysteria, 'I want you to know this: I am as decent and kind and generous as anybody. I may have had – a little bad luck – in some things, but that doesn't change what I am inside. I believe there is some chance for Eliza and me – some chance. I'm not going to leave here, Haila. I'm going to stay here until I find out.'

For a long moment their glances held, unyielding and hostile across the leaf-strewn deck, while around them wood-sounds and night-sounds grew louder with the final dying of the day. A group of children went chattering homeward along the road, a dog barked somewhere among the pines, from one of the cabins below by the river the wind carried up-canyon the deli-cious smell of charcoal-broiling steaks. When she finally responded it was in a weary but understanding tone.

'Well, dear, if that is your final decision, then of course there is nothing I can do about it except give Elizavetta my own con-sidered judgment. And I am afraid that it is exactly what I've been telling you. It couldn't possibly work. You know it couldn't. But if you aren't mature enough to accept the fact, then I'm afraid' – she gave a little shrug – 'I'm afraid events will just have to take their course.'

'Just so,' he said evenly. He stopped at the foot of the steps and turned back to face her as she stood above him, perfectly coiffed, perfectly gowned, apparently in perfect command of herself and the situation; as, he felt with an inward shiver, she had been of every situation since she first became sentient sixty-three years ago.

'Stay out of this, Haila,' he said quietly. 'You can't play God to everybody.'

'Only to those I love, Bill. Or care for.' She smiled for a second in a way that looked curiously helpless and open – perhaps the only moment, he realized later, that she was ever really honest with him. 'That's another thing you're mistaken about. People don't always understand me, either, you see. I really did like you, Bill. I really was your friend. But I can't sit by and let you inflict the hurt of your own heart upon another heart that has done nothing to deserve being hurt. Surely you can understand that.'

'I understand nothing except that there may be a chance for me – a chance. And you and this damnable camp want to destroy it if you can. And I won't let you. *I won't let you.*'

Again the twilight pressed in upon them as they stood silently gazing at one another. It was growing colder and the smell of steaks, he realized incongruously, was making him hungry despite the high singing tension to which their interview had brought him. He half-expected some further pronouncement from her, but knew instinctively that she was too clever for that. There was only a gently sad expression, a gently worried, thoughtful shake of the head, one hand raised to tuck a straying hair into place on the trim grey head.

'Well, dear,' she said finally, 'I don't care about myself, but I *am* sorry you misunderstand Greenmont so. We've only wanted to help you, all of us. But—' she looked off across the darkening canyon with a wistful little smile, 'I guess that's life.'

'I guess it is,' he said evenly. 'Good night.'

'Good night,' she said. 'See you tomorrow.'

And so she would, he thought as he went back across the ravine to the MacAleer cabin, and so would they all, in their happy, cosy, self-cannibalizing way. And so they did, when he went again to the Meadows next morning after a tossing, unrestful night. But he managed to play an outwardly relaxed game of tennis with Louise, who gave him several encouraging wise-cracks and comments, and then lazed by the pool with Einar and Sally-Jane, who were equally friendly. Under their per-suasions he began to relax a little his general antagonism for Greenmont, though it revived again when Haila appeared with Viola Townsend. She gave him a little wave and a wistfully chiding look when he passed near them as they sat gossiping with Mother Magruder in the Grove. What they were talking about he could only imagine, and his peace of mind was not increased when, just after he passed Mother Magruder, she gave her whooping, wheezing cackle of laughter and the words 'thought he could get away with a thing like that in Greenmont!' came clearly to his ears. Who 'he' was, or what he had done, the major had not way of knowing, but he thought he could guess clearly enough.

He went back to the cabin and snapped at Gray, which made the boy cry so that he had to spend some time apologizing, which left him further contrite and upset. Finally he went into his bedroom in the midst of the drowsing afternoon, quiet and humming with the softened sounds of nature at half-speed, and flung himself on the bed for a nap.

Sleep did not come, however, for it was Friday afternoon and the busy week-end was about to begin. By two o'clock the first carloads of husbands and guests were beginning to grind up the road past the cabin, and presently, knowing who he wanted to see yet feared to see, he went out on the deck and sat there pretending to read as the stream of arrivals grew.

Shortly before 6 p.m. the old green convertible poked its nose around the bend and went steadily by. He rose, his heart pound-ing painfully, and lifted his hand in the hesitant start of a wave, but the driver looked straight ahead. She was wearing another of her floppy hats, he noted, and some kind of purple-looking dress, and the impatient thought shot across his mind: Of all the damned nonsense. It was succeeded by another, more pain-ful: Why didn't she speak? And then, still more painful, the honest answer: You know exactly why.

His gesture of greeting died half-formed, a deeper pain took up residence in his heart. So it was to be a battle: so she did not understand and would not forgive. His heart, of late all too willing to expect antagonism, all too ready to accept the idea that people were against him, did so again. How hard life made things for people: or, at least, how hard for him.

He knew he must stop this dangerous and weakening self-pity, but Haila had done her work too well. In spite of his strongest intentions, his trust in Eliza had been shaken, his ability to meet the situation calmly had been eroded. Now Eliza was making it worse. New tensions rose in his heart and be-laboured his being. I must stop this, he told himself, I must: it is damned nonsense. But such exhortations made no difference. His heart did not respond and his mind was not sure enough of itself to make his heart behave.

Nor did the remaining events of the day assist him. The Drummonds invited him for dinner and he went up to their cabin without much appetite. She had invited Elizavetta too, Louise confided when they went into the kitchen to mix a drink together, but Eliza didn't come. Her absence caused Jerry to dwell at great length on his problems at the ranch during the week, and the conversation, for once, stayed off the subject everyone was interested in with a diligent avoidance that soon grew painful. He went home to bed early, not daring to look too closely at the cabin across the ravine for fear he might see her there, and finally dropped off into the deep sleep his physical exhaustion and emotional tension demanded.

He did not know what the week-end held for him, but what-ever it was he knew he was not in much shape for it. His last conscious act was to shove the whole matter to the back of his mind and try to pretend that it did not exist. Eventually this was enough to trick his mind into sleep, though it gave no assurance for the coming day.

THREE

The pleasant sounds of morning, given a little extra excite-ment by the knowledge that the week-end was beginning, that many extra people were in camp, that almost every cabin was full, came to them clearly as they moved about the Drummonds' deck readying breakfast. From all around among the little groves and along the river bank dishes clinked silverware rattled, there were scrapings of chairs being pushed up to tables and the cries of irate parents attempting to secure the presence of their wandering young. The balm of another perfect day lay upon the great river canyon, and in it the noises of humanity and nature blended in a kindly chorus gentle to the ear and comforting to the heart.

'The thing that worries me,' Louise said as she came out of the kitchen with a platter of scrambled eggs and bacon, 'is that he's taking it all so seriously. If he'd just ease up a little it would be so much better for everybody.'

'How can he?' Jerry demanded, following with a pitcher of orange juice and a wicker basketful of doughnuts, 'with Haila around? I gather she's being extra-double bitchy about the whole thing.'

'What shall we do to her?' Einar asked lazily from the air-mattress where he lay sprawled full-length, looking up through the pine-tops with a cherubic air into the cloudless ten o'clock blue. 'Weight her down with golf-clubs and throw her in the pool at midnight? Get old Mr Stafford to shoot her next time she crosses his property on the way to Soda Springs? Lure her up-river and push her on top of a rattlesnake? Drown her at The Falls?'

'I want us to be serious, now,' Louise said. 'What are we going to do about Bill? This man needs help.'

'I tell you what,' her husband suggested. 'Let's all help him by just – not helping him!' He gave a bright smile. 'Wouldn't that be an original idea?'

'It wouldn't work in this place,' Einar said, stretching luxuriously and trying without success to grab his wife's ankle as she passed on her way to the kitchen. 'We've got to *do* something. You know that, Jer. Everybody around here has to *do* something. Even my Ma is thinking of getting into the act, and you know what that means.'

Louise groaned.

'God forbid. I haven't tangled with Mother Magruder since you and Sally-Jane were romancing, and I'd rather not now. Kindly tell her to go away and not bother us, will you?'

'I'll try,' Einar said thoughtfully. 'Poor Bill needs all the help he can get.'

'There you go helping again,' Jerry said, sitting down and pouring the coffee. 'Why don't you just—'

'Well, I like the guy, let's face it,' Einar said, leaping to his feet in one smoothly co-ordinated movement and moving to the table, where he sat down with a satisfied thump and cradled his arms protectively around the basket of doughnuts. 'He deserves better than he's got so far.'

'Better than he may get,' Louise said soberly. 'I *wish* he didn't take it so hard.'

'Maybe he has reasons,' Einar suggested. 'We've none of us thought of that, you know, but maybe the guy has reasons. Has that ever occurred to you?'

'It's occurred to me,' Louise said drily, pulling a chair up to the table and parcelling out the scrambled eggs. 'I even know something about what they are. But even so—'

'Even so,' Jerry said, 'lots of people have unhappy marriages and get divorced. It isn't enough to end the world for. At least, not often.'

'Nothing's worth ending the world for,' Sally-Jane observed thoughtfully from the other end of the table where she was filling the juice-glasses, 'unless you think it is. Then it is.'

'By George, you're quite the little philosopher,' her husband told her with an admiring look. 'Have a doughnut.'

'Well, it *is*,' she said, making a face at him, 'so stop being smart. Now maybe that old divorce was one of those messy things that just tears you to pieces. Or maybe—'

'Or maybe he let it be,' Jerry said. 'You've got to have some proportion about these things.'

'You, too, philosopher,' Louise told him. 'Since when were you ever divorced? Or maybe you have some plans you haven't told me about?'

Her husband chuckled.

'Did it seem that way last night?'

'Last night?' Einar inquired with an air of innocent interest. 'We find,' he said, ducking with dignity the spoon his wife threw at him, 'that it's much better in the morning. At least it is on week-ends, when you don't have to get up right away and go to w—'

'Very *well*,' Louise said, blushing in spite of herself. 'Now just stop all this brilliant repartee and let's get back to Bill. I get the feeling it was a messy divorce, but I also get the feeling that he made it a lot harder on himself in some way I don't quite

163

understand. I had a talk with him at the Grove on Thursday after we got back from the Valley. He seems to feel he's very inadequate in some way.'

'Well, now,' Einar said, expansively, pushing himself back so that his chair teetered on two legs, 'I'll be glad to take him aside and give him a few hints on how to—'

'For heaven's sake,' his hostess said, attempting to kick his chair out from under him, but not succeeding as he hastily brought himself down again, 'grow up! I'm talking about something serious. Something psychological he can't seem to overcome. He thinks the world's against him, for one thing.'

'Of course it isn't,' Einar agreed. 'Only Greenmont.'

'I don't think that's quite fair, honey,' Sally-Jane said slowly. 'I don't think Greenmont is really against him. We're not, and lots of people aren't. They might be, though, if he keeps on thinking so.'

'Which he will, if we don't leave him alone,' Jerry said. 'So there – we – are.'

'I don't think it's that simple,' his wife said, frowning thoughtfully. 'Anyway, Haila won't leave him alone.'

'Yes, I understand she's already had it out with him,' Einar said, finishing his bacon and eggs and passing his plate for more.

Louise looked surprised.

'Who told you that? I hadn't heard about it.'

'Oh, just some of the kids,' Einar said airily. 'They happened to be passing along the road at the time. Susie Hendricks said the major and Mrs Buxton seemed awfully mad about something.'

'I don't think Bill gives in much,' Sally-Jane remarked thoughtfully. 'He may be unhappy about things, but I expect when he really wants something he sticks to it.'

'Except that wife, whoever she was,' Jerry pointed out. 'And whatever it is the lack of which makes him feel inadequate, if you follow me. Anyway, what does he want – Eliza? And where, by the way, *is* Eliza? Why doesn't *she* give him some help, if that's what he wants?'

'Well, after all, lover,' Louise said with some impatience as they finished eating and sat back for a few moments to savour the gorgeous day before leaving for the Meadows and their tennis game, 'there are such things as human delicacies, you

164

know. People do hesitate to barge right in, sometimes, when their most intimate feelings are involved.'

'No doubt that's right,' Jerry agreed. 'But I must say, coming into it again after a week away, that I do seem to teeter on a thin line between sympathizing with the guy and saying: For God's sake, straighten up and stop whimpering! After all, he's a grown man.'

'Life isn't always too easy for even grown men,' Einar observed. Louise snorted.

'Now, there, sweetie, speaks a charity I didn't expect to find.'

'I agree with Jerry,' Sally-Jane said as she finished her last cup of coffee and stubbed out a cigarette in the bottom. 'I wish he'd go at it with a little less earnestness. I'm on his side, but I think maybe he defeats himself sometimes by the way he reacts to things. He's so serious.'

Jerry nodded.

'I also wish Eliza didn't take things too seriously. Or more seriously. Or however the hell she does take them. Anyway, I hope she gives him the go-sign soon and puts him out of his misery, it that's what he wants. Although why anyone would want—'

'Sweetie,' Louise said firmly, 'for the hundredth time, that question is neither here nor there. Who knows why anyone wants anything. Apparently, he does.'

'Or thinks he does,' her husband remarked as they all arose and began stacking the dishes to take them back to the kitchen before leaving.

'Which is the same thing, as good old S.-J., Doctor of Philosophy, was driving at earlier,' Einar said, lifting his wife off her feet and whirling her around a couple of times before kissing her thoroughly and setting her down.

'My only concern,' Louise called from the kitchen where she had begun running water over the dishes to rinse them and leave them in the sink, 'is, how do we encourage them to get together so they can have any chance at all of working it out?'

'Just leave them alone,' her husband told her, picking up his racquet and preparing to head for the Meadows. 'Just leave them the God damned hell alone. If you'll forgive my French.'

Louise shook her head.

'You can't do that with Haila on the warpath. Somehow

165

we've got to head her off at the pass, first.'

'She's probably just like us,' Jerry said as they started along the tree-tunnelled road in the glorious morning. 'She just wants to help.'

'The only thing I want to do,' Haila remarked with the line Greenmont knew so well around her lips, 'is be of some assistance in a sadly mixed-up situation. I just want to *help*. Does that make me such an ogre?'

'I don't think it does at all,' Viola Townsend said, giving her skirts a defiant little tug as she sat on the Buxtons' porch swing. 'I think you are being perfectly reasonable about it. I know Louise doesn't think so, but I do.'

'I wish Louise didn't think she had the answer to everything,' Mrs Buxton said. 'It makes her so difficult to get along with, sometimes.'

'Sally-Jane and Einar always egg her on so, too,' Mrs Townsend said with a sniff. 'Really, those *two*.'

'I don't want to think I'm interfering where I'm not wanted,' Haila said, 'but after all, somebody has to take a firm hand and get things straightened out.'

'Old Haila's a real straightener,' her husband agreed admiringly. 'Never knew anybody to straighten out as many things as Haila's straightened out, over the years. Don't know where Greenmont would have been without her.'

'I don't know where you would have been, anyway, dear,' his wife said pleasantly. 'Now I want your honest opinion, you and Bob: am I really interfering too much? Should I just forget about it all?'

'I don't think you should for one minute,' Viola Townsend said loyally. 'I don't know what Elizavetta would do without you. And as for—' she lowered her voice and gave what she conceived to be an imperceptible nod at the still-silent cabin across the ravine '—*he* ought to be grateful, too.'

'I do honestly feel I've got his best interests at heart,' Mrs Buxton said. 'He may not agree with me right now, but after it's all over and he's had time to think about it less emotionally—'

'All over?' Jim Buxton echoed in some surprise. 'I didn't

166

realize you'd decided that was the best thing for them.'

His wife gave her head a grave little shake filled with sadness and wisdom.

'*Much* the best thing. After all, Jim, can you imagine Eliza and the major married to each other? I can't.'

'Well . . . Marriages don't always depend on other people being able to imagine them, do they? I mean – that's not the only criterion, is it?'

'If people don't conceive of it,' Haila said crisply, 'it seems to me it's a pretty good indication the people contemplating had better stop, look and listen.'

'But hadn't *they* better stop, look and listen? What I mean is, old girl – should you?'

'Jim, dear, you *can* be so obtuse,' his wife said with an impatient air that made Viola Townsend nod vigorously in agreement. 'Elizavetta turns to me as to a mother. I also flatter myself that Bill, however much he may object to what he regards as my interference at the moment, also respects my intelligence and my logic and is grateful to have an expression of them for his guidance. He needs guidance, Jim. That boy is a wandering soul trying to find port.' '

'Don't think he'll find it on his own, eh, Haila?' Bob Townsend looked grave. 'Well, maybe not, maybe not. Give him a steer, then! Give him a firm hand on the tiller. That's the ticket!'

'Thank you, Bob. You always get at the heart of it.'

'I try to,' he said complacently.

'You succeed. Admirably. As I think anyone would who fully grasped what is involved here.'

'What's that?' Jim inquired mildly. 'I'm probably a little stupid, but—'

'No, dear,' his wife said calmly. 'Not a bit of it. You just aren't familiar with all the facts. The major is a really sick boy.'

'He does seem a little odd to me,' Viola Townsend observed. 'I must say he did from the first moment. Quite bitter. Not at all the sort of person one is used to meeting in Greenmont.'

'Or anywhere, for that matter,' Haila said. 'He is taking this much too seriously. He even has it in his head that Greenmont is to blame, in some way, whereas in reality everyone has been perfectly friendly to him from the moment he arrived. All

167

of us have done everything we could to make him feel at home. Then he goes off the deep end and writes this extraordinary letter to Elizavetta. It doesn't make sense. Normal people just don't do that kind of thing.'

'People under pressure sometimes do do odd things,' Jim said thoughtfully. 'We don't know what the pressures are, do we?'

'Apparently just an unhappy marriage and divorce,' Mrs Buxton said. 'Which he went into much more explicitly than necessary to Eliza, thereby upsetting her dreadfully.'

'She did cry most of the way through lunch,' Viola Townsend said. 'I've never seen Eliza so upset since her parents died. She's usually so placid about everything.'

'Maybe,' Jim Buxton said. 'Maybe. But I've sometimes wondered about Eliza.'

'Oh, of course she's lonely,' his wife agreed. 'There's nothing surprising about that. But she leads a life filled with many good things. She keeps busy, and she's kind to people. I don't think she's felt too lonely. But I think she does now, quite suddenly. Thanks to our friend across the ravine.'

Bob Townsend frowned thoughtfully.

'Cut the ground out from under her, did he? That can be pretty devastating sometimes, when you're clinging to a pattern to make yourself think it's all worth while. Wonder how he justifies that?'

'I don't think he does,' Viola said indignantly. 'I think all he sees is his own selfish interests. I don't like to say it, but I think he's a completely cold and self-centred individual. I really find it hard to forgive him.'

'He's created a situation that's completely impossible,' Haila Buxton said. She paused for a moment to wave down to the road where five small Albertsons were trudging by on their way to the pool, yanked forward by an excited fox-terrier and trailing inner-tubes, air mattresses and other well-used items of aquatic equipment. 'Absolutely impossible.'

'Now, Haila,' her husband said mildly, 'don't get too fierce. I'm sure he didn't intend to. Probably just reaching out for a little help himself. Anyway—' he paused and grinned at Viola Townsend, earnest and dumpy and purse-lipped before him, 'anyway, I seem to recall that you girls were all hot for it yourselves just a few days ago, weren't *you*? I don't think this romance with Elizavetta was his idea originally, was it? Seems to me you kind of pushed them at each other with all your might and main. Or am I mistaken?'

'Jim, dear,' his wife said firmly, 'I am sure that if any of us had known the type of individual we were dealing with we would never have countenanced any such thing. We simply didn't. The only excuse is ignorance. It was a dreadful mistake. The only solution now is for him to leave Greenmont at once and forget all about it.'

'It's the only way,' Viola Townsend agreed. 'The only way.'

'Oh, now, come,' Jim protested. 'That does seem pretty rough. I don't want to see you girls drumming anybody out of camp, especially a nice boy like the major.'

'But he isn't a nice boy,' his wife said. 'That's what we're telling you. And there are rules in this camp, after all, concerning immoral behaviour.'

'Never enforced, thank God!' Bob Townsend said with a sudden chuckle. His wife gave him a severe look. His hostess went right on.

'To say nothing of the ordinary rules of decent society, which he has violated by his treatment of Elizavetta. I think you are being much too charitable, Jim. Much.'

'Well, of course you girls are closer to it than I am, but I don't think he's done anything immoral, has he? I mean, not in the sense—'

'In the sense of violating another person's privacy and stability,' Haila said, 'he has. That's immoral enough, in my mind.'

Her husband nodded judiciously and spoke with a perfectly straight face.

'Well, I know you never do anything like that yourself, so you're in a better position to judge than I am. Maybe he should go, if he's as bad as you say. But – I don't know. We can't make him. He's supposed to stay here until Mary and Buck get back and keep an eye on Gray, for one thing. What would you suggest?'

'We could always send them a cable and say Greenmont would appreciate it if they'd ask him to leave,' Viola Townsend said. 'Any of us could take care of Gray.'

'Well, now,' Bob Townsend said. 'Just a minute now, you girls. I agree with Jim here, there's no point in getting rough. I think we're all getting a little hysterical about it, myself. After all, it's only a little love affair, as I see it. I certainly wouldn't want you sending any cables, Viola. The man has some rights.'

'Not if he violates others,' Mrs Townsend said. 'Not if he comes into camp and upsets everything and everybody.'

'Doesn't seem to me he's upset much of anybody but Eliza and you two,' her husband said. 'I'm not defending that, you understand, but everybody else seems reasonably happy.'

'They're not,' Haila Buxton said, shaking her head with finality. 'They're not. I was talking to Mother Magruder about it yesterday, and she agrees with me that—'

'Oh, well,' Jim said. 'Oh, well, oh, well. If it's spreading like *that*, then everybody *will* be getting the word.'

'I've discussed it with quite a few myself,' Viola Townsend reported. 'Everybody at the upper end of camp is quite shocked. Janie Rupert said she didn't know what we were coming to.'

'I'm blessed if I do, either,' Jim said. 'And as for the poor old major—'

'You just watch when he comes to the Meadows,' Haila said. 'I think it will be quite obvious that everybody is concerned about it.'

'You've convinced me,' her husband said. 'I'm sure they are. What will this do to him and Eliza, I wonder? All this popular concern?'

'After the way he has treated her and treated me and treated Greenmont,' Haila said, rising and beginning to clear the table, 'I am afraid, my dear Jim, that I really don't care what it does to him. As for Eliza, I don't think she is seriously concerned about him. She is upset, but I think only on the surface. In any event, the best thing for her would be for it to end altogether, and as soon as possible.'

'Such assurance,' her husband said admiringly. 'I wish I were so certain of a lot of things.'

'Your uncertainties are what have given me all these grey hairs over the years,' Haila said in a tired tone, 'but that is neither here nor there. The important thing is the major and Eliza. You say we can't make him leave, and I don't suppose we can. But we can make it clear to him that we would appreciate it if he *did* leave. Then he might, of his own free will.'

'Not much free will about it, as far as I can see, eh, Jim?' Bob Townsend said with a chuckle. 'When these gals get on the warpath, look out!'

'Look out is right,' Jim agreed, tapping out his pipe carefully and depositing the ashes in the outsize ashtray standing at his elbow. 'I think I'd better go over and warn him.'

'I think you'd better just let things take their course,' his wife said. 'Over-sentimentalizing is what has created this situation. It is time for us all to stop it.' A screen door slammed and abruptly her voice changed and her hand came up in a wave.

'Good *morning,* Bill!' she called as they all swung around to stare curiously across at him where he stood on the MacAleers' deck, the dappled sunlight falling upon his stocky figure clad in t-shirt and gaberdines, looking tired but defiant. 'We hope you slept well.'

'Yes, thank you,' he called back. 'And you too.'

'Like a rock,' she said merrily. 'Like a rock! The just, you know, and all that.'

'Yes,' he said. 'I know.'

'Can we give you a bite to eat?' she went on in the same comfortable voice, while her husband looked at her a little strangely. The major shook his head.

'No, thanks. We have breakfast almost ready over here. I'll see you all at the Meadows, I expect.'

'We'll be there,' she promised lightly.

'So will I,' he replied. And added, on an impulse that made Viola Townsend shift indignantly on the swing, 'With bells on.'

'I hope so, dear,' Haila told him with a comfortable little laugh. 'We'll all be waiting for you.'

'I'm sure of that,' he said, still smiling but with an edge definitely in his voice now. 'It wouldn't be like you if you weren't.'

'Let us know if you need anything,' she said, returning to her domestic tasks as he started back inside. 'We'll be happy to help.'

'Thank you,' he called back over his shoulder as he disappeared, 'but, no, thank you.'

Silence held for a moment after the second slam of the screen-door and then Haila said in a voice suddenly cold with anger:

'There! You see what I mean. Did you ever hear such insolence? I tell you, Jim, he doesn't *deserve* anything from Greenmont.'

'Probably not what he's going to get, at any rate,' her husband remarked. Bob Townsend gave a rueful chuckle.

'Poor devil! Doesn't know what he's up against.'

'You boys get your golf clubs and run along,' Haila suggested. 'Viola and I will wash up and be along a little later.'

'Best we do that,' Jim said, untangling his bony legs and rising to his heron-like height, 'before old Haila here explodes entirely.'

'Well, it isn't funny, Jim. It *really isn't funny.*'

'I know that,' he told her as he picked up a putter and took a couple of balls from a coffee-tin on the shelf in the corner. 'It gets unfunnier all the time.'

'Just doesn't know what he's up against,' Bob Townsend repeated with conviction. 'Poor devil.'

But in this he was mistaken, for their neighbour was under no illusions as he returned to the kitchen of the MacAleer cabin and prepared to join Gray for breakfast. He knew what he was up against, it dismayed him, but he told himself savagely that he was not about to give in to it. A pack of gossipy old bitches would find their work cut out for them. It would take more than their stirring around to drive him off and make him abandon what he wanted. He was tougher than that, and they would find it out.

And having stated his defiance so strongly to himself, naturally it collapsed in the next instant, for it was obvious that Greenmont could do him great damage indeed if its inhabitants really set their minds to it. Under the sunny air and the clear blue sky, beneath the gentle surface of the lovely, placid days, the idle skein of summertime could suddenly be tightened in a way that would, if not literally at least with finality, strangle both him and his putative romance. It need not even take the form of direct hostility to him, though he knew that Haila would never forgive him their angry conversation of two days ago. It need only take the form of old friends talking to Eliza, and the deed would be done.

172

If he were only certain of her, if he only knew what she was thinking. If there were only some way to communicate again without running the gauntlet of the Meadows' prying eyes, the children who reported, the elders who discussed. The sensible thing, and probably the only one that would meet the situation, would be to follow Louise's advice and throw himself upon Eliza's mercies, tender or not tender as they might be at this particular point. At least, if untender, they might be persuaded to change by a personal talk; and certainly, if tender, nothing would be lost and much gained by giving them a chance to find expression.

'Buddy,' he said abruptly as he came back to the redwood slab and sat down to it, pulling the cereal and cream towards him in a matter-of-fact fashion, 'how strong is the pact these days?'

Gray gave him a shyly pleased smile.

'O.K., I guess.'

'Is it strong enough to stand taking a note to Eliza – and without telling Tommy Rupert or anybody else, this time?'

The boy gave him a startled glance and suddenly looked on the verge of tears.

'I didn't know you knew that,' he said in a stricken voice. 'I didn't mean to tell him. *Honest*. He made me do it. He's a lot bigger than me.'

'I know he is,' the major said calmly, continuing to eat his breakfast in a non-committal way.

'I really didn't mean to. Honest, I really didn't. I didn't tell anybody else. But I guess' – he looked sad – 'I guess Tommy must have.'

'Sure he did. What else did you think he would do?'

'Well, I just didn't mean to,' Gray repeated, the tears glistening in his eyes and threatening to fall. 'I won't ever do it again. I promise. Anyway,' he added hastily, 'I didn't know what was in it, or anything. I didn't do *that*.'

The major gave him a searching look, and after he decided that it had gone on long enough, relaxed into a half-smile.

'I know you wouldn't. I trust you, buddy.'

'You do?' Gray said uncertainly, and now the tears did start to fall. 'I don't know why,' he said in a muffled voice, dashing them savagely out of his eyes. 'Especially after I went and told

173

Tommy ... I suppose he went and told everybody,' he added miserably.

'Not everybody,' the major said with a grim little humour. 'Just one. And one told one. And *that* one told one. And one and one make two, and two and two make four, and four-and-twenty blackbirds gossiping by the pool can cook up a hell of a pie. But: I do trust you. So wipe off and eat up, and I'll tell you the latest. You like Elizavetta, don't you?'

'Everybody likes Elizavetta.'

'Why?'

The boy looked puzzled for a second and the major could see he was really trying to analyse it. Two cars met each other on the road, voices called, a committee of blue-jays went screaming over the cabin and quarrelling away into the distance. Gray finally spoke in a thoughtful tone.

'She's kind.'

'I think I agree. Anything else?'

The boy gave a tentative little smile.

'She treats kids like people. So do you.'

'Mmmhmm. Is that all?'

'Well ... She doesn't hurt anybody, and she's – she's kind of – different – in a nice way, I mean. And—' he paused. 'I-I guess that's about all I can think of. She makes you feel like you're a real friend. Everybody likes her, here in Greenmont. Some people—' he paused again and a wistful little smile came into his eyes, '—some people in Greenmont don't like other people, but everybody likes Eliza.'

'And you want to help and protect her and help and protect me,' the major said. The boy gave him a quick, earnest look.

'Oh, yes. Oh, *yes.*'

'Well, we're in trouble, you know. Greenmont doesn't want us to be friends any more. Or at least some people don't want us to be.'

'Mrs Buxton doesn't want anybody to be friends,' the boy said. His voice trembled a little and again his eyes started to glisten. 'She doesn't want my father and mother to be friends.'

'I got a phone call from them last night,' the major lied promptly. 'They said to tell you they're getting along all right.'

'Why didn't they call me?' the boy demanded in dismay. 'Are they going to call me?'

174

'They will in the next few days,' the major said, cursing himself for lying but reflecting instantly that he had to do something to lift his ward's morale. Why in hell hadn't they called him, as a matter of fact? He made a note that he must make good on this as soon as possible by sending Buck a cable telling him to call his son.

'Don't you worry now,' he said firmly. 'Everything's going to be all right. But you're right about Mrs Buxton. She does meddle into things. Now she's after Elizavetta and me. It's going to take a lot to stop her. The pact is going to have to be pretty strong. Can I count on you?'

Gray nodded earnestly, diverted from his own problems, a sudden pleased excitement in his eyes. Thank God we got by that point, the major thought.

'All right, then, listen. While you clean up these dishes for me I'm going to write Eliza another little note and I want you to take it right up to her. She's probably still at her cabin, so you can do it quietly without anybody seeing you. O.K.?'

'I will,' the boy said fervently. 'I really will.'

'Good. Now get at these dishes and I'll write it out and you can take it.'

'Oh, sure,' Gray said, jumping up and starting to work. 'I really will!'

And so again he wrote to Eliza, very briefly this time, not pausing much to think or polish, relying on brevity and honest intention to protect him from any further inadvertences that might aggravate inflamed feelings. It was very simple and straightforward, after all: he had to see her and this was how he thought it might be done with least notice. If she were agreeable.

It occurred to him wryly as he finished what an absurd little two-penny-romance device it was, this business of communicating by secret note, arranging – or so he hoped – a secret tryst. How trivial it could be made to seem to the hostile eyes that he felt were on the watch around him.

But events, however absurd and ridiculous to the watching world, are only trivial in the degree to which the burden of human emotions is put upon them: and the burden here, he knew on this serene and beautiful morning, was explosive indeed.

He folded the paper several times securely and dispatched his fellow pact-member off up the road with it, reflecting as he did so that he could probably not have explained, had anyone been there to ask, why he should again be slipping his head into the noose of written communication after it had trapped him so disastrously once before. But some faith in Gray, some trust still in the ultimate decency of Greenmont, some desperate feeling, again, that you had to trust some things some time, and could not always be crafty – plus, he was honest enough to admit to himself, some childish fear of meeting her face to face without preparation – prompted his action. And, really, even if it should be discovered, what of it? All he contemplated was a talk; some attempt to solve, as two rational beings, the sad little tangle they had got themselves into, so that it could move forward to an outcome happier than that which now seemed assured for it.

He was suddenly conscious that the cabin across the ravine was silent and deserted. He did not know how long it had been so, but he was glad of it. He would have to face them all again in a little while, and he did not want another skirmish before he was ready for it.

He went in to shower and shave with a deliberate slowness designed to steady his nerves, before, carrying in his hands a golf club, a tennis racquet and a wayfarer's uneasy heart, he set forth for the waiting Meadows.

ᴇᴅ FOUR ᴆᴡ

Eight or nine foursomes were on the golf course, both tennis courts were filled, along the pool and on the benches of the Grove the week-end crowd was gathering as he came into the Meadows. Wild hoots and exclamations resounded from the lower court where the Drummonds were once more locked in deadly combat with Einar and Sally-Jane, equally hilarious noises came from the upper court where the junior Bill Pursemans were beating Rudy and Sarah Whitman. From the golf course could be heard the violent protests of Father Magruder as he missed a hole-in-one, the raucous jubilation of Bob Townsend as he made one, and from all corners of the wildly agitated, sparkling pool echoed the excited shouts of dozens of children and adults as they disported in the ice-blue ice-cold water. The denizens of Greenmont were home and happy, and over all their right little, tight little world in back of Beyond lay the perfect unity of friendship and spirit that made all their days together so relaxing and so pleasant.

Except, of course, for him. Was it only imagination, or did the cries from the courts, the shouts from the golf course, the uproar in the pool and the gossip on the benches suddenly diminish as he came in view? Was he utterly and foolishly over-sensitive, or did a certain wary watchfulness creep abruptly upon the lovely scene? He told himself he must be imagining things, yet knew that, essentially, he was not. He was being observed, all right, though not in quite the obvious way his over-sensitive, over-wrought feelings told him. Nor was it necessarily a hostile observation. It was just that Greenmont was hearing things about this man, and Greenmont intended to look him over even more thoroughly than it had before.

Trying with reasonable success to act as though he did not know it, he walked slowly across the golf course, threading his way between players who paused briefly to smile and speak and give him swift, studying glances, until he came to the benches, already well-filled with their customary week-end complement of knowing and perceptive ladies. He waved to Janie Rupert, nodded to Mary Elliott and Betty Albertson, stopped to speak briefly to Lila McCall, hoped to be able to get past, without exchanging more than the most cursory of greetings, Mother Magruder and one of her many offspring. But this was not to be.

They hailed him with their customary loud good-humour and he found himself, at least momentarily, trapped.

'Well,' said Mother Magruder, mountainous and complacent. 'Up for a little game, eh? Guess you don't think we're so bad, after all!' She gave her wheeze of laughter. He attempted to respond with a reasonable good-humour.

'I don't think you're so bad. I think you're great.'

'That's not the way Haila tells it!' she informed him with a cackle. 'If,' she added with a sudden malice, 'you can believe Haila.'

177

'I don't know,' he said cautiously.

'I hope you can't, anyway,' she replied, her mammoth folds of flesh falling away in quaking chuckles, 'because if you can, then *you* said some very naughty things about Greenmont. We should all hate you, really.'

'Did I?' he said, trying to make it sound puzzled and disinterested, though he felt dismay. 'I don't recall it. Maybe I said something she misinterpreted. I've found,' he ventured, 'that Haila sometimes has her own way of looking at things.'

'That's good!' Mother Magruder cried with an abrupt squawk of laughter that turned heads all along the benches and even caused those nearest in the pool to hesitate a second in their turbulent splashings. 'Her own way of looking at things! Haila has her own way of looking at things ! Yes, she certainly does. She *certainly* does!'

'Yes,' he said. 'Perhaps we can't always place as much reliance in them as we'd like.'

'Can't believe her, eh?' Mother Magruder cried in the same loud voice. 'Can't believe Haila! Well, she'll be glad to hear *that*!'

'I didn't say that,' he said hastily. 'It's a matter of interpretation.'

'Well, what did you say?' demanded Mother Magruder, her shrewd little eyes suddenly staring straight into his from their deep pockets of flesh, a sharp hostility coming abruptly from behind the rollicking joviality. 'What did you say about Greenmont? That's what we want to know,' she repeated loudly. 'What did you say about Greenmont?'

He was suddenly aware that now everyone around them was listening, behind the masking rustle conversations carefully lowered to permit their participants to hear him more clearly.

'Greenmont's very interesting,' he said lamely. Mother Magruder gave a snort.

'Is that all you think of us? We're just interesting? Well, well!'

'Very,' he said, and suddenly, against all common sense, breaking through his carefully held control, a cold impatience overcame caution. 'And at times quite insufferable. As I told Haila. Now, if you will excuse me—'

And he turned and walked purposefully towards the lower

178

tennis court. Behind him he heard Mother Magruder cry. *'Well!*
Did you hear that? Did you hear that Greenmont's insufferable?
Well, well! Well! Well! '

The conversations resumed, more loudly now, and with a
new note of relish and excitement.

So he had done it, on a foolish impulse too strong to control,
brought Greenmont itself into challenge, given Haila not only
her own word but his own to justify her position, made even
more uncertain the outcome of his relationship with Elizavetta.
He felt that he badly needed allies. Four he thought he had
were playing their noisy game on the lower court. He hurried
towards them and took a seat on a bench alongside the net
where Einar was standing, waiting for Sally-Jane to serve.

'Greetings,' he said. 'I saw you talking to my Ma. I hope she
didn't get you into any trouble.'

'No,' the major said with an attempt at a smile. 'No more
than I got myself into.'

'Well,' Einar said, instinctively leaning out of the way of one
of his wife's wilder serves that narrowly missed his right ear,
'don't let her throw you. She's a little formidable at times, but
it's just a matter of standing up to her.'

'Yes,' the major said with a grim ruefulness. 'That's just what
I did, unfortunately.'

'Don't worry,' Einar told him as he sprinted across court
to try to intercept Jerry's return, missed and came back to the
net, breathing strenuously. 'I'll talk to her about it.'

'It's too late. I'm afraid I made the mistake of attacking
Greenmont.'

Einar paused and frowned.

'Well, that's not good,' he admitted, 'but we'll try to get you
out of it.' He grinned. 'I've done it myself, at times.'

'But you're a Member.'

Einar gave a startled little laugh as Sally-Jane got over a
perfect serve, Louise swung at it with a frantic energy, wailed,
'Oh, *no!* ' and missed.

'I don't think it's fatal.'

'Oh, no, probably not fatal,' the major said. 'It just compli-
cates things because of my own damned foolishness. As if they
weren't complicated enough already.'

'What's that, sweetie?' Louise asked as service changed hands

179

to Jerry, Einar dropped back to his base-line and she came to the net. 'What's complicated now?'

'The whole damned thing,' he said. 'The Whole Big Picture. Life. The Universe. Me.' His voice lowered. 'Elizavetta.'

'Mmm,' she nodded thoughtfully as Jerry prepared to serve. 'Well. She ought to be coming down to the Meadows pretty soon and then we'll know more about it. I think it's going to be all right. She's a reasonable girl. Don't worry.'

But as their vociferous game went on and the tides of victory surged back and forth across the net, he did worry, increasingly, in the bright blue day astir with the soft, warm morning breeze. The outcries in the pool, the gossip in the Grove, the shouts of glee and chagrin from the golf course rose again to their normal level and went beyond it, but still it seemed to him that there was one underlying note in everything, a constant observation and discussion of himself and Elizavetta going on all over the green meadow where Greenmont's residents disported. He recognized that this was largely his own fault for allowing his inner tensions to explode into his hostile argument with Haila and his comment just now to Mother Magruder, but it seemed to him beyond the bounds of common decency that any group should be so obsessively concerned with what was, after all, a private matter involving two people. His mind refused to accept the fact that this was perfectly normal behaviour on the part of society. He still attempted to insist to himself that simply by insisting to Greenmont that it was a private matter, he could put the past week back in the box and make it so.

He was shaken from this forlorn fantasy by the arrival of Viola Townsend from the upper end of camp and a glimpse of Gray hurrying past with an air of apparently guilty speed.

Viola's appearance was hailed by Louise with a cheerful cry of, 'Welcome, O harbinger of glad tidings!' which Mrs Townsend ignored with a sniff as she marched past the tennis court and took a seat among the ladies of the Grove. At once, it seemed to the major, the tempo of conversation in that busy area increased. It seemed so to Einar, too.

'Madam Quack is talking sixty to the dozen,' he remarked as he came to the net again.

Several minutes later Gray appeared from the same direction, started to pass near the courts on his way to the pool and then changed course when he saw the major. So abrupt and so guilty did his change of direction appear, in fact, that the major's hand, half-raised in greeting, fell back in dismay.

'What's that bright little boy up to, major, honey?' Sally-Jane inquired. 'Looks to me like he's been in somebody's jam-pot.'

Mine, I'm afraid, the major with a sickening jolt of apprehension, though he could not quite bring himself to believe that the boy had betrayed him again after being so conscience-stricken about it earlier.

After that there was only one thing left to wait for as the day moved towards noon and the healthy uproar of the Meadows reached its week-end crescendo. Shortly after twelve it occurred, and again he could sense the sudden diminution of sound, the hasty diverting of attention from less intriguing matters to this. Elizavetta and Haila appeared, framed by the pines that flanked the road where it entered the Meadows from the upper end of camp. At once it seemed to him that everything became curiously muffled, not only around him but inside his head, so that sound appeared to drop away and be succeeded by a curious buzzing silence. His vision also seemed to be strangely concentrated, peripheral things blurred oddly away so that the only thing he saw was the brightly dressed, awkwardly hesitant figure as it stood beside the elegantly thin, perfectly poised one on the edge of the Meadows.

'There she goes, there she goes,' Louise carrolled, 'all dressed up in her Sunday clothes! Except that this is Saturday. Eliza! Come down here this minute and referee. We need you. These children are beating the pants off us again.'

The two figures hesitated, there was apparently some quick comment by Haila, Elizavetta moved irresolutely and paused. Louise persisted.

'Come on, sweetie. Your expert assistance is absolutely imperative if Jerry and I are to squeeze out the victory so richly deserved by superior character and ability.'

'Better help out, honey,' Sally-Jane agreed. 'We're the ones who need it, not those two vultures.'

'That's right, Eliza,' Einar said, pausing in mid-court as a lob from Jerry lifted successfully over his head and fell just inside the base-line. 'You see how it is.'

As clearly as though they were standing an arm's length

away, those at the court could sense Haila's firmly repeated, *I don't think I would if I were you*. Again Elizavetta moved with an awkward indecision. *Damn it,* the major urged inside his mind, *you have to see me some time. Come on, damn it. COME ON.* And of course the moment their little tableau broke into life and she and Haila started towards them, all sorts of doubts and terrors sprang up in his heart and he wished himself far away.

But Eliza had made the decision, apparently, and he told himself the least he could do was be grateful for what he knew must be an act of great courage, here in the eyes of camp, and meet it with an equal fortitude. He rose as they approached. They would have to pass him – and so they did, even as he prepared to speak, Haila looking pleasantly straight into his eyes without a word, Elizavetta staring determinedly off into some vague sector of the sky where he did not exist, walking with a determination verging on the comic – had either of them been in condition to appreciate it – in its fixed severity.

Almost before he realized what was happening they had brushed past and left him standing ludicrously, mouth half-open, hand half-outstretched, alone in the laughing universe.

'I'd like to, Louise,' Eliza said in a clear voice that trembled a little, 'but I think Haila and I would rather sit in the Grove and talk.'

For a moment or two no one said anything. Then Jerry gave his racquet an impatient swing and headed for the serving line.

'O.K., now,' he said decisively, 'let's go!'

'Wowee,' said Einar softly as he and Sally-Jane fell back to receive, 'I guess we'd better.'

'Should we?' the major asked dully; and then, with an abrupt shift of mood and a rising impatience, *'Should we.'*

'Sweetie,' Louise said hastily, 'don't you think you'd better—'

'I don't think I'd better do anything but talk to Eliza,' he said in an increasingly angry voice. 'I think that's what I'd better do. Don't go away now,' he said to their startled and perturbed faces. 'This may be quite a show, so don't go away.'

'But, *sweetie*—' he heard Louise's voice fade away behind him as he strode forward blindly towards the gossiping Grove. Again the world narrowed down, all else blurred away, he heard nothing, saw nothing but the garishly dressed figure

182

walking with a tensely controlled dignity ahead of him.

'Pardon me,' he said, too loudly he knew, but he could not help it, 'I would like to talk to you.'

'Oh,' she said in a frightened voice. 'Oh! But I—'

'Just talk to you,' he said, unaware of the silence all around, the way his voice rang out through the attentive Grove. 'Without Haila or anybody. Just talk to you. Is that all right?'

'But I don't,' she began, 'I don't—'

'Of course you do,' he said harshly, rushing ahead on a tide of emotion he could not control, 'of course you do. Now where shall it be, here or where I suggested?'

'Really—' Haila began indignantly, and he snapped:

'I'm not talking to you, Haila! For once, be quiet!'

He was dimly conscious of a startled and approving burst of laughter from somewhere along the benches. Haila turned quite white.

'How utterly impertinent! How utterly—'

'I am talking to you, Elizavetta,' he said, lowering his voice abruptly so that only the three of them could hear it. 'Without right, without warrant, without anything but the certainty that I must. Now will you talk to me privately as I want, or shall we do it right here? Because I am going to talk to you, Eliza. I'm not going to stop now.'

'Oh!' she said, turning to stare at him from enormous eyes filling with tears, *'why do you bother me so?'*

'I don't mean to bother you,' he said, a sudden wistful kindness in his voice. 'Oh, my dear, I don't mean to bother you. I just want us both to be happy, that's all. And we can't be unless we can talk it out alone.'

'But I don't want to talk to you,' she protested helplessly.

'Yes, you do,' he insisted gently. 'You know you do. Now, why can't we—'

'Eliza, dear,' Haila said. 'I think we had better walk on, now.'

'I think *you* had better walk on,' he said in a savage whisper. 'Yes, I think *you* had better. Eliza—'

'Oh, all right,' she said in sudden capitulation. 'All right, all *right.*'

'Good,' he said, feeling amazingly happy. 'Then I'll see you where I said, all right?'

'Yes, *all right,*' she said, turning her back on the Grove so that its occupants could not see her face, the tears beginning to come in earnest. 'Now, go away.'

'My dear,' Haila said, 'I think I had better go with you. I don't think you are safe with this man, in this mood.'

'Eliza knows she is safe with me,' he said, a singing in his heart and gentleness in his voice. 'Eliza knows I wouldn't hurt anyone, don't you, Eliza?'

'Not physically,' Haila said. 'But you carry hurt within you and it hurts others. That is what I worry about.'

'Not for Eliza,' he said softly. 'And not for anybody else, either, however you want to twist, horrible old woman. Now please leave us alone and we will work it out, won't we, Eliza?'

'I said I would see you,' she told him through her tears. 'Now, go away.'

'Yes,' he agreed happily. 'And don't worry. Everything is going to be all right.'

'I hope so,' she said in a tone of desperation and desolation that shook his heart with an agonizing tenderness. 'Oh, I hope so!'

He was conscious of the renewed buzz of talk in the Grove, the watching eyes all around, as he bowed gently and turned away, but they did not matter. He went to the pool as in a dream, ignoring them; swam gravely back and forth a dozen times, threading his way between shouting children and keeping exact count as though his life depended upon it; got out, dried himself, took some sun. His friends did not come near him nor did anyone else, and he missed them not at all. In precisely twenty minutes he arose, gathered together his things and walked slowly down the sun-flecked road to the cabin.

Gray was nowhere to be found and he did not feel like eating. Instead he lay on his bed, eyes wide open, hardly thinking, hardly feeling, as the hours drifted by to the appointed time. A strange serenity lay upon his heart, untroubled and clear of doubt.

It never occurred to him that she might not meet him. He knew she would, as certainly as he knew that he would greet her, when she did, with a loving kindness that would resolve, for their forlorn and battered hearts, all things.

Secret and warm, the little glen with its overhanging rock and carpet of pine-needles might have been dropped into the world from some ancient time before man with all his petty and peculiar problems came along to upset the sensible and well-ordered savageries of nature. No rusty beer cans, no empty cigarette packs, no mementoes of the finer niceties of civilization lay about its pleasant confines. Not yet had the thoughtful rearrangements of organized recreation and the kindly attentions of the bulldozer ventured in, and with luck never might. So it was and so it had always been. So, presumably – if the planned six-lane divided highway scheduled to go in next year across the mountains stayed as far away as Greenmont's residents fervently hoped – it would always remain.

At this moment, on the placid slope of mid-afternoon, it was a playing-ground for squirrels, a convention site for chipmunks and field mice. Above their squeaky cavortings robins and flickers and a blue-jay or two bickered lazily in the branches. At one point a bob-cat dashed across in a series of bounds that scattered other occupants in hysterical disarray in all directions. Later a pair of deer drifted past like living sunlight, cropping leaves with a nervous stateliness and soon departing for other places. A rattlesnake flowed slowly in, coiled for a while on a sunny rock and dozed the moments away. A skunk came by, hopping like a little fluffy-tailed mechanical toy through the bear-clover and the moss-covered stones where an ancient stream once ran. A mother quail and six chicks went whistling and chuckling over the glen floor searching for nuts and grubs. A coyote paused for a moment at the edge of the clearing, causing great alarm, then thought of something else and ran off without bothering anyone. A red-headed woodpecker pounded on a tree. The world drowsed.

Into this quiet scene, scattering chipmunks, squirrels and mice, causing the quail to skitter off over the rustling leaves, provoking the birds into indignant chatter and prompting even the rattlesnake to decide, after a moment or two of disdain, that it might perhaps be better to slither off to some other spot less inhabited by inimical sounds and smells, there presently came crashing Man, and a moody one at that.

He had arrived as promised, and because he did not at once

185

see the one he had come to see, was dashed immediately out of his hopeful dreams into a disturbed uncertainty. Where was she? Where was she? He was here, the glen was here, no one else was here: where was she? He had used the trail that skirted through the woods behind Greenmont so that he would not be observed, thinking that at any moment he might overtake her doing the same. But he had not, and now he stood irresolute in the gentle afternoon, all senses sharpened, listening intently. Somewhere a branch snapped as though stepped upon, he turned eagerly towards the sound. But no one came, it was not repeated. Quite without looking, he sat down moodily upon the rock fortunately just vacated by the rattlesnake and began aimlessly pegging a handful of stones, plucked from the primeval creek-bed, against the nearest pine.

It was thus she saw him when, a little later, she came silently along the trail and stood without speaking for a moment, concealed by the giant corpse of a fallen redwood at the edge of the glen.

'Well,' she said finally in a breathless voice. 'I'm here.'

He jumped up and turned towards her, face alight.

'So you are. Thank you for coming. I appreciate it.'

'You sound so formal,' she said, a slight smile breaking through the nervousness. 'After all, you hardly gave me much choice.'

'No,' he said with a tense little laugh. 'I really rather didn't, did I?'

A genuine amusement touched her voice for a second.

'I think you quite frightened Haila.'

He said, suddenly grave, 'But not you.' She shook her head.

'No, not me . . . Do you mind if I sit down?'

'Be my guest,' he said, giving an elaborate bow, spreading an imaginary cloak. She smiled a little and took her place upon a segment of the redwood near the overhanging rock, tossing the big hat carelessly on the pine-needles, spreading the folds of the fiercely flowered skirt over the aromatic, rust-coloured shreds of ancient wood.

'I think I was five years old when I first came here. What were you doing at the age of five, fighting with the world?'

'Oh, now,' he said, starting to sit down close to her, hesitating at her slight, instinctive withdrawal, taking his seat carefully a little further off. 'That's hardly fair.'

'Are you fair?' She gave him a sudden direct glance from troubled dark eyes in which a little humour managed to gleam. 'I hadn't noticed it, too much.'

'I have an awkward heart,' he said simply, though a great pain within him protested the injustice of it. 'I'm sorry.'

'Oh,' she said hastily, 'I didn't mean to—'

He shrugged with a sort of defiant unconcern.

'You meant to do what you did, which was to tell me I'm not always fair. I was just saying I don't necessarily mean to be unfair. It just happens. Does that make understandable sense to you?'

She gave him a long, thoughtful stare during which he was suddenly acutely conscious of the warm, slumbering afternoon, the wood's smells, the muted forest sounds, the sense of being far away from the world. That was what he had wanted: what would come from it? Probably nothing: and wasn't that what he really wanted, in his awkward heart? He could not say, unable as he was to debate with himself in the midst of his tumbling emotions.

'I think you make sense,' she said slowly, 'if I can only grasp what it is.'

He took a deep breath.

'You didn't understand from my letter?'

He sensed an immediate coolness and withdrawal and cursed himself for going too fast.

'It was very strange,' she said finally. 'I tried to understand it, but it just – hurt.' Her eyes looked suddenly brighter with the possibility of tears, but she did not give way to them. Instead she reached down and dislodged a portion of the rotting redwood, crumbling it in her fingers, brushing from them the ochre dust of two thousand years.

'Well,' he said. 'Well: I wanted you to understand. But—' his voice grew forlorn for a second before he caught himself and strengthened it, 'I guess you didn't.'

'I tried to. I read it many times.' A faint suggestion of a smile came again to her lips. 'I probably could quote it to you right this minute, I read it so many times.'

He responded with an answering, rueful little smile.

'I could too, believe me.' A desperate urgency entered his

187

voice. 'Oh, Eliza! What are people supposed to do if they can't talk to each other frankly about what they feel? How can they ever help each other?'

'I want to help you,' she cried with a sudden harsh protest that startled him. She shook her head in a puzzled way. 'But you make it so difficult.'

For a long moment he did not respond, crushed by the world's unfairness. Then he burst out, 'Why do I? *Why do I?*' in a tone equally harsh, that frightened them both. 'I'm sorry,' he said humbly. 'I'm no good, I care too much.' He gave a dry and bitter smile. 'Or not enough. Which is it, Eliza, can you tell me? I only wish somebody could. Then maybe it might all make sense.'

Again they were silent, the universe adrift in the limpid heat of mountain afternoon.

'I'm sorry,' she ventured at last, with a curiously old-fashioned, little-girl politeness, 'that your marriage was so – so – unhappy.'

'Thank you,' he said in an equally artificial tone. Neither said more. The silence grew. The silence shouted. His heart died, all the bright glorious hopes disintegrated. He stood up.

'I'm sorry,' he said bleakly. 'I'll go.'

'*No!*' she said, holding out her hand in a quick gesture of protest. 'Oh, please, no!'

'Oh, yes,' he said, though the renunciation cost him so much he wondered if he could draw breath to speak. 'I'm not playing games with you: you don't want to talk to me, we have nothing to say to each other. It was all in my mind that we might have.'

'No, it wasn't,' she said in a half-whisper, an expression close to hopelessness touching her face. 'Oh, no, it wasn't. I want to be friends.'

'Friends!' he said with an anguished mockery, though he did sit down again upon the ancient weathered log. 'Is that all you understand, friends? And do you call these – these *people* here in camp your friends?'

'They are my friends!' she said, with a glance full of pain but unyielding. 'They are my friends. They have been my friends all my life. Why can't you see that?'

'And all your life,' he said harshly, 'they've kept you in

188

exactly the mould they want you. Good old Eliza, our pet old maid!'

'Oh!' she cried bitterly. 'Why do you strip me down to nothing? Why do you have to be so cruel? Why do you have to hurt so? Isn't it enough to be hurt yourself, without hurting me?'

'That sounds like Haila,' he said harshly. 'There speaks Haila! She isn't content just to interfere, she has to fill you full of jargon about me. She has to tell you I want to hurt people. I don't want to hurt people! All I want is for people – my God, all I want is to love people and have them love me. But they don't understand. They don't ...'

She gave him a strained, direct stare, and when she spoke it seemed to him that it came through trumpets, so ringing did it seem to sound against the soft quiet of the glen, so shattering was it to him.

'Are you sure that isn't *your* mould? Are you so sure you don't want to be misunderstood? Isn't that easier for you than the task of fulfilling your obligations to other people? Isn't it easier to blame them and run away than face them and find love wherever it is among their imperfections?'

'I haven't found it,' he whispered. 'I haven't found it. I've given it – or I've tried to – but I haven't found it.'

'It's there in most people,' she said in a softer tone, 'somewhere. At least I've seemed to find it, almost everywhere.'

'And I nowhere.' He felt the lovely day as ashes in his mouth, nothing was left now, it was over, whatever it had been. There was a terrible crying in his heart, but it didn't matter. He stood up. 'Let's go back. They'll all be waiting. And wondering. And gossiping. We'd better go.'

But again she made a gesture of protest and remained seated; and after a moment he sat slowly back down again, not looking at her, staring through the tree-tops at the distant sun-softened crags above, gentle and shimmering in the haze.

'It's probably true,' she said at last, forlorn but doggedly honest. 'They probably have kept me in a mould, and I've probably let them, because for me that's been easier, too.'

A rending pity, so sharp it seemed to stop his breathing, rushed into his heart.

'Oh, no. Oh, my dear, no. I didn't mean to be so harsh. I

shouldn't have. I have no right.' He gave a haunted little smile. 'Who am I to talk, after all? I didn't mean to – I shouldn't have.'

'I probably deserved it. In my way I suppose I must sound pretty smug, too. But I'm not. God knows I'm not. I'm just funny old Elizavetta Berrenger – just funny old Eliza,' she said, almost losing control of her voice but managing to hang on, 'whom everybody loves.'

'They do,' he assured her earnestly. 'They do. There's no doubt about it. Everybody loves you. I haven't heard anyone say anything unkind about you.'

She made a wry little face.

'Don't worry. Sooner or later everybody in Greenmont says something unkind about everybody else. But we get over it. Maybe that's what holds us together in the long run. It's just part of being friends: we survive each other.'

'What an odd way to put it,' he said, struck by her words, taken out of himself for a moment. 'Maybe that is what people have to learn to do – survive each other, good and bad and everything together. Maybe that's what I haven't learned to do.' His expression darkened abruptly. 'But no. *No.* I won't admit that. I've tried. I have tried, Eliza. And it just doesn't work, for me.'

' "It's possible I have a heart that isn't capable of loving," ' she quoted. 'But you don't really believe that or you wouldn't have written it. You wrote it because you wanted to be told you do – because you know you have.'

'Then why doesn't it succeed?' he demanded in a tortured whisper. '*Why doesn't it?* Am I so unattractive or something? Am I an ugly old monster? Is it because I have' – his voice trembled between pain and laughter – 'b.o. or halitosis or something? Should I change my toothpaste or my soap? Advise me, Eliza! I need your help!'

The dark mascaraed eyes gave him a glance oddly composed of compassion and disbelief. Her answer could not have surprised him more.

'You don't want anyone's help. Not really. I think you enjoy this. I think you like to be alone against the world.'

He felt literally as though the redwood log had reared and struck him a heavy blow, so devastated was he by the terrible

190

injustice of her mistaken and defensive remark. But he managed to remain seated, and to go on, even though the conversation, he now knew, was doing irreparable things to them both.

'That's Haila again,' he said in a strangled voice. 'More jargon. Oh, God damn that woman, God damn her! Why can't she leave anyone alone?'

'I won't defend Haila,' she said, staring unseeing into the sheltering woods across the glen, 'but there you go again, blaming someone else.'

'And are you so perfect?' he cried bitterly. 'Is everything so wonderful for you? My God, Eliza, I'm offering you a chance – some chance – at least I'd like to think I was – a chance—'

'A chance for what?' she cried with an equal bitterness. 'To go through this sort of thing for the rest of my life? What sort of chance is that?'

'But it wouldn't be,' he protested desperately. 'It wouldn't be, it would be peaceful and happy, I would make it that way for you—'

'Like your other marriage?' she asked, and he realized in a startled way that marriage was indeed what they were now discussing, in some fashion brought about by life, which had hurtled them into it, almost, it seemed, without their conscious volition. 'That didn't sound so peaceful and happy to me.'

'I tried to tell you,' he said, forcing himself to speak in a quieter, more patient tone, 'how that was. I tried to make it very clear so that you would know all about it, and understand. I guess maybe I was – too frank. But I wanted you to know it all, so you could understand. I thought you were grown up and I could tell you. But I guess I just shocked you, instead.'

For a moment she did not speak and he did not dare look at her. The afternoon shivered slightly, a little breeze rose quickly in the pines and quickly died. Before long the world would begin its long sweet passage into evening.

'I was shocked,' she said slowly, 'at first. Then I became sorry for you. You will never know,' she said in a half-whisper, 'how sorry I became for you. You just won't ever know.'

'Why not?' he demanded in an anguished voice. 'Why won't you tell me? Isn't that a start on love?'

She gave a strange sad little shake of her head.

'Who said love? Not I.'

191

'Then I,' he said desperately. 'I said love. Don't you want it, Eliza? Are you so shut off from it by the years that you don't want it? How can you be? Everybody wants it, you aren't any different.' A humble note came into his voice, desolate and sad, beseeching and gentle. 'Are you?'

And now he perceived that she was crying, not noisily but with a soft intensity that she did not attempt to control, the tears running down her cheeks, the mascara beginning to run with them, dripping on her hands as she held them to her face, spilling over, bespattering and marking the loudly-coloured dress.

'Here,' he said, for at the moment he did not know what else to say, 'take my handkerchief.'

Their hands touched as he gave it to her, and suddenly her hand was clinging to his with a woeful desperation. But she did not move closer to him, and he knew that if he tried to move closer to her it would not be accepted. Their hands lay linked on the deeply corroded wood as she daubed awkwardly, with the handkerchief in her left hand, at her reddened eyes. He had a sudden mental picture of a frustrated God looking down and wondering what to make of two such hapless little souls.

'You don't know,' she said finally, her voice still shattered frequently by sobs, 'how hard the pretending is. Always being bright and cheerful, always being Good Old Eliza! Always being alert and interested and entering in, always acting as though this kind of life were just exactly what you wanted, always being anxious to make everybody feel that they don't have to worry, Eliza's getting along all right, they can ease their consciences about *that*! Always smiling, always being a good sport, always just – just—'

'Always being brave, I think,' he said softly. 'I think that's about it, don't you? Always just being brave.'

'I don't want to be brave!' she cried, but before he could respond with whatever offering of solace he might have in him, honesty reasserted itself and her voice, even amid sobs, became filled with a basic common sense. 'But of course one has to be. Nobody could live, otherwise.'

'Unless you let someone else be brave for you,' he said urgently, and now he did turn towards her and she did not flinch away from him as he fully expected her to do. Instead

192

she stared at him through tear-filled eyes and asked a question that would have been hurtful and offensive were it not asked with an honesty that eased its bluntness.

'Who?' she said in a disbelieving tone. 'You?'

'Yes, me! Why not, Eliza, why not? Can you answer me that, *why not?*'

'Don't shout,' she said with a breathless little gasp of laughter that almost made him laugh too, incongruous though it was in the midst of all their tearing emotions. 'Haila might hear you.'

'Haila'd better not,' he said ominously; and raising his voice he shouted mockingly, 'Hey, Haila! Are you there, you old battle-axe? And if so, are you getting an earful?'

'She isn't here, she doesn't know about this. I don't think anybody's here but us.' Her face darkened, the impulse to laughter died. 'Not that it matters to anyone.'

'But us,' he said quickly, taking both her hands in his. Again she did not protest or withdraw, and neither did she renew or strengthen the desperate pressure he had been aware of earlier.

'I don't know that it even matters to us,' she said in a miserable tone. 'I don't really know why – why I came here at all.'

'Because I asked you to. Because you do want me to help you and be brave for you. Because you must feel something of what I do, or you wouldn't be here. Isn't that true, Eliza?'

'What *do* you feel? I can't figure it out. I don't know whether it's genuine or whether it's just – just something you dreamed up about me that isn't true.'

Again the black unfairness of it threatened to overwhelm him, but he fought it off and spoke with a dogged hope.

'But you want it to be true, don't you? You hope it's true, don't you? Eliza, look at me! You *hope* it's true, don't you?'

She shook her head with a troubled expression.

'I don't know what I hope, when you hammer at me so! Yes – yes – *yes,* I hope it's true! Does that satisfy you?'

'If you mean it,' he said simply, and for a second thought she would cry out again. But instead she only looked about her at the quiet glen as though she had never seen it before, as in one sense, the sense of an urgent emotion, she never had.

'I don't know what I mean. I just know I want something' –

193

she gave a lonely little half-sob – 'somebody – I can depend upon! That's all I want.'

'But that's what I want!' he said with a happy urgency, for now at last it all seemed to lie clear ahead, the pathway to this other beleaguered heart, to happiness for them both. 'Don't you see that, Eliza, don't you see how well we suit each other? We're both alone, we both need someone. What could be more perfect for us?'

But again, as he might have known, the crippling of the years was too much.

'Is that all it takes?' she asked with a sadly sceptical and disbelieving look. 'I may not have as – as much experience of – of – things – as you have, but even I know better than that. That would be too easy, and life isn't that easy.'

'Did Haila tell you that?' he demanded sharply, frustrated and dismayed by this recurring refusal to acknowledge and accept. She did not withdraw her hands or her now steady and candid gaze.

'Common sense tells me that,' he said quietly. 'Doesn't it you?'

'Common sense,' he said harshly. 'Common sense! What could anybody ever do in this world if all he listened to was common sense!'

'I think we'd better listen to it,' she said, 'or we'll get into something we might regret.'

'Get into what?' he asked scornfully. 'Bed?'

'That,' she said, without flinching, 'and other things. Into hurts and pains and things that can tear people apart if they don't watch out.'

'But look at what you can gain!' he protested, a growing anguish in his heart. 'Look at the love you can have! You can't get anything in this world without some risk, Eliza, God knows you can't.' He stopped abruptly and gave a bleak and hopeless sigh. 'Yet that seems to be what you want.'

'I've told you what I want,' she said, and her eyes began to fill again with tears. 'I just want someone who can – who can—' her voice trailed away.

'But, my dear,' he said softly, 'I *am* someone. *I* am someone. Why do you refuse me?'

'I don't know,' she said miserably, and now the tears began to come in earnest. 'I don't know. I don't even know that – that I do refuse you . . . for sure.'

'Well, then,' he said, and now the glen was very still around them, the sun was receding, first shadows were beginning to come, the only sound was a gentle whispering in the trees, 'well, then . . . If you don't refuse me . . . then you must accept . . . isn't that so, Eliza?'

Her hands still rested in his, she was making no attempt to stop the tears which once more descended full-tide. Then abruptly she did, yanking back her hands, dabbing furiously at her eyes with the soggy handkerchief he had given her, crying out in angry little muffled sobs as she did so.

'I'm such a mess, such a mess! Everything is so mixed-up!'

She stopped swabbing her eyes, the sobs diminished, she stared with a look of a thousand miles at the woods across the way, now beginning to fill up a little with the secret darkness where the Weendigo walks. He expected her to rise and leave, his heart was preparing itself to receive this last, to receive this last, most crushing blow. Suddenly she spoke.

'Shall we go – back there – behind the rock?'

'But—' he said, almost stammering in the astounded confusion that now swept over him, 'but – are you sure – are you sure you want—'

'I don't know,' she said with a woeful little sob, 'but I won't ever know, until I find out.'

The squirrels, mice and chipmunks left the glen, the mother quail and her chicks whistled quietly to one another for a bit and went to sleep. The bob-cat returned and bounded off again, the deer drifted through once more, the skunk, meticulous and dainty, hopped prissily by in a last search for grubs, the rattle-snake retired to his secret nest. The globe turned, afternoon plunged into dusk. Mountain coolness ended the lingering warmth of the golden day. Night claimed the world. A twig snapped, back in the forest, where the Weendigo walked.

'Well, well,' said Einar to Sally-Jane, peering out the Magruders' kitchen window at the wildly agitated figures of Mrs

Buxton and Mrs Townsend almost running down the road in the gathering dark. 'What's up with Lady MacBeth and Madame Defarge?'

'Sweetie,' said Louise to Jerry, pausing on their deck as she handed him a second martini, 'there goes little Gray. I wonder if he and Bill and Eliza would like to come to dinner?'

But little Gray hurried on by without answering her call and as for Bill and Eliza, they were nowhere to be found when Jerry ambled through camp a few minutes later, glass in hand, in search of them.

◆§ SIX §◆

Sometime around 10 a.m. he awoke, disturbed by some sound from the Buxtons', or a car droning by on the road, or children shouting, or some disturbance of nature striking at last through his drug-like sleep – he could not say what it was, and for several moments thereafter he could not say where he was. Then everything came flooding back, and with it a great happiness. The world was suddenly in place and all was well.

The reasons for this he could not exactly define, though he felt them to be unassailable. Surely it could not have been anything unduly exciting or perfect in all that frantic, awkward grappling on the pine-needles, for she had been too frightened and he too tense for it to be anything exceptional. Exceptional in its inadequacy, perhaps, notable for its failure to set the heavens alight and the mountains singing, filled with the sort of horribly humorous irony with which the act of love is so often filled when dream finally becomes reality at the wrong time in the wrong place under the wrong circumstances; nature's supreme wonder turned, as so often, into nature's little joke – often especially reserved for Americans, who think sex is the answer to everything. It had happened, and according to all the books he had ever read, he should now be walking on air, dancing on the clouds, leaping through the universe ten feet high – only this wasn't all the books. It was just odd little Elizavetta Berrenger and lonely little Bill Steele, a combination of modest hearts and easily-damaged hopes that the books somehow never took into account in all their clinical details and their naïvely romantic hymns to the infallible efficacy of proper techniques, properly applied.

So the proper techniques, which he did not need books to tell him, had not been properly applied in every detail; so hearts and hopes had become lost in the rush, bowled over by bodies that wouldn't wait for them to catch up; so awkwardness and earnestness and too much tension had made everything awkward and earnest and too tense; so they had flunked the exam. And out of it he had come loving Eliza and she, hopefully, had come loving him; and what did the books have to say about that? What the hell did the books have to say about that? he asked them with some exuberance as memory made his body tumescent again and he desired her with a consuming desire. Where did all this fit into their endlessly childish, endlessly romantic view of a world in which everything, supposedly, could be solved by the expert orgasm?

His and Eliza's hadn't been very expert, so desperate had been their coupling; yet far from dismaying him, this had only made him love her more. Now a great concern and kindness filled his thoughts, a great tenderness filled his heart. He wanted to cherish and protect her, he wanted to help her always. At last he had found someone to take care of: he knew it now beyond all doubt. And so sure was he that she felt the same way, so certain was he in his heart that she was what he needed her to be, that he was filled with a surging happiness as he rose and began to ready himself for the day.

He was indeed walking on air, dancing on clouds, leaping through the universe ten feet high – not because his union with his love had been perfect, but for a reason much more fundamental and important: because it had not.

Showered, shaved and ready for breakfast, he gave a shout for Gray, who did not answer. Coming into the kitchen he found a bowl and a milk glass standing in the sink, a box of cereal open on the table, some curious and puzzling sense of early and possibly hasty departure. For a second this disturbed him; then it was swept away in his happy mood. Probably the boy had rushed off to the Meadows for some engagement with his friends, no doubt he would see him later in the day. The major felt completely rested and ravenously hungry. He got a bowl and a couple of glasses, poured orange juice and milk, ate two helpings of cereal in rapid succession. Everything was perfect, the warmth of another gorgeous day was beginning to invest the beautiful canyon, nature and his mood conspired to fill him with a satisfaction so deep he thought he had never known anything to match it. He and his love were not on safe ground yet, he knew they had a journey to go before they reached snug harbour, but he was absolutely certain they were on their way. After so many months of unhappiness and uncertainty, this was enough to fill his heart to overflowing with love for the world and everything in it.

He was in the bedroom, whistling happily to himself and getting his gear together, when he heard a scamper of feet on the deck, the slam of a door, the slam of another, and once again the sound of crying from his housemate's room. What the hell, he wondered, his attention deflected momentarily from himself, his mood disturbed a little but not deeply concerned: now what? He stepped across the hall and rapped sharply on the door opposite.

'Hey, buddy! What's the matter in there?'

The crying ceased abruptly. A muffled voice said:

'*Go away!* I don't want to talk to you!'

He opened the door and stepped in. There was a convulsive movement on the bed, a pulling-up of blankets and hiding under the pillows as before.

'What is it?' he asked patiently, sitting on the bed. 'Better tell me all about it.'

'Don't want to tell you!' the voice said. And then abruptly, startling him out of his euphoria, 'I hate you!'

'Now, wait a minute,' he said sternly. 'Wait – a – minute. What do you mean, you hate me? What kind of nonsense is that?'

His charge sat up abruptly, throwing off the pillows and blankets. The major was genuinely shocked and now, suddenly, greatly disturbed, by what he saw. The boy's T-shirt was torn, one eye was beginning to turn black, and in his hand he clutched a bloody handkerchief with which he had been attempting, without too much success, to staunch the flow from his nose. The major whistled.

'Jiminy Christmas! Whatever happened to you?'

But there was no response of humour to his deliberately youthful expletive. Instead a troubling fright, a shattered and homeless faith, looked back at him from the reddened eyes. The only audible response was another deep sob.

'What's the matter, buddy?' he repeated softly. 'What's this all about?'

He was aware that the boy was staring at him as though he had never seen him before. A little fear began to rise in his heart.

'I said,' he repeated, more sharply than he would have without the spur of it, 'what is this all about? You must tell me, Gray, if I'm to help you. What is it?'

'I had a fight.'

'I can see that. Who with, and what about?'

'Tommy Rupert.'

'And what about? Not,' he said, and a growing dismay began to blight the beautiful morning, for he was sure of the answer already, 'about me?'

Gray gave him a long, slow, anguished look, then nodded.

'But why?' he asked, trying to make his voice reasonable and patient, though he had some difficulty with it since the dismay was becoming deeper as all sorts of wild imaginings crowded his mind, withering its happiness, destroying its calm. 'Why did you fight Tommy Rupert?'

'Because,' Gray said, his eyes if anything more frightened and more stricken than before. 'Just because!'

'That's a kid-reason, "just because",' the major said, trying, though he did not feel like it, to inject a little humour to drive back the demons that seemed to be coming nearer through the gorgeous day. 'And it doesn't go with the pact, either. Now tell me what—'

'There isn't any pact! The pact's all gone! There isn't any pact!'

'But,' he protested, 'but I thought—'

'There just isn't any pact,' the boy repeated, and suddenly a great sob welled up and tears started into his eyes again. 'You ruined it!'

'*I* ruined it?' he said, and now his dismay was almost comical, so taken aback was he by this unfounded accusation. 'How in hell did *I* ruin it?'

'You just did. You just did, and you know it!'

'Now, see here,' he said with a recurrence of sternness, for it

199

seemed the only way to bring some sanity back into the conversation – if a conversation with a twelve-year-old about a secret pact could be called sane. Except that it was sane, and, he now knew, desperately serious as well. 'Just see here. What *is* this all about? Why did you and Tommy Rupert fight, what did you fight about, and what has it got to do with the pact? I want you to tell me, Gray. I don't want any more nonsense, now. Out with it.'

The boy looked at him for a long moment and he had an impression of some forest thing trapped, frightened of him and equally frightened of the consequences of whatever move it might make. But finally Gray spoke, almost in a whisper.

'I fought him because – because—'

'Because what?' the major demanded sternly, and in a flash the boy was out of bed and standing by the door, ready to run.

'Because he said you did dirty things to Eliza!' he shouted. 'And I fought him, but it's true! I saw you, and it's true. It's true, it's true, it's true!'

And with a wild burst of renewed sobbing he slammed the door behind him before the major could move, and took off, down the hall, across the living-room, across the deck, down the stairs, out and away.

For some minutes thereafter the major hardly stirred, hardly thought. Very carefully, as though he were suffering from some grave injury, as indeed he was, he leaned back against the crumpled pillows at the head of the bed and rested there, staring straight before him without expression. He seemed to hear nothing, see nothing, feel nothing. It was as though the morning, once so bright and brilliant and full of happy hopes, had turned to an impenetrable wall through which he could not define the outlines of things and, in fact, had really no desire to define them. It was better, perhaps, to leave them as they were, muffled, obscured, mysterious and unclear: though they were not, of course, unclear. They were clear with a clarity that shattered his heart. They were clear in a way that hurt him as he had never been hurt before.

It was not surprising that he sat on, not wanting to move, not wanting to think, not daring, for a while, to let his mind contemplate what he must endure, when, as he knew he would presently have to do, he shored up his broken defences, put on whatever armour he could find for his lacerated feelings, and ventured forth up the sunny road to face Greenmont.

There came in due course a moment when he raised himself from his reclining position on the bed, managed to get to the bathroom where he dashed cold water in his face until his daze was at least partially broken, and then started slowly, with a sigh so profound it would have shocked him had he realized it, into the living-room to pick up his athletic gear and prepared to leave.

Even as he did so there was a sudden movement outside, a sudden crashing in the bushes and rustling in the leaves, the sound of youthful voices filled with a half-thrilled, half-frightened, deliciously excited amusement:

'Around the corner – and under the tree – The gallant major – made love to me!'

Now he knew what had awakened him. It came again as he stood absolutely still in the middle of the living-room, his tennis-racquet dragging on the floor, his golf-club aslant over one shoulder:

Around the corner – and under the tree – The gallant major – MADE LOVE TO ME!'

And a wild burst of giggles, quickly stilled; a scurry of feet; and silence, in the lovely day.

⌇ SEVEN ⌇

'Around the corner, and under the tree,' Einar sang cheerfully as he and Sally-Jane entered the Meadows, 'the gallant major made love to me. He kissed me once – he kissed me twice – ta-da-da-da-da – Ta-da-da-de-*dum* – And that was pre-tty nice!'

'Einar Magruder,' Sally-Jane said firmly, 'I want you to stop that, now. I've told you sixty-seven times it isn't funny, and it isn't. Now, stop it, hear?'

'But how can I get in the right mood if I don't sing a little mood-music? Now, look there,' he added, pointing to a corner of the pool where familiar figures were already gathered, something about their attitudes and postures indicating clearly that an argument was already in progress. 'Haila's obviously called a council of war and we're all going to get into it and raise hell.'

'I don't care what that old bitch has called,' Sally-Jane said with a snap in her eyes and a crackle in her voice. 'I want *you* to behave. Whose side are you on, anyway?'

'Oh, I'm on Bill's. And Eliza's – if Eliza is on Bill's, that is. Which is another matter. I don't see her anywhere, do you?'

'I should hope not! Why should anybody come down and face this pack of wolves?'

'I'll face them,' Einar said with relish, 'I'm one of them. Let me at 'em! . . . Good morning, all!' he called out merrily as they reached the pool. 'Everybody happy and bubbling this morning? *That's* nice!'

'Einar, lamb,' Louise remarked from her place on the concrete apron beside the dancing water, 'why don't you, for once, wait until you're spoken to? It might be better, this time.'

'Indeed it might!' Viola Townsend said, shifting herself indignantly on the bright blue air-mattress where she sat with Bob. 'I think we can do without your puppy-dog insolence this morning!'

'I believe we can,' Haila Buxton agreed, not even bothering to glance up from the beach towel she occupied with an air of calm assurance.

'Now, wait a minute,' Einar began, losing a good deal of his cheer, 'now, just wait *a* minute. What the—'

'Serious matters are under discussion here,' Haila observed, still not looking at him. 'It may be they are too profound for children.'

'Well, damn it!' Einar said angrily. 'Just who do you think—'

'I think we'd best all cool down,' Jim Buxton said mildly but with a note of authority so unexpected that it startled them into at least a momentary compliance. 'These girls don't mean to be rough on you, Einar, boy, but everybody is rather upset about what's happened and we are discussing it quite seriously. Anything you have to contribute of a constructive nature will be welcome. I can't see,' he added with a chuckle that attempted to break the tension, 'that the rest of us are making much progress so far.'

'Personally,' Jerry Drummond said, 'I think the whole thing is a tempest in a teapot. How come you and Viola know all

202

this anyway, Haila? Did you peek?'

'I am not accountable to you, Jerry Drummond,' she said, blushing a little but standing her ground. 'The facts are as we state them, and you know it.'

'Sure I know it, but my attitude is, what of it? They aren't the first people who ever had a little romp in the woods, even in Greenmont. Perfect though it is. Now, are they?'

'That isn't the point,' Viola said stiffly. 'There are standards in this world—'

'Oh, pfui!' Einar said, recovering his flying-speed a little as he and Sally-Jane spread beach towels and settled down. 'We aren't talking about standards here, we're talking about two human beings.'

'Well,' said Viola tartly, 'you and Sally-Jane should know.'

'And lay off me and Sally-Jane,' Einar said with a sudden ugly edge in his voice. 'We've just about had it, from you.'

'All right!' she said. 'All right! But there's something you should realize, both of you. I am *not* just a funny old woman. There *are* standards in this world. There *are* decencies that have to be observed if society is to hold together. It *is not right* for promiscuous love-making to go on all over the place—'

'Oh, Viola, stop it!' Jerry said. 'Cut it out! You make it sound as though we were holding a constant orgy up here all the time and you know very well we're not. This is all damned nonsense, for my book. I can't see why it matters if two grown people want to—'

'It matters because we have to have certain rules of behaviour if everything isn't to fall apart,' she said, red-faced and hard-pressed but sticking to it with a dogged honesty. 'It matters because there are children here, for one thing, and we can't have them exposed to this sort of thing before they have to face it. That's why it matters!'

'That's right,' Bob Townsend agreed. 'I do believe she's right on that, you know, Jerry.'

'Well,' Jerry said more slowly, 'you may have a point there, I'll grant you. But why do children have to know about it?'

'In Greenmont?' Louise inquired with an unamused smile. 'Oh, sweetie, come on! I'll bet Gray knows.'

'Gray knows,' Haila Buxton said grimly.

'Again I ask,' Jerry said, 'how do *you* know that, Haila? It

203

seems to me you've been keeping an awfully close watch on this whole thing. Anyway, Einar's right on one point. Let's don't forget there are two people involved here, and they've been hurt enough. If they can make each other happy, I say more power to 'em.'

'It isn't enough just to say that,' Haila told him. 'It would be nice if it were, but it isn't. There *are* standards, and all of us who are responsible have to see that they are observed. Whether that includes you or not, Jerry, you will have to be the judge.'

'Oh, will I?' he said, his tone sharpening despite Louise's hand on his arm. 'All right, I am. I say we've messed this thing up enough for them by hanging around them and watching everything they do and interfering all the time, and I say it's about time to leave them alone to do what seems best to them. Who are we to presume to get so high and mighty about it? That's what I want to know.'

'It has got beyond such easy philosophies,' Haila said, 'now that it has become a public scandal—'

'Because you made it so,' Jerry retorted. She shot him an angry look.

'Oh, I'm the one? I'm the only one. Well, well. You just said yourself all of us were involved. Very well, then. Let's keep on being involved until we've taken care of it as it should be taken care of.'

'Mrs Buxton, honey,' Sally-Jane suggested sweetly, 'have you all thought of talking to Eliza about this and seeing how she feels? Just maybe she doesn't want all this help from all of us any more. Maybe Bill doesn't either.'

'I am quite sure that what Bill wants or doesn't want is quite immaterial to me. He is a totally selfish and unfeeling individual, only out for what he can get with no regard or consideration for common decency or the feelings of anyone—'

Jerry snorted.

'A typical male, in other words: what bastards we all are. How do you know how he feels? Have you talked to him since yesterday?'

'I haven't talked to either one of them,' Haila said with dignity, 'but I know Eliza, as we all do, and I think most of us who have any perceptions have formed an impression of Bill in the

204

past week also. Mine is not favourable. Anyway,' she said with a sudden impatience, 'I have already consulted Mother Magruder about this' – Einar made a protesting movement but she went firmly on – 'and she and Viola and I have decided to act, even if the rest of you won't. She is going to mention it to the Board today, and Viola and I have already taken steps.'

'That has an ominous ring,' Jim said with an air of hopeful humour. 'Now, what might it be that you girls have done?'

'We told you the other night what we thought we would do,' Viola said. 'We did it.'

'Oh, no!' Jim said, genuinely dismayed. 'Surely you didn't!'

'Now, really,' Bob Townsend said with an equally unhappy expression. 'Now, I think that's a damned shame! I wish you'd consulted me, Vi. I really do.'

'What is it?' Louise demanded in alarm. 'What on earth have you two done, Haila?'

'Someone has to make decisions and do things,' Haila said firmly. 'There comes a time when talk does not suffice. We called Buck and Mary in Hawaii and told them we thought it would be best if they asked the major to leave. And we told them why.'

'Oh, my God,' Jerry said. 'My *God*. You're insane.'

'I am not insane. It is you who are insane to think Greenmont can sit idly by and allow a public spectacle to be made by a man with the morals of an alley-cat and the hide of a rhinoceros—'

'How nice,' Jerry said bitterly. 'How nice to be you and be perfect. God save *me* from such perfections.' He stood up abruptly. 'Louise, I'm going to play tennis. Are you coming with me?'

'No, I don't think so,' she said thoughtfully. 'I think I'll stay here and apply first-aid to Bill if he comes up to the Meadows. I think he's going to need it.'

'I think I'll stay with you,' Sally-Jane said.

'And I,' said Einar.

'I think you and I had better go and play golf, Bob,' Jim Buxton said soberly. 'I give up on this. I don't know what's going to happen now.'

'The only thing that can happen,' said Haila, unmoved, 'when one transgresses.'

'But these *are* people,' Jerry protested angrily, making one last attempt. 'You can't just crucify someone—'

'There he comes!' Viola interrupted excitedly. Her lips pursed in a prim disapproving line. 'And he doesn't look crucified to me. He looks very well satisfied with himself.'

'I suppose it would please you better if he were crawling,' Einar said harshly. 'That would be about your speed.'

'I'm going,' Viola announced, breathing hard with a combination of indignation and strain as she heaved herself up and turned towards the busy benches of the Grove. 'I shall leave you here with your – your *wastrel*!'

'Please do,' Einar said coldly. 'What about you, Mrs Buxton?' he demanded, rounding on her. 'Don't you think you'd better go, too?'

She gave him a look of serene contempt and put on her straw hat, her beach robe, her sandals and sun-glasses, with an air of great deliberation.

'I shall, you impertinent child. Eliza needs me and I am going to her. It is too bad the Magruder good breeding ran out in you, as I shall tell your mother.'

'I believe she knows,' Einar said, 'but I'm sure she'll be glad to have you confirm it.'

'I believe she does,' Haila said calmly, 'and I shall. Please, all of you, try not to give the major the feeling that everybody approves of him and everything is all right. We don't and it isn't.'

And, tall and angular, righteous and self-assured, she walked away.

'Christ!' said Einar. '*Christ!*'

'Yes, sweetie,' Louise said, 'it's all very well to say *Christ!* but the girls have a point, and you know it.'

'So do we have a point, damn it! You've got to have a little charity and compassion in this world. You can't always be forcing everybody into tight little patterns. They don't always fit.'

'You can't have too much of a rebel around, either,' she said thoughtfully. 'Viola's right on that.'

'Rebel! He hops into bed with Eliza, who's been dying for it for twenty years, we all do our best to push him into it, and then when he does—' He shook his head angrily. 'And all

206

because two old harpies went spying! How hypocritical can people get?'

'Lover,' Louise said, 'you're just beginning to find out. Wait a few years and maybe you'll begin to have a slight start on a small inkling of the full extent of it . . . . Well.' She made a gesture of dismissal. 'Here he comes and it's up to us to do what we can to put Humpty-Dumpty together again.'

'I'm not sure we can,' said Sally-Jane. 'Are you?'

'That,' said Louise, 'depends, I think, on Humpty-Dumpty.'

And they turned to stare across the teeming Meadows filled with life and laughter in the rollicking noon-time, perceptive and disturbed enough to realize that in the simple act of walking over a green lawn towards a swimming-pool they were seeing a fellow-being doing one of the bravest things he ever would do.

Again he saw them waiting for him – it seemed to his beleaguered mind that life in Greenmont was a series of recurring etchings, each generally similar to the one before, yet each cut a little more deeply by the acid of his mounting turmoil and unhappiness – and again he had the sensation that there was no one else in the world, that sight and sound were narrowed down to one tiny segment with all else excluded. To it he clung with a haggard determination as he approached them, deliberately refusing to hear or see anything else, the chattering voices in the Grove, the shouting frolickers in the pool, the crows of truimph or wails of sorrow from the golf course. It was true that he could not see them very distinctly, his eyes seemed to have a strange inability to focus as clearly as he would like, he was apparently looking at them, not directly, but with a painful sidelong glance from half-closed eyes as he came along. But such as they were, they were the only real friends he felt he had in Greenmont at that moment. To them he went with a desperate blindness, not knowing what their reception would be or what they would say, but feeling somehow that if he could just gain the other side of the pool where they sat he would have gained, however temporarily, some small haven from the world.

'Sit down, Bill,' Louise said kindly. 'You look bushed.'

He managed a weak and apologetic smile and dropped down beside Sally-Jane, who moved over for him with an encouraging

207

pat on the beach-towel.

'I am. I felt fine when I got up, but . . .' he passed a hand over his eyes – 'I feel tireder now . . . I'm glad to see you don't think I'm a leper, anyway.'

'Why, Bill, honey, what do you mean?' Sally-Jane began with a wide-eyed innocence. Then she gave an honest little frown. 'No. I won't be social and pretendy. We know what you mean. We don't think you're a leper. Some,' she added drily, 'do.'

'Apparently it's all over camp,' he said glumly.

'Or soon will be,' Einar agreed.

'And the ironic thing is – you won't believe this' – and he looked as though he did not know whether to laugh or cry – 'but the ironic thing is that I really and truly just thought we'd talk. I really did. I didn't have any – any plans. I'm not excusing myself, but it was – it was really quite a surprise to me. I didn't know she – that she'd – I only did it because she—'

'Maybe you'd better not go on,' Louise suggested. 'We get the picture and we'll keep it to ourselves. Because,' she added with a wry little smile, 'nobody in Greenmont would believe it if we told them, anyway.'

'Does anybody in Greenmont ever believe anything but what they want to believe?' he asked, with some revival of acerbity that seemed to break the cone of silence around him. Now he could hear the voices, the shoutings, the exuberant splashes from the pool, the whole glorious day pounding in suddenly with a curiously raucous insistence he had never seemed to notice before.

'Probably not,' Louise said. 'Which makes it tough. Tell me,' she said, lighting a cigarette and peering up at him with a candid glance, 'what comes next, in your plans?'

'I want to ask her to marry me.'

'Why?'

He gave her a glance equally candid, straight and direct.

'Whoever knows? Whoever really knows? Because I do, that's all.'

'Do you think she will?' Einar asked.

He looked off at the high peaks, stark and gleaming in the hot sun.

'I don't know.'

'She didn't give you any idea? I should think you'd—'

'I don't know,' he repeated with a sudden impatience. 'It wasn't exactly a debating society we were conducting at the time.'

'O.K., O.K. Take it easy. I didn't mean to—'

'You never mean anything,' he said with an abrupt bitterness he did not really mean to show them, but could not contain. 'You none of you ever mean anything. But somehow things happen, don't they?'

'Now, listen, sweetie—' Louise began. But he flared up, badgered beyond endurance by the unrelenting annoyance of things.

'Don't sweetie me, I don't like it.' Then his expression changed, he became remorseful at once at her half-hurt, half-angered look. 'I'm sorry, Louise. I apologize. I appreciate your friendship, I value your help, but somehow everything just – builds up. I don't mean to be rude.'

'Well,' she said, a little doubtfully, a little sharply, 'I hope not, because you're going to need all the resources you can find.'

'I think so, Bill, honey,' Sally-Jane said soberly. 'You don't want to get mad at the only – at the friends you've got.'

'Particularly,' Einar remarked thoughtfully, gazing over the rollicking Meadows, 'when the roof may be about to fall in.'

'What do you mean by that?' he said, outward scorn contending with the apprehension that rose suddenly in his heart. 'How could it more than it has, with everybody knowing?'

'Oh,' Louise said with a rueful smile, 'that isn't all the possibilities Greenmont can muster when it sets its mind to it.'

'What have you all done now?' he demanded with a sick dismay that could not be softened even by the knowledge that these really were his friends, that he must not alienate them or he would have no one. 'What on earth have you all done to me now?'

'We haven't *all* done anything,' Louise began, but he interrupted with a sudden almost frantic anger, beyond caution, beyond decency.

'What is it?' he demanded harshly. 'What is it in you people that makes you act this way? Why do you take such pleasure in hurting the stranger?'

'But—' Louise protested in almost comical indignation, 'but—'

209

'It isn't right,' he said, shaking his head in an harassed and baffled way, speaking almost as though to himself alone. 'It just isn't right.'

'Well, I'll be damned,' Einar said softly into the silence that followed. 'That's the kind of reward we get for being friends. Well, I'll be damned.'

'I don't know who's a friend and who isn't,' he said in a tired voice, not looking at them, staring blindly down the canyon misty and blue in the noon-time heat. 'And I don't know, any longer, that I care.'

'Bill, honey,' Sally-Jane said thoughtfully, 'I think you need rest. I really do, I think you need rest real bad.'

'I need to be let alone,' he said with a last flicker of wry unamusement. 'And, not knowing it, I came to a place where it just isn't possible.'

'Oh, hell,' Einar said. 'Where in hell is it? Do you know of any place? Inhabited place, I mean?'

But he did not answer, continuing to stare off down-canyon as though somewhere in its shimmering depths he would find the answer to whatever it was he sought.

'Well,' Louise said, standing up, 'I know you're under strain, Bill, and I know you'll think better of it later. Meantime, I guess I will play some tennis. I know Jerry doesn't really want to play with the Grossmans and they're about to trap him over there. Coming, competition?'

'Yes,' Einar said in a disgusted tone. 'I'll have to break away when my Ma comes to the Meadows and try to argue her out of talking to the Board – I still want to make *that* contribution – but there's no point in further conversation here.'

'Major, honey,' said Sally-Jane, gently reproving, 'you just don't know your friends, that's all.'

But again he did not answer as they arose and gathered their racquets and walked away to the courts leaving him alone by the pool in the midst of the darting, running, splashing, shouting, crying, laughing kids of Greenmont. He would have cursed himself for flaring up at them, except that he was too tired and too depressed to do it: he just couldn't seem to make the effort. His world was spinning ever faster towards some climax he could not foresee, though its half-hinted, half-guessed outlines were ominous enough in this perfectly peaceful, perfectly happy, perfectly secure little principality of playtime behind the mountains.

So lost was he in his musings that he did not notice that at the caretaker's cabin someone shouted at the kids, that one of them detached himself and went running across the bridge over the river, that he apparently received a message and then came running back to stand, panting and excited, before the major. It was not until the boy said breathlessly, 'Tommy Rupert, sir!' that he looked up with a sudden expression of annoyance.

'Yes?' he said sharply. 'What is it?'

'You're wanted on the telephone at the caretaker's cabin,' Tommy said. 'It's long distance!' he announced to the pool. 'All the way from Hawaii!'

'Thank you so much,' the major said, aware that the noise all around had abruptly diminished, that Greenmont was paying attention to him now with a care and intensity unmatched in his previous experience of its curious mass contemplation of the outlander. He got up, trying not to act awkward and self-conscious, knowing he was, hating himself for being so, hating them for making him so. Somehow he crossed the lawn and reached the telephone booth, stepped inside and closed the creaking glass door as tightly as it would go – not quite tightly enough, he could see, to shut out the sounds of the Meadow, or, conversely, to shut in conversation against the golfers who played alongside, the kids who darted past, the casual strollers who happened to pass near by.

'Hello?' he said, and he had to say it twice, for something seemed to be closing his throat, choking off his breath, cutting down his voice to half its normal volume. 'Hello, Buck, is that you?'

'Hey, there, boy!' a faint voice called, and even though the connection was not too good, there was a humming and the little tintinnabulations that accompany long-distance danced along the line, the salutation called up at once the manner too hearty and the face too red. 'How's it going, up there in our happy heaven? Everybody treating you right?'

'Pretty good,' he said, managing so speak more loudly, cupping his hand around the mouthpiece to shut his responses as much as possible away from near-by listeners. 'It's O.K. up here.'

211

'It is?' Buck shouted, and the major thought he could detect a curious and disturbing note of scepticism coming over the ocean. 'Well, how's Gray?'

'Just fine,' the major called back. 'How are you?'

'Oh, we're fine, too . . . So everything's O.K., eh?'

'Yes, it is. Why, do you hear anything different?'

There was a moment of silence before Buck replied, long enough for the major's heart to constrict painfully.

'Well, to tell you the truth, pal' – an excessive chuckle came across the Pacific – 'better watch yourself, there, boy! Those old biddies will talk!'

'What do you mean?' he demanded sharply, but Buck hardly seemed to notice his tone, so busy was he with his chuckles.

'I mean, pal, nobody minds a little hop in the hay even with dear old you-know-who, bless her silly heart, but – you have to be careful about these things, you know, particularly up there at camp. People will talk, you know, people *will* talk!'

'All right,' he said harshly, 'so people talk. So what about it?'

'Well – nothing, pal, except that it kind of puts us on the spot, you know. I mean – guest of ours rapes local beauty' – again there was a burst of chuckles – 'my God, boy, *Eliza*! How *could* you? – but, I mean, guest of ours does it, and it kicks up a storm, you know, and – well, they kind of expect us to do something about it, I guess.'

'What?' he demanded, still in the same harsh tone though his heart was pounding so fast he thought something fearful was about to happen to it. 'Do you want me to leave?'

'Well, hell, no! But you know how it is, pal, with Haila and Viola and Louise and all of them getting excited—'

'Is Louise excited? She didn't tell me.'

'Well, Haila said she is. Anyway, boy, whoever it is who's excited, they seem to have the whole damned camp pretty much in an uproar, and—'

'*Do you want me to leave?*' he repeated in a carefully level tone, though it cost him greatly to keep his voice from trembling.

Again there was silence.

'Why – hell, no, boy, that's too damned drastic. I refuse to do it. After all, it's your business and Eliza's. Except,' he added with a ruefulness that came clearly across three thousand miles, 'nobody's business is private, in Greenmont. But, hell, no, I'm damned if I'll do it! After all, it's your—'

'But you would prefer me to leave.'

'Well—' Buck said, and paused. 'No, God damn it, I'm damned if I would! After all, you're my old buddy, you know, and anyway, there's Gray – though I guess somebody could take care of him if you – but, no, now, I'm not saying *that*. We want you to do whatever you think is right. You do what you think is best, boy. You stay there and tell 'em to go to hell. After all, they aren't going to lift our membership for it, are they, now?' He gave a hearty laugh. 'You do just what you think is best.'

'Very well,' he said, his voice drained of emotion and feeling, exhausted and, finally, defeated. 'I'll leave as soon as I can get packed. I'll ask Louise to keep Gray. Enjoy the rest of your visit.'

'No, now wait, boy!' Buck cried vehemently from the distant shore, the green and lovely island, 'now, I didn't say – oh, now, God damn it, I don't think that's right, that you should have to – that we should have to ask you – that you should be forced to – just because some old biddies – just because—'

'Good-bye, Buck. Thanks for the use of the cabin.'

'Oh, damn it!' Buck cried. 'I think that's unfair, now, I really do. I think that's God damned unf—'

'This has cost you a mint,' the major said, removing his ear from the receiver, cutting off the still loudly protesting voice, the hearty reiterated regrets, the voluble, relieved concern. 'Good-bye.'

He came out of the phone booth and for several minutes stood unmoving in the sun, oblivious to all the busy life of the Meadows as it swirled about him. Presently things began to focus again, he looked towards the courts where the others were now busily romping about in their customary noisy game. For a moment he considered going to them, then rejected it: they were enemies too, now, strangers to a stranger who had finally given up his attempts to penetrate their all-knowing, self-centred, self-preoccupied little world. He heard the gossip diminish in the Grove, the shoutings soften in the pool: he knew he was again the centre of Greenmont's attention but he did not

213

care. There was only one thing left to do before he left this pleasant paradise to which he had been unable to find the key, and with a heavy sigh but a still hopeful heart he left the Meadows and started up the road to do it.

At the point where the path turned off to old Mr Stafford's and the Mineral Springs he saw approaching down the road the rolling gait and monumental bulk of Mother Magruder. The sharp little eyes set deep in their buckets of fat gave him a quick and hostile glance, the narrow little mouth opened for some stinging comment, but before she could say it he forestalled her.

'Try to do as much harm as possible today,' he called, and as he passed he heard the raucous and malicious cackle.

'Get out!' she cried in a voice filled with a spiteful relish. 'Just go on and leave, and Greenmont will be happy!'

He did not reply and behind him the spiteful squawk welled up again from amid the mountainous flesh.

He shuddered and went on.

At the Berrenger cabin all was silent as he approached. The river rushed along through the cavern of the trees, the sun filtered down in light and shadow, a few birds called sleepily: no human disturbance broke the mood of mountain noon. A terrible dismay shot through his heart. Surely she had not left, fled from Greenmont without a word – surely she would not desert him, now that they stood at last on the threshold of their life together. Surely for her, too, their union, however awkward, had opened the way to peace and happiness! A door opened, Smudge hurled himself yapping against the screen. Haila Buxton stood inside, managing to look dignified and stately despite beach-robe and sandals.

'Where is she?' he said loudly, though again his breath constricted, his heart began to hammer, a dreadful tension dragged upon his being.

'I do not believe,' she said, perfectly calm, perfectly poised, 'that that is, or should be, any concern of yours.'

'Oh, don't you! Well, it is. Now, where is she? *Where is she?*'

'You needn't shout,' she said quietly. 'I am right here. Furthermore, there are neighbours, right over there. I should think you would feel you had made a sufficient spectacle of yourself in the eyes of Greenmont, already.'

He shook his head with an air of disbelief.

'You are fantastic. Did God appoint you guardian of everybody, or did you just volunteer for the job? Now, I want you to tell me if Elizavetta Berrenger is in this house. If you won't tell me, I shall come in and look. In fact' – and he half-started up the steps towards her – 'I think I may do that, anyway.'

'And what shall I do, you ridiculous man?' she inquired, not retreating an inch. 'Scream for help? Wouldn't that be a nice spectacle for camp to see? Major,' she said, and suddenly her tone was cold and matter-of-fact, 'if you do not want to be taken out of here by the police, you will stop this nonsense at once and leave.'

'Nonsense! *Nonsense?* Our lives are nonsense, in your view? How can you say such a thing?'

'I can say it because it is the truth. Everything I have said throughout this whole sorry episode has been the truth.'

'As you see it,' he said bitterly. She laughed, without amusement.

'How else is truth ever defined? Yes, as I see it. And as Greenmont sees it. And now, finally, I think, as Elizavetta sees it too. So, Major, I think you had better abandon this fantasy and leave us, now.' She put a hand up and adjusted her already perfect hair. 'We aren't stupid people here in camp, you know, whatever else you may think of us. All of us have reached this judgment, though we began by being your friends. You have made it impossible for us to continue on that basis, and now there is nothing left for you here.'

'I have made it impossible?' he asked in a wondering voice. '*I* have made it impossible? How can you have the monumental gall to say such a thing?'

'I know,' she said calmly, 'that it is sometimes hard for people who are emotionally involved to see themselves in a given situation as others see them. Particularly people in your' – she hesitated for a moment and chose her word with delicate care – 'disturbed condition. So it is understandable. It does not make it forgivable,' she gave a coldly tolerant little smile, 'but it makes it understandable.'

'I must see Eliza,' he said with a desperate calm, fighting down blind anger, mastering himself in a great internal battle.

215

'With your permission – "permission", for God's sake! – or without it. You will open the door, or I will come through it. And Haila, darling,' he said quietly, 'I don't give a good God damn if you scream your fool head off. I am coming in, for reasons you will never understand if you go on devastating the world around you until you are a hundred and one.'

'You spare yourself nothing, do you?' she said, paling a little but otherwise showing no alarm. 'What is your conception of this, you fantastic being? Is it your idea that I am holding her prisoner? Do you think she wants to see you and I am not letting her? How on earth could I do that to a grown woman? She doesn't *want* to see you. She doesn't *want* you around. Major, believe me, *she does not want you.*'

'I don't believe it,' he said in a ragged voice, though his mind was suddenly not so sure, his heart was beginning to pick up an erratic and sickening rhythm. 'I don't believe it.'

'Very well,' she said, and even in such a moment he was almost able to offer some jape at her obvious theatricality, the dramatic way in which she drew back from the doorway and left it momentarily vacant. 'Ask her, then!'

But he did not, of course, ask anything, so shattered was he by swirling emotions, so unable to form words for which there might be no meanings, express meanings for which there might be no words.

Enormous, red from weeping, filled with things that could have meant everything, or, equally easily, nothing, the dark eyes stared out at him from behind the screen as though disembodied in the cool shadowed depths of the cabin. Their message must be one of rejection, for that was what Haila said it was, and no words of contradiction came from Eliza. Yet for several moments he remained so, staring with a terrible desperation as though by this look he could force her to break the fearful silence that held them. Finally he broke it himself, with a strangled sound that was half-voice, half-croak:

'Elizavetta . . . *Eliza!*'

But she only continued to stare in silence until at last, flinging her hands to her eyes and letting out a single tearing sob, she turned blindly and disappeared.

'And now, I think,' Haila Buxton said, closing the door with a slow finality in his face, 'everybody has been hurt enough.'

Again life in Greenmont repeated its small, familiar patterns; again he found himself, not knowing how he got there, at the Mineral Springs; again it seemed to him that in the roiling waters as they raced across the ancient rocks he might be drawn to his death if some miracle did not save him: and now no miracle would. Once more he sat upon a boulder above a deep green pool tossing pebbles at the flirting fish; once more a water-ouzel bobbed and busted in the icy stream. But where before he had told himself that he had no defences and had been playing games in the telling, this time he had no defences and it was no game. Where before he had in some curious fashion half-pretended an unhappiness he knew instinctively would lift, now he knew there was no pretending, it would not lift. His mind was numb, his heart crushed. Through his being there flooded the knowledge that all men have but most manage to live with sufficient for the working day: the instinctive, implacable comprehension of the endless sadness of things . . .

This time he knew he could not escape it.

If there had been some response from her, some indication, some little sign, however small, upon which to hang a shred of hope, then it might be different. There had been none. He could see again those dark, enormous eyes, filled – or empty – with things he could neither fathom nor determine. They had told him nothing. She had permitted Haila to talk for her and in so doing had acquiesced in Haila's harsh dismissal. He had come to her for help and she had given him nothing. Once more he had been rejected, and this time by a heart as kind and decent as any – but so afraid. So afraid! He had tried to tell it not to be, but years of habit could not be overcome. It cowered in its cabin like a woods-thing, hiding behind Haila's pompously self-righteous figure, buttressed in its panic by all the prying eyes and gossiping tongues of Greenmont. He had contested with Greenmont for it and Greenmont had won. The battle was over and nothing was left for him now.

Not only was nothing left for him here, but what was left for him anywhere? He had tried as best he could to make some sense of the world, to convince it that his was a loving heart that asked only love and the chance to give love in return. The world had not believed him. It had not cared to accept his generosity. It had said: Some understand love and give and receive it without difficulty, but your road is not so simple. Your road has many turnings and you may not find your way. You may never find your way. You may always walk alone, seeking surcease you will never achieve, your naïvely trusting hopes made a mockery, the gifts you would bring to others dashed to the dust. Why continue on your road, which apparently leads, always and for ever, nowhere?

In a last desperate attempt to restore some sanity to the crumbling universe he tried to tell himself that if this were six months from now, if more time had intervened to deaden the anguish of his divorce, he would not be feeling so terribly what he was feeling now, it would not matter so dreadfully to him, he could survive it better.

The attempt did not work. It was not six months from now, he did feel it dreadfully, and he was not sure, at this moment, that he could survive it at all.

How long he sat there staring at the plunging waters he did not know, or when it was that he became conscious of the water-ouzel as it danced and dodged and ducked along the stream-bed; but presently his mind began to play a little game with it, and so intently did he become engaged, so desperately important did it begin to seem to him, that he did not even hear Gray's approach or know that he was there until a small voice said at his elbow:

'I'm sorry.'

'What?' he asked dully; and then, as he looked around and down at the small figure trembling beside him on the rock, 'Oh ... That's all right, buddy. It doesn't matter.'

'But it does matter!' the boy insisted, frightened by his absent air, his tone of really not caring, about this or anything. 'I got scared and did an awful thing. I hurt you, and you're my friend.' His eyes widened with a pain he was just discovering but would know more of. 'I don't mean to hurt my friends.'

'I don't either, buddy,' the major said in the same sad voice, 'but somehow it just – happens to people, in this world. Look!' he said, nodding across the stream. 'There he goes again!'

'What?' Gray asked, startled, seeing squirrels, jays, a chipmunk on a branch. 'I don't see what—'

'The water-ouzel,' the major said as the little brown bird

teetered and bounced and prepared once more to plunge beneath the surface. 'I have a little bet with him, buddy. I've been betting that if he gets from that big rock over there to that big rock over there, under water, then maybe I'll find – maybe I'll find someone who will – who will—' His voice trailed away and it was apparent to the boy that some devastating struggle was going on inside.

'But he never does!' the major cried in a strangled voice. *'God damn it, he never does!'*

And quite suddenly, frightening Gray terribly, he clenched his fists and began to cry, great savage sobs that shook him violently as he sat upon the cold bare stone, his body rocking back and forth a little, rigid and unyielding in every line except for the convulsions of pain he could not control, that shook it as he wept.

'Oh, don't,' Gray said desperately. 'Oh, please don't! I didn't mean to hurt you, honest I didn't! You're my friend. Honest I didn't!'

But the major was unable to speak, though he attempted to nod his head in a way to indicate that it was all right. The terrible sobs went on and ran their course, while the river plunged and gurgled and chuckled along at their feet, the dappled sunlight grew ever warmer in the heat of noon, and the water-ouzel, satiated at last with the grubs it had found along the bottom, darted away downstream.

At last he stopped, exhausted, surprised to find that no one had come, since it had seemed to him that his sobs had been great shouts; surprised to find that Gray was still crouched terrified beside him. He put out a tentative hand and touched the boy's head.

'I'm sorry, buddy,' he said in the husky whisper which was all his tortured throat could muster at the moment. 'I didn't mean to make such a spectacle of myself . . . You didn't do anything.'

'Yes, I did,' Gray began with a miserable honesty, but the major shook his head.

'No, you didn't. Or if you did, I know you didn't mean it. Some people do, but you don't . . . Now,' he said, more firmly, 'I want you to promise me something. I'm going down to the Valley this afternoon—'

'Why?' Gray cried. 'You aren't going for good?'

'I'm afraid I must.'

'But why?' Gray demanded in dismay. '*Why?*'

For a second the major looked as though he would break down again, but after a moment he went on.

'Because, buddy, people up here think I should. Greenmont doesn't like me, and Eliza—'

'She likes you! She does too!'

'No, I don't think so. I don't think so. Anyway, if she does, she – doesn't know how to show it, and so it's best for both of us that I go. It'll be best for you, too, buddy, I think. You shouldn't have to be involved in – things like this – at your age.'

'I'm twelve!' Gray said stoutly. The major managed a shred of smile and tousled his hair.

'So you are, and a good troop, too. I hope you'll always be on my side, even if – if we don't ever see each other again.'

'But you'll come back,' Gray said. 'You've got to come back!'

'To Greenmont?' the major said with a weary little attempt at a laugh. 'No, buddy, I don't think so ... Now, you can stay with Mrs Drummond and she'll take care of you until your folks get home. You tell her I said so and she won't mind. O.K.?'

'I don't want you to go!' Gray said desperately. 'I don't want you to go!'

'I don't want to go, buddy,' the major said quietly, 'but sometimes grown-ups have to do things they don't like.'

'I hate grown-ups!' Gray said. 'They mess everything up!'

'They do, rather,' the major agreed, 'so that's why I want you to promise me something. When you get to be one, I want you to promise me that you'll try to be kind to people. You won't always make it, and it won't always get you anywhere, but – you try. For me. O.K.?'

And he looked again very hard at the turbulent water because he did not trust himself to look at the small stricken face beside him.

'O.K.,' Gray said, so low it was hardly audible. 'I'll try.'

'Good,' the major said, holding out his hand. 'Now, you run along and play and stay away from the cabin for a while so I can pack. I'll try to be out of there by the time you come back.'

'But I don't want you to go,' Gray cried desperately again,

clinging to his hand. 'I don't want you—'

'Please, buddy,' the major said, disengaging himself gently. 'It's the pact. Be brave, now, and just – run along. I'll write to you some time.'

'But—' Gray said in a desolate voice. 'But—'

'I'm not going to talk any more,' the major said, turning back and concentrating intently once again upon the racing stream. 'I'm going to watch the river. You go have fun.'

And after a little the boy obeyed, his last view of his house-guest that of a hunched, tightly controlled figure sitting on a rock by the water, looking as though it would never move again, so rigid and wounded were the lines of the body curved protectively against some unseen terrible blow at the hands of some unseen but dreadful adversary.

In the Meadows all was life and laughter as the boy ran by. Abruptly he stopped and stared for a long moment at the happy golfers on the green, the shouting frolickers in the pool, the noisy players on the tennis courts, the comfortable gossipers in the Grove, all the bright felicitous scene so gay and carefree in the sun.

'I hate you!' he cried suddenly in a high, anguished voice. 'I hate you!'

'What's got into little Gray?' Bob Townsend inquired blankly on the seventh tee.

'I don't know,' Jim Buxton said, though something in his voice and eyes indicated that perhaps he did. 'Your putt, isn't it?'

⋐ NINE ⋑

'Honey,' Sally-Jane said half an hour later as they finished their peanut butter sandwiches and milk in a relatively quiet corner of the Magruders' strident porch, 'I'm worried about something.'

Einar nodded.

'Me too. Want to go find him?'

'I think we'd better.'

At the MacAleer cabin they did, having checked the Mineral Springs, made a quick survey of the Meadows, and received from Haila Buxton, whom they overtook walking slowly down the road, a terse but triumphant review of the episode at Eliza's.

'I'd like to tell you what I think of that,' Einar said, 'but I haven't got the time to waste on someone so – so—'

'Neither have I,' said Haila calmly, 'so save yourself.'

'I guess with you around one has to!' Einar snapped. Sally-Jane placed a hand on his arm.

'Honey,' she said firmly, 'that really is beside the point, right now. Bill needs us, I'm sure he does. Come on, now.'

'Perhaps you can lend him a key to the gate,' Haila suggested as they brushed on by. 'I don't believe he has one.'

But this was one of the few things in which she was mistaken, for he did. It lay in his palm as he looked at it, pausing for a moment in his packing in the silent cabin. It let you in and it let you out, but it did nothing for you while you were there. MEMBERS ONLY, the sign said. If there was a key to that, he had not found it.

Now he was almost finished, finished with his packing, finished with the cabin, finished with his sorry 'vacation', finished with Greenmont. What else he might be finished with he could not say, though some deep and ominous burden seemed to hang over the somnolent afternoon, dulling his thoughts, dragging on his body, making him feel heartsick, mind-sapped, bone-weary, all together. He moved like an automaton through the deserted rooms. The Weendigo was not supposed to walk in daylight, but he felt its presence now. He was almost ready for it, now that all his earnest, loving naïve hopes had been destroyed so completely in this sheltered, pleasant place.

He was in the bedroom when he heard footsteps on the deck. His first instinct was to hide. But his car stood at the foot of the steps below, his suitcases and duffle-bag were open in the living-room, the books he had not had time nor energy to read were still piled upon the table. Obviously he could not escape, though he dreaded having to face any at all of the peculiar, helpful-unhelpful, encouraging-discouraging, kindly-hurtful, mixed-up people of Greenmont who had taken his mixed-up

222

heart and made it ten times more so in the space of a week.

You have killed me inside, he told them silently in his mind: go away and let me rest.

But it was obvious in a second that they were not about to, and when he heard their voices he relaxed just a little, though his weary defensiveness did not decrease. At least these two had tried, according to their lights, to be genuinely friendly. Perhaps they would let him get away with only a little more bruising.

'Bill, honey!' Sally-Jane called in a dismayed voice from the living-room. 'You aren't going down, now, for sure? Why are you going to do that, now?'

'What's the matter, pal?' Einar called in a voice he tried to make sufficiently hearty and unconcerned, though a genuine worry sounded through. 'Can't we do something to help?'

For just a second he was moved to make the same retort he had before to these cheery offers of help which was no help, concern which was concern only for that which would make the most delicious item of gossip in the Grove. But with an exhausted sadness he refrained. What good did it do, any longer, to show up their pretences? No doubt they were convinced of their own good-heartedness; why try to expose their belief in it for the fraud it was? It was all over now, it did not matter.

'I'll be out of the way in a few minutes,' he said quietly, coming into the living-room with a final armload of clothing, putting it in a suitcase, snapping it shut.

'But, *Bill*,' Sally-Jane protested, sitting down on the raised stone hearth, crossing her legs and leaning forward, chin on hand, too earnest to be conscious of how pretty she looked. *'Why?'*

'Why?' he echoed, and despite the fearful weight that seemed to be pressing down upon his head and body, some slight ghost of asperity tinged his tone. 'My God, you ask me why? How can you?'

'Now, look, pal,' Einar said, trying to sound reasonable and suddenly sounding very young, 'I think you're getting it all wrong, here. I think you're taking this too much to heart. I think...' His voice trailed away at the major's look of disbelief and saddened scorn. 'Well,' he began again, 'I'll admit a few people up here have been pretty tough on you, but we haven't, now, have we? And Louise and Jerry haven't, either. And,' he finished abruptly, 'we don't want you to leave, damn it.'

'That's right, Bill,' Sally-Jane said softly. 'We want you to stick it out.'

He sat down abruptly on the lumpy old leather sofa. He gave a weary smile, so bleak it touched them greatly.

'Now I'll say, why? Why should I? Has Greenmont done anything but hurt me?'

'Greenmont—' Einar said. 'Greenmont is funny. You have to understand it, and I guess sometimes that's hard for an outsider to do. It has its bastards and it has its problems and it gossips too much, and all that, but it also has some wonderful people in it, and we have some wonderful times up here, it's so peaceful and relaxing' – again the major gave him a look – 'yes, it is too,' he said firmly, 'it is wonderfully peaceful and relaxing, and it has a sort of – of family feeling about it that's wonderful, over the years. I mean, we keep coming back, year after year, and after a while that builds up something that – well, it doesn't *matter* if people here are bastards sometimes, they're just – people, that's all. They're friends. I mean, you forgive them and forget it, and we all go on together, and we know each other, and we understand each other, and – and that's how it is. I know it's hard to describe, but if you've known since the age of three how the people around you are going to react, and if you've all grown up together and have very few secrets left from each other, well, then – it makes life *solid,* somehow. It means there's one place in the world that you can always come back to that doesn't change, when God knows everything else is … So we forgive Greenmont a lot, for what it does for us … Of course,' he admitted, his voice becoming more rueful, 'I guess it can be pretty hard sometimes on a stranger.'

'It was hard on me,' Sally-Jane said quietly, 'and I haven't forgotten it or forgiven it, Einar Magruder, even if you have. It's no fun being an outsider if this place turns against you. I'm not impressed by Dear Old Greenmont. But I am impressed by the argument that there are decent people everywhere, including here, and I think Bill should be too. Some of them are still his friends and want to help him. So I hope he'll stay … Maybe,' she said, and a little twinkle broke through her seriousness, 'maybe I'm getting loyal to Greenmont too, in spite of my talk.

I really don't want him to go away thinking badly of us.'

The major gave a tired little smile and shook his head.

'If charm could do it, I think you two could almost persuade me. But it isn't all that simple or easy. I can see it's relaxing and pleasant in some ways, yes, but to me it's been prying and hurtful. And,' he said, standing up with an air of finality, 'it's beaten me and I can't fight it any more, and I've got to go.'

'Does Eliza want you to go?' Einar asked. An expression of remembrance and pain came into the major's eyes.

'Apparently so. She had the chance, and she didn't say anything.'

'Maybe Greenmont was too much for her,' Einar said, and then realized what he was saying and added hastily, 'But that doesn't mean—'

'It means all it has to mean to kill it,' the major said. 'What more does it have to mean?'

'I'm sure Eliza will think differently about it in a day or two,' Sally-Jane said. 'Give her a little time to think it over and it will be all right.'

'I need her now,' the major said simply. 'And she isn't here.' His voice sank to a hurt, baffled whisper, and he spoke to himself as though they weren't even in the room. 'She just isn't here.'

'But—' Einar began, and then his voice died too.

'If you'll excuse me,' the major said, 'I've got to finish packing and go down. To somewhere.' He gave a bitter little smile. 'I don't know exactly where, but – somewhere . . .'

Einar and Sally-Jane exchanged a quick glance.

'I think,' Einar said, 'that I'll help you finish packing and then we'll follow along down to the Valley with you.'

The major stopped abruptly with a strange expression of annoyance and anger and something else they could not define.

'Why?' he asked sharply. 'I'm not going to commit suicide, or anything.'

'You might,' Sally-Jane said, making her tone deliberately unimpressed by his vehemence. 'You're not in a very good mood, right now.'

'People with less cause than you have driven over that grade,' Einar observed. 'All *they* had was one drink too many. Nobody's ever been killed, but—'

'This is silly,' the major said harshly. 'Absolutely silly. And

225

it's also an invasion of my privacy. God damn it, will you people up here never learn that people have a right to *privacy*? Now, leave me alone! *Just leave me alone!'*

'We're not going to leave you alone, so God damn it yourself, *be quiet!'* Einar said loudly. 'We're at least going to follow you down to Big Smith and see that you get off properly from there. So, *shut up!'*

For several moments they stared at one another with a naked hostility while outside the afternoon hummed quietly along towards its zenith in the drowsy canyon air and somewhere a dog barked, off among the pines.

'Now,' Einar said, breathing hard but managing to speak more reasonably, 'where do you want those books, in the other suitcase?'

'That's obvious,' the major said shortly, turning away and starting to put some of them in himself. 'Where else would they go?'

'Well,' said Sally-Jane as Einar smoothly negotiated a hairpin turn, the major's car moving steadily forward one curve below,

'I think that's a real good idea,' she said, 'I really do. I know Smith. *I* sure need one!'

'Lord, yes,' her husband agreed. 'I also hope we can persuade him to come back. I'd like to invite him up again in a few weeks when everything's quieted down, and see if it doesn't work out all right with Eliza then. We can't have him at our place, Ma would never stand for it, but maybe Jerry and Louise—'

'I think that's a real good idea,' she said, 'I really do. I know they'll go for it. Let's go up to their cabin tonight when we get back and talk it over.'

'You see?' Einar said wryly. 'We *are* nice people. Why can't he get it through his head?'

'You are, anyway,' she said, snuggling closer while the cars twisted and turned and hairpins multiplied on hairpins.

'Thank you,' he said, taking her hand and squeezing it hastily before returning his own to the wheel. 'I'm glad my services are appreciated.'

He glanced at her with a quick grin, and even as he did so

saw her eyes, which had never left the major's car, widen suddenly. His own swung back instinctively to the road as she gave a little gasp.

'Honey,' she said swiftly in the clear, practical tone he had already learned meant *Step lively*, 'I do believe Bill is going over the grade.'

'Oh, my God!' he cried, tromping on the gas and swerving his own car dangerously on the next turn in an attempt to catch up. 'Bill! *Bill!*'

But nothing stopped the forward lunge of the car ahead. With a sickening screech of scraping branches along its sides it shot over the edge and disappeared with a crash in the trees below.

❧ TEN ❧

'I think he looks pretty good,' Gray said seriously somewhere off in a fuzzy distance.

'Oh, so do I!' Elizavetta agreed fervently from the same far region.

'I think it's much better,' Haila Buxton remarked, somewhat closer, '*much* better, that he be right here where his friends can help him, rather than down in Big Smith where he would be all alone. I think we've made much the best decision.'

'I do, too,' Viola Townsend said, comfortably. 'You can cook for him right here, and Eliza and Louise and I can come and take turns sitting with him, and everything will be all right in no time.'

'I guess you gals have it all figured out, don't you?' Jim Buxton said with a comfortable chuckle.

'They always do,' Bob Townsend agreed heartily.

'You can say that again,' Einar said drily, and somewhere off in the background Louise and Sally-Jane and Jerry said in a low, sardonic chorus, perhaps a trifle hysterical with relief, '*Yeayyyyy*, brother!'

And somewhere inside, through a wild amalgam of pain and amusement as though all the world were at one and the same time fiercely hilarious and utterly insane, his mind struggled up out of blackness to suggest to his body that it check a few aches here and there: found nothing insurmountable: and then sank

227

back into blackness for a while. But not before it gave him a tired, ironic message.

You couldn't even do that, it remarked before he drifted off again; you couldn't even do that.

And, so here you are with your friends in Greenmont again. Whatever made you think you could escape?

THREE

For three days and nights he slept, coming vaguely half-awake only at far-spaced intervals to hear about him the relieved, complacent voices of his friends, his pummelled body conspiring with his exhausted mind and heart to force quiescence until nature could repair him.

When this was accomplished he awoke.

A wry amusement took dominion of his mind. With it was a curious light-heartedness. He was aware of everything but no longer shattered by it. Desperation and despair seemed to have been lost over the grade. In one searing instant he had evidently recaptured common sense.

The world appeared to be back in place.

For this he congratulated himself with a secret satisfaction, indicated only by a pleased little smile about his eyes, of self-irony and self-humour. Where were all the storms and tempests of a week ago? Who was that who had fought with Haila, been devastated by the silence of Elizavetta, cried before Gray at the Soda Springs, sent his car in one wild, insane, not-really-meant moment over the mountainside to come to rest with a sickening crash against an impervious redwood, damaging the car considerably, his body considerably less, and freeing instantly, in some strange and inexplicable reason, his sad, uneasy heart?

Surely that had not been Bob Steele – 'You remember Major Steele from Fresno, dear. But, of course, *you* would!' – surely not good old, troubled old, mixed-up, loveless Bill Steele from the Valley!

That was someone else, he told himself with a pleased inward excitement; that was some other wayfarer through Greenmont, not this confident and steady being, once more in command of himself, who lay here on the sofa in the MacAleers' living-room while Haila Buxton busied herself in the kitchen cooking his first real lunch since the accident.

That so desirable a result should have come from so impulsive and chaotic a moment was, he told himself as he watched the soup being heated, the hot tea briskly prepared, the ice cream portioned out with a firmly efficient hand, just one more of those ironies he was apparently fated to meet as long as he remained at Greenmont. That he would remain, now, until Buck and Mary returned, he had no doubt; that he would in all probability return often to this pleasantly peculiar, peculiarly pleasant place, he was equally sure. Buck and Mary would invite him back, Louise and Jerry would do the same; even Mother Magruder might relent and allow Einar and Sally-Jane to have him in the house. He might even – and this almost made him laugh aloud – he might even buy a cabin himself some day, if one became available and he could persuade Greenmont not to blackball him. Such was the nature of this chameleon-like place, with its long-standing feuds and its unpredictable affections, that it might well take him to its heart for ever now that he had proved he really meant it. Maybe that was the key to all this kindness he now found himself overwhelmed with as he came back to a full awareness of the world: now they knew he had really meant it . . . It hadn't all been a game, after all.

'Haila,' he called out in a shaky but confident voice that startled her so that she dropped a spoon with a clatter on the soapstone sink, 'do *you* think I really meant it?'

'Meant what, dear?' she inquired in a solicitous tone as she turned towards him, looking, he noted, as calm and self-assured as ever. 'Goodness, you surprised me! The doctor said you would be coming back to us any minute now, but still it's quite a surprise. Welcome to Greenmont!'

And she gave a merry laugh, perfectly comfortable, perfectly friendly.

'Yes,' he said, and a slight irony edged his increasingly stronger voice, 'welcome to Greenmont, indeed. What I mean is, do you think I really meant it about Eliza – and all that?'

'Why, of course, dear. Of course! I don't think anybody has any doubts about it at all.'

'Mmmmmm,' he said. 'That's quite a change, isn't it?'

'Why, I don't know, dear,' she said thoughtfully. 'I don't think *I* ever doubted it, even when – even when I felt it best that – well, that— But, there, you naughty boy!' she cried with another jolly explosion. 'The doctor *said* you'd probably want to start taxing yourself by talking too much right away. He said you shouldn't do it. We must obey the doctor, you know! Now, dear,' she said, abruptly serious, 'tell me how you feel. Are the

232

aches and pains still there, or are they beginning to go?'

'I feel fine, Haila,' he said, a trifle drily. 'Outside and in, too ... If that's O.K.,' he added with a sudden cheerful grin that he hoped would catch her off balance, but of course it didn't. The only difference was that now he no longer seemed to mind.

She chuckled.

'Why of course it's O.K., you foolish boy! It's marvellous news ... Now, let me see,' she suggested like a school-teacher with a slightly recalcitrant but well-loved pupil. 'Let's see you move the arms, one by one ... that's right. And now lift the legs, one by one ... that's right! And no pains, honestly, now, nothing in the back or the neck or the head or the tummy or anywhere?'

'Not *anywhere*,' he assured her with another grin. She smiled back with complete approval.

'Well, I am so glad. So *glad*. And everyone else will be too. I'll go up after lunch and spread the word in the Meadows, and before you know it we'll have seventeen-eleven people down here paying you visits. *Everybody* has been *so* interested.'

'I'll bet. Where is everybody?'

'Well, of course you know it's Thursday – but of course you *don't* know it's Thursday – and so most people are down in the Valley, as usual. Most of the men are, except Einar, of course. That boy,' she observed with a wry air, 'manages *more* vacations. And Eliza, of course, is down in Big Smith, running the library. But,' she assured him with a surge of coyness, 'they'll all be back before long, just as always!'

'How is she?' he asked, and was pleased to find that he could ask it in a perfectly casual way. Haila gave him a pleased smile.

'She's just wonderful, dear. Just – simply – wonderful. She can't wait to get back and find out how you're doing. She calls every day, you know.'

'No, I didn't know.' Surprisingly, a little excitement began to stir beneath his calmly confident, above-it-all, no-longer-caring, in-command-of-himself assurance. 'Why does she do that?'

'To find out about you ... Dear,' she said, and she placed a warmly encouraging hand on his arm, 'I'm not the only one who's been doing some thinking since Sunday night!'

'Well, I'll be damned,' he said with some irony, though again he could not suppress entirely the odd little feeling – surely it

233

could not be excitement! – that seemed to be stirring in his heart. 'Wonders never cease, do they? Particularly in Greenmont.'

'You and Greenmont,' she said with another chuckle. 'You and Greenmont! Are you reconciled to us at last, you silly child? You seemed so *determined* to have a feud!'

He gave her a startled look, half-humorous but firm.

'Now, Haila, see here. Just see here. I don't want to upset this new-found harmony that's flourishing all over the place, but I'm not going to let you get away with that. That isn't honest, and you know it.'

'Well, dear,' she said, not at all perturbed, 'let's say it wasn't all on one side, shall we? I think you'd have to admit that *that's* honest, now, wouldn't you? The provocations weren't all on our side, were they? You did provide a few yourself, didn't you? Come, now!' she urged with a completely amicable coyness. ' 'Fess up!'

'I'll 'fess if you will,' he replied with a wry smile. She nodded, agreeably and, apparently, with an entirely matter-of-fact sincerity.

'Why, certainly, dear. What makes you think it's an issue?'

He shook his head with a wonderment equally sincere if not quite so matter-of-fact.

'Haila, you're an amazing woman. You really are.'

'No, I'm not. I'm just intelligent enough to know when I've made a mistake, and honest enough to admit it. I was wrong, Bill. *Wrong!* Is that so amazing?'

'I don't know,' he said, staring at her thoughtfully. 'I truthfully don't know.'

'Well,' she said comfortably, 'don't worry about it. Good heavens!' she turned hastily to the stove. 'That soup is almost burned-on. What will you think of the cook!'

'As a cook,' he said with a sudden grin, 'I think very highly of her.'

'As a friend, too, I hope,' she said with an abrupt seriousness as she returned from the kitchen with his tray. 'I do hope so, Bill! ... now, let me get you steadied here' – she plumped some pillows behind his back, straightened his bathrobe neatly around his shoulders, and helped him sit up, which he did with some dizziness but a reasonable ease – 'and see if some real food won't make you feel better. Can you manage the spoon by yourself?'

'Oh, sure,' he said, taking it from her with a smile. 'I really do feel pretty good, you know. I'm going to try walking pretty soon.'

'After lunch,' she said firmly, 'and after a nap. We don't want to overdo it the first time out. Viola will be along around two with news of Eliza's call, I expect, and then Louise will be by at three to sit with you for the rest of the afternoon while Viola and I go up to the Meadows to play some golf. Louise will probably bring Gray, he's been staying with her since Sunday, but I expect now that you're with us again he'll be moving back. He's been very anxious to, but we thought it would be best to wait until you felt better. And now you do, and before you know it, everything will be back just as it was!'

'Good God,' he said, but with a genuine amusement that took the sting out of it, 'I hope not!'

She responded with an equally genuine laugh, filled with the comforting sense that all was well, the world was orderly again and moving once more along respectable and well-defined ways.

'Well, you know how I meant that.'

He gave her a quizzical look.

'Do I?'

She patted him playfully on the arm.

'You foolish fellow! Of course you do.'

But of course as he finished his lunch, managing to get down a good bit of the soup, most of the tea, all of the ice cream, he was not so sure. All this sweetness and light seemed just a little too good to be true, somehow. His last vivid mental picture of Haila before his departure, stern self-righteous Demeter closing quaking Persephone's door in his face, was somehow not quite compatible with this warmly friendly mother-image, slaving away for him over a hot stove and candidly confessing all her errors. Nor was he so sure that the rest of Greenmont had fallen in line, either. The only thing he was sure of – and here, too, his little stir of excitement at the mention of Eliza's name and the news of her telephone calls raised a certain small but insistently uncomfortable question in his mind – was that he had emerged

235

steady and whole and once more in command of himself. But somehow even that seemed a little dubious now. In some way he could not exactly define his conversation with Haila had undermined it a little. Welcome to Greenmont! was right.

His mind was filled with a good many things as he obediently drifted off to sleep again after his nurse had whisked up the kitchen and gone back to her own cabin for a nap. The last thought he had before sinking away was that he would have to find out from his real friends if everybody really meant it. He certainly couldn't tell from Haila.

Nor, it appeared, was he going to be able to tell from Viola, who arrived promptly at two as promised, bustling and agog with the latest word from Elizavetta. She came puffing up the steps and into the living-room with hardly a rap, apologizing breathlessly as she came but obviously not to be deterred.

'Stuart Grossman said,' she explained, plopping her ample self down in one of the tattered leather armchairs, 'that once you began to come around – you know he's been your doctor, don't you, or don't you? – that once you began to come around, we shouldn't let you go on sleeping too much. He said we should wake you up at regular intervals and try to get you back on a normal sleeping schedule as soon as possible. How are you, anyway?'

'I'm fine,' he said with a smile. 'I'm sorry I got camp so upset—'

'Oh,' she said comfortably, 'anybody can make a mistake, particularly on *that* grade. Good heavens, it's all I can do to keep from yelling at Bob, sometimes.'

'Yes,' he agreed, hoping, though not with much confidence, that this might be the generally accepted version of what had happened, 'it is rather tricky if you don't know it. I hear you've all been taking care of me. That's very kind.'

'Oh, yes. There was some argument about it at first, the ambulance people from Big Smith wanted to take you down to the hospital there, but Stu said no, as long as it was just a superficial shaking-up with probably only a very slight concussion and maybe a rib or two, that you'd be better off right here with

236

your friends. Haila agreed with him very vigorously, and that did it.'

'Haila is a vigorous agree-er,' he said with a smile. 'And it apparently wasn't even a rib or two.'

'No, I guess not. Your car was pretty badly banged up and Jerry's having it fixed for you in Big Smith, but other than that you came through in great shape.'

'I was just lucky.'

She nodded quickly.

'Oh, you were. Indeed you were. And in a way, it was good for all of us. We had the impression that when you left, you were – annoyed with us, and this gave everybody a chance to re-think everything and more or less – start over, you might say. Which I think,' she added, blushing but saying it out, 'was a good thing. I think we – I think some of us – may have been a little harsh . . . about some things. I am sorry for my part in that,' she said firmly. 'I just didn't understand.'

'Well, thank you, Viola,' he said, genuinely touched. 'I guess things got a little hectic for all of us.'

'*Also*,' she said importantly, 'Haila and I called Buck and Mary and told them all about it, and they said for you to just make yourself at home and take it easy and they'll see you when they get back. Buck said to forget anything he – he may have said earlier.'

'I have, long since,' he assured her. 'Something like that accident wipes the slate clean of a lot of things.'

'Oh, it does . . .' She put her hands on her knees with an almost playful clap and leaned forward. 'Well! Guess what!'

'I couldn't possibly. You tell me.'

'It concerns A Certain Person,' she said, clearly enunciating each capital.

'Surely not the President!' he exclaimed. 'That *is* kind of him!'

'Oh, you silly!' she said, with what, in one less matronly and substantial, might almost have been considered a giggle. 'What a silly! No, not the President. Someone closer, and – should I say it – dearer—'

'Old Mr Stafford!' he said, looking pleased. 'He is such a doll.'

She giggled again.

'You know *perfectly* well who I mean. She called just a little while ago and wanted *me* – to tell *you* – that—'

'Go on, go on, Viola!' he urged. 'I'm breathless!' – and found, to his annoyance, that he was, a little.

'That she had decided to take the rest of the week off and come up and help us take care of you!' Viola said triumphantly.

And even that took her three days to get up sufficient courage to do, he thought; but, even so, his heart gave a jump. He caught himself with a growing impatience. Stop *that*, he told himself. It didn't matter, it really didn't matter, because that was all over and he was his own man again.

'That's very kind of her,' he said gravely. 'Is she sure she can afford the time? I wouldn't want her to upset the library's routine just because I'm not up and romping around camp.'

'Oh, she doesn't *mind*! Gracious, you don't think she *minds*, do you? Actually she wanted to stay on Sunday, but Haila suggested that perhaps it might be better if she went down for a couple of days and got things in shape to leave and then came back.'

'Oh, Haila did, did she?' There was sufficient in his tone to make Viola look flustered and hurry on.

'Now, don't get mad at Haila again!' she told him, tucking up one of her many wandering grey hairs with a nervous hand. 'Haila feels very sorry for everything, she has *broken her back* to take care of you and to see that everything will work out so that you and – so that you and Eliza—'

'My Lord, I'm on a merry-go-round,' he said with a weird amusement. 'The Greenmont merry-go-round! This is where I came in, Viola. Don't you recognize the scenery?'

'Well, now,' she said stiffly, 'I'm sorry I said anything about it, because when I just talked to Elizavetta I can tell you she wasn't thinking about Haila or me or anybody but herself and you. That's the honest truth, now. And you really *mustn't* get suspicious of everybody again. That was half the trouble, before.'

'Half, maybe,' he said softly. 'Not all.'

'Well, anyway, you just mustn't. You said yourself the accident had cancelled a lot of things. Now, let them go!'

'Yes,' he agreed abruptly, for he realized suddenly that there was a genuine change in his heart, he did not feel annoyed at Haila, he felt instead an amiable amusement towards her, a genuine gratitude towards Elizavetta for being willing to devote the time. 'How long does Stu think I'll have to stay in bed?'

'He told us last night, when he finally went down,' she said, looking relieved at the change of topic, 'that as soon as you felt rested and could walk, you could do anything you pleased. He suggested regular naps and early-to-bed, but he said you'd feel tired enough for a while to do that of your own accord, anyway.'

'I'm sure of that ... Here,' he said, raising himself to a sitting position, swinging his legs over the side of the sofa, holding out a hand, 'give me a hoist, here, and let's see what happens.'

'Good!' she said, pushing herself up with a wheeze and taking his hand. 'Steady does it!'

And with a little tugging from her and a not too difficult effort from him, steady did, so that in a couple of minutes he was standing on his feet, woozy but determined.

'Now,' he said, 'let go, and I'll try to make it to the deck.'

'Well,' she said nervously, 'take it easy, now—'

He smiled.

'I will. Stay close and grab me if I start to topple.'

'Well!' Haila cried from across the ravine as he emerged, shaky but triumphant, on the deck and eased himself slowly into the yellow plastic chaise-longue. 'There's our conquering hero!'

'Not very conquering, Haila,' he called back, 'not much of a hero: but here I am. What a beautiful day!'

'Greenmont never fails,' she said with a happy complacency, coming down her steps and along the path between the cabins, golf-club swinging casually from her hand, looking fresh and rested and ready for the afternoon.

'No, it doesn't,' he agreed. 'It's lovely.' He grinned. 'Particularly when one might, of course, be dead.'

'Now, hush,' she said, while Viola looked startled and disapproving. 'Hush, hush, hush, hush, *hush*! We aren't going to talk about that any more. It's all over and done with and everything is starting anew. What did Eliza have to say?'

'She's coming up tonight,' Viola said. Haila looked pleased.

'There, now! That ought to make you recover in a hurry!'

'Like a flash.'

She tapped him lightly on the shoulder.

'Don't be so sure it won't. You may find yourself surprised.'

'I may,' he said, giving her a sudden direct glance which she returned steadily. 'Or again, I may not.'

'I know which I'd bet on, if I were a betting woman,' she said, and before he could make some quick and no doubt provocative retort, she had turned to Viola.

'Louise will be along in about half an hour and then we can go.'

'Go ahead now,' he said; and at Viola's hesitation, 'I'm perfectly all right. I'll just sit here and enjoy the afternoon.'

'Well—' she said doubtfully. He waved them away.

'No, no kidding, I'm fine. Let me commune with nature. Let me comfort my soul. Let Greenmont work its magic!'

'It will, Bill,' Haila said with a comfortable laugh as they started down the steps. 'I think I can promise you that. It will!'

And though not, perhaps, in the way she meant, the magic of Greenmont did come back as he sat there on the deck in the slumbering afternoon. Far away somewhere there was a world of clashing purposes and bitter, angry men; far away great forces rent the nations and hapless humanity suffered from the Blight. Not in Greenmont. Here the sunlight fell as always dappled on the paths, the jays and squirrels bickered in the trees, the sky of absolute blue played host to the clouds of absolute white, the canyon slept in near-primeval innocence, the river roared, the high peaks soared, the universe for ever floated on a lake of perfect peace . . .

He sat for what seemed a long time, though it could not have been more than half an hour, once again hardly moving, hardly thinking, allowing himself to drift, allowing the slumbrous day to work its restoratives upon his heart and mind. For the first time, perhaps, since his first day in Greenmont, he began to understand the hold it exerted upon those who loved it. With the understanding came a surge of affection for it, and for its unpredictable, inexplicable, difficult but likeable people. They were characters, many of them, true enough: but, then, so was he. And perhaps now that they had finally come to some appreciation of one another's personalities, they could go forward, if not as bosom friends, then in any case no longer as constantly contending enemies.

At least he hoped that he and Elizavetta could, now that

whatever had been in his turbulent heart had apparently vanished down the mountainside in the accident. The terror of that strange moment in which he had wanted – not wanted, sought – not sought, desired – not desired – that strange instant when some power beyond himself had kept his foot hesitating on the gas-pedal, his hands trembling on the wheel, until suddenly, in one blind, chaotic impulse, it had forced them into action and sent him over – came briefly back to shake his being and take away his breath. Then it passed, as suddenly as it had come – as suddenly as it had then, so that even as he heard the car screaming through the clutching branches he had cried out, 'No! No!' to Someone who, apparently, had listened – and again he was at peace. It was indeed, as Haila said, over and done with; and so apparently, was the hunted mood and devastating emotion which had preceded it. Once again Elizavetta was just an awkward, lonely, exaggerated sort of girl – kind and decent, as he now knew her to be, but nothing to throw his world away for, nothing to agonize over, ever again. A friend, and, he hoped quite sincerely, for life: but only a friend. Nothing more.

His security and satisfaction in this peaceful conclusion to a hectic ten days lasted approximately five minutes: then he began to wonder, not in the self-torturing, self-wracking way he had before, but in a calmer, more objective, idly curious, really quite humorous, inward fashion. If this really is the case, old buddy, he asked himself wryly, why all the palpitations when Haila mentioned her name? Why all the flips and flutters at the news of her telephone calls? Why the eager attention when Viola rendered her report? Why the leap of heart, accompanied though it was by a flicker of the old annoyance at her timidity, at the announcement that she would be back tonight to join the local chapter of Volunteer Workers In Charge Of Mixed-Up Majors? How about that, old smug-and-sure?

He grinned to himself as he sat there on the deck, a perfect example of a silly son of a bitch who certainly ought to know better by this time. Well . . . so he did. He could tell it from the mood in which he found himself. The ache was gone, the anxiety was gone, his own exaggerations were gone. The approach was sensible now, the attitude was self-assured, the touch was light.

Or was it?

'God damn!' he said, aloud and, perhaps, not quite as humorously as he would have liked to believe, 'you'd think I was still in shock ... In fact,' he added softly to a gorgeously-marked grosbeak as it alighted on the deck railing to peck at the breadcrumbs Haila had left out, 'you'd think I was still in Greenmont ...'

There was a race of feet down the road, a dash up the stairs, arms flung around his neck, a wild, convulsive hug.

'Good Lord, buddy,' he said mildly, extricating himself with some difficulty, 'you'll strangle me to death. How've you been?'

'I've been fine!' Gray said. 'But I'm better now that I know you're O.K.'

'That's good,' he said with a grin at Louise, following along up the stairs. 'Hi. Aren't you going to hug me too?'

'I ought to take a belt and tan your hide. That's what I really ought to do. After *that* performance.'

'Mrs Drummond doesn't mean things like that,' Gray explained. 'She just does it to be funny.'

'I know. She's a very funny lady. But we like her, don't we?'

'She's great! When are you coming up to the Meadows?'

'Slow down, lover,' Louise said, flopping down on the deck-swing all knees and angles and quirky expressions. 'Give your boy ten minutes to make the world stop whirling. He probably can't even walk straight yet.'

'I got out here,' the major pointed out. 'Not without leaning on Viola's ample bosom, I'll admit, but—'

'Sufficient to cushion any fall,' Louise assured him, lighting a cigarette and pulling over the coffee-can-nailed-to-tree-stump that served as ashtray. 'Better than three eiderdown quilts and a bucket of styrofoam.' She shot him a sudden penetrating look. 'How are you, anyway?'

'Pretty good,' he said, a little warily, as he knew she perceived. 'How are you?'

'I'm fine. But I didn't take Lover's Leap in a Karmann Ghia. Are you sure everything is still in place?'

'It's still in place,' he said with a grin, 'but I haven't had a chance to check it out and discover whether it still works, of course.'

242

'Ever the quipster,' she said. 'Ever the riotous rogue. You should be thankful you're still sitting here in dear old Greenmont exchanging merry jests with ageing females.'

'Oh, I am,' he said, suddenly sober. 'Don't worry: I am.'

'Everybody in camp wants to know how you are,' Gray announced abruptly.

The major smiled.

'You look a little fidgety, buddy. Why don't you run along and tell them?'

'O.K.!' Gray said cheerfully. He gave a mischievous grin. 'I'll tell them you'll be up to play golf and swim at four o'clock.'

'Oh, you will, will you?' he said, kicking out at the boy playfully and then saying, 'Ouch!' as Gray giggled out of reach and dashed off up the road.

'Rivet loose, eh?' Louise inquired. 'I thought you were too high and mighty... This small, significant jar,' she said, handing it to him, 'is some preserves from Mother Magruder. A peace offering.'

'Mother Magr—' he said blankly. 'Mother Magr – *not* Mother Magr – I mean, *not* Mother *Magr*—'

'All right, all right. Knock it off. Yes, Mother Magruder. The most amazing people have got religion since you went over the cliff. You should have done it sooner.'

He grinned.

'The circumstances have to be just right for that sort of thing. You can't just do it any time.'

'And they were right just then?' she inquired with a shrewd glance.

'Frankly,' he said, giving her look for look, 'it was just an accident.'

She snorted.

'Sweetie, you don't fool Louise. Or actually anybody. The first thing Jerry and I heard about it was when Tommy Rupert came crying through camp, "Major Steele's committed suicide! Major Steele's committed suicide!" This instantly became the official version, and knowing Greenmont, it always will be though you live to be a hundred. If you come back here in 1995, somebody – probably old Mr Stafford' – she chuckled abruptly at the thought – 'will come sidling up and say, "Now, about that time you tried to commit suicide" – And,' she added,

243

serious again, 'you did, didn't you?'

'Did I?' he asked, serious too and looking far out across the canyon to the misty blue mountains across the way, feathered neatly now with the start of shadows as though a giant magnet had drawn the filings of the trees all one way in the descending afternoon sun. 'Louise, I honestly do not know. I think there was an impulse – an impulse. But whether it was an impulse to die – or an impulse to live – and certainly if it was an impulse to die, it was succeeded instantaneously, believe you me, by an impulse to live' – he shivered – 'my God, what a feeling! – I really don't know. All I know is, I came out of it, and for that I'm thankful, O.K.? Will Greenmont leave me that, that I'm glad to be here? Even here?'

And he gave her a look partly humorous, partly quizzical, partly prepared to be defensive. She stubbed out her cigarette firmly, shrugged, and lit another.

'I think Greenmont will leave you that,' she said slowly, 'if you'll leave Greenmont a few things.'

'Well,' he said shortly. 'I don't want to go into all that again. I feel, and I hope I'm right, that I lost a lot of things over the mountain. I really feel differently about' – he considered it carefully – 'almost everything.'

'Even Eliza?'

'Even Eliza.'

'Is that good or bad?'

He started to retort and then thought better of it, or, rather, decided in mid-breath that he really didn't know what to say. Instead he busied himself for a moment drawing his bathrobe more tightly around his legs against the little wind of afternoon, shifting himself more comfortably in the chaise-longue.

'Well, which is it?'

He smiled.

'There you go again, old Eagle-Eye Drummond, pinning me down . . . It's good, isn't it? It's what everybody wanted. As nearly as I could gather,' he added with a rueful little grin, 'about the things that Greenmont wants.'

She gave him a quick glance and spoke with a deliberate bluntness.

'You have too many scapegoats. Face yourself, once in a while.'

His first impulse was to flare up, but again he thought better of it: his new mood thought better of it. All that hair-trigger business really was over. He smiled.

'You know, Louise, if this is a test, forget it. I've passed.'

She returned the smile but didn't yield.

'Not a test, sweetie. More fundamental than that.'

He nodded.

'Yes, I face myself. I have faced myself. I told you, many things changed in a moment's time. Eliza is – is—'

'What?'

'A nice old maid I met in a screwball paradise at the back of nowhere. Once upon a time.'

'You think you can relegate her into yesterday as easily as that?' She gave one of her hoots. 'Come on, now, Bill.'

He shrugged.

'All right, then,' he said, 'you tell me what she is. What am I supposed to think about her? What does Greenmont want me to do now?' He smiled, more savagely, perhaps, than he intended. 'Tell me, lady. Tell me, do.'

'I think Greenmont wants you to marry her,' she said matter-of-factly. 'And furthermore, I think you want to.'

'Louise,' he said, managing to be humorous but with a growing edge to it, 'are you insane?'

She nodded cheerfully.

'I certainly am, sweetie.'

'In the first place,' he said patiently, although he really could see no reason for treating it as a valid question, he didn't know why he was even discussing it with her, 'I don't want to. And in the second place, what about all this awful moral issue everybody was making such a fuss about? Am I forgiven for' – he smiled a little – 'for being a willing victim? I thought everyone was on the warpath about that. It hardly seems very consistent now to turn right around and—'

'Pooh!' she said with a grin. 'Who's consistent? When were human beings ever consistent? You've become Greenmont's project ever since you went over the grade. That makes everything all right. Don't tell me you can't understand it!'

'I've been Greenmont's project, in one way or another, ever since I set foot inside the gate. I almost got projected to death. I'd rather be relieved of the burden from now on. If,' he added in a level tone, 'you don't mind.'

'I don't mind,' she said blandly, 'but how can you fight City Hall? . . . Say,' she added abruptly, 'would you like something to drink? I'm thirsty.'

'There were some Cokes in the ice-box on Sunday,' he said, aware that he was being given time to think about it, but falling in with this obvious move because, in his new mood of confidence and serenity, it didn't really matter. 'If Haila hasn't been doing some solitary drinking, they're probably still there.'

'Have to watch that Haila,' she told him, and they both laughed. 'Now,' she said, returning with the glasses, giving him one, settling back down in a comfortable sprawl on the swing. 'Why are you afraid to accept it?'

'I'm not afraid to accept it,' he said amicably. 'I love to accept it.'

'Well,' she said with a chuckle, 'at least you aren't taking off my head about it, which does represent a gain. You would have, a week ago.'

He smiled.

'Oh, no. I've told you what I think about Eliza. I mean it.'

'You really sound as though you do,' she conceded. 'On the surface.'

He shrugged.

'Everybody lives on surfaces. The world lives on surfaces. So let's leave it on the surface, shall we?' Again an acid edge crept into his voice, despite his determination not to let it, and his newly placid mood. 'I know this runs counter to all the tenets of Greenmont, but—'

'Ah ha!' she said with a grin. 'There's our boy, about to come out snapping and snarling. Why are you so defensive?'

'Louise,' he said, laughing in spite of himself, but, again, with a growing annoyance in his tone, 'damn it, I am not defensive! Now, will you stop heckling me? You're going to drive the patient into a relapse.'

'Sweetie, you don't fool me for a minute. And furthermore, why should you want to? Nothing has changed at all, really, despite your attempt to get down to the Valley by the most direct route. She's the same, you're the same. Even Greenmont is the same.' She chuckled. 'It's shifted gears and gone into reverse again, but it's still the same.'

'Well,' he said bluntly, 'I'm not. So Greenmont had better go slow, unless we all want to have another hassle.'

'Oh, pish-tush. Too bad you didn't lose that chip off your shoulder, too. It must have been the first thing you picked up after the crash.'

'Louise—' he began. 'Louise—' and suddenly, quite genuinely and with no longer any annoyance at all, he began to laugh, such a hearty sound in the sleepy afternoon that she presently joined in.

'Well!' she said when it ended. 'That was fun. What did it mean?'

'It meant that I really don't care what you think, or what Greenmont thinks, or what anybody thinks, I'm on the mend, and I'm feeling fine, and I'm going to be here for another couple of weeks, probably, and I'm really relaxed and I'm going to enjoy it. So!'

'So! yourself,' she said with a grin. 'That makes it inevitable.'

'Inevitable?' he said cheerfully. 'How do you figure that?'

'I always knew if you ever got to the stage where you could really relax, it would all work out. You just had to learn not to care too much, in order to get what you care about. Now you have. So what you want will come to you. It's that simple.'

'O.K.,' he said with an answering grin. 'O.K., you have it all figured out. Dream away, O Seeress of the Sierras, dream away. You can't bother me any more. Have fun.'

'We both will. Me watching and you doing.'

'Oh, nonsense,' he said amicably. 'Nonsense, nonsense, and *you* know it's nonsense.'

But he didn't, of course, and as the afternoon declined and he managed to lead her away from that topic and into other concerns of Greenmont about which they gossiped companionably until almost six, he had to fight quite sternly to keep from admitting to himself that it might not be nonsense. He told himself that he was being made the target for one of the most obvious games in the feminine repertoire: *Oh, yes, you do, now! Yes, you do! You just think you don't, but you really do!* – until you began to concede it a little validity, you let yourself begin

247

to believe it just a little, and then before you knew it, you were hooked.

There really was no reason, he told himself firmly, why he should fall for this ancient gambit, especially since it wasn't true. That was the thought he must hold to (and suddenly realized he was holding to it so firmly that at one point he was actually grinding his teeth and his palms were sweating) – it just wasn't true.

'Well, sweetie,' she said at last, 'I must be off. Janie Rupert and a couple of the girls and I have a bridge supper in the works and I've got to contribute the salad. So be good, now. The night shift will be along in a minute ... In fact,' she said, peering up the darkening road, 'here they come now. Hi, competition!' she hollered. 'Your victim awaits you!'

There was a sound of running. Einar and Sally-Jane, arm in arm, came full tilt down the road and roared up the steps to collapse, out of breath and laughing helplessly, into deck chairs.

'Here's the bedpan brigade,' Einar announced when he got his breath. 'Boy, I know more about your functions that you do, after these last four nights.'

'On which note of grace and high culture,' Louise said, 'I shall leave you all to spin away the hours until Cinderella comes along in her old green pumpkin. Keep an eye out for her, Sally-Jane. Prince Charming here is getting anxious.'

'I'm not—' he began. Then he laughed.

'Sure. Bring her on. I can hardly wait.'

Launched on that basis, his conversation with the bedpan brigade naturally ran towards more of the same. He knew it probably would have, anyway – Louise was right on that, the subject still seemed to be Greenmont's major preoccupation – but by the time supper was finished and a gin-rummy game under way, he found himself stretched to a tension he had not thought possible earlier. His reserves of good humour and calmness were substantial, now, but under the prod of Einar's constant joshing they were beginning to wear a little thin.

'Einar, honey,' Sally-Jane said finally, 'don't you think we've

about exhausted that subject, now? I think Bill's been remark-
ably patient, I really do. He says it's over, so it's over. Now,
quiet down.'

'But,' Einar objected, 'you girls haven't talked about anything
else since Sunday. I don't see why I—'

'Because I said so,' she told him calmly. 'Now give me that
ace you've been holding back, so I can gin.'

'You see, Bill?' Einar said, 'you see what you get into.
Married six weeks and she's already laying down the law. My
advice to you is to stay clear of it. Eliza may be the most
glamorous thing that ever reached the mountains, but there's
a tiger underneath. There is with all of them. Watch out!'

'I think you'd better watch out,' he suggested with a sufficient
amicability, 'or S.-J. and I are going to beat you, and the loser
has to buy a bottle of bourbon, you know.'

'To drink at your engagement party,' Einar said with a grin,
and then looked elaborately startled as his wife said, *'Hush,
now!'* in an indignant tone.

'What's that?' the major inquired with a startled but amused
expression. 'What sort of a joke have you got going now? Who's
talking crazy this time? Tell me the gag: it must be a real
funny.'

'Not funny at all,' Einar said. 'Dead serious! You know
Greenmont.'

'Einar Magruder,' his wife said, 'that is neither here nor
there. You know very well it was just a joke the other night,
and he regretted it right away, poor old Jimsy, you could tell
from the way he looked—'

'Oh, sure,' Einar agreed. 'Jim was innocent, he's always innocent, he just has a habit of getting caught in the middle. But I
noticed all the rest of you certainly snapped it up in a hurry.
Haila to cook this, Viola to cook that, Louise to make the salad,
Ma to fix some preserves—'

'Now, wait a minute,' the major said carefully. 'Let me get
this straight. This is an engagement party that's being planned
for us?'

'Not seriously,' Sally-Jane said. 'Really, now, Einar, you can
be so *annoying* at times. It's just a joke, Bill. Some of us were
sitting around in here Sunday night after the – after you – when
they brought you back here and we knew everything was going

249

to be all right – and Jim Buxton just grinned and said, "It would be just like Greenmont now if he went right ahead and married the girl, after all. Maybe old Haila here and the rest of you had better start planning the engagement party." And right away' – she dimpled prettily – 'everybody did. But it was just a joke. You know Gr—'

'If somebody says that to me just once more,' he promised with a certain grimness under the humour, 'I shall take off like a rocket. Yes, I know it. And I hope you'll help me persuade it to forget the whole thing, because it isn't going to happen.'

'Well, the party's going to happen,' Einar said blandly. 'It's all set for Saturday night at the Falls. So, engagement or no, we're going to have a high old whoop-de-do-ing time, and *you*, Bill, might just as well laugh and enjoy it. Of course it *would* be nice if you should – if you did – it would be a sort of *pièce de résistance* – a sort of soufflé à la Sierra, as it were – a sort of – sort of—'

'Yes,' he said shortly. 'Well, I've told you it isn't going to happen. So forget it.'

'But you will come to the party,' Einar suggested drily. 'After all, it's free.'

'I don't know,' he said in the same sharp, unamused way. 'I rather doubt it. Anyway,' he added, though of course it was of no concern to him, he didn't care, 'what does Eliza say about this?'

Sally-Jane smiled.

'Naturally she'd already gone home when the subject came up. That part of it really was just a joke, Bill. It's mostly just to be a get-well party.'

'Well,' he said, still shortly. 'All right, then. Einar, it's still your turn to play.'

'But I'm sure she could be persuaded,' Einar remarked softly.

'I said it's your turn to play,' he repeated evenly, and for the first time since the accident something of the old annoyance was back in his voice as he spoke to Greenmont.

Annoyance, however, was of no profit in Einar's present mood, and so he presently decided he might just as well ride with it – that would be more in keeping with his concept of himself and his own detached and confident mood. He began conducting an elaborately exaggerated conversation, outlining plans for the wedding, ideas for a honeymoon, where he thought they might settle down, the kind of house they might like, how many children they would probably have. This kept up until shortly before nine, when he began to feel suddenly tired and Sally-Jane started making I-think-we'd-better-quit signs to Einar. They were adding up final scores when they heard a car come grinding up the road. Conversation ceased. They listened intently.

Just as it came around the bend below the cabin, the car hesitated, slowed down . . . crept along for a moment . . . almost stopped. Then with a sudden nervous roar it took off. The sound dwindled rapidly away up the road, and again the night was still save for the distant talking of the river, the sleepless stirring of the trees.

'Still afraid,' Einar remarked thoughtfully. 'It's too bad.'

'What do you mean, still afraid?' the major demanded sharply. 'How do you know – what right have you got to assume that—'

'Of course it was,' Einar said. 'Do you have any doubt? I don't.'

'You can't prove it,' he said angrily. 'And you have no right to accuse her of – of—'

'O.K., O.K.,' Einar said. 'It strikes me that for a guy who doesn't care any more, you're awfully—'

'I'm going to bed,' he said abruptly and started to stand up. But the room whirled and he staggered and held out an arm. Einar linked it around his own neck with one hand, grasped him around the waist with the other, and steadied his body against his own.

'O.K., Battling Billy,' he said with a grin. 'Let's go.'

'Well,' he said with an attempt at dignity, and a returning humour, 'there still isn't any proof it was—'

'Oh, it was, Bill, honey,' Sally-Jane said, 'and we all know it. However. That will have to be tomorrow's problem. You're out on your feet, right now.'

'You can say that again,' he conceded with an enormous yawn. 'You folks don't have to stay the night, though. I can manage all right from now on.'

251

'Aw, shucks,' Einar said. 'It was such fun getting you potty-trained, especially when you were under all that dope Stu gave you. You've no idea.'

'Go home,' he ordered drowsily. 'I'll see you tomorrow.'

'We'll stay until Gray comes in,' Sally-Jane said. 'There's some water and a bottle of sleeping pills by the bed. Stu wants you to take one.'

'I may take them all if Greenmont doesn't stop romping all over me again,' he said. Einar gave him an amiable yank towards the bedroom.

'Come on, funny boy. If you were any more hilarious, we couldn't stand it.'

'Me, either,' he confessed with another yawn. 'Oh, Lordy! Me, either.'

Some time around 3 a.m. he awoke in the silent cabin to hear the river, sharper and more distinct now in the absence of all human sound, plunging away down-canyon. Somewhere a peculiar yowl, probably a bob-cat, broke the stillness. An owl hooted plaintively. Looking up through the trees from where he lay he could see the moon, nearly full, riding overhead. The world was bright and shining and quite cold. He drew the covers more closely around his head and continued to stare up for several minutes at the luminous sky.

'Engagement party,' was it? Well, well. What a strange, fantastic place this was, still. He would never really understand it, never get over it. It would remain, in some ways, a mystery always. And as for Eliza – so, perhaps, would she. He could understand her hesitation on the road, but to decide finally not to stop at all, to decide finally that she didn't dare, when he was so calm and so willing to greet her, now, as a friend, was too much. Really too much. Secretly he had agreed with Einar, though of course he had felt he must defend her. Any decent friend would do the same. It meant nothing.

Tomorrow's problem, Sally-Jane had said. But – no problem. He could joke his way out of the 'engagement party' with the others as he had with the two of them. And with Eliza, as soon as they saw one another again, he knew he could move into an easy friendship that would prove comfortable and rewarding for them both as the years went by and they returned again and again to Greenmont; both, in time, no doubt, with partners who would give them just that peculiar combination of caring enough but not too much that they had been unable, for all of Greenmont's erratic and basically well-meant sympathies, to give each other.

The moon swam on through the bright night sky, the bob-cat screamed once again upon the mountainside. The Weendigo walked no more in this good world. It did not occur to him that it might just be hiding. He sank away into sleep again with a pleased little smile upon his face.

❧ TWO ☙

Morning came, bright and sparkling, sharp and clear, one more inevitable addition to Greenmont's steady progression of lovely days. The smell of frying bacon, mingled with the smell of pines and bear-clover fresh with dew, drifted through the canyon on the cool yet gentle wind. Off among the aromatic trees doors slammed, voices called. Underlying everything, the river's steady throb, half-heard, half-sensed, tied the world together. Vigorous with life yet peaceful and serene, camp came awake around him. He felt happy and hopeful and glad to be alive.

Assisted by Gray, who took his duties seriously and became quite stern when his house-guest tried to do too much, he got up and was already beginning to putter around the kitchen, feeling steadily better and more like himself every moment, when Haila arrived from across the ravine.

'Now, Bill,' she said with a reproachful little smile, 'you know you're not supposed to be doing that. That's my job.'

'He's feeling fine,' Gray declared stoutly. 'I'm taking care of him.'

'I know you are, dear,' Haila said kindly. 'Aren't you about finished with your breakfast and ready to go and play, now?'

'No, I'm not,' Gray said firmly. 'I haven't started. I'm going to eat with him.'

'Well, dear,' she said with a comfortable chuckle, 'I guess you may if you like. After all, it's your cabin.'

'You can stay until we finish breakfast, though,' Gray said. 'I guess you'd better wash the dishes.'

The major laughed.

'I guess that assigns you *your* duties. But I tell you, buddy: we can probably help Mrs Buxton, can't we? After all, she's been taking pretty good care of me, too, you know.'

'Well,' Gray said doubtfully. 'Can you make pancakes?' he asked Haila. 'I don't know whether I could or not. I'd sure like to have some.'

'Suppose you set the table,' she suggested, smiling over his head at the major with a perfectly relaxed and companionable air, 'and I'll see what I can do ... Bill,' she said a little later, readying the frying-pan and mixing the batter, 'do you think you'll be needing me this morning?'

'No, thanks. I'm feeling fine. Why, are you going down today?'

'Nothing like that.' A coy little expression came into her eyes. 'I've just got a secret. *That's* all.'

'What's that?'

'*You'll* see.'

'I suppose,' he said – though there was really no reason to ask, except that he had a perfect right to be idly curious about it, it was perfectly natural that he should inquire – 'Elizavetta will drop in some time today, won't she?'

'That's it,' Haila said with a pleased smile. 'You've guessed my secret. Eliza will take over *all morning long*. No one else will *come near*.'

'Oh, my God,' he said in a dismayed voice, 'that's great. Just simply great.'

'Well, isn't it?' she demanded. 'What better way for you to have A Little Talk?'

'Gosh,' Gray said, 'with everybody knowing?' And he gave Haila a sudden, half-furtive, half-frightened look in which the major thought he detected some shared knowledge. Suddenly he knew what happened at the glen. That was why the boy had avoided him last week, that was why Haila had been so implacable, that was why ... that was why.

But that was also past, and he told himself with a considerable effort that there was no point in reviving it now. Instead he managed to keep an impassive expression in his eyes and a reasonable note in his voice.

'Exactly. Gray knows the problem. How can we have any kind of talk when it's so – so stage-managed? Really, Haila? Honest to God, are you people really that obtuse?'

'No one is obtuse,' she said coldly, and for just a moment there came back into her voice the Haila he knew. Ah, there, he thought drily, I knew you were hiding in there somewhere, all the time! But her tone changed at once to one of playful banter. 'Now Bill! Please don't be foolish about this. Eliza is here – we all know it – she couldn't sneak in incognito – she wants to come and see you – we want her to – there's only one way for her to do it – and that's *do* it. So what's the fuss?'

'She did want to?' he asked, and, absurdly, a little quickening of interest and hope touched his heart. 'Are you sure you just didn't put her up to it?'

'Bill, Bill!' she admonished in a motherly, chiding way. 'I've told you your concept of my influence with Eliza was naïve, and it is. She wanted to see you, from the first.'

'But you didn't want her to until you could arrange it so that we could be alone. You wanted it to be the perfect little scene. And *you wanted to plan it*. Now, didn't you?'

And despite his words, which would have sounded hostile standing alone, his expression and tone were more amused than not. He truly did feel amused, amused and relaxed. Greenmont was being so – in character, somehow. He almost laughed aloud.

'Well,' she confessed lightly, responding to his tone, 'you may be right, Bill. You may just be right. But, after all, it wouldn't have been any advantage to you to have a town meeting about it, would it? The two of you couldn't have talked with everyone here, now, could you? How would that have helped matters? Surely you see that!'

'Haila,' he said, and a quite genuine humour came into his eyes, 'I can always see the perfect logic of everything you propose. The minor fact that I sometimes don't agree with it has nothing to do with its logic. You are *logical*, ma'am! Of that there is no doubt.'

'Very well, then,' she said complacently. 'Take advantage of it and don't be a silly boy.'

'Will that earn me an extra piece of cake at my engagement party?' he asked, and was pleased to observe that for a second she looked quite flustered. Then she laughed heartily.

'I can see we can't keep *any* secrets from *you*. Not any.'

'I've kept one from you, though,' he said cheerfully. 'It isn't going to happen.'

'I don't know why,' Gray said unexpectedly from the end of the table where he was finishing the enormous pile of pancakes she had placed before him. 'I still think it would be great.'

'There! ' she said with a chuckle. 'Reinforcements from the only person you trust in all of Greenmont.'

'Oh, now,' he said, aware of its truth but, childishly, a little hurt by it.

'Almost, Bill,' she said, giving him a shrewd glance. 'Almost.'

'And why should I—' he began tartly, and then broke it off abruptly. Another minute of this and they would be into things that really would sting. His post-accident mood would not permit it. Instead he turned to Gray with a smile.

'Buddy, I think you'd better run along and play, now. Mrs Buxton and I can finish up.'

'O.K. Shall I tell Eliza you're ready for her to come on down?'

'No, thanks,' he said, giving Haila a quizzical look. 'I have an idea she'll get here right on time.'

And so, of course, she did, for anything else would have been unthinkable. The directress and the company wouldn't have permitted it. Greenmont Productions Inc., wanted heroine to enter left centre, up stairs to deck, indicating suitable timidity. That wasn't what he wanted her to indicate, but, then, he wasn't in charge. And as a matter of fact he wasn't all that calm, himself. To his surprise he found that he was, in reality, quite tense.

'Hello,' he said, standing up, gesturing to one of the deck chairs, holding out his hand. 'This is kind of you.'

'Oh, don't get up,' she said hurriedly, giving his hand a quick, nervous squeeze and dropping it. 'Just go right on with whatever you're doing.'

He smiled.

'I haven't been doing a thing but sit here and wait for you. What kept you so long?'

'Well,' she said, sitting down carefully in one of the chairs on the far side of the deck, taking off the floppy hat, arranging the bright orange skirt, not looking at him. 'I had to finish up around the cabin before I could come down, and Haila said you probably wouldn't be through breakfast until about ten.' She glanced hastily at the big open-faced watch she carried on a big open-link brass chain around her neck. 'It is ten.'

'I'm sure of it,' he said, and sat down abruptly on the deck-swing, since he found that his legs were trembling so that it was a case of sit down or fall down. 'How did you leave things in Big Smith? Everything all right at the library?'

'Oh, yes,' she said quickly. For the first time a faint smile came into her eyes. 'Everything's always all right at the library. It isn't the world's liveliest place. Or Big Smith's, either.' The smile grew a little, though it was a timorous thing, ready to retreat. 'If you knew Big Smith you'd know what that means.'

He nodded.

'I can imagine. I grew up in one of those little Valley towns myself. There are areas of a sort of shabby liveliness, but the nice kids don't see too much of them ... So you've come to help take care of me.'

'Yes,' she said, looking at him for the first time and then looking quickly away. 'How are you?'

'Fine. I expect I'll get up to the Meadows tomorrow.'

'Maybe we can play some golf,' she said, and again a little smile broke through.

'With at least ten partners, I'll bet,' he said with an answering smile. 'How have you been, anyway?'

'Oh,' she said, suddenly shy again, 'I've been fine. How have you been?'

'Oh, fine. You know how it is: eat and sleep, sleep and eat. But I'm really fine ...' He gave a sudden little grin. 'Well, I guess we've exhausted that topic. What else shall we talk about?'

'I don't know,' she said, looking as though she were on the verge of rising and running. 'Can I get you anything from the kitchen, or some books, or something?'

'No, thanks, I'm not hungry. I just finished breakfast, you know.'

She nodded hurriedly.

'Yes, I know.'

'And I don't feel like reading. I—' he paused. 'I rather

257

thought we might talk. Isn't that what Haila wants us to do?'

'I suppose she does,' she said, and again a tentative little smile appeared. 'But do we always have to do what Haila wants us to do?'

He uttered a surprised little laugh.

'My dear girl, that's heresy. Particularly,' he said, for it was best to get it out in the open at once and laugh about it, before Greenmont could upset her with it, 'since what she seems to want us to do is to get married. Isn't that a typically silly Haila notion? What you might call an Hailucination,' he added for the sake of something light, however feeble.

But she did not smile, and for a moment she did not answer. When she did, it was very low.

'I don't know.' Again she gave him a quick glance, and glanced away. 'Is it?'

'Well—' he said blankly, so surprised was he and yet, in some curious fashion, so intrigued and almost, absurd though it was to say it, excited. 'Well ... Well, but ... I don't know,' he finished lamely. 'What do you think?'

'I wouldn't think you would want to after what I did,' she said unhappily.

'Oh,' he said, relieved now that he knew what the trouble was. 'I could understand that. You couldn't very well say anything with her standing right there. It hurt me at the time, but I understood it later.' He smiled, though it cost him a little effort, remembering the searing despair of that moment at the door. 'I forgive you, if that will make it better.'

She shook her head miserably.

'No, I don't mean that. I mean—' her voice almost trailed away and he realized that she was blushing furiously under the heavy tan. 'I mean – before that.'

'Oh,' he said. 'Oh.' And for several seconds he literally could not think what to say next, except that he knew he must say something or the moment would become intolerable for them both. 'Well ... that's all right, too. I mean – it really is.' He knew he mustn't joke, yet a curious flippancy overcame him, prompted by sheer nerves. '*I* enjoyed it, anyway.'

She gave him a startled look and for a second he thought she would literally get up and run. But she remained, and after a moment spoke again, very low, in a crushed voice.

'What you must think of me! Oh, what you must think of me!'

'Now, why?' he asked, and suddenly his voice became stronger. 'Now, why, for heaven's sake? It was perfectly natural. We're grown people. What of it?'

'It wasn't for me,' she said in a half-whisper, still blushing, still poised as if to run. 'I wasn't brought up that way.'

'Well,' he said a trifle tartly, 'I wasn't either. But you learn, out in the big bad world. And you learn it isn't all that scarey. You also learn,' he said, more softly, 'that with love it's everything and without it it isn't much.'

'That's what makes me feel so – so unclean,' she whispered. 'I just don't know if – if there was any love in it.'

'I'll tell you what makes me feel unclean,' he said vigorously, and a sudden anger with Greenmont drove him forward to say what he knew he shouldn't, but he could not stop himself, it came out anyway, 'and that's being spied upon like a – a couple of animals by your precious Haila and your precious Viola!'

'Oh,' she whispered, looking absolutely stricken. 'I didn't know. *I didn't know.*'

'I'm sorry,' he said, instantly remorseful, for it had indeed been a frightful thing to say, instantly he was unable to explain what had prompted it, 'I shouldn't have said that. Don't worry about them. They'll never mention it to you. In fact, if we get married, they'll never mention it to anybody. Which is by no means,' he added quickly, 'any reason why we should.'

'I couldn't have Greenmont saying things like that,' she said, still stricken, still almost inaudible. 'They would never stop. You just don't know this place.'

He gave a grim little laugh.

'Oh, yes, I do. Pretty well by now, I think. You're one of theirs. They won't talk about you. They may damn me for ever, but even that they'll get over in time. But just keep it in mind next time you feel like trusting Haila. She doesn't deserve it ... Anyway,' he said, his voice suddenly gentle, 'who said there wasn't love in it? That's what I brought to it.'

For the first time she looked steadily at him, a pained but analytical gaze.

'I think you brought to it – a search for somebody else. I

think that's what you've been conducting ever since you came here. Maybe even ever since your divorce. I don't think you brought any love for me ... I—' her voice broke a little but she went on, 'I – I wanted to think so, for a while, but I ... just ... don't.'

'That isn't true,' he said quietly, and believed it. 'That isn't true. That's gone from me, now, I swear. First, meeting you drove it out, and then my – accident – drove it out, and now it's gone altogether ... If it ever was there. I really did offer you love, Elizavetta. I didn't think you wanted it, and by now I'm convinced of that, but I offered it, anyway. I'm glad I did.'

'I want it,' she said in a tortured whisper. 'From somebody – *some time* – before I get too old and there isn't ... any hope ... at all ... for me.'

For a minute or two he did not respond, though his heart was filled with a sudden staggering pity. It was different for him, he could go away, now, purged of his hurts, free to find someone else who could give him what he needed. But not Eliza, trapped in the library and Big Smith and Greenmont for the rest of her life. He felt abruptly that he must help her somehow, though he did not know exactly how it would be.

'Well,' he said, because he knew he had to say something, 'I wish' – and astounded himself greatly, for he did not know he wished this until he said it – 'I wish it could be me ... Yes,' he said, more strongly, in response to her startled look, for now he was quite sure he meant it, everything was reversed, the world was changed again, determinations, intentions, resolves, new mood, new confidence, new detachment suddenly seemed unimportant and unworthy in the face of her sad forsaken look and lonely threatened heart, 'I wish it could be me. I don't mean,' he added hastily, 'that it can be . . . necessarily. But . . .'

His voice trailed away, so that they sat staring directly at one another at last with hesitant, wondering expressions, in the fresh singing beauty of the mountain morning.

'Louise says,' he remarked at last with a shaky little laugh, 'that nobody's consistent, and maybe I'm not. But – if you want – if you like – I mean, I'm not much, really, and I did – go over the grade. But that was because,' he assured her earnestly, 'I was unhappy about us. Basically.'

'Were you?' she asked, still almost whispering. 'Or were you unhappy about – her – and about me – because I wasn't her?'

'Oh, no!' he declared, though he was struck again by that faint, elusive resemblance, 'No, no. That's all over ... I thought,' he said with a wistful little smile, 'that this was, too. But' – he spread his hands upon his knees and looked down upon them as upon those of a stranger – 'maybe it isn't.'

'I wish I knew what you really feel,' she said, 'what you really think. Then maybe I'd know what I ought to do ... I think,' she added, so quietly he could hardly hear her, 'that I could help you. I think we might be happy together. But I ... I just don't know.'

'Whoever does?' he said, aware that somewhere he had heard or said all this before, struck anew by life's repetitiveness, but sure that this time he meant the words as he had never meant them before. 'It's a chance: a chance.' He stared across-canyon at the mountains, stately and serene in their well-ordered, un-troubled world. 'I think,' he said, very softly, 'I would like to take that chance.'

There was a silence. He did not look at her, he almost forgot for a moment that she was there, so confused and chaotic were his contradictory, whirling thoughts. Everything came rushing back, his divorce, his unhappiness over that, his strange jumble of feelings towards Eliza; his serene conviction after the accident that both were finished and he was freed of ghosts at last, and now this abrupt reversal, this strange surrender, this plunging back once more, unexpectedly but apparently quite willingly, into the turmoil from which he had thought himself extricated; the overtones and echoes that this involved, as she instinctively perceived; his worries, his doubts, his pity – his pity! – and possibly, although he wasn't sure, he perhaps would never be sure – his love.

It made no sense.

Or it made all sense.

He realized in a shattering flash of insight he was powerless to deny or escape that he would never know.

At last she broke the silence with a trembling little sound that he realized with a surge of – what, hope or dismay? Again, he would never know – to be laughter.

'I hate to let Haila think she's right again, but I guess there's

261

nothing for it, is there? I guess . . . if you can take a chance . . .
I can.'

And now what filled his heart? Was he happy or unhappy,
sorry or glad? Again there was such a jumble he could not
say. He thought he was happy, and at least he acted like it: held
out his hands to her as she came towards him with a little half-
cry held her in his arms for an awkward, nervous kiss during
which he knew she was intensely worried lest anyone see them,
sat back and looked at her with a relieved and kindly and loving
expression in his eyes when she stood before him a second later
fidgeting with her dress, pushing at her hair, laughing with an
excitement, pathetic in its intensity, that rendered him helpless.
What had life done to him, coming thus upon him by surprise?
How would he bear the trust it had in this strange fashion imposed upon him? And did he want it, really? And where, in
what great Explanation, did one ever find the reason for such
things?

'Well,' she said finally, 'if you think you'll be all right for –
for a few minutes, I think I'll go up to the Meadows and tell
Haila and the others.'

She laughed again, a current of nervousness running strong
beneath it. He smiled at her, trying to put into it as much reas-
surance as he could.

'Sound happy,' he said gently. 'You're supposed to be.'

She laughed once more, shakily, as she started down the steps.

'It may take me a while. I'm not so – used to it, you know.'

For the rest of that day he did not lack company, nor loud
conversations, not many cordial friends hovering about with
hearty, congratulatory statements. Einar and Sally-Jane came
first, scarcely fifteen minutes after, bringing the car and insisting
that he get dressed and come to the Meadows. He protested
good-naturedly, feeling a little unsteady still, but did so. Haila,
Viola and Mother Magruder were waiting at the Grove when
they arrived – 'Ah!' said the latter's son irreverently, 'The Three
Graces!' – and he found himself swiftly established on a bench,
from which, surrounded by the ladies in the nature of an
honour-guard, he and Eliza held court for several hours. During
this time her nervousness seemed to decrease, his own weird

262

jumble of contradictory emotions to diminish. When in time he became tired and indicated that perhaps he had better go back down the cabin to rest, they were reasonably relaxed and comfortable together.

'Not the most ecstatic bride and groom-to-be I've ever seen,' Louise confided privately to Sally-Jane, 'but I think they'll make it.'

'They're on the Greenmont toboggan,' S.-J. murmured back. 'Nothing can save them now.'

At the cabin he fell deeply asleep, with Eliza and Gray keeping vigil in the living-room; awoke for dinner, and to receive quick greetings and jovial congratulations from Jim Buxton, Bob Townsend and Jerry Drummond when they arrived from the Valley; and once more fell asleep, so soundly that Eliza soon left him in Gray's care and went off to her cabin, exhausted too.

They had no further chance to talk alone, nor, indeed, did either of them seem to want to. Life was rushing them along and it all seemed right yet somehow very strange. There probably was nothing to say anyway, though he hoped there would be later in their lives.

He reflected with a grim little inward smile just before he dropped off that, at any rate, he was committed at last. That had been what Greenmont and the whole wide world had wanted of him, had they not? Now they had it. In an age that made a fetish of commitment he had finally offered his obeisance. He told himself ironically that he hoped the world would be as happy about it as he knew he and Eliza would be.

Or as the world knew he and Eliza would be.

THREE

From the Falls the canyon widened abruptly and then dropped evenly away on both sides to form a natural amphitheatre perhaps thirty miles in length, leading on down through an almost perfectly-tiered succession of gradually diminishing peaks until finally, very far away and just visible under the constant layer of heat-haze that enshrouded it in summer, the eye could faintly discern the geometric interlacing of bare brown plains and neatly cultivated green fields that covered the floor of the great hot Valley. Out of that fertile furnace came the food for half a nation, desert made to bloom by the skilful application of just such waters as those that teemed for ever over the jagged limestone lip of the Falls, filled the deep green pool above, plunged forward to fill the deep green pool beneath, then surged on over still another ledge of limestone to fall again, and pool again, and so, in an endless progression of big falls and little falls, turbulent sluiceways and quiet reaches, descend at last to the Valley and the sea.

Now it was 4 p.m. on Saturday – Engagement Saturday, and they had all been right (though in a sense, perhaps, wrong) and he had been wrong (though in a sense, perhaps, right – but he had told himself last night to close his mind on that debate for ever) – and here they were, joking and laughing and clattering their pans and baskets as they scrambled down the brambly path from the road to the secluded area along the river where they planned to eat. Flanked by Eliza and Gray, his two faithful attendants, he stood at the last level turning in the path before it descended sharply its final 100 feet to the Falls, and surveyed them all against the panorama of receding ranges below: Einar and Sally-Jane, flushed and boisterous, no doubt from some last-minute encounter in the bedroom before jumping in the car to make the three-mile run down from Greenmont; Viola Townsend, moving heavily on the narrow, tortuous walkway, red-faced and puffing, her solemn round face careful with the effort of maintaining her balance; Haila coming after, lean and angular and perfectly turned-out in her suède jacket and tweed skirt, showing a surprising agility as she clambered down; Louise, uttering jocular 'Heys!' and 'Ho's!' and 'Steady, there old girls!' as she slipped and slithered along; Bob Townsend and Jim Buxton, carrying the liquor and urging one another heartily to, 'Watch it, there!' and, 'Be careful, boy, be careful!' as they half-walked, half-sat their way down, holding lovingly aloft their precious gurgling burden without which no party, of course, could be complete; next, ironic and surprising, Mother Magruder, her enormous bulk assisted and supported on the turns by a sweating and occasionally profane Jerry Drummond as she wheezed and cackled along; and, finally, his earnest little housemate, serious but excited, at his side, and on the other, looking pleased and for once reasonably well-relaxed, his lady-love in one of her most sportive outfits, all spangles and streaks and loud, insistent colours.

Greenmont! There they were, this oddly assorted group, quarrels forgotten, clashes put aside, their crisis over his disruption of their placid unchanging routine smoothed out and safely behind them – Einar and Sally-Jane calling jolly japes to Haila and Viola, those two dignified ladies replying comfortably in kind, Louise and Mother Magruder joshing each other amicably as they negotiated the tricky trail, the men happy and jovial in the promise of the party to come.

'We're friends,' Elizavetta had told him: 'we survive each other.'

And so they had, once again, surmounting one more of the many little crises that from time to time disturbed their lovely mountain paradise. The crises were never very big – sometimes, he told himself ironically, nothing bigger than the crisis of a heart – and after they had been successfully disposed of, Greenmont returned to the even flow of its perfect days and all was jollity, mirth and friendly frolicking again.

'Hey, there, you observers!' Louise shouted up from the edge of the water, which she and Haila had reached at last. 'Don't stand there gawking! Come on in, the water's fine!'

'I'll bet it is,' he called back. 'All of fifty degrees, I'll bet.'

'Forty!' Jerry called over his shoulder just before grabbing desperately but successfully for Mother Magruder, who had turned to look up, slipped on a bear-clover, given a startled whoop, and almost gone over. 'Forty – but – you'll – love – it!'

'I expect to,' he replied, for here below the narrower passages where Greenmont lay, out in relatively open country and exposed to the direct drive of the sun, the canyon still held considerable heat from the fading day. 'We're coming right down.'

And placing a hand on Gray's shoulder, holding Elizavetta's arm, which trembled a little under his touch but at least did not pull away, he safely negotiated the steep descent, finding that by now he was in almost complete command of himself again, his aches and bruises no longer painful, his dizziness almost entirely gone, rested and comfortable physically whatever the lingering ills that might lurk elsewhere.

Beside the Falls, where three enormous slabs of rock furnished them space on which to spread their picnic hampers, Jerry and Louise disappeared into a little clump of trees to change into swimsuits, and when they came out Haila and Viola went to do the same. Jim Buxton remarked with a humorous chuckle that he expected he would just sit by in case old Haila had to be dragged out when she hit the water, and Bob Townsend declared himself in jovial agreement. Mother Magruder wheezed that it had been ten years since she had gone swimming at the Falls, and anyway she didn't want to displace all the water and dry it up for everybody else, so she would watch with them. Eliza and Sally-Jane changed next, the major and Gray and Einar followed quickly. Ten minutes after their arrival Jerry Drummond dived off a high rock into the pool that measured perhaps fifty by seventy feet and emerged spouting and blowing on the far side to let loose a bellow that literally echoed back and forth for a moment between the peaks above.

'My *God*, that's cold!' he shouted. 'Hurry up, you sissies!'

A moment later they were all in, shouting and laughing at the fierce initial shock, thrashing about to restore the circulation, gradually relaxing as their bodies adjusted to the fierce pounding of the racing, steely waters.

'Be careful, now, sweetie,' Louise cautioned, coming alongside as he drifted towards the lip of the Falls. 'It's a thirty-foot drop to the second pool and you're not in much condition to try it. Again.'

'That's right,' he agreed, managing a grin between shivers as they came to the limestone edge and rested a moment, paddling against the insistent surge of the river which would, if it could, send them hurtling over. 'What a view!'

'It is that. A great place for a party. And,' she added lightly, 'a great occasion for one.'

'Do you think so?' he asked, quite seriously for a moment, so that she turned away from the vista below and gave him an equally serious look.

'Do you?'

'I—' he ducked his head abruptly under water and out again as if to clear it. But he did not return her look, only staring away down the canyon. 'Sure. Of course. Why not? Certainly.'

'It's a little late,' she told him with some severity, 'to be going

266

through that kind of performance again. Snap out of it, Bill. You've made the decision, now stick with it.'

'Did I make it?' he asked, giving her a quizzical sidelong glance to which she replied with a frown of real annoyance.

'If you don't know,' she said sharply, 'then I pity you.' And turning abruptly she braced her feet against the edge of the Falls and shoved off across the pool with a determined stroke that swiftly left him behind.

'Hey, Bill!' Einar shouted from the diving-rock. 'Watch Gray and me do our Olympic turn!'

'O.K.,' he shouted back. 'Just give me a minute to get on dry land, though. I'm frozen to death.'

'Come over here,' Haila called. 'You'd better get out now, anyway. You're officially an invalid, you know.'

'I know,' he said, attempting to pull himself up on the rock beside her but finding that his arms were too weak still to support him, so that he had to swim ten feet downstream to a shallow spot and walk back, 'I guess I really am,' he said with a smile. 'Now, go ahead,' he called to Einar, who promptly did a double jack-knife. Gray followed with a quite commendable half-gaynor. Everyone applauded lustily, the three non-swimmers from the first slab, where Mother Magruder was already methodically unpacking the hampers, the others from various vantage points around the pool where they had paused in their splashings to drift with the racing current and watch.

'Entertainment courtesy of the management,' Einar said cheerfully, surfacing alongside Haila. 'Dancing girls later. Or did you bring your own?'

'She's over there with Viola,' he said, and so she was, the two of them paddling about sedately in the shallower section on the other side.

'Yeah,' Einar said, preparing to take off. 'Why aren't you with her? You act like an old married man already.'

'That's right,' he said, and for a second an almost puzzled expression came into his eyes. 'I do, don't I?'

'That's much better, Bill, honey,' Sally-Jane assured him, appearing suddenly behind Einar and splashing him vigorously. 'It makes everything much calmer for everybody.'

'Ho!' her husband said. 'When did you like it calm? I haven't been aware—'

'Quiet,' Sally-Jane said, placing her hands on his shoulders and shoving his head under. 'Don't let them bother you, Bill,' she flung back hastily before starting a sprint-stroke and dashing away just ahead of Einar, who came up blowing and indignant and ready for battle. 'Easy's best!'

'It really is, Bill,' Haila said comfortably as he settled down beside her and they watched Einar and Sally-Jane's noisy race for a moment. 'And, you see? Things work out – things work out. All the tangled threads come together, and things work out.'

'It's comforting,' he observed, not without irony.

'It is,' she said placidly. 'It's nice to know that no matter how complicated things may seem to be at a given moment, sooner or later they will straighten themselves out if we just keep calm and give them time.'

'Coming from you,' he said gravely, 'I shall treasure that thought.'

She chuckled.

'Without a little bite, Bill, we wouldn't know you. And life would be so much duller for us all.'

'Good,' he said with a smile that was not too unfriendly. 'At least I'm good for something: laughs.'

'Try a few, you silly boy,' she said lightly. 'You'll be amazed at their therapeutic value. Anyway,' she added in a firmly josh-ing tone, 'you're the happy engaged one, and I refuse to let you be serious. Eliza! Eliza! Come over here and tend to this beau of yours! I'm going to get dressed and help Mother Magruder get things ready for dinner.'

But Eliza, looked embarrassed, called out, 'I'll help you,' instead of coming over, so he sat alone on the rock while Louise and Viola joined her and Haila behind the clump of trees. Presently they emerged to start bustling about with Mother Magruder while Jim and Bob Townsend began laying a fire in a sharp cleft of rock, forming a natural flue leading up towards a leaning half-dead pine above, that bore the smoke-marks of many a previous picnic.

Soon Gray, blue-veined and chattering, clambered out beside him, then Jerry and Einar, after a couple of final turns through the darkening water. Then they too were dressed and gathering around the picnic rocks. The day began to die, in that strange golden light, filled with summer yet carrying the first cool hint of summer's ending, in which it sometimes seems that all the world must be about to cry.

'Autumn coming,' Louise remarked quietly beside him, and shivered a little. 'The years don't wait.'

He nodded gravely.

'No.'

'How brave people are,' she remarked, still quietly. 'Not about the big, dramatic things, but just the ordinary business of getting through the days – the little things that tear you down.' She gave a wry little smile. 'What guts it takes just to *live*, let alone get dramatic about it.'

'My goodness,' he said with an answering smile. 'I'm the one who ought to be gloomy, not you.'

'And not you, either,' she told him firmly. 'You're on your way, and it's going to be all right.'

'Do you think so?' he asked, glancing across the slabs, now spread with paper tablecloths and napkins, cluttered with the paraphernalia of picnics, to the place where Elizavetta knelt before the fire assisting Jim and Bob. 'I hope you're right.'

Half an hour later, first drinks consumed, seconds in hand, food ready for cooking, they stood about the leaping fire while the night drew rapidly in. Far down, the last faint remnant of day, a thin band of lemon light, still defined the level horizon of the Valley. Above, the rising moon was already beginning to cast the jagged peaks into steadily sharper outline as it came from behind them to the east. Very soon it would climb free into open sky and the world would turn luminous, eerie, soft and white. A million stars were out. Suddenly it was quite cold, the air had sharpened, sweaters were welcome, the fire was cosy, warm and good. The faces around him became increasingly relaxed, increasingly kind, friendly and intimate. Greenmont was repeating itself again, in one of its most pleasant manifestations. A tide of good-fellowship washed over them all.

'Come on, everybody!' Mother Magruder cried. 'Time to fix the chow! Let's get to it!'

'You heard my Ma,' Einar said. 'She's given you fair warning! If she gets it all, it will be your own fault.'

'Stop being an insolent pup,' his mother ordered jovially, 'and

269

fix me a drink. Don't worry about *this* crew. I've never known any of 'em go hungry, yet.'

'Eliza and Bill, honey,' Sally-Jane said, 'why don't you find yourselves a good spot, now, and let the rest of us look after you. After all, it's your party, isn't it?'

'You bet it is, Sal,' Bob Townsend agreed. 'That's a fine idea! Come on, now, you two!'

'Well—' Eliza began hesitantly, looking at the major with an expression in which shyness and a pleased excitement mingled. 'If you think—'

'Of course I think,' he said, smiling directly into her eyes, excluding the rest, moving forward to tuck her hand firmly under his arm. 'Of course I do.' He addressed her again as he had that very first day, at the gate. 'Where will it be, Princess? You choose the throne.'

'I don't think it had better be too far from the fire,' she said with a sudden little smile at her own practicality. 'It's cold.'

'That's our girl,' Jerry said as they all laughed. 'Here's to Common-Sense Hints on Romance, by E. Berrenger.'

'I'll drink to that,' the major said, lifting his glass, and, with another burst of laughter, they all followed suit.

'I think it had better be right here, then, sweetie,' Louise said, dusting off a place on the rock nearest the blaze, which now was beginning to form a bank of glowing charcoals beneath its dancing surface. 'You can keep warm, and we' – she chuckled – 'can keep an eye on you.'

'That figures,' he said, and again they all laughed, perfectly friendly, perfectly happy. 'But don't get me wrong. We love it!'

'Might as well, boy,' Jim Buxton said in his carefully humorous way. 'You're going to be part of us from now on.'

'What have I done,' he asked, but with a grin that made it acceptable, 'to deserve so curious a fate?'

'Just got yourself engaged to the most devastating female in the entire Sierra Nevada range, that's all,' Einar told him. 'We've all suspected she was, all these years, and now we know.'

'Let's drink to that,' Bob Townsend suggested. 'Come on, Vi!' he added at the slightly disapproving expression that came automatically to his wife's face. 'This is an occasion!'

'Oh, I suppose it is, really,' she said with a sudden smile. 'After all, once in a while I have to stop being Stuffy Old Viola!'

'I'll drink to *that*!' Einar said, and for a second she looked like Stuffy Old Viola indeed. But then, as they all shouted merrily and raised their glasses and rushed the moment along, away from all their little family bickerings and into the happy spirit of the occasion, even she relaxed and took a drink.

'You see what you've accomplished, you two,' Haila told them with a chuckle. 'You've made us all your willing slaves.'

'Which reminds me,' Louise said briskly, 'that it's about time to start the hamburgers and let your slaves feed you and themselves. Jerry, cook up!'

'Yes, ma'am,' he said, placing an iron grille over one side of the fire. 'Viola, unwrap your gourmet goodies and let's get this show on the road.'

Sitting a little apart in their special place by the fire, he and Eliza watched in silence the pleasant scene, firelight illuminating the happy, vigorous faces, the busy bodies bustling about in final preparation.

'How strange it all is,' she said finally, in a voice so low it barely reached his ears. 'So many stops and starts – and here we are.'

'Are you glad?' he asked, giving her a quick glance, aware that they were being watched, not wanting to look too intently or ask with an air into which others might read too much significance. Yet what could be more significant, he told himself abruptly. What a curious thought to have!

'Are you?' he repeated, more strongly.

'I don't know whether gladness is the word,' she said, looking at the far peaks now stark and blazing in the full triumph of the moon. 'I think maybe gladness is something we'll have to earn, over the years. I don't know whether we have it yet. Do you?'

'I know I want to give it to you,' he said, reaching for her hand as though in some way physical contact might clarify the uncertain clamour of the heart.

'And I to you,' she said, returning the pressure with an almost anguished desperation. 'I do, I do.'

'Eliza—' he said with a sudden rush of emotion, forgetting the others, turning towards her, taking both her hands in his, a des-

271

peration loving yet almost frightened in his eyes, 'Eliza—'

'Hold it!' somebody shouted, a flash-bulb popped, the world was momentarily wiped out in a blinding flash of light.

'Good for you, boy!' Bob Townsend cried. 'You'll be a real photographer, yet!'

'I hope so,' Gray said shyly, gradually materializing as the major's eyes began to focus once more and he became aware that they were all looking and laughing and applauding while the boy advanced the film in his little box camera and threw the spent bulb into the fire where it expired with a decisive pop! Elizavetta's eyes were wide and startled, momentarily frightened as they looked into his, but trying to convey to her the thought *We must laugh* he did so himself as he turned towards his friends of Greenmont, contriving by some miracle of control not to drop her hands guiltily but rather to continue to hold them firmly in his.

'I guess you got one for the books that time, buddy,' he said with a laugh that managed to be quite amused. 'We'll make it number one in our album.'

'Einar told me to do it,' the boy said with a pleased smile. 'We didn't think you'd mind.'

'We don't, do we, Eliza?' he said, gradually and naturally relinquishing her hands, which fled back to her lap and trembled there.

'Why, no,' she said with an uncertain little laugh. 'I hope you got it focused right, Gray.'

'I'm sure it's perfect,' Jerry said in a tone that indicated he didn't really approve. 'Get some plates, somebody, and let's eat. The hamburgers are done.'

And with Viola's hamburgers, Haila's beans, Louise's salad, Mother Magruder's preserves, Sally-Jane's chocolate cake, the pickles, the relish, the catsup, the mustard, the lettuce, the onions, the sliced tomatoes and the potato chips, the moment passed and the party moved to a new and less intimate plane filled with the details of eating, the comfortable noises of nutriment, the slower and lazier tempo of increasing internal satisfaction. It was a good picnic, one which was often remembered in later conversations as having been, ironically, among the best ever held at Greenmont, and for a time even he and Elizavetta were allowed to occupy themselves with enjoying it. There were things he would have liked to say to her, perhaps – although he really had no idea – things she would have liked to say to him. But where was the chance? The occasion stopped them all.

'Now, then,' Jim Buxton said at last, getting up and reaching for the bourbon, 'help me fix everybody another drink, Bob, and we'll have a toast.'

'Sure thing,' Bob said, rising a little unsteadily but with great enthusiasm despite Viola's protesting hand on his arm. 'Nothing like a toast for a time like this.'

'Now,' Jim said when glasses had been refilled, even Gray's grape soda, and everyone was sitting back again relaxed and happy, 'old Haila, here, has a word or two to say.'

'Oh, no,' Einar murmured, but Sally-Jane put her hand over his mouth, so he bit it and his protest was lost in a scuffle that ended in giggles when his mother reached over, wheezing, and swatted them with an unopened bag of potato chips.

'Dear friends,' Haila said, standing beside the fire, the moonlight picking up the silver in her hair and throwing her confident figure into sharp relief against the backdrop of the mountains below, 'this is indeed a happy occasion for all of us in Greenmont. One who is *very dear* to us has found – ('Finally,' Einar whispered, irrepressible, and this time it was Louise who pushed him, so that he fell backwards and almost went in the water. Haila went on, pretending not to notice) – 'what we hope – what we *know* – will be a great happiness.'

My God, the major thought: she really means it. Would that all of us were so positive.

'In so doing, she has added to our family in Greenmont a new friend, one who we know will become, in time, equally dear. There were moments,' Haila said, and a little coyness came into her tone, 'there were *some moments* when the course of true love did not seem to run smooth. But we knew – *we knew* – that everything would work out for the best. And so it has!'

'Hear, hear!' said Bob Townsend loudly, and there was a scattering of applause. Haila stopped for a moment during which they could hear the wind rustling in the pines around them, the muffled crash of water as it reached the bottom of the Falls thirty feet below, the snap and crackle of the fire on to which Jerry had just thrown another log.

'Whatever problems there *have been*,' she went on, 'whatever

273

problems there *are* – whatever problems there *may be* – we
know they *have been, are being* and *will be* overcome by these
two wonderful people who mean so much to Greenmont.

'Bill, Greenmont welcomes you!

'Eliza – *dear* Eliza – your old friends wish you well! '

And amid other loud cries of, 'Hear, hear! ' and 'Good old
Eliza! ' and 'Good old Bill! ' – rather like a moonlit version of
the Mad Hatter's Tea-Party, as Louise was always to remark
later in recounting the events of that gorgeous, fateful evening
– glasses were raised and toasts were drunk and the picnic
became even more amiable than before.

For a moment or two he did not know whether he should
answer, or should let Eliza do it, or whether they both should.
Mother Magruder decided it for them.

'Response! ' she whooped. 'Response, you two! First Eliza
and then Bill! We won't settle for less, you know! We won't
settle for less! '

Obediently Elizavetta stood, outwardly calm though he could
sense her trembling as she stood beside him in the almost blinding luminescence that poured down from the sky. She had refused liquor all evening, so now he held out his glass to her in a
gesture that brought more laughter and applause, and after a
moment she took a deep swallow and then folded her hands
tightly together against her breast as she began to speak.

'Haila, and all of you: you *are* my friends, my old and dear
friends. I—' she paused for a second and then said, 'We,' firmly,
and Jim Buxton said, 'Brave girl! ' and everybody laughed –
'we thank you for your kind wishes. I know it has been a – perhaps a strange experience for – Bill' – the major realized with
a start that it was the first time she had ever used his name – 'to
come to Greenmont, not knowing us or our ways—'

'Which,' Louise murmured, 'are, like those of some others,
peculiar.'

'—and not, perhaps, always understanding us. Sometimes we
talk about being just one big family at Greenmont, and in some
ways, I think we are. At least,' she said, and suddenly her voice
trembled, 'you are *my* family, and you have been for many
years . . .'

There was a little silence filled with memories and emotion,
and then she went on, more strongly.

'I don't know – I don't suppose anyone ever knows, really – how things will work out for us, but – we start with your love, and that means a great deal. Thank you all.'

Again there were loud sounds of approval, given a deeper and more tender note by their old friendship for her, their old liking which was indeed, as she said, love or close to it, all the many days and many things they had shared together, so many memories stretching back down over thirty years to the time when she had been just a little girl, long before she grew up to work in the library at Big Smith, wear odd clothes, and worry about The Blight.

Haila and Viola frankly wiped away a tear, Louise and Sally-Jane were touched, Mother Magruder wheezed a couple of times in a very emotional manner, and Bob Townsend blew his nose. Silence fell and the major stood up.

Abruptly as he did so a new mood fell upon them, a strange moment in which, possibly for the first time and possibly – for who knew, with all of life's chances and the swift, dulling nature of time and habit? – the last, they looked clearly at one another, there in the moonlight on the rocks by the Falls.

Ten people who had pretty well ruined his life for ever, or come so close to it that only a miracle had pulled him back; ten people who had proceeded to give Humpty Dumpty a great fall and then had tried to put him together again as hastily and contritely as they could. Apparently they had succeeded. Or had they? He was not sure even now as he stood there facing them in the clear cold whiteness; any more than they were sure, as he perceived in some instinctive flash of perception, that the effort had been worth it, or that he really was the prince they wanted for their wistful, worrying, woebegone sleeping beauty.

And what about the sleeping beauty herself? He gave her a sudden quick, wondering glance as she sat quietly beside him in the moonlight. Her little speech had been graceful and touching, it had mentioned him by name, it has used 'we' and 'us', though none of these without some hesitation. She, like himself, seemed to be in the grip of a determination to go ahead, to take some definitive step, to do something, to be committed at last and get it over with and thus – perhaps – and possibly – and if they were very lucky – find some end to loneliness, some answer to the heart's sad crying, some surcease from all the little doubts that underlie the world.

'My friends of Greenmont,' he began, and Bob Townsend said comfortably, 'You see, he calls us friends. What were you girls worrying about, Vi?' which caused his wife to say, 'Shhhhh!' and look embarrassed – 'and, yes, Bob, I do call you friends, because we have been through a lot together. Isn't that what you told me once, Elizavetta? How did you put it?' – she gave him a startled, almost warning look – 'We've survived each other. Of course,' he said, and he could see they obviously weren't sure how they should take it, so he grinned – 'I almost *didn't* survive, for a minute or two, there. But,' he went on in an amicable tone, and he could see them visibly relax, 'the Lord was with little William, and somehow I managed. And so here we are.

'Here we are. I would ask of you – *we* would ask of you – a little patience, a little charity, a little slowness in judging, a little hesitation to condemn. Greenmont, I will admit' – and again he grinned – 'comes, possibly, as close to perfection as man can get on this imperfect planet, but once in a while – take it easy, O.K.? Remember everybody's human, and we all make mistakes, and we all have our own way of looking at things, and what seems this to you may seem that to me, and so – be kind. It isn't much to ask.'

'I'll say "Hear, hear" to that,' said Einar loudly, and in the curious little stillness that had come over them the major could hear Sally-Jane say, 'Likewise,' and Louise make a firm, agreeing sound.

'As for me,' he said, for he knew he had pressed the thought far enough, it was best to let it rest and work in them, if that were possible, in its own good time, 'I'm a mess. Oh, yes, I am,' he said in response to Haila's murmured, 'Oh, now, *Bill!*'

'Or was. A real, gone mess – all mixed up about a lot of things when I came here. But maybe I'm beginning to get everything sorted out at last. Maybe with Eliza's help – and your help – it will continue to make sense. That is what I ask of Greenmont: to give us a chance . . .'

His voice lowered and everything around seemed brighter and stronger and more emphatic to them – or would when they remembered it later: the moonlight whiter and more blinding, the wind's rustle louder and more searching, the river noisier and more insistent as it surged over the Falls, the mountains bigger and grander and more overwhelming as they loomed above and fell away below. His listeners were absolutely still when he spoke his final words, very softly:

'Give *me* a chance.'

'Hurray!' Bob Townsend said, after an awkward little moment. 'Er – hurray! Great speech, great speech!' And at once they were all talking and applauding and laughing and relaxing, rather nervously perhaps, but still with a determined enthusiasm and friendly cordiality designed to erase any unfortunate tensions that might have crept in during his rather odd little talk. 'Really *strange*,' as Mother Magruder was to describe it so often in the years to come, with a rather puzzled cackle that always began full-blast but then trailed out into a rather thoughtful grunt. '*I* didn't know whether he was happy or not, or how *we* were supposed to feel.'

Obviously the others had the same reaction, but after the first flurry of slightly uneasy noise they quickly assumed that everything must be all right. After all, he had smiled at Eliza, and even bent and kissed her gently on the forehead, before he sat down, which brought a special burst of applause and made their friendly noises even louder and more relieved. A moment later Louise had started a tune, off-key as usual, but vigorous, and quickly they were singing in perfect comfort and good fellowship, all doubts forgotten, all tensions banished, the world once more well-ordered and recognizable under the compulsions of old friendship and shared memories of the same ritual many times repeated in the long, happy history of Greenmont.

They must have sung for half an hour or more, and in the midst of it he sat beside Eliza holding her hand in a dutiful but absent-minded grasp whose nature she apparently came to realize, for in time she removed it. He gave her a smile of perfect friendliness, but as though from a great distance, and for a moment she looked deeply troubled. Then 'Waltzing Matilda' rollicked over them, echoing raucously back and forth between the cliffs in the silver serenity of the night, and when he automatically reclaimed her hand and began to sing, she looked less uneasy and did the same. Inside, he still was at a great distance.

277

This was what it had all come to at last, his unhappy searching, his bitter, crippled flailing about to break loose from the bondage the past had placed upon him, his attempt to forget the paralysing agony of his divorce and all it had meant to him in the way of love rejected, hope made laughable, self-respect grievously shattered if not altogether destroyed. Liberated on his own recognizances, coming to Greenmont by a set of curious chances, he had found – Elizavetta. Shy and lonely and unhappy, too, she had become for him – or had he, he wondered, required her to become – the answer to all this. Odd, awkward, exaggerated, frightened, yet in some curious fashion reminiscent of the other who had made him so unhappy, she had also proved herself to be decent and generous and good and kind as the other could never be, within the limits permitted her by her friends and the tight little world in which they had lived so much of their lives together. Because of those limits he had said to her, and said to them, things he would never have dreamed of saying at other times in other circumstances. On far too many occasions he had spoken with a brutal directness and an offensive candour that had passed the bounds of sense and decency. He had let their game of idle and essentially good-hearted gossip entrap and entangle him until he had almost died of it. He had taken it seriously, because the whole thing was serious to him. And yet somehow, out of all their strange little battle that had raged back and forth over the fragile ground of Elizavetta's hesitant affections, something had emerged that might possibly – just possibly – give him peace.

To this he was committed, now, and must not look back; or was he, and would he? Suppose it did not succeed, suppose it was all a mistake, suppose the commitment had been to a memory, or a dream, or an impossible figment of his tortured need? 'You're trying to make me something I'm not,' she had protested several times. Perhaps she was right.

His friends of Greenmont swung into 'I've Been Working On The Railroad', and he shivered in the midst of their happy clamour. Once again, momentarily, the Weendigo went walking.

But, no, it could not. It could not. He had made his decision, he had pledged his heart, he had said: 'Take a chance,' and, finally, the one he had appealed to had agreed. He could not betray that now: he could not betray her, or himself, or his concept of himself. With her it might all prove right, with her the terrors that stalk the mind and sap the heart might vanish in a gentle and growing happiness for them both. With her the commitment might prove valid. With her he might truly be able to achieve some real and genuine peace, or at least keep his heart at bay until enough years had passed so that it would grow too old and tired to keep on yearning for what it could not have, and trouble him no more.

When they had finally stopped their singing, gathered up their picnic gear and begun the slippery, dangerous climb up the narrow path to the cars parked along the road, he stopped for a moment on the level place from which he had studied them at the picnic's beginning. There he turned and looked back down the long sweep of river and ranges to the Valley. The others passed him, joking and laughing, Elizavetta paused for a moment to stand with him, then went on a little hurt, a little puzzled, as he smiled automatically but did not speak nor attempt to detain her.

He looked at the moon, the stars, the enormous brilliant night. His heart cried out, words and thoughts tumbled half-formed and incoherent about his mind. There was nothing to say but desperately he wished to say it. He raised his arms to the mountains and a strange little cry, not very loud, not very sensible, anguished, incomprehensible, stricken, broke from his lips.

There was something for him somewhere but he did not, even then, know where.

'Sweetie,' Louise said suddenly two hundred feet above, pausing by the door of the car, picnic hamper half-in, half-out, her whole body suddenly tense and rigid. 'I smell smoke.'

'The hell you do!' Jerry said with a defensive lightness, though instantly his body, too, tensed with the instinctive dread that haunts all who live in the mountains, and on the back of his neck the hair began to rise with the awful thought of what might happen to them and to Greenmont, lying peacefully in the canyon above, if it were true, and if—

He hurried around the car and smelled the air intently.

279

'Yes,' he said quietly, 'the hell you do.'

And lifting his voice in a wild, warning shout, he grabbed an axe and a shovel from the car and hurled himself, slipping and sliding, half-cursing and half-sobbing from fear, rage and excitement, back down the tortuous trail to the Falls.

⤶ FOUR ⤷

Of the confused, chaotic events of the next forty-five minutes, only the most confused and chaotic memories remain in Greenmont. Nobody, in the first place, ever has known exactly how the fire started; certainly the major, when Jerry came plummeting down the path with Einar, Jim and Bob close behind, was as amazed as anyone. It took him, in fact, a second or two to grasp what was going on, but the moment he realized – when the word, 'Fire!' finally emerged from their largely incoherent shoutings – he assumed command. 'I think he was communing with his soul when we reached him,' Jerry was to say later, 'but it sure didn't take him long to forget it.' It was then that Haila usually murmured, 'Such a waste. *Such* a waste!' in a troubled voice and, occasionally, brushed away a tear.

In any event, things moved fast when they began to move. From the level landing where the major stood, he and his companions could see below them in the luminous night a small pillar of smoke rising serenely in the scarcely-moving air. At its base the first little orange tongues of their enemy were moving upward on the trunk of the big dead pine above the picnic-area, beginning already to flicker through the tinder-dry brush and oily bear-clover surrounding it. Even as they watched the air began to stir, the wind turned, an evil little gust raced up-canyon and the fire leaped twenty feet up the trunk of the tree and flared out as though from a suddenly-opened blast-furnace thirty feet along the ground on either side.

For just a second they were paralysed by the ancient, primordial fear, they cowered in their cave amid the half-eaten bones of mammoths and looked out at the monster threatening to engulf them. Then civilization and training reasserted themselves, the major shouted, 'Come on, damn it, let's get down there!' and he and his little crew began to scramble forward.

'Are you sure you're all right?' Einar managed to call to him as they went. 'You're not very strong yet, maybe you'd better go back—'

'Back, hell!' the major shouted angrily. 'I've been fighting fires in these mountains since I was sixteen. You and Jim take the left there and try to get ahead of it and start chopping down everything you see. Bob and Jerry, you do the same on the right. We'll get you, you son of a bitching bastard!' he shouted directly at the fire, which now was a personalized enemy for them all. 'You bet we will!' Einar echoed with a wild exuberance, and even Bob Townsend yelled, 'Yes, God damn you!' with a startling if somewhat liquified vituperation.

After that, the situation became rapidly more confused. The wind, joined in perverse association with the fire, moved ever faster up the canyon. Within ten minutes an area roughly two hundred yards in diameter was burning around and up from the Falls. Above on the road Louise, Sally-Jane, Elizavetta and Gray felt as though they were looking into a vest-pocket edition of Hell in which flames leaped ever higher and the figures below swirled in and out of sight in the sinuous smoke until finally they could be seen no more and only shouts and curses signified that life still existed. By the time Haila's car reached the gate, having paused only long enough at the store so that she and Viola and Mother Magruder could scream, 'Fire at the Falls!' to the startled cowhands lounging there, they could see, looking back down the moonlit chasm, a great smudge of grey against the unearthly brightness of the sky.

'Oh, dear!' Viola wailed as she scrambled back in, 'I forgot to lock the gate!'

'It doesn't matter,' Haila said, grimly fighting the wheel as she trod on the gas and sent the car leaping ahead, 'it will have to be open, anyway. Stop blubbering and reach over here and keep honking this horn. Mother, I'm going to slow down at every cabin we come to and you yell, "Fire at the Falls! Men go, women and children come to the Meadows!" '

Thus organized for their part of it, they careered up the road, blaring through the night, so that within fifteen minutes from Louise's first exclamation cars filled with the excited segments of Greenmont's Saturday night, some in good condition to fight a fire and some not, were already beginning to screech back down towards the Falls. Within five minutes after that a call

281

had been put in to the ranger-station fifteen miles down-river and Haila, breathing a little hard but otherwise perfectly calm, was already making mental plans for assigning the women and children to the remaining cars and starting them on their way out. 'If it just doesn't jump the road,' she kept saying quietly to herself. 'If it just doesn't jump the road.'

By some miracle, considering how many other things were against them, it did not do so as the little band from the picnic fought on. Eyes half-blinded, windpipes half-choked, unable to see one another for minutes at a time in the steadily mounting inferno around them, they chopped and cut and slashed and dug with the axes and shovels they had all brought to the picnic and which, theoretically, should have been used to prevent just what was happening now. Yet as they fought, and in hasty flashes of memory reviewed the final moments before their departure, none could remember where the fault had come. The fire had apparently been out, drowned in water, the last charcoals had seemingly been dispersed and killed – Einar, in fact, had scooped up most of them and shovelled them directly into the pool. Most, but apparently not all. But if there was any guilt on anyone, no one would ever know. And no one, really, cared. It had happened, as fire sometimes does happen in the mountains, even among those most constantly aware of its possibilities, and now it was up to them to hold it, if they could, until help came.

Strangely the wind, abruptly reversed for no reason they could tell, was blowing back down-canyon at the moment, giving them valuable assistance. So was the configuration of the canyon, for it narrowed sharply a hundred yards or so above the Falls into a cleft measuring perhaps 400 feet in depth from river to road. Along its upper edges Bob and Jerry on the one side and Jim and Einar on the other worked grimly on, Bob and Jim beginning to feel their years, increasingly and excruciatingly tired, Jerry and Einar scratched and aching but still relatively fresh, the major, first on one side then on the other, shouting encouragement and directions as he hacked and chopped at the stubborn undergrowth.

'Get on up a little way and start working towards each other,' he shouted finally when they reached a point where the canyon began to become both narrower and shallower. 'I'm going to try to get ahead and start a back-fire if the damned wind doesn't cross me up.'

'You watch it, now!' Einar shouted. 'You ought to let me do that, you're in no condition to—'

'Let me do it for Greenmont!' the major shouted back, and they always remembered the strange note of irony, half-bitter, half-humorous, entirely mocking, that was in his voice. 'It's the least I can do, for all you've done for me.'

'Oh—' Einar began, not knowing exactly what to say but feeling he must protest this odd comment, shouted through the smoke to them at so odd a time, riding mockingly over the evil crackling of the fire and the crash of branches that were beginning to fall in increasing numbers all around. 'Don't be a damned fool!'

'It's got to be done,' the major called back, his tone once more impersonal and business-like. 'Come help me if you like, but Jerry, you and Bob stay where you are and work towards Jim. Pray the wind doesn't change again, or we've had it.'

For the next few minutes no one said more, as the wind continued steadily down-canyon and the fire, temporarily thwarted, turned in upon itself and began to chew at the few tall pines that had managed over the centuries to find footage in the narrow cleft. Bob Townsend's heart was thumping violently, Jim Buxton felt a knifing pain in his side, even Jerry was beginning to slow a little as he slashed away at the clinging underbrush and the snake-like willows. Einar, too, was becoming increasingly short of breath, and it was only by deliberately closing his mind to what the major's physical condition must be by this time that he managed to fight his way up the river to a point perhaps fifty yards above the uppermost fringe of the fire, where he found him waiting, panting, at the base of another dead pine.

'I still think you'd better not—' Einar began, but with a savage anger the major turned on him.

'Shut up, you damned silly kid! This is a man's job and if you're not a man, get the hell back on the road with the women! Now,' he said, more calmly though it was obvious he was having some difficulty breathing, 'go back down there and bring me a couple of burning branches. Move!'

'All right,' Einar said with a bitterness of his own, 'but you don't have to worry. You'll be a hero! '

'I won't if you futz around until the wind changes! ' the major snapped. 'Now, *move!'*

'That must be the crew from the ranger station,' Sally-Jane said, pointing down the canyon. Far beneath, the lights of three vehicles twisted and turned and climbed with agonizing slowness towards them through the ghostly night.

'Somebody ought to be coming from camp soon, too,' Eliza-vetta said in a trembling voice. 'Where *is* everybody! '

'I'm sure the girls are there by this time,' Louise said. 'It won't be long before we get reinforcements, if the boys can just hold it down there.'

'I think it's slowed down a little,' Gray told them, peering over the edge with a fascinated fear and excitement.

'The wind's changed,' Louise noted. 'Let's pray for it not to change back.'

'How can you be so calm about it?' Eliza demanded, starting to cry. 'Your husband is down there—'

'Your husband may be, if he lives through it,' Louise said crisply. 'What good does it do to bellow? That isn't any help to them.'

'Oh, I hate this place! ' Elizavetta cried. 'I hate it! Everybody is always so calm and superior about everything and it doesn't matter if people get hurt or if – if—'

'Stop – that! ' Louise said evenly, and slapped her straight across the face. Gray gasped and looked absolutely horrified.

'He may or may not be worthy of you,' Louise said, breathing hard, 'but, my girl, I'm not so sure as I used to be that you are worthy of him. *Do you want him?'*

'I – I—' Elizavetta began, but Louise did not relent.

'*Do you want him?'*

'Yes! ' Eliza cried out in a sudden harsh voice that further terrified the boy but satisfied Louise. 'Yes, yes, yes, yes, I do! '

'Very well,' Louise said, more softly. 'Then pray for him and stop acting like a ninny . . . I'm sorry, pet,' she said, stooping down and putting her arms around Gray. 'Big people have to be rough sometimes if they're' – she gave a shaky little laugh – 'if they're to survive each other.'

284

But whether he who had survived them could survive nature, Eliza's knight was in no way sure as he stood panting at the foot of his pine tree waiting for Einar to return with the torches with which he hoped to set the back-fire. The wind was capricious again, for a second it paused and he held his breath with a sudden terrible constriction in his chest before it resumed again in a steady flow down-canyon. He thought of all the excitement occurring at this moment all around, he could imagine the electrifying news as it shot through Greenmont and picture the overloaded cars that must even now be roaring on their way with assistance, he could see the ranger-station from which no doubt fire-trucks were coming, the ranger-station he had not been told about but which he knew must be there, there was always a ranger-station, providing only its men could arrive where they were supposed to be in time—

He thought also of the past three weeks, and of the days that had come before, and of the days that might come after, if he survived this. Ah, there, Eliza, he thought drily, where are you now, and have you crossed the ice? And will you wait for me on the other side? Or must I hang down my head and die, poor boy, while there's a hot time in the old town tonight and the swallows come back to Capistrano?

'Damn it, hurry up!' he shouted to the struggling Einar, now clambering back up holding two branches, flaming at the tips, as carefully as possible above his head. 'Thanks,' he said, grabbing them out of his hands. 'Now get back down there and tell the others to clear out back to the road, and you clear out, too.'

'Back with the *women*?' Einar demanded with an indignation so startled it would have been laughable in some less frightful circumstance. 'What the hell do you mean? I got your branches for you, I did what you wanted me to—'

'Back there out of the way of the backfire, you jackass! Go on, go! I'm tired of you!'

'I'm not going to leave you,' Einar shouted angrily. 'I'm not going to just run out and leave you to – to maybe—'

'Look,' the major said with an elaborate patience. 'The wind may change any second. If I do this right, everything will be O.K. I can't do it if I have to worry about an hysterical amateur who's probably already wet his pants—'

'I haven't,' Einar said furiously, 'but I tell you, buddy, if I had the time I'd do it right in your—'

'Go on and get,' the major said in the same tone of elaborately tired patience. 'Go on, go on. For Christ's sake, *go on!*'

For another furious moment Einar stood glaring at him. Then with a mixture of anger and scorn and worry and regret that came out as a bitter, choking, unintelligible sound, he grabbed his axe in one hand and his shovel in the other and threw himself up the side of the canyon towards the road, using the tools to gain purchase and drag himself forwards as he scratched and scrambled and clawed his way up the cliffside. The major watched him go, a curious expression of satisfaction mingled with a grim affection in his eyes. Fifty yards below, the fire, still at bay, churned and twisted among the snapping branches with a steady rush and roar, its outlines concealed in the billowing smoke.

The major waited, forcing himself to count out three minutes by sixties, which he thought would give the others time to seek shelter, too. The branches, one in each hand, burned steadily closer to his fingers, sparks already dropping from them and beginning to ignite some of the pine-needles around his feet.

Many things passed through his mind in those short moments. None made any particular sense or had any particular coherence. How about that, old Weendigo, he thought with a sardonic humour as he reached 57 – 58 – 59 – three. How's this for a commitment – and to dear old Greenmont, at that? And somewhat awkwardly, for by now he was beginning to feel quite weak, he ran to one side of the steep-sided V in which he stood and tossed one burning branch into the underbrush, turned as swiftly and ran back across the narrow space and tossed the other against the other side.

Instantly the flames leaped across the narrow space, driving him back down towards the main fire as they dissolved the bushes and reached eagerly for the dead pine above. When he had retreated down about sixty feet, so that he was approximately half-way between the two lines of flame, he paused and looked back. The wind continued steady down-canyon, his scrutiny convinced him the back-fire was burning beautifully. Get out of here, you fool, he told himself as he had told Einar. *Move.*

But, curiously, for no reason he would ever know, he did not move. Nothing held him there, nothing compelled him to remain. The dead pine became a torch to its top, its enormous branches like enormous arms stretched against the sky, the pale moon shining through them in a haze of smoke. The canyon above was a roiling mass of flame, the canyon below was the same. His escape path was narrowing rapidly. Get out, get out, his mind warned him. *Go.*

But he did not go. He thought of Eliza, he thought of Greenmont, he thought of his old love and of his new, he thought of all his mixed-up, uncertain, groping attempts to find something he had thought, for a brief, pathetic time, he had – he knew with a terrible certainty that he did not have it – he felt tired and sick and unhappy and afraid, where only minutes before he had tried to persuade himself against his better knowledge that he was calm and happy and certain and secure. He did not move.

The blazing pine made a sudden splitting, tearing, cracking sound and began, ever so slowly, to descend.

Why, yes, he thought, as it moved faster and faster and the wind began to scream through its fiery branches.

Why, of course.

There you are.

The great arms embraced the sky and the world went out.

'Where *is* he?' Jerry shouted five minutes later as they stood at the edge of the road, the entire stretch of canyon from backfire to Falls a solid blaze, the fire beginning to die upon itself. *'Where is he?'*

'Oh, my dear,' Louise said, holding Elizavetta and beginning to cry. 'I don't know, I don't know ... Wouldn't you know,' she said with a miserable little shred of a laugh as the first cars from Greenmont began to roar around the bend above them and the first ranger-station truck ploughed importantly around the bend below. 'Here's everybody, just too late.'

But for quite some time, Elizavetta and Gray refused to believe that it was too late. Long after the last remnant of fire

287

had been scientifically damped out, long after the last smouldering tree-trunk had been chopped down and tossed in the river, long after the last wisp of sodden smoke had climbed and dissipated against the moon-washed sky, they continued to stand on the edge of the road, huddled close together, looking down. It was not until he was found, resting quite peacefully under the branch that had struck him down, still quite recognizable, for it appeared he had been suffocated rather than burned, that the lonely, awkward girl and the frightened little boy would believe that it was indeed too late.

It was not until four men from the ranger-station brought him up, jarring and jogging on a stretcher along the tortuous trail, that they finally knew that his difficult and uneasy spirit would trouble them no more.

It was then that Elizavetta let out a cry such as Gray never hoped to hear again, filled as it was with such anguish and such lost hope and such lost happiness and such realization, at last, that all those things had indeed really existed and were now, indeed, really lost.

Even as she did so, one of the many stars of summer fell behind the mountains. She did not see it through her tears and only the boy, crouched shivering by her side, observed its golden death, which may have meant something or, quite possibly, nothing at all.

And so he went down the mountain for the last time, after a brief return to Greenmont where his things were collected from MacAleers' cabin and placed beside him in the ambulance; passing once more and for the last time beneath the sign which says MEMBERS ONLY, going again by the blackened area of the fire, silent and deserted now, traversing safely, now, the hairpin curves and treacherous turnings that scarcely a week ago had almost exacted the price exacted now; passing on down through Big Smith to the great Valley itself, passing out of the mountains, out of Greenmont, out of the world; having failed, for whatever reason, to achieve that peculiar grace and respectably uncertain peace which, while denied to those who Aren't Members, is always, of course, achieved by those who are.

THAT was what happened to the major when he came to Greenmont: a rather odd little tale, and one which all of us have discussed many times over cocktails at the Drummonds', hamburgers at Einar and Sally-Jane's (they bought the Rupert cabin when the Ruperts moved to Chicago) and steaks at the Buxtons', in the long, cool summer nights when the wind sighs through the pines and the last of lovely twilight fades upon the high, bare peaks.

Somehow he didn't get along here.

We have never really known why.

Louise, of course, has a theory, and so do several others. Louise thinks, with her casual air and her flippant grin – which, however, always shadows when she discusses the major, for she, like the others of us, was genuinely fond of him – that it was simply a case of rebound, and that what he saw in Elizavetta was just a slightly exaggerated version of his first wife whom he still desperately loved. Louise may know better than the rest of us, for she indicates that she did have a couple of confidential talks with him which seemed to hint as much. But, again, she may have misread it. This may be entirely too simple.

Haila, on the other hand, while conceding what he did for Greenmont, has none the less reverted to her original conclusion that he was simply a cold-blooded, selfish, self-seeking individual, dreadfully mixed-up and probably guilty about it all, who invaded our peaceful little paradise and raised havoc with one of our sheltered maidens for his own selfish physical purposes. Viola and Mother Magruder agree with this. There are moments when Haila has some difficulty defending her thesis, for Louise under sufficient provocation will sometimes make some elliptical references to 'virtue begging to be otherwise', which causes Haila to blush and move swiftly to something else; but, in the main, this is her belief. Haila has a way of re-adjusting the past to suit her conduct in it, and her interpretation of course frees her from any responsibility for what happened.

Sally-Jane, surprisingly for one who is still so pert and fluffy despite increasing years and responsibilities, seems to lean to a deeper and more sombre view. She talks at times, rather vaguely, about, 'Things that really get to people' – and, 'After all, we all have our problems' – and, 'Who can ever say exactly

289

what impels a human heart?' This usually prompts Einar to call her 'Socrates' or something equally witty, and that diverts the conversation. None the less there are times, when we are finally confronted with the full memory of his last three weeks on earth, and, above all, with the realization of what he did for Greenmont, when we think S.-J. may be groping towards it, whether or not she will ever finally arrive. Maybe it all did exist in those inward reaches of the heart where each individual has his own compass, unique to him, and no one else can know, but only guess.

For the men, of course, it is exactly the realization of what he did for Greenmont that gives him his special place in all our hearts. What he did to Eliza, or what he may have done to himself in the process, is something we don't worry about too much. After all, Eliza isn't the first girl who got it in a summer romance, and anyway, she lived through it. He didn't, and the reason he didn't is because he gave his life for us: he died to save Greenmont. There may have been other reasons, as the ladies perhaps half-perceive in their puzzled speculations, but the essential thing is that he did it. That was what he shouted to Einar in those last few minutes, and Einar won't let anyone forget it.

'We wouldn't be sitting here right now,' Einar always said, 'if he hadn't saved us. Greenmont would be gone and this whole canyon would be just a – just a wasteland.'

The thought of our beloved Greenmont being a wasteland is enough to make everyone choke up, and that usually ends the argument. He did die for Greenmont, which after all didn't do too much for him, when you come right down to it. We all feel a certain guilt about that, too, which also terminates it at a certain point. Nobody wants to get too specific about who did what to whom; it isn't the sort of thing a place like Greenmont likes to remember. After all, to use Eliza's phrase again, *we* have all survived each other. Why couldn't he? And why must we always be reminded that we may have had some responsibility for it? This camp isn't a place in which to take responsibility, it's a place to get away from it. You spoil the whole premise if you begin thinking along those lines.

What Eliza's own theory is – and the subject, I will say for Greenmont, which usually isn't that reticent, is never raised in her presence – we perhaps will never know. She has never mentioned his name since the night of the Fire. Neither has she changed, in any discernible way, her mode of living or her general approach to the world. Did she really love him, as would seem to be indicated by her last wild outburst when they brought his body up the trail? Did she really regard him as her last chance for love and happiness, a chance that might never come again – that never has come again, as far as we know, and apparently, now as the years draw on, never will? Does she, too, feel a certain guilt that she did not respond more eagerly, return more fully the love and kindness he was evidently, at least towards the end, ready to give her? We will never know. She doesn't say, and even our curiosity stops at last at the politely impenetrable barrier of her concern for Causes and her good-hearted, never-ending worry about The Blight.

As for me, I don't know either. My ideas generally seem to run along the same vague lines as Sally-Jane's. Was he prevented from taking his own life – which, at the moment he wished to, would have been quite pointless – so that he could be saved to contribute his life for Greenmont – which then gave the sacrifice some point? Or, in his mind, would it have had more point if he had been allowed to take it when he wished to? And was giving it for Greenmont, to him, quite pointless?

Or there is another possibility. Was he, perhaps, one of those people to whom the world insists: 'You must give us more of yourself. You may think you are giving us enough, but we say you aren't. You may think you are sincere in what you offer, but we know better. You must let us violate your personality even more, you must let us invade your privacy even further, you must let us force you to act as we think you should, or we won't believe you. You must, you must, you must!

Perhaps that was what lay at the heart of his ruined marriage. Perhaps that was why he could never quite make the commitment that Greenmont demanded of him. There are such people, completely convinced that they are giving enough of themselves, never quite convincing society of it. There is no reason any objective observer can see – certainly no reason they themselves can see – why they should evoke this response from those who, quite possibly crippled and inadequate themselves, are always quick to attribute impairment and inadequacy to others. Yet evoke it they do, and damned be he who attempts to escape it.

The devouring hungers of a thousand hearts will wear him down, try to evade them though he will.

These are the sort of questions that occur to me. But, like the others, I do not know.

One thing I do know, though, and that is that I finally settled my score with Haila. It took me a while, after my parents reconciled and came back from Hawaii, to even get to the point where I could talk to her, and all told, it took me about ten years after that to really fight back. After she had kept me in my place for a decade, in a little private war nobody else knew about, I finally got up enough nerve to break that particular chain binding me to my childhood, and told her off. She asked for it and I let her have it, figuring that at twenty it was about time.

'Well, Gray, dear,' she said with a sweet smile and a chuckle one day when we happened to meet crossing the Meadows and no one else was near, 'have you delivered any notes for anyone lately?'

'If I have, Mrs Buxton,' I said sharply, 'I haven't used them to try to drive a man to his death.'

I think it was the only time I have ever seen her really upset. For a moment she looked livid. Then her mouth got that pursed, tight little smile we all know so well, and she said gently, 'Well, dear, perhaps we won't say any more about *that* subject.'

'I guess not,' I said shortly and brushed on by, an exhilarating action I only wished I could have repeated several times, I enjoyed it so. And since then, we never have.

And now here it is fifteen years later and it's almost eleven o'clock on another Fourth of July, and pretty soon we'll have the Annual Meeting and then the barbecue. This year Einar is president of the Board and Sally-Jane is pregnant again – this is the ninth time, Einar breeds like all the other Magruders – and with a very few exceptions, everybody is here. As I sit on a bench in the Grove scribbling these last notes hastily before someone comes along and looks over my shoulder and asks what I'm doing, everything is much the same as it was on that other Fourth of July, and indeed as it has always been, and please God always will be, in Greenmont.

Mother Magruder and the first members of her innumerable

clan are beginning to gather around the pool. Einar himself and Sally-Jane are on the lower court with the Drummonds, getting in a last game before the meeting, and also before S.-J. has to bow to the inevitable again and retire from competition for a while. There in the distance comes Haila, putter swinging complacently from one hand, about to meet Viola, who at this moment is sitting, plumped forward and trying not to peek too obviously on the bench next to mine. They will join Jim and Bob, already waiting impatiently by the first tee. Soon Elizavetta and Mr Smudge the Third will be coming along, too. This year she's on some sort of advanced poetry kick, and she and Haila read lots of books about it and exchange notes and comments at every opportunity. This baffles the rest of us, and Sally-Jane and Louise are full of remarks, but Eliza and Haila go right ahead with their enthusiasm. They always have and, no doubt, always will.

Basically, nothing ever changes, at Greenmont. You would never know we had all been through that summer together, just as you would never know we have been through some other things I could tell you about.

Greenmont goes on. It is, as Einar remarked that time Viola caught him and Sally-Jane at the Mineral Springs and they had to get married a lot sooner than they intended, bigger than all of us, with its comfortable, lazy, lovely life, its placid, even, carefree days, its curious combination of innocence and sophistication, its easy-going, wisecracking, self-centred distillation of all the busy, bright uncaring of the world.